Books by Lindy Bell

BEYOND THE BADGE SERIES
Brotherhood by Fire
Brothers in Service: Through Thick & Thin
To Become a Brother (Young Adult Novel)
Embattled Brother

OTHER BOOKS
Jane Austen Celebrates: Holidays & Occasions Regency Style

EMBATTLED BROTHER

LINDY BELL

Editor: Dr. Laura Cheshier
Cover Designer: Dar Albert,
Wicked Smart Designs, wickedsmartdesigns.com
Interior Book Designer: Sandra Jonas

Library of Congress Control Number: Pending

ISBN: 978-1-7365604-8-8 (Paperback)
ISBN: 978-1-7365604-9-5 (Ebook)

Printed in the United States of America
30 29 28 27 26 25   1 2 3 4 5 6 7 8

To Jeremy Wolfe

A Firefighter's Firefighter
who serves his community and the men who serve
under his command with fierce devotion
and heartfelt passion.

I'm honored to have had you as such a vital
part of the Beyond the Badge series.

AUTHOR'S NOTE

EMBATTLED BROTHER IS A work of fiction. Any resemblance to actual events or persons is entirely coincidental. Members of the fire service are dedicated and wholeheartedly serve not only their community but also their fellow brothers and sisters in the fire service brotherhood. While there may be an instance of a rogue member in the fire service, these types are rare and typically vetted out long before rising as high in rank as the character Milton Carr.

ALOW HUM OF VOICES could be heard through the glass of the receptionist's window as she smiled up at Lucas from the other side.

"I'll let them know you're here, sir. You're welcome to take a seat. They'll be with you shortly."

Lucas nodded and turned, looking around the small waiting area. A row of photos in black frames on the far wall drew his attention and he walked over. He recognized it as the Abernathy Department's memorial wall for firefighters who had died in the line of duty.

Scanning the row of framed pictures, Lucas's breath caught as his hand reached out instinctively. His fingertips grazed the engraved plate at the bottom of the frame containing a photo of Mr. Andy.

Firefighter Andrew H. Garrett
Years of Watch 1994–2001

Mr. Andy was gone? And had been all this time? Lucas had been looking forward to seeing Mr. Andy again for so long only to discover now, that he'd died years ago. It just didn't seem . . . fair. Lucas and his mother had moved from Abernathy at the end of 2000. Mr. Andy had died only months after? How was it possible the smiling, laughing firefighter who had sat across from him at the cafeteria table in second grade and eaten lunch with him, had listened to him, and advised him was—gone?

Lucas straightened from leaning over, sensing someone's presence beside him more than he'd heard him approach. He glanced to his right to see an older man, a deputy chief, standing solemnly beside him, staring at the photo and plaque as well.

"Did you know Firefighter Garrett?" Lucas asked the man standing beside him, the question's past tense feeling wrong.

The older gentleman beside him seemed to come to himself and stuck out his hand. Shaking Lucas's hand, he said, "Deputy Chief Bentley. You must be Deputy Chief Matthews."

Lucas worked to gain control of his unsettled thoughts. Today was an important day, and he had to focus on what was at hand. He'd have to deal with what that photo and small plaque meant later.

"Yes, sir. Lucas Matthews. It's a pleasure to meet you."

"Likewise. We've heard great things about you and look forward to finding out more. Everyone is waiting, but first, yes, I knew Andy. We worked together."

"You didn't happen to work at Station 2 together, did you?"

"Why, yes. We did. The Deuce. How did you know that?" Bentley asked with a note of surprise.

Lucas smiled wistfully and studied the man before him. About Lucas's own height with the same medium build, Deputy Chief Bentley had close cropped salt and pepper hair with short sideburns. His face was a bit worn but his brown eyes were bright with curiosity and reflected a wisdom that only came through experience.

"Mr. Andy—err, Firefighter Garrett conducted a field trip there for my second-grade class."

Bentley nodded slowly. "Were you in Katie—Mrs. Garrett's class?"

Lucas couldn't help but smile. "Yes, sir. She is my all-time favorite teacher. And Mr. Andy, well, he's the reason I became a firefighter."

A sudden look of alarm crossed Lucas's face. "She's not . . . Mrs. Garrett's not gone too, is she, sir?" Lucas asked with a quick glance back toward Andy's photo. "I'd planned to go by and see them after the interview today."

Bentley smiled and clapped Lucas on the shoulder. "No, Son. She's fine. I'll give you her address after the interview. And you know, when I saw your name on the list of candidates, I thought it sounded familiar but couldn't think why. You were the kid Andy had lunch with at Katie's school. Is that right?"

Lucas ducked his head and looked back up at Bentley with a slight grin. "That was me. He changed my life in those few short months. I'd hoped to tell him how much and surprise him today, but now . . . now I know that's not possible."

Bentley studied Lucas. "You know, I remember him talking about you. It was evident you meant a lot to him. I have no doubt Katie is going to be thrilled to see you and hear that from you. But, in the meantime we have an interview to do. Are you good or do you need a minute?"

Lucas straightened. Clearing his throat, he tugged at his black uniform tie and smoothed his white officer's shirt.

"I'm ready, Deputy Chief Bentley. I've been working toward this moment since second grade."

"Well, let's get to it then. And good luck," Bentley said with a warm smile. He motioned toward the door leading into the office area, and opening it, he stepped through to lead the way.

Lucas followed, taking in the layout of the space. It was a short hallway with office doors along either side. As they took a left turn, Lucas caught a glimpse of a plaque outside the corner office on his right and noted it read "Chief." Bentley pointed out various offices and a training room. Lucas glanced into the offices, opening off the hallway, acknowledging those he passed with a quick nod.

A young lieutenant stopped Bentley to ask a question, and Lucas paused outside the doorway of a nearby office. The officer behind the desk inside stood and walked to the door, eyeing Lucas with scornful curiosity.

Lucas nodded as their eyes met but the other man only stared, crossing his arms over his chest as he leaned against the door.

"Right this way, Chief Matthews," Bentley said with a furtive glance at the man in the doorway. Lucas looked away from the officer, continued down the hall behind Bentley, and entered the conference room.

He had been told there were three active-duty deputy chiefs. One was a final candidate for the chief's position so would not be participating in Lucas's interview. Since Deputy Chief Mike Bentley was retiring, he had been placed in charge of this phase of the interview process. As one of the three finalists, Lucas had already met with the city manager and members of the city council. This interview with the department's ranking command staff was the last step in the process.

Taking a deep breath, Lucas took a seat at the opposite end of the conference table from where Deputy Chief Bentley took his seat beside the other two deputy chiefs who would conduct the interview. As they prepared to start, Lucas looked around the small but orderly room with a dark wood cabinet with bookshelves on one side and a large window overlooking the back parking lot opposite. Framed pictures of what must have been local fires hung on the other walls. The air in the room was a bit stuffy and the scent of strong coffee lingered. A cup of coffee sounded good, but Lucas was grateful for whoever had provided the bottle of water sitting in front of him. It might be a long afternoon, but he was ready for this. He was so ready.

LATE THAT AFTERNOON, LUCAS drove through Abernathy neighborhoods, sipping the coffee he'd gotten at a coffee bar he'd found near Station 1. He glanced casually from side to side as he drove, searching for anything that looked even remotely familiar from those few months he and his mom had lived here. Abernathy was a comfortable, homey mid-size town. It was just far enough away from the Dallas/Fort Worth Metroplex for easy access but far enough away to maintain that small town feel. A move would be a big change for him and his family, but if he got the job, he also had no doubt his family would be happy here. He took another sip of coffee. It was hot and strong, very strong, just the way he liked it.

His thoughts drifted back to the interview. It had gone really well, he thought. They asked key questions about his vision for the department, his management style, any immediate goals, his thoughts on technological advancements in the fire service, and in light of his background and answers, why he would be particularly qualified to lead the department. They had all been pertinent and relevant questions and ones he felt particularly prepared to answer.

He needed to call Jill and let her know how it had gone. She'd be anxious to hear, but right now, he just wanted to be here, in Abernathy, in this moment. He wanted a few minutes just to think about the past, where he'd come from, what he'd mentioned in the interview that had gotten him to this point, and where he hoped he was headed.

As he had left the over three-hour interview, they had said they'd let him know something as soon as a decision was made. A time frame hadn't been shared so he didn't know if that meant it would be today, tomorrow, or next week. He had no control over it, so he wasn't going to waste time worrying. It would be business as usual for him. Whatever was meant to be would be.

Even though he'd grabbed a quick snack with the coffee, he was still hungry and thought about stopping for a late lunch before going to see Mrs. Garrett. He was still trying to wrap his thoughts around Mr. Andy being gone. He wanted to be a bit more prepared before seeing her since the surprise of it was still so new.

His phone rang just as he turned down a side street that led to a corner shopping center with a cafe he'd spotted earlier. He picked the phone up from the seat beside him and glanced at the caller's ID. Kirk Lorimar, Abernathy's City Manager. That hadn't taken long. This could be a really good sign or a really bad one.

Lucas cleared his throat and tapped to answer. "Lucas Matthews."

"Good afternoon, Chief," Kirk Lorimar said, his voice warm and friendly.

"Good afternoon, sir. I hope you're doing well," Lucas said, his voice calm, but his heart racing.

"Doing really well, but I'll be even better if this call goes as I hope," Lorimar said with a slight chuckle. "From everything I've heard about your interview with the chiefs, you blew them away, and I must say, from the conversations you and I have had, I'm not surprised. We feel that you have the experience, skills, and innovative thinking we'd like to bring to the Abernathy Fire Department. I'm happy to say we had an overwhelming consensus which makes this easy. Lucas, it's my pleasure to officially offer you the position of Fire Chief for the City of Abernathy. If you need some time to think about it and get back to me, I understand and that will be perfectly fine."

Lucas pulled his truck over and couldn't stop the smile spreading across his face.

"Mr. Lorimar, thank you, sir. I appreciate it, but I don't need time to think about it. I am extremely happy to accept the offer and the position. My wife and I have discussed this opportunity and are in complete agreement. I am truly honored," Lucas replied trying, but failing miserably, to contain his excitement.

"Excellent!" Kirk Lorimar boomed into the phone. "We look forward to you joining the city and the department. Ruth Bingham, our HR Director, will be in touch later today to get the paperwork started. Let us know what notice you need to provide, and we'll plan your start date accordingly. And, Lucas, please, you can call me Kirk."

Lucas chuckled. "Of course, Kirk. Thank you. And you can call me Lucas."

"No, no," Kirk said with a slight laugh. "With what I've already learned, a fire chief deserves his title. We are honored to have a man and officer of your caliber join us. We can't wait for you to get started. We'll talk again soon. Call if you need anything or have any questions."

"Thank you, Kirk. I will. I look forward to getting started too."

The phone's screen went blank when Kirk hung up. Lucas laid the phone on the seat beside him and rested his forehead on the steering wheel. The job was his. He was incoming Fire Chief for the City of Abernathy. So many thoughts raced through his mind. So many things would need to be done. He looked up and silently thanked the Lord for this opportunity and for giving him the skills and experience he needed. And just as he had at every other level he'd held in the fire service, he asked for guidance and help to do the best job possible for the men he would lead, for the city he would serve, and for his family. "Thank you, Lord," he breathed softly as he picked up the phone and hit the speed dial for Jill's phone. He couldn't wait to tell her.

J ILL SLOWLY LAID HER phone down with Lucas's voice still ringing in her ears. She could hear the excitement beneath his usually unshakably calm demeanor. He'd gotten the job, and they'd be moving to Abernathy. She was excited—no she was thrilled—for Lucas. Becoming fire chief and going back to Abernathy had been Lucas's goal and dream for almost as long as she'd known him. Over the years, he'd talked constantly about Andy Garrett and about serving with him one day in the same department. Andy had advised Lucas, listened to him, and talked to him—just talked. He had also instilled the dream of becoming a firefighter in Lucas, and Jill knew how much Mr. Andy meant to her husband.

She'd also heard sadness in Lucas's voice when he'd told her Andy had passed away and how soon it had happened after he and his mom had moved. Andy would never know the drive he'd instilled in Lucas to join the fire service, but it was fitting for that goal to culminate with Lucas becoming chief in Abernathy where it all began. She couldn't imagine the conflicting emotions Lucas must be experiencing, but she also knew her husband was as solid as they came—steady, and always in control.

Lucas was on his way to see Katie, Andy's wife. Jill hoped seeing her would help Lucas process this new grief and disappointment.

The family picture on her desk caught Jill's eye, and she reached over to pick it up. She smiled as she surveyed her family's happy faces looking back at her. The twins, Jon and Jessica, were fully ensconced in their sophomore year of college. Even though they were twins, they looked nothing alike. It was a bit ironic that Jon was a replica of her with his blond hair and big, startling blue eyes while Jessica looked just like Lucas with a mop of long, golden-brown hair she tried to tame without much success. Her brown eyes were filled with the same kindness that always filled her dad's, but while Jessica had her dad's quiet spirit, Jon had Jill's lively, talkative nature. The twins had been back in school a little over two weeks, and Jill missed the good-natured bickering that filled the house when they were home. They were her and Lucas's pride and joy. She knew they'd be as excited about their dad's new job as she was, but she wasn't sure how they'd feel about moving from Fort Collins, which they'd called home their entire lives.

She and Lucas had built their house, a neat ranch style with large rooms and some acreage, not too many years after they'd married, wanting lots of space for a growing family. Their plans changed though when, after so many attempts and heartaches, Jon and Jessica had thankfully been born but without the hope of having any other children. The Lord knew what He was doing, of course, and those two had filled the house with so much fun and energy that Jill wondered now if she would have been able to keep up with any more children. Jon and Jessica were developing lives of their own, so they'd be okay with the move so long as they still had access to both sets of grandparents, and Jill knew the grandparents would make sure they did.

From the corner of her desk, the small French clock interrupted her thoughts and signaled the afternoon slipping away with its signature melodic chime. Lingering, Jill looked around the special space she'd designed for herself, which reflected not just her love of interior design, but her other interests and hobbies as well. Books about unusual travel destinations filled the built-in bookshelves while a basket with her latest needlework project sat next to a deep, comfy chair. Several books were stacked on the nearby table, vying for her attention. Warmth permeated the comfortable, muted furnishings, the deep upholstered chairs, colorful paintings, the cabinets, and the large flat desk she used for work that Lucas had built from designs she'd drawn. She sighed and paused briefly before grabbing her pen and making a note to talk to her Realtor friend, Alexandria, tomorrow about a possible contact in Abernathy and putting this house on the market.

She was sure they'd find a beautiful home in Abernathy, a place they'd both love, and one they'd enjoy calling home with enough space to entertain the new friends they'd be making. This move was going to be great. If she was with Lucas, she would be content and happy, and his dream was coming true. She looked at his face, smiling back at her from the photo she still held. Touching two fingers to her lips, she smiled and touched them to Lucas's face, grinning at her from beneath the glass. "Congratulations, Chief Matthews," she said softly.

She set the picture back on the desk and took one more glance before picking up a pen and sliding a notepad, curly q designs decorating its corners, in front of her. There was a lot to be done, and she'd best get started. She had a move to plan.

MILTON CARR HUNG THE phone up after talking with Kirk Lorimar, who had thanked him for his time and interest in the chief's position but then explained quickly and succinctly that the job had gone to someone else. The offer had just been made and the candidate accepted. Lorimar had gone on to say he hoped Deputy Chief Carr would continue with the Abernathy Fire Department, providing the same exemplary performance he'd been giving as well as providing complete support to the incoming chief. Exemplary performance? If his own performance was so exemplary, Carr thought, why hadn't he gotten the job? And full support? Not likely.

Milton Carr, middle-aged, his dark hair thickly streaked with premature gray, was formidable when he chose to be, which was most of the time. He was of average height but used his stocky and muscular frame for intimidation when the situation warranted and sometimes even when it didn't. His steel gray eyes were cold and unforgiving, easily boring a hole through anyone who even threatened to cross him.

His hands shook with anger as he picked up a pencil and began thumping the papers on the desk in front of him with loud thuds. He was furious. No. He was livid, and it was taking every ounce of self-control he had to tamp down his frustration. He couldn't be seen losing his temper while at the office, but really, who could blame him? That job was supposed to have been *his*. Who was this outsider they were bringing in anyway? It had better not be the guy he saw this afternoon on his way to interview. The guy's name, Carr had learned, was Lucas Matthews. He hadn't looked like much. In fact, he looked way too young to have the experience needed for a chief's position.

Carr angrily shoved the file and papers from a meeting earlier that afternoon across his desk. He shot up from his chair. Thrusting his hands into his pockets, he glowered at the empty space on the desk where the papers had just been. The voices from the hallway reminded him to be careful not to make a scene. He glanced around his sparse office. He'd never taken the time to personalize it since he thought he'd be moving to the chief's office sooner rather than later. Its emptiness and barren walls hadn't bothered him before, but now they seemed to be closing in on him.

He'd been so confident that he would be the obvious choice this time. How had he *not* gotten the job? He shook his head and ran his fingers though his hair and pulled at his collar in frustration. He should have listened to his wife. His mind drifted reluctantly to the conversation they'd had the evening he'd submitted his application.

He'd stood at the workbench in his shop, relishing the smooth feel of the gear shift and tools in his hands. This shop was his sanctuary and rebuilding his '65 Chevy C10 truck was his stress release.

Progress, slow as it was, on the truck's restoration was still satisfying. Everything moved at its own pace, and he'd discovered the key was to adjust to that pace. And that was the hard part. While he worked, his mind drifted to the posting of the chief's job opening, which he knew was imminent. Bracken surprised everyone when he'd announced his retirement and then left abruptly. That had been a little over a month ago, and the process to replace him was moving slowly. Carr knew, of all the deputy chiefs, his tenure would be the longest. The only one who would stand in Carr's way would be Bentley, but there were rumors he was planning to retire. If so, the pathway to the chief's job would be clear. The position was supposed to have been posted weeks ago, and Carr had been checking daily.

Even though the hour was late, he decided to take one more look at the job site—just in case. He pulled a rag from the back pocket of his jeans and wiped his greasy hands before reaching for the computer's mouse sitting on the workbench. As the screen came to life, he looked over his shoulder at the Chevy. He couldn't help a small grin. This truck was a labor of love and had been for years.

Carr picked up the coffee cup he kept filled and heated on its own warmer and took a sip as he clicked his way to the appropriate screen. He blinked and blinked again. The job was posted—applications were open for Abernathy Fire Chief. He felt his heart racing with excitement. He'd kept his resume and other requirements for the job updated and ready. In fact, everything had been ready for weeks. It took only minutes for him to complete the information and submit the application. Leaning back on his stool, he put his hands behind his head, lacing his fingers together and smiled. The process was now underway, and it was just a matter of time before he would be sitting in the corner office with a plaque that read "Chief."

He sat up and stretched before glancing at his watch. It was late. He should get to bed. He had just started flicking off the lights when Brenda appeared in the doorway, stifling a yawn and pulling her robe tightly across her to ward off the evening's chill.

"Everything okay?" she asked as she stepped inside and pulled the door closed behind her. Stopping near him, she leaned forward, placing her elbows on the workbench. Brenda Carr was a couple of inches shorter than her husband, her hips a bit wider than her shoulders; her clothes strained as she moved. Her round face was framed with dark brown curly hair while her hazel eyes were set above soft rounded cheeks and a full, dimpled chin.

"What are you still doing up?" Carr asked, bending close and kissing her on the forehead.

"I've been working on my latest craft project," Brenda answered proudly. "It's wonderful finally having my own workspace. I'm starting out small for my first project—new curtains for the kitchen window—but from there, who knows?"

Carr chuckled as he lightly pinched his wife's cheek. "You do remember your new craft room is still Casey's old room, and she's going to need it when she comes home from college to visit. Right?"

"Of course. Of course. It will always be Casey's room, but when she's not here, it's my craft room, and I love it. But you still haven't answered my question—everything okay?"

"It most definitely is. I just submitted my application for the Abernathy chief's position."

Brenda's eyes grew round. "The job posted?"

"Yep. It must have just been posted when I saw it. Honey, I'm pretty sure I'll be the only internal candidate. They'd be crazy not to go with someone who already knows the personnel, Abernathy's operating procedures, the city and staff, and a dozen other things specific to our department. This is my time. I can just feel it."

Brenda studied her husband's excited face. She didn't want to put a damper on things, but she also wanted to make sure he took things one step at a time. She gently placed a hand on either side of his face, forcing him to look at her.

"Milton, before you get too far down that path, think for a minute. Please don't shoot the messenger but remember what happened the last time you thought the job was yours."

He opened his mouth to protest but Brenda put a finger to his lips, stopping him before she went on.

"You'd be an awesome chief, and I agree, they'd be crazy not to hire you for all the reasons you've mentioned and many more. But, please, take things one step at a time. I couldn't bear to see you hurt and disappointed again."

Carr pulled away from her with an exasperated huff and sat down heavily on a stool a few feet away.

"Well, thank you for that vote of confidence," he said sarcastically, picking up a nearby pen before throwing it back down in frustration.

Brenda came and stood behind him and put her arms around his shoulders, squeezing affectionately.

"I'm in your corner, Milton, and only thinking of you. I just don't want you to get your hopes, up but I do know you'd be an amazing chief."

Brenda kissed him softly on the cheek.

"You're right. I know," he said softly. "I don't mean to get ahead of myself, but . . ."

"You just want it." Brenda finished for him as Milton turned and rested his forehead to hers. "I understand. I do. Use the interview process as an opportunity to show them what a valuable asset you are and that you're the right person for the position. Okay?"

Milton shrugged. "Okay."

It had all seemed so simple then, Carr thought as he shook himself from his reverie. Today's reality, however, was anything but simple. He'd been working toward a chief's position his entire career. There were a few minor incidents he knew were in his personnel file, but they shouldn't have affected his advancement. He'd be a great chief, so he couldn't—he wouldn't let this go. He wanted this job too badly. This wasn't over—not by a long shot.

LUCAS SMILED AND WAVED to Mrs. Garrett as he drove away. It had been a wonderful visit, and it was so incredibly good to see her again. She looked older, of course. He did too. But now, when she smiled, the light didn't quite reach her eyes as it had before. It was there occasionally, but those times were when she talked of Mr. Andy or glanced down at the open scrapbook on the table. Her love for Mr. Andy was still evident on her face, in her actions, and the way she looked at his photos. It was a true testament to everlasting love, Lucas thought. It was the same kind of love he and Jill were fortunate to share. Lucas smiled as he drove beneath the neighborhood's canopy of trees, the leaves casting flickering shadows in the late afternoon sun. He couldn't wait for Jill and Mrs. Garrett to meet. He had no doubt they'd hit it off and become good friends.

Lucas glanced at the clock on the dash. Bentley and Katie had both mentioned a new Station 2 from the one where Mr. Andy had served. He'd like to see it. As it turned out, he wasn't far from The Deuce, as Station 2 seemed to always be nicknamed. He pulled into the parking lot and parked in one of the guest spots in front of the office entrance. He got out of his truck and stepped back, taking time to survey the outside of the station.

For an almost forty-year-old building, it was in great shape, as was the lush landscaping into which it nestled. Bentley had mentioned a re-grand opening coming up, but unfortunately, it was scheduled before Lucas would start. He walked to the visitors' entrance and reached for the door handle, but before he could open it, a bronze plaque on the side wall caught his eye. Letting go of the handle, he stepped closer to get a better look. *Andrew H. Garrett Memorial Fire Station 2* glowed golden in the bronze. The relief of Mr. Andy's face was an exact replica of him and just how Lucas remembered him. Lucas fingered the same years of watch the engraved plaque in the administrative office lobby had held. He shook his head and sighed sadly. Oh, how Lucas wished for just one more conversation with Mr. Andy to let him know how much he'd done for him and the impact he'd had on his life! That conversation wasn't possible, Lucas knew, but he was still going to carry on Mr. Andy's legacy just as he'd promised himself and Mrs. Garrett he would do.

He took another look at the station and its three bay doors on the other side of the building. The red paint on the vertical doors shone brightly in the late afternoon sunlight, the window in each door sparkling. The station was obviously well-maintained. Above the bay doors in big block letters, it read, "City of Abernathy Fire Station 2." There was a large office window between the bay doors and the office door entrance, all surrounded by a dark red brick exterior. The office window, too, sparkled in the sunshine, the desk inside, visible through the window, neat and orderly.

With one more glance, Lucas pulled the door open and stepped into the small entry with the standard window, looking into the front office, and a locked door straight ahead. City announcements and information were pinned neatly to the bulletin board on the wall to Lucas's left. No one was at the desk, or in sight, so Lucas rang the doorbell and waited. No one appeared, and everything remained quiet. He'd seen the engine and the ambulance through the windows of the bay doors, so he knew the firefighters were there.

Lucas went back outside and started around the side of the building, following a narrow walkway off the drive. He began hearing voices coming from inside the bay as he got closer to the back of the station. Some were excited yells and shouts echoing off the cinder block walls while others sounded more like grunts. When Lucas stepped around the corner and stood just inside one of the large bay doors, he stopped short and smiled, seeing the frenzied activity. They were playing office chair hockey.

He was glad they hadn't seen him, conspicuous as an officer in his white shirt. They continued to play, perspiring, their faces red with effort as the chairs rolled quickly, and sometimes dangerously, back and forth on the pristine cement floor. Their brooms and mops were being expertly wielded as whacks were made at the hard plastic pickle ball flying between them. A firefighter with blond, almost white hair, hit a shot hard that went wide and headed straight toward Lucas. That was when they saw him, and their faces froze in horror as the ball whizzed harmlessly past Lucas and bounced off the wall behind him.

Lucas didn't say anything but casually turned and walked to where the ball had rolled to a stop. He picked it up and, turning, started to where the group stood in a huddle, their chairs now pushed aside, mops and brooms in disarray on the floor beside them. Each man stood rigidly, their faces betraying the dread they evidently felt.

Lucas walked slowly toward them, tossing the ball casually in one hand. Reaching them, he stopped and looked at each man before bending over and picking up one of the discarded brooms.

"Who's winning?" he asked, studying the broom.

"I'm sorry—what?" one man asked, who Lucas surmised was the station's officer.

"Who's winning?" Lucas asked again, looking at the man without a hint of a smile.

"The red team," another man spoke up from the back of the group and motioned to a ragged red armband tied around his upper arm.

"Yeah—only because blue is playing a man short," a burly man to Lucas's left groused irritably with a furtive glance toward the officer.

"You want supper don'tcha?" another asked, receiving a glare from the officer.

"Could the blue team use another player then?" Lucas inquired, motioning to the man wearing a blue armband who'd spoken.

The men exchanged uncertain glances, but Lucas waited patiently. It never ceased to amaze him how quickly word spread in a fire department. They must have already heard a new chief had been hired, and if so, he knew what must be going through their minds. Should they go along with the new chief or decline based on decorum.

"Don't worry. I haven't started yet. Lucas Matthews," Lucas said, shaking each man's hand as the five men introduced themselves.

After a few seconds of awkward silence, Lucas said, slightly narrowing his eyes as he looked at the group. "It's nice to meet all of you, but the question remains, could the blue team use another player? I have a bit of experience with office chair hockey myself."

Lucas casually dropped the ball, whacking it with the broom he held before the ball hit the floor, sending it sailing toward the other side of the bay and the makeshift goal at that end.

Grins broke out as each grabbed a chair, making sure Lucas had the one that rolled the smoothest. Thirty minutes later Lucas was as winded and red in the face as the rest of them.

"Score?" he gasped as they stopped mid court. The others rolled up, gasping for air as well.

"Red four. Blue five," the man, Jeffries, who'd spoken up originally, panted as he leaned back in his chair, breathing hard.

"And I'm calling time," the station officer, Lieutenant Briggs, said with a chuckle. He wore a familiar blue armband.

The group started to groan but catching their lieutenant's eye and his slight head jerk toward Lucas, they stopped mid groan.

Lucas laughed and stood, handing his broom to a nearby firefighter.

"You guys have any water? I'm buying," he said as he pulled the firefighter nearest him to his feet.

"Follow me, Chief," the outspoken Briggs said and headed toward the door to the station while the others began putting things away.

"Sixth man cooking?" Lucas asked as they passed through the door from the bay into the station and the aroma of dinner cooking greeted them.

"Yeah. Station rookie, Chandler, is cooking tonight. First time, so we're not exactly sure how it's going to turn out," Briggs said, leading the way down the narrow hall.

"If the smell is any indication, I say it's going to be a success," Lucas replied as they walked past the doorway of the recliner room. Glancing in, Lucas came to a sudden stop. Mr. Andy's picture, a very large picture, hung on the wall behind the rows of recliners.

Briggs stopped and returned to see what had caught Lucas's eye.

"Firefighter Garrett," Briggs said succinctly. "Station is named for him. Never knew him. You?"

"Yeah. I knew him," Lucas said under his breath before turning to Briggs. "He's the reason I became a firefighter."

Briggs took a step back. "Oh, I'm sorry, sir. I didn't know . . ."

"Of course, you didn't. No worries. I called him Mr. Andy when I knew him. I was in second grade. He was—well I guess still is—my mentor." Lucas grinned sheepishly. He clapped Briggs on his shoulder and said, "Now, where's the kitchen and this rookie chef I need to meet."

Chuckling as they headed to the kitchen, Briggs added, "Please, sir. Don't give him any ideas about him being a good cook. We're just hoping it's edible."

"Hey! You don't have to eat it," the rookie said, throwing a dish towel over his shoulder as they entered the kitchen. It looked like every pot and pan had either been in use or was currently being used. The stainless-steel island was covered with food in all states of preparation.

Briggs jerked his head over his shoulder. As Lucas came around the corner, Chandler's eyes went wide.

"Sir. Chief . . . sir," he fumbled.

"Something sure smells good in here," Lucas said, ignoring the stumbles and holding out his hand to Chandler. "Lucas Matthews."

Chandler took Lucas's offered hand and shook it firmly. "Brett Chandler, sir. I'm the station rookie—as of last shift."

"Well, welcome aboard." Lucas paused and chuckled. "But it looks like you're ahead of me. I don't start for a few more weeks." Lucas glanced around the messy kitchen and back to Chandler. "I hope you're doing the dishes too, or you're going to have some upset guys."

Chandler looked around and grimaced. "Yeah, I should probably do some damage control before dinner."

Chuckling, Lucas nodded and picked up some of the bottles of water Briggs had set on the island as he pulled them from the refrigerator. "Sorry you were busy and couldn't compete in the hockey match," Lucas added, his arms now full.

Chandler looked at Briggs, his eyes wide.

"The Chief here is a pretty fair hockey player," Briggs said with a shrug as he closed the refrigerator door.

"Well, I'm sorry to have missed it, too," Chandler said, eyeing Lucas appreciatively, "but someone has to cook. Today was my lucky day." He stepped to the stove and stirred a large, steaming pot.

"Hope it's our lucky day too," Briggs said, starting back to the bay, carrying some of the bottles of water.

Lucas chuckled, picked up the remaining bottles, and followed Briggs.

"Chief, stay and eat with us," Briggs was saying to Lucas as he popped the door open and stepped into the bay, Lucas and Chandler behind him.

The four firefighters who'd remained in the bay were standing in a semicircle around an officer, his white shirt a stark contrast under the florescent lights to their navy shirts and pants. The officer was talking, his back to Lucas.

Color drained from the faces of the four firefighters when they saw Lucas approaching as the guy in front of them said, "Yeah. Hired him out of nowhere. He has no idea how we do things in Abernathy. I've been around twenty plus years—five as deputy chief, so I know how it's done—inside and out. Doubt he knows much. He even looks like a kid, so if he thinks I'm going to train him, well, he's got a . . ."

The officer trailed off, seeing their eyes move from him to something behind him. He turned to see Briggs and Chandler standing on either side of Lucas, all holding bottles of water.

"Uh, well . . . sir. I didn't expect to see you . . . here," Carr managed haltingly.

Lucas recognized him instantly as the officer who'd watched him on the way into his interview. The name of the internal candidate hadn't been shared with Lucas, but this must be him, Lucas surmised, mentally sizing the man up.

"That's a bit obvious," Lucas said, handing bottles of water to the four waiting firefighters. "Lucas Matthews. And you are?" Lucas said, holding his now empty hand toward this guy who seemed more put out that Lucas was here than he was embarrassed at his inappropriate remarks. Lucas's eyes narrowed reflexively as he stepped closer to the man, his hand still extended.

After several long seconds of Lucas holding out a steady hand, never breaking eye contact, Carr took a small step forward and gave Lucas's hand a short and less than enthusiastic shake.

"Deputy Chief Milton Carr," the man said, his chest puffing out with exaggerated importance.

"Deputy Chief Carr, it looks like we'll be working together soon. Perhaps we can have lunch after I'm officially on board. To talk," Lucas added pointedly.

Carr looked Lucas up and down, a slight sneer pulling one lip upward, as he gave the merest acknowledging nod.

Turning dismissively from Carr, Lucas stepped toward Briggs. "It was a good workout, Lieutenant," Lucas said with a nod toward the mops and brooms now stowed in a corner of the bay. "Can I look forward to another?"

"Absolutely, sir, but can you stay for dinner? Can't promise how good it will be, but we'd love to share the pain or—the joy with you," Briggs said with a cheeky grin in Chandlers' direction.

"You know—" Lucas began just as his phone rang.

He held up a hand, signaling the group to wait and moved a few steps away.

Carr glared at Briggs, who was pointedly not looking in Carr's direction.

Carr fumed. They'd invited this new guy to dinner but were snubbing him?

Lucas turned back to the group as he dropped his phone into his shirt pocket.

"Sorry. I'll have to take a rain check. That was HR. Paperwork awaits. I'm anxious to get things rolling, so I appreciate them working late to get it pulled together. I certainly wouldn't want anything to delay my starting," Lucas added with a pointed look at Carr who returned Lucas's look with a glare.

Lucas turned to the others with a grin. "It's been a pleasure. I'll be seeing you guys around."

Moving toward the crew, he shook each of their hands before he turned and noticed Carr had stepped several feet away, eyeing Lucas pensively. Lucas headed toward the bay door where the early evening dusk was beginning to settle in. The cool night air drifting in felt good.

Turning the corner, Lucas took a quick glance over his shoulder to see the firefighters moving toward the station door, leaving Briggs alone with Carr. Briggs was obviously trying to join his crew and escape the conversation Carr was seemingly determined to have. *Use your rank effectively*, Lucas remembered Mr. Andy saying. Not as a bludgeoning tool to get someone to listen when they obviously don't want to, Lucas thought.

Lucas made mental note of the situation and of the man. He'd dealt with guys like Carr before, and it looked like he was going to have to do it again. This time, though, it would be in his role as chief.

Reaching his truck, Lucas climbed in and closed the door. Putting the key in the ignition, he started it and after backing out, turned toward City Hall. He knew this job would have its challenges—both seen and unseen. It looked like he'd just met one of the more visible ones.

SITTING OUTSIDE HIS PARENTS' house, Chase Carr squirted mouthwash into his mouth, hoping to cover the remaining odor of the cigarettes he'd smoked after school. He huffed into his hand to test his breath and thought it was passable. He was supposed to have gone to basketball practice that afternoon, but he was still trying to find the right time to tell his dad he hadn't made the team because . . . he hadn't tried out for the team. Basketball had been his dad's idea—not his. Chase wasn't good at sports and had no desire to try to become good. His dad had plenty of ideas and fully expected his son to embrace them without question.

Chase hadn't felt like doing his homework either, so he'd stayed away from home as long as possible. Time had run out, and he had no choice now but to go inside for a dinner where he'd either be interrogated or ignored.

When his sister, Casey, had been home, things were better. He'd managed to get through dinner then, along with the rest of the family, listening to his dad drone on about the fire department and things that were of absolutely no interest to anyone else. His dad never asked a single question or made even a cursory inquiry as to how anyone else's day had gone, how they were doing, what they might be dealing with, or plans they might have. Nothing indicated interest in anyone but himself.

Chase smiled, thinking of Casey. She would entertain him by making subtle faces at him across the table or kicking him in the leg when she knew he couldn't respond. He sighed. Casey was off to college now and out from under their dad's dictatorial dominance and strict rules. Chase envied her—and missed her.

He waited a few more minutes before getting out of his two-door hatchback coupe. Its dark blue paint was coated with dirt and dust. He might wash it—someday. He walked as slowly as possible through the garage and to the door into the house. It was almost 6:00—and he was expected to be on time for dinner.

Once inside, Chase slid into his chair at the dining room table and took a quick drink of the iced tea his mom placed beside his plate. His dad, glowering in his seat at the head of the table, acknowledged Chase with the merest nod. Placing a napkin in his lap, Milton Carr reached for the salad and serving tongs in the center of the table.

"Do you want to talk about it, dear?" Chase's mom asked tentatively with a glance toward Chase, followed by a concerned look down the table at her husband.

"Talk about what?" Chase blurted out before he'd thought better of it. He nervously bit his bottom lip and wished he could take the question back.

A heavy silence fell across the table. Chase looked first at his mom, whose head was bent over her empty plate, and then to his dad, who had paused with the salad bowl in his hand.

Unable to hold back, Chase asked, "What? What's happened?"

"Your Dad just got some, uh, disappointing news at work today."

"Disappointing?!" Milton Carr suddenly raged, slamming the salad bowl on the table, pieces of lettuce and small tomatoes bouncing out of the bowl as he tossed the tongs down with a clatter.

"Disappointing?! My entire professional career has just gone up in proverbial flames, and you describe that as 'disappointing?!'"

"Milton, calm down. Please," Brenda Carr said with another glance toward Chase. "You're only going to work yourself into a fit. I know it's disappointing, but you still have a job you love and are so good at. Try to remember there are bright spots in all of this. Who knows if this new guy is even going to last? Everything is going to be okay. You'll see."

Seemingly oblivious to Chase, his parents continued their conversation, his father raging and his mother trying to calm him and smooth things over.

Chase forked a bite of salad into his mouth as he looked across the table at Casey's empty chair which made him feel even more alone. He felt lonely, that was the word. *Lonely.*

"Chase, finish your meal," his dad said, jerking Chase back to the present. "We've got more to do than sit here and wait for you to stop daydreaming. Eat."

Chase obediently chewed, not tasting the food. His mind went to the same old topic and problem that didn't seem to have an answer—making his dad notice him—approve of him. Even if he couldn't play basketball, there had to be something else. But since his dad was so upset about not getting that job, he'd probably be even more focused on work than ever. If there was a way he could help his dad, Chase thought, and where it mattered most—his job—maybe that would make his dad notice him. It was up to Chase to figure it out. And he would.

WITH CHASE IN HIS room, the door supposedly closed, Brenda Carr joined her husband in his workshop inside their garage. The evening was unseasonably warm, so they propped the door open for some fresh air. Brenda stood behind her husband and placed her chin on his shoulder. Resting her head against his, she could feel the tension in his body as she put her arms around his shoulders.

This shop was her husband's refuge, especially when something major like not getting this job had him down and, in this case, extremely angry. She had to agree, it was disappointing. She knew how badly he'd wanted that job, and this time it had seemed like it might actually happen.

It was quiet, only their neighbor's dog barking or an occasional car passing by broke the silence.

"Any luck yet?" she asked in a hushed whisper.

Milton Carr shook his head without taking his eyes from the computer screen. "Why are you whispering? There's no one here but us."

Brenda laughed self-consciously. "Oh, I don't know. It just seems like the appropriate thing to do since we're doing detective work."

Milton didn't smile. He just shook his head and continued studying the screen.

"Nothing's showing up. But I have a feeling something's out there, just waiting to be found," he said as he swished the mouse and clicked on a different search link.

"Think out of the box and definitely outside of the fire service," Brenda encouraged. "He can't be that squeaky clean."

Milton had researched the background of the other finalist earlier, looking for any information he could use. He'd researched Lucas Matthews too, but it had only been a cursory search. At that time, the chances of Matthews becoming chief had been remote, so it hadn't been worth Carr's time to dig too deep. But he knew Brenda was right. Nobody was perfect, and he was determined to find something—anything—he could use against Matthews.

After forty-five silent minutes of his doing searches on the laptop and Brenda on her iPad, he found something they hadn't come across before. Lucas Matthews came up in a search in the Fort Collins newspaper. There was a series of articles, long ones, about a high school student—Lucas Matthews—who had overdosed on Fentanyl and survived. There was a big trial, and drug dealers who had forced the overdose were basically sentenced to life in prison. Milton read the first article aloud ending with, "Lucas Matthews survived the drug overdose, and it was his dramatic testimony that resulted in the three defendants being sentenced to lengthy prison terms with no chance of parole for decades."

Milton met Brenda's gaze as he looked up from reading.

"Drugs," he said pointedly. "Matthews is associated with drugs."

"But he was the victim—not a willing participant," Brenda protested. "That's no help."

"Come on, Brenda. Think!" Milton retorted sharply. "Who is going to research a little rumor? If word just so happens to spread on its own that Matthews is associated with drugs, his credibility is going to be in doubt. Rumors in the fire department have a life of their own, and a story like this is going to take off like wildfire."

Brenda looked skeptical as Milton huffed his frustration.

"But Milton, by spreading these rumors, you could destroy a man's reputation—going as far as saying he did drugs when he didn't. You'd have to be really careful not to cross the line into slander and have liability. I don't know . . ."

Milton shook his head.

Brenda sighed tiredly. "Fine then. I'll leave it up to you. I'm going to bed."

She kissed Milton on the cheek and, stepping outside the shop door, walked quickly back to the house as leaves scattered across the driveway in the wind. The house was quiet and still at this time of night. The only sound was a distant motorcycle and the rumble of the ice maker dumping ice. One lamp in the living room and the light over the stove in the kitchen were the only lights on. Brenda started down the hallway, but hearing a soft click, she paused and turned. She glanced down the hall at Chase's door. She shrugged and continued down the hall. Chase had gone to bed hours ago, and it was long past time that she did too.

T HE NEXT FOUR WEEKS were a flurry of travel back and forth to Abernathy, packing, unpacking, goodbyes, send-offs, and best wishes. Lucas and Jill were both exhausted. He'd just kissed her goodbye and sent her on the three-hour drive back to Fort Collins where she'd finish packing up the house and get it on the market. Watching until the taillights of her SUV disappeared around the corner, Lucas went inside the place he'd call home for the foreseeable future. Jill had just spent the weekend settling him into the townhome they'd rented with the sparse furnishings he'd need until they would buy a house and move in.

He could still feel the softness of Jill's lips against his as they'd kissed goodbye. He hadn't wanted to let her go, and they'd lingered as long as possible, murmuring 'I love you's' and kissing before she'd left. As barren and cold as the furnishings of the new townhome already were, they seemed even colder and emptier without her there.

Jill had done her best to make the place comfortable and feel like home, but as hard as she'd tried, this townhome was a poor, albeit temporary, substitute for what they were leaving behind. Thinking of his study in their home in Fort Collins, Lucas flopped down on the boringly beige, lumpy sofa and thought back to the evening that put the wheels of this move into motion.

HE'D HOVERED THE CURSOR over the shutdown icon of his computer and clicked the mouse. The screen went blank as he reached up and slowly closed the cover. Lucas leaned back in his worn leather desk chair, comfortable, just the way he liked. He breathed a heavy sigh as he looked around his study. He loved this room—his space. Jill's design talent of capturing the owner's personality was evident here. The warm glow of the honey-colored paneling, the bookshelves lined with his fire service awards, recognitions, and memorabilia sat alongside his favorite books and the training manuals he'd poured over for so many years. His dad's medal took the most prominent position on one of the shelves to his left where he could see it easily.

The worn and faded upholstered chair where he'd spent so many hours reading and studying for promotional exams sat near the fireplace. The plantation shutters covering the room's one large window were closed against the night, but the nearby lamp's glow reflected off them, giving the entire room a homey, settled feeling. He took another look around. Was he ready to give this up and move? One minute he was but the next, he wasn't. Was he ready to give up what he and Jill had built here to follow a forty-year-old dream? He ran his fingers through his golden-brown hair, still a bit long for a firefighter, he knew, but he'd stopped worrying long ago about conforming to details that didn't really matter in life's big picture.

He picked up the family picture off his desk. It'd been taken a week before the twins headed off to college. They'd gone back to campus a little over a month ago to start their second year. He couldn't believe his son and daughter were already college sophomores. They were happy and enjoying college life, but where had the time gone? When Jill told him they were having twins after they'd been hoping for children for so many years, he'd been thrilled, but that feeling had immediately been followed by panic. He needn't have worried. Jill had everything under control as she always did, and beginning a family with two tiny infants had been no different. Being a family had come easily.

Lucas had to admit he didn't miss changing diapers or the 2:00 a.m. feedings, but he did miss watching Jon play high school football and Jessica sing in the high school choir. They were both so talented, so well adjusted. Lucas had worked hard to make sure they'd had the stable, happy family and home life he hadn't had until Coach and Patsy brought him into their home to join their family. Lucas and Jill had successfully navigated the twins' growing up years, and now, they had two amazing adult children they loved and grew prouder of every day.

Lucas took a deep breath and set the picture back on his desk; he stood and pulled the chain on the desk lamp he'd used since high school. The pool of light across his desk was immediately extinguished, and the room was enveloped in shadow. He glanced around one more time before walking across the room and into the darkened family room as the clock on the fireplace mantel chimed eleven times before settling back into its regular soft ticking. Lucas could hear the low tones of Jill's voice coming from their room down the hall. He smiled. She was on the phone with either Jon or Jessica as she was at least every other night.

When Lucas came to the door, he saw Jill sitting in bed, the phone to her ear, leaning back against a fluffy pillow. The room glowed softly from the lamps on the night stands on either side of the bed. She looked up as Lucas entered, a smile lifting the corners of her lips.

"Jess, your dad just came in. Gotta go." Jill hesitated just a second before adding to what Jessica must have replied, "Love you too, dear. I'll tell him. Let me know how the test goes."

Jill ended the call with a slight tap on the phone and looked back to Lucas, a crease forming between her brows.

"Jess said to tell you hi and that she loves you, but what's up? It looks like something's bothering you." Jill held out her hand and Lucas crossed the room to take it and sat on the edge of the bed, the mattress dipping under his weight.

Rubbing his thumb across the back of her hand, Lucas looked into the beautiful blue eyes he'd known since first grade. So much had happened through the years but the one thing that always held true was Jill. When they'd found each other in high school, purely by chance after being separated in first grade, he knew he'd never let her go again.

She was studying him closely now, a question in her eyes.

"Something's on your mind, Lucas. What is it?" She gave his hand an encouraging squeeze. She knew him so well.

Lucas looked down. His breath caught with an excitement he couldn't deny. "The chief's position is open in Abernathy," he finally said. "I'm thinking about . . ."

". . . about applying," Jill finished for him, smiling. "And you will. Of course you will! Lucas, this is wonderful news. It's what you've been waiting and hoping for. Aren't you excited?"

Lucas's eyes searched hers.

"Well, yes . . . I'm excited but . . ."

"But what?! You've been working hard all of these years to get to the point where you could apply for this exact position. You're one of the youngest deputy chiefs in the service. Your work and commands have been exemplary. Chief Matthews—doesn't that sound great? Have you submitted your application?"

Relieved, hearing her excitement, Lucas chuckled as he pulled Jill to him in a tight hug, her silky blond hair cascading over his bare arms as he held her.

"Are you sure about this though?" he asked as he leaned back, looking at her closely as he tucked a strand of hair behind her ear.

"What? Of course, I'm sure!" Jill said, placing a hand on either side of Lucas's face and looking at him intently. "I know how happy this will make you, and your happiness is my happiness."

Lucas shook his head.

"I've got to be the luckiest man in the world," he said as he leaned forward and kissed Jill, her lips smiling beneath his.

Jill pulled back and took a breath as Lucas's lips hovered near hers.

"You're right, Chief Matthews. You *are* the luckiest man in the world," Jill chuckled softly. "I couldn't love you more even if I tried. You just keep making it so . . . easy . . . to . . . love . . . you," she said, punctuating each word with a kiss. Lucas's dark brown eyes glowed with love as he looked at her.

"So? Have you?" Jill asked, grinning at the confused look that crossed Lucas's face.

"Have I what?" he asked, sitting back, tilting his head.

"Submitted your application!" Jill laughed with a teasing swat.

"No. I wanted to talk to you first, but if you're okay with it . . ." Lucas drifted off.

"Come on." Throwing the sheet and comforter back, Jill stood and grabbed Lucas's hand, tugging him behind her down the hall and to his study. Pulling out his desk chair, she sat him down and opened the laptop.

"I know you, which means I also know you keep your resume up to date and ready to go, so we're submitting your application right now."

"Now?" Lucas asked, his head swiveling so quickly his head nearly collided with Jill's as she leaned toward the computer.

"Yes, Chief. Right now," Jill said, giving Lucas's cheek a quick peck. "I can't wait to meet Mr. Andy and Mrs. Garrett."

Lucas grinned like a young boy. "You're going to love them, and they're going to love you." He entered his password and pulled up the recruitment website. He really was the luckiest man in the world.

Two months had flown by, and tomorrow was his first official day as fire chief of the Abernathy Fire Department. Lucas glanced down at the binder and neat folders his new assistant, Lindsay Andrews, had dropped off that afternoon to add to the ones she'd started bringing each weekend he and Jill were in town. Lindsay was a dynamo and had a wealth of knowledge about both Abernathy and the fire department. Even though Lucas wanted to form his own opinions about the department—procedures, personnel, facilities, equipment—Lindsay was a tremendous resource.

He and Jill had moved his things into his new corner office at the fire administration building that afternoon with Jill adding her special designer touch to the space. She had successfully personalized the office to Lucas's taste, making sure everything was set and arranged where he would feel most comfortable. Lucas was very pleased with the results as they'd proudly surveyed the room late that afternoon.

They were able to shift the large desk just enough to give the office a new feel. Jill placed two comfortable guest chairs in front of the desk with two more matching chairs grouped around a small conference table for more casual conversations, which made the entire space feel more relaxed. They'd hung photos from previous fires Lucas had fought on the walls while the bookcase behind his desk held framed certificates, training manuals, fire mementos, his helmet from Fort Collins, and a replica of his father's medal. The original medal stayed safely in his home office. And just inside the door, so it would be the last thing Lucas saw each time he left his office, Jill hung a plaque on which she'd hand lettered Lucas's mantra, ". . . and then some."

Lucas had been a bit skeptical about the fire hydrant that came with the office when he'd eyed it the first time. It sat in a corner, near the windows on the front of the building that overlooked a busy thoroughfare. The hydrant held individual plaques with dates of service of each preceding Abernathy fire chief. When Lucas found Chief Jerry Hamilton's plaque with his years of service and remembered how highly Mr. Andy had talked of Chief Hamilton, Lucas changed his mind and decided the hydrant was a good tradition to maintain.

The space felt like a chief's office but not a pretentious one, and Lucas looked forward to putting it to use.

Glancing back down at the folders on the coffee table in front of him, Lucas picked up the one on top. He'd learned that Lindsay prioritized things, placing the most important material on top where he'd see it first. Flipping the folder open, he studied his schedule for tomorrow.

His phone buzzed, and he picked it up, expecting a text from Jill but grinned when he saw it was from Jessica: *Will be thinking about you tomorrow, Dad. Abernathy is lucky to have the best fire chief EVER! Will be anxious to hear how your first day goes. Love you!*

Lucas texted back: *Thanks, and love you, Sweet Girl.*

He laid his phone down just as another text pinged, this one from Jon: *Go gettum, Dad. Leave no prisoners.*

Lucas chuckled before sending: *You know it, Kiddo. Go study.*

He sent both texts with a thumbs-up emoji. His kids were the best.

Lucas reached for the soft drink cup from his and Jill's drive-through dinner that evening and sipped his Dr. Pepper while studying tomorrow's schedule. He'd already set up some meetings himself, so even before seeing this, his calendar was pretty full. No time, however, had been allotted to visit the stations, and to him, those visits were a priority. He appreciated the jump start Lindsay had provided, but it was up to him to set the pace and that started now.

He made notes on his calendar and sent Lindsay an email with the changes before opening the next file. Personnel. Lucas exhaled deeply as he read through the names, ranks, and assigned stations. He was anxious to meet these people and get a firsthand feel for the department. Lindsay had included the City's organization chart as well, which detailed who was who and who did what. Lots of people to meet, but Lucas was looking forward to it. He was pretty good with names; plus, he thought he had a pretty keen sense of observation and an avid ability to read people.

He thought he knew, but actually, he had no idea how much he would have to put those skills to the test.

S HIFT CHANGE WAS AT 6:30 a.m. Since Riley Sullivan's promotion to battalion chief and his transfer to Station 1, he'd made sure to arrive no later than 5:45 or 6:00 a.m. at the latest. As battalion chief, it was his responsibility to make sure Abernathy's nine fire stations were fully staffed before the official start of B Shift.

When Riley arrived, some of the B Shift crew were already in the bay checking the apparatus and equipment, making sure everything was ready for the day. Riley gave each a nod as he walked through to the station door. When he opened the door, he couldn't help but smile as the aroma of bacon and baking biscuits greeted him. He knew there was probably a mound of scrambled eggs in the process of being cooked as well. Riley chuckled to himself as his stomach growled in response.

He bounded into the battalion chief's office but stopped short when someone he didn't recognize stood behind A Shift's Battalion Chief Tyler Forney, studying the computer screen over Tyler's shoulder. The man looked up and straightened as Riley stopped just inside the doorway. This must be the new chief. Besides the obvious designation of an officer by the white shirt and five bugles on his collar, this man exuded authority. He had a confidence that was evident in his bearing and in the straightforward way he moved from behind the desk toward Riley, extending his hand.

"Lucas Matthews. You must be Battalion Chief Sullivan."

Riley took Chief Matthews' hand and smiled warmly.

"Yes, sir. It's great to meet you. We've been looking forward to your coming."

"Well, I'm happy to be here. I've been looking forward to this for over 40 years."

At the surprised, then confused look on Riley's face, Lucas chuckled. "Not to worry, Sullivan. I'm sure you'll be hearing the story sooner or later but for now, it looks like you're up."

Tyler looked up from the computer and nodded at Riley. "Sully, just a few things to bring you up to speed."

Riley took a step toward the desk and set his gear down, his full attention on Forney.

"You needed two over timers today, and they've been notified. I've made note of who and where they're going. Engine 5 is in the shop after the crew crushed their tailpipe on a tall curb, and they have switched to a reserve. Ladder 7 crew slammed another unsecured breathing apparatus regulator in the door of their truck and broke it. They're on their way here to pick up a spare, so they're out of district. Paperwork on all of that has been completed. Oh, and Firefighter Graham called in sick. He's almost out of sick leave if you want to check on him."

Riley nodded as Forney listed each item. Lucas watched and listened closely to the level of detail being exchanged.

Tyler stood and, stepping around the desk to the side chair, picked up the gear he was taking home. In the office's cramped quarters, Lucas stepped back to allow Tyler to pass while Riley moved behind the desk to take a seat at the computer in the wobbly desk chair.

"Have a great shift, Sully. I fueled up Battalion 1 for you last night. You're welcome."

Riley looked up briefly and grinned. "Thanks, Forney. I appreciate it."

"You owe me. Nice to meet you, Chief. I look forward to working with you," Forney said, shaking Lucas's hand before swinging his duffel bag over his shoulder and stepping toward the door.

"Likewise," Lucas replied as he moved to stand behind Riley.

Riley stiffened. He was a bit put off by the new chief wanting to watch him work. Riley knew he was the department's newest battalion chief but did Chief Matthews doubt his capability already?

"Relax, Sullivan," Lucas said, leaning against the cabinet behind the desk. "I'm just trying to get familiar with the names on each shift and station assignments."

"Sorry, sir," Riley said with a glance over his shoulder.

"Nothing to apologize for. We've all got to get to know each other," Lucas said, watching Riley's computer screen over the top of his mug. Drinking the last bit of coffee, he set the mug on the cabinet next to where he was leaning.

"Yes, we do, sir," Riley replied distractedly as he studied the screen.

Lucas chuckled, scanning the chart as Riley made changes. "It's good to finally be putting some names and faces together. Forney was just giving me some back history on some of the staff and your name came up as next BC on duty. All I've had to go by is a list of names, the station where they're assigned, and the barest bones on each. I believe the strength of the department, and my priority, is the personnel—getting to know them, and by getting to know them, I mean more than just a name on a list."

Lucas glanced at his watch and stood. "I do need to check in at the office, meet everyone there, and, of course, start the inevitable meetings, so I'll leave you to it. Rather convenient Station 1 and the administrative offices are just across the bay from each other. I expect I'll be seeing you often."

Tearing his eyes from the screen, Riley nodded and stood.

"Yes, sir, I imagine we will. It was nice to meet you, and welcome," Riley said, shaking Lucas's hand. "I look forward to working with you."

"As do I with you, Sullivan," Lucas replied with a warm smile as he walked to the doorway. Turning, he added, "And Sullivan, I've heard good things about you. I look forward to hearing more."

Taken by surprise, Riley could only nod before Lucas turned and was gone.

"SULLY!" JEREMY ENNIS BURST through the door to the battalion chief's office where Riley was putting the finishing touch on B Shift's assignments.

Riley gave a start then glared at his best friend, who plopped down unceremoniously in one of the guest chairs, dropping a box piled high with an assortment of objects beside him and cradling his bunker gear in his lap.

"What on earth are you doing here?" Riley asked before hitting the submit button to finalize the shift's needed adjustments. "Don't you have an office now where you can go and annoy someone there?"

Jeremy chuckled and held up his bunker gear before pointing to the box by his chair. "Of course, I do. I'm moving in today but thought I'd drop by on my way and check in. I hear the new chief starts today."

"He was just here. He'd been looking at shift assignments with Forney when I got here," Riley answered, straightening some piles of folders on the desk, sliding one in front of him and opening it.

"Well? What did you think of him?" Jeremy asked, leaning forward eagerly. "Nice guy? Do you think he'll be easy to work with?"

"Yeah. Nice guy—actually, really nice. I like him—seems laid back.

The conversation wasn't long, but one thing he said I really liked, and I think is going to make a difference . . ."

Before Riley could continue, the Station 1 officer, Brody James, stuck his head in the door. "Breakfast is ready, Chief. FYI."

"Thanks, Brody. On my way," Riley said, standing and sending a pointed look at Jeremy.

"Ah, come on, Sully. You can't say that much and not finish it. What did he say?" Jeremy asked, standing and picking up his box, waiting.

Riley grinned. "He said he believes the strength of the department is in the personnel. He said his priority is getting to know everyone beyond a name on a roster and which station they're assigned."

Jeremy nodded thoughtfully.

"A bit different from what we had before, isn't it?" Jeremy asked, shifting his load.

"Yeah, but a good kind of different. Time will tell. Now, go on. Chief Matthews headed to admin just a few minutes before you barged in here. I imagine he's going to want to meet his new Fire Marshal."

"What?! Dang it, Sully. You should have told me! I'd planned on moving into my office over the weekend, but Allie and I, well, we got a bit sidetracked looking at houses. I thought I was early and planned to be moved in by the time he got here." Jeremy paused on his way to the door and turned with a grin. "Fire Marshal Ennis has a nice sound to it, doesn't it?"

"Yeah. Yeah. So does knucklehead Ennis, so go on."

Jeremy chuckled but stopped short when another figure appeared in the doorway.

"Hey, guys! Glad I caught you both here!" Cade Marshall said, stepping around Jeremy and his load.

Riley sighed. "Come on, guys. This is not the local diner where you can pop in for a chat and cup of coffee. I've got work to do, and besides, Cade, the new chief started today. We all need to be on our best behavior."

Cade plopped down in the chair Jeremy had just vacated while Riley remained standing, looking at Cade with a slight glare.

"I'm serious, Cade. I've got things to do."

"Yeah, yeah. We've all got things to do but thought you'd like a heads up on some information I got about your new chief."

"Oh right. You know more about the new chief than the rest of us?" Jeremy said with an exasperated huff.

"I've got my own network of campus resource officer contacts, you know."

"Uh-huh," Riley said, walking to the door. "I didn't think you were in the mix with the officers much anymore since you're over the entire resource officer program for the tri-county area now. Either spill what you're so anxious to say or walk out with us. Jeremy needs to get to admin, and my breakfast is getting cold."

Cade stood and crossed his arms over his chest, looking between the two. "Your new chief is one seriously bad dude, according to an officer who knew him when he was in high school."

Riley scoffed. "High school was a long time ago, Cade. Just because you deal with high schoolers every day doesn't mean that's recent history for everyone else."

"I know. I know," Cade replied impatiently. "But this guy's background . . . Well, don't say I didn't warn you. He's tough. Really tough, but the thing is—you'd never guess it."

Jeremy stepped back into the room and asked, "What exactly have you heard?"

Riley rolled his eyes and threw his hands in the air. "I gotta go."

"He survived an attempted murder by drug overdose when he was a senior," Cade stated flatly.

Riley stopped mid step. "He did what?"

"Bullies," Cade said, grinning with satisfaction that he'd gotten their attention. "He ended up testifying against them, and they got life terms. All of them. I hear they'd hounded him through middle and high school, but when it came down to it, he came out on top. He's got a quiet demeanor, but I'm telling ya, from what I've heard, don't ever underestimate him."

Jeremy let out a low whistle and exchanged a look of surprise with Riley, who was nodding thoughtfully.

"That's not what I was expecting to hear but it's good to know. He said he'd share his story with us, but I'm not sure he meant as far back as high school. Thanks, Cade," Riley said, stroking his chin thoughtfully.

"Oh, you're welcome. You know me. I'm the helpful one," Cade said with a flourish of his hand.

"Why don't you be the gone one?" Jeremy asked, hefting his gear up.

"Just what I was about to say—gotta go. Meetings to get to . . . you know, I may go back to being a CRO. I actually miss being on campus."

"I'm not sure Emily would go along with that. You've got two young boys to corral, and she might like a little help," Jeremy said, walking to the doorway followed closely by Cade and Riley.

Cade's face softened, and he grinned. "Yeah, the campus days were fun, but the boys . . . they're even more fun. I never knew how great kids could be." The smile on Cade's face dimmed. "Sorry, Sully. I . . ."

Riley clapped Cade on the back. "No worries. It will happen for Maggie and me one day."

The three exchanged brief nods as they parted at the end of the hall.

Riley could smell breakfast as he stepped into the kitchen. As he started filling his plate, he glanced at the group of firefighters assembled around the table eating. He couldn't help but think about what Cade had said about the new chief and wonder how much their working lives were about to change. There evidently was a lot more to the new chief than met the eye.

L UCAS STOPPED SEVERAL TIMES to meet firefighters starting their shift as well as those going off shift as he started across the bay toward the administrative offices. He was impressed with the quality of personnel he'd already met and continued to be impressed as he met more. He was winding his conversation down with B-Shift's engine driver when Lucas spotted Deputy Chief Carr entering the administrative offices through the back door. Head down, Carr walked with a determined, stiff gait, yanking the back door open and barreling inside.

Lucas took a deep breath and exhaled slowly. Clearly, the situation hadn't gotten better, so he just needed to deal with it. As Mr. Andy used to tell him, *Best to address a difficult situation head on. Don't let it come to you.*

Lucas walked across the bay and followed Carr into the slight vestibule that opened into the back hallway of the administrative offices. Carr had stopped at Lindsay's desk where they were chatting amiably. Lindsay was laughing at something Carr had just said, but with Lucas's approach, Carr cut Lindsay off, ending their conversation abruptly. Confused, Lindsay gave Lucas a questioning look.

Lucas smiled and nodded, greeting Lindsay with a good morning as he came to a stop in front of her desk. He turned to Carr.

"Deputy Chief Carr. Good morning."

Visibly bristling, Carr turned to Lucas, the genuine smile he'd worn talking to Lindsay was gone, replaced with a pasted-on version.

"Chief Matthews," he managed with a slight nod in Lucas's direction.

"Chief Carr, I believe you and I need to visit. Get to know one another. Why don't we do that now."

"My calendar is pretty full," Carr began self-importantly. "I'll see if I can work you in later."

Lindsay's eyes grew round as she looked between the two. It was an understood departmental rule of protocol that when the Chief said he wanted or needed to see you, his request took priority.

"Deputy Chief Carr, now *is* a good time," Lucas said and motioned for Carr to move ahead of him.

Carr stood, frozen to the spot, looking at Lucas venomously before reluctantly starting down the hall.

Lucas gave Lindsay a reassuring smile and followed Carr.

Carr stepped just inside Lucas's office and came to a stop, taking in the changes. Lucas followed him in and gently closed the door behind them.

"Please have a seat," Lucas said, motioning to one of the two side chairs at the small conference table. He hoped by having this conversation in a less formal setting, it might smooth away some of Carr's animosity. Lucas watched as Carr looked around the office. It was quick, but Lucas thought he detected a hint of approval before Carr's face regained its stony mask.

Carr took a seat as Lucas eased into the chair across the table from him. Lucas studied Carr for several seconds before leaning forward and saying, "Chief Carr, I understand you were one of the three finalists being considered for the chief's position. Is that correct?"

Carr's only response was a jerky nod. His steely gaze remained fixed on Lucas.

"Well, let me tell you up front," Lucas went on, undeterred, "I understand what a disappointment it must be to have your hopes and sights set on something that didn't work out. But let me also tell you I've reviewed your record with the department and took an especially close look at the Personnel and Training Division which you lead. Personnel and training are both hot button topics for me. What I found in looking at the records and in meeting the personnel I've met so far, is that you run a tight division. It's quite impressive. I'd like to discuss some very minor tweaks with you at some point but certainly not anything that has to be addressed today or even this month, but soon. I hope we can work together to make this entire department the absolute best it can be. I have an open-door policy, so I'd like for you to feel free to share your thoughts."

The small clock beside the computer monitor on Lucas's desk ticked off several seconds in the charged atmosphere.

Eyes flashing, Carr responded in low, measured tones. "Chief Matthews, I'll be more than happy to share my thoughts. I do a damn good job, sir. My division has been and will always be 'tight,'" Carr said, motioning air quotes with his fingers. "I don't need somebody from the outside coming in who knows absolutely nothing about this department, its history, or its personnel to tell me how well they think my division is being run. I don't need to hear about any so-called 'tweaks' they think are needed just so they can leave their mark on the department. I don't understand why they picked you to lead this department, but there is one thing I do know.

I will continue to do my job just as well as I always have and expect there to be no interference from you. Is that up front enough for you?"

Lucas casually leaned back, never taking his eyes from Carr. His calm demeanor on the outside was a direct contrast to the frustration roiling inside him. This man ran a strong division vital to the department. Lucas had seen the records and data to prove it, but how had Carr advanced so far in the service with such blatant defiance of a commanding officer? Carr was acting more like a petulant child than a deputy chief. Lucas took his time to formulate an appropriate response, waiting for several long, uncomfortable seconds, allowing Carr's hateful words to hang suspended in the air.

Exhaling a long, slow breath, Lucas tapped his fingers lightly on the table's polished surface. Thrumming his fingers one last time, Lucas looked Carr in the eye.

"Well, Deputy Chief Carr, you have made yourself perfectly clear, and thank you for your candor. But, let me also be perfectly clear about what we have in front of us. My record and my reputation in the fire service, as well as my citizenship in the community I serve, all speak for themselves. The fact remains I was selected by Abernathy City management to serve as the new Chief of the Abernathy Fire Department. Not you. It is true you have been in Abernathy for several years and know the history of the city and the department. You know the personnel—their weaknesses and their strengths—and I need that depth of knowledge to best serve this department and the citizens of this community.

"Starting today, I am chief of this department and under my tenure as chief, things will be changing. This department will be moving forward, and it will move forward with . . . or without you. It is my sincere hope it will be with you. I respect your service and the condition of your division.

I am determined to believe the best of you and give you a fair chance. I expect you to do the same for me." Lucas paused then added, "Do we have an understanding?"

Carr stood and walked stiffly to the door. Placing his hand on the knob, he turned to face Lucas and said, "Chief." With a curt nod, Carr opened the door and walked out, closing it solidly behind him. The framed certificates and pictures on the walls vibrated slightly as Lucas leaned back and turned to stare out the window at the sun dappled park next door. There always seemed to be one stubborn holdout at every level. Lucas felt confident he could bring him around. He usually could.

Today was his first day, and a new chief was an adjustment for the entire department. Carr might just need a little time, but only a little, to adjust to the new scheme of things. Carr would come around—or else.

J EREMY BARRELED THROUGH THE back door of the administrative office area after half running across the bay that separated the offices from Station 1. He noted several offices were still dark, their occupants not having arrived yet. He also smelled coffee when he passed the break room. He'd have to come back for a cup, but right now, he just needed to get to his office.

Even though he was officially early, he had intended to arrive even earlier to set his new office up. He had just graduated from the police training academy, and today was his first official day as fire marshal. Fire investigation, arsons in particular, were typically few and far between, and when they did happen, they were usually routine, but there was always the off chance of something bigger happening. State regulations for a town the size of Abernathy required each department have a fire marshal, and at the rate Abernathy was growing, it was past time the city had one.

After having shared an apartment with Cade for five years while Cade was still a full-time patrol officer, Jeremy had the opportunity to see things from an officer's perspective, so when the announcement was made about hiring a new fire marshal, Jeremy was all in. Being fire marshal meant an increase in pay, and with him and Allie expecting their first baby, that was nice. Even though he would be on call, he would be off regular shift duty and have more time at home. He already missed working in the stations, but he was excited about the job and his new responsibilities.

He hurriedly turned the corner into the hall where his office would be but abruptly ran headlong into something—or someone—and dropped his box with a clank, his bunker gear landing in a pile beside it. He didn't recognize the face until he looked down and spotted the five bugles on the collar of the guy's white shirt. Chief Matthews. Jeremy groaned to himself as he straightened, leaving his pile on the floor.

"My apologies, sir. I was . . ."

"Evidently in a hurry," Lucas replied, studying Jeremy somberly.

Chief Matthews was about average height, slender but muscular. His golden-brown hair was a bit long for a firefighter, Jeremy noted, but it was the Chief's eyes that were the most noteworthy. They were brown but more importantly, they were kind and . . . knowing. As they appraised each other, Jeremy quickly became aware of the new chief's compelling air of authority.

Jeremy's face reddened. "Yes, sir. My apologies. I'm . . . Well . . . sir . . . I was . . . I am just moving into my office. It's my first day. Well, actually it's not my first day, but it is my first day as fire marshal. I was about to set up my office." He was rambling and told himself to shut up.

Lucas nodded. "That must mean you're Jeremy Ennis. I'm Lucas Matthews—Chief Matthews to be exact. It's nice to meet you." Lucas stuck out his hand which Jeremy shook firmly.

Lucas looked down and eyed the box Jeremy dropped along with his bunker gear before looking back up at Jeremy.

"Fire Marshal Ennis, I see you're carrying your bunker gear with you. I strongly suggest you stow it in a sealed compartment in your vehicle and not in your office. We're going to be looking at some new protocols for gear, based on recent studies. I don't want to bore you with it now, but just know that gear retains a significant amount of carcinogenic materials even after it goes through an extractor."

Jeremy's eyes grew large. "I hadn't heard about those studies, sir," he said, swallowing hard.

"We'll be talking about it more, but it's always better to be safe than sorry. Stow your things and join us in the conference room."

"Yes, sir. I'll be right there," Jeremy said, stooping and gathering his things. He hoped the red in his face would be gone by the time he walked into the conference room.

STILL SIMMERING ABOUT HIS exchange with Matthews, Carr snickered as he watched the scene unfold from his office doorway. He wasn't surprised at Ennis. Carr had recommended Darryl McCracken for fire marshal to the now-retired Chief Bracken. However, when Ennis expressed an interest in attending the police academy and moving from battalion chief to fire marshal, Bracken hadn't considered anyone else. Carr believed Darryl McCracken was the superior candidate, their longtime friendship notwithstanding. Carr sighed to himself. He sure could have used McCracken as an ally in the office. McCracken would have had his back, advising him of the challenges it looked like this new chief was going to present.

Chief Matthews continued down the hall, approaching the conference room, and acknowledging Carr with a nod as he walked past. Carr turned to his desk and picked up a notepad and the mug of hot coffee he'd just poured and walked the short distance to the conference room for the Monday morning staff meeting.

Matthews had claimed a seat at the head of the table, placing a portfolio, notepad, and his own cup of steaming coffee in front of him. He took a deep breath and stood, waiting to greet the department's senior command officers.

The other two deputy chiefs, Jack Weston "West" and Nathaniel "Nate" Baldwin, filed in shortly after, taking seats on either side of the table next to Matthews. Fire Marshal Ennis and the Public Information Officer, Captain Elise Stephens, quickly followed and took their seats while Carr continued to linger momentarily in the doorway before closing the door and taking the seat at the opposite end of the table—furthest from Lucas.

L ucas looked at the officers seated around the table's oval length, silently appraising each. From those wearing the white officer's shirt and black pants, to those wearing the navy shirt and pants, Lucas had noted the condition of each person's uniform as well as their boots as they'd come into the room. A pressed, neat uniform and polished, well-kept boots said a lot about an officer while a wrinkled, unkempt uniform and dirty, scuffed boots did the same.

This group was to be his inner circle and those he would rely on most to run the department at optimum efficiency and safety. They were waiting for his first words to them as Chief, and Lucas knew the next few minutes would set the tone for what kind of chief, and man, they would size him up to be. First impressions were important. He had been thinking about it and knew what he wanted to say. He just hoped he could convey it effectively.

Lucas took a silent breath and eased into his chair, sliding his portfolio in front of him and pulling out the agenda he'd compiled. No one yet knew his thoughts about the department, where he envisioned it going over the next several years, or how it would affect their specifically assigned areas, and even possibly, what other roles they might be expected to fill. He already had a pretty good feel for what he could expect from the officers in front of him. Most were strong, competent professionals with just as powerful a heart for service as for perfection in doing their job.

Nate Baldwin, Deputy Chief of Emergency Management, sat to his right. He was a tall wiry man with dark brown hair and a bald spot on top. He fidgeted occasionally and had yet to look Lucas directly in the eye. From personnel reports Lucas had read, Baldwin was a good officer and had the respect of the men but was a nervous, anxious sort in his job performance. By all accounts, Baldwin was solid and did a great job managing EMS Services and Emergency Preparedness. He was also the Abernathy Department's ambassador to other departments and liaison to any visiting dignitaries or guests.

As Baldwin picked up his mug to take a sip, Lucas's eyes slid across the table to Jack Weston, Deputy Chief of Support Services. According to his personnel file, he preferred to be called West. Like Baldwin, West was tall but instead of wiry, he was athletically built. His sandy brown hair was a bit longer than a crew cut, making Lucas feel like they might already have something in common. However, where Lucas had a quiet, authoritative demeanor, West was a forceful and vocal presence. He was anxiously watching Lucas's every move, evidently ready to get things underway. West had significant responsibilities, including overseeing Procurement, Fleet and Apparatus Management, as well as day-to-day equipment maintenance and readiness of equipment such as all vehicles and apparatus, radios, and bunker gear, among other items. He also oversaw facility management, making sure stations were well maintained.

Sitting next to West was the Public Information Officer and community liaison, Captain Elise Stephens, who was a little taller than average, with straight dark hair cut into a blunt bob, striking green eyes, and an athletic build. From what Lucas had read in her file, Elise had been with the department seven years and had been promoted into the captain and public information officer roles two years ago. Lucas had researched and read some of the Abernathy Department's press releases and media reports Elise had produced as PIO, and they were excellent. She was at ease and comfortable in front of news cameras and gave concise factual accounts when needed. She could also be a warm and friendly face for the department when working with public relations duties. The department's social media presence was consistent, informative, and upbeat thanks to her. She was a solid, hard worker.

On the other side of the table from Captain Stephens sat Jeremy Ennis, the new fire marshal Lucas had just bumped into in the hall. Reports in Ennis's file were extremely positive, detailing a quick rise through the ranks after being a firefighter/paramedic for several years. His work was exemplary, especially as a paramedic and officer. Lucas tried not to smile, thinking of their encounter in the hall, Ennis's head with its curly brown hair bent over the box he'd dropped in the hallway, his face flushing red with embarrassment when he'd looked up. That, evidently, was not indicative of his quality of work. Fire marshal was a difficult and very demanding job, but from everything Lucas had read and heard about Ennis, he had every confidence Ennis was going to be solid in his new role.

At the opposite end of the table sat Deputy Chief Milton Carr. His primary area of responsibility was personnel and training. His record of handling his job responsibilities was extremely positive. However, several instances reported by various officers, were noted in his file that revealed a different side of the man. He had been belligerent and argumentative on the noted occasions. None of the instances had reached official complaint status, but they gave Lucas some insight into what he might expect from Carr.

In light of those documented instances and Carr's behavior so far, Lucas knew he had a challenge on his hands. Personnel and training in particular were critical components of Lucas's vision for the department. Carr also oversaw IT, another critical area. Lucas needed a reliable officer handling all of these areas, one who would be on board with the changes Lucas envisioned and make sure they were implemented.

Lucas cleared his throat and looked at each of them before he began. "Good morning. If I haven't already met you, my name is Lucas Matthews, the new Chief. I look forward to getting to know each of you and working with you. I have dreamed of working with this fire department, and my wife and I are thrilled to be moving to Abernathy. We're looking forward to becoming part of the community.

"I'll be meeting with each of you individually to discuss your role and your current areas of responsibility in detail—and I do mean detail. For now, what you need to know is that my number one priority for this department is its personnel, whether that means the latest in training techniques, or the best and safest equipment and gear, or clean, well-maintained stations, or qualified commanding officers. I expect the best from each of you and the best from our personnel."

Lucas stood and leaned forward, placing his hands on the table, looking each officer in the eye before continuing. "Actually, I expect the best of everything you've got, and then . . ."

He had their complete attention as they looked at him, their eyes wide.

"I repeat," Lucas said, his tone measured, his voice earnest. "I expect the best of you, the best from our personnel, the best of everything you've got . . . and then some."

Lucas straightened.

"Questions? Comments?"

Those at the table let out a collective breath and leaned back in unison. Unaware, they had moved to the edge of their seats.

"No, sirs," chorused from around the table except for Carr, who only looked defiantly at Lucas.

Lucas gave Carr only a cursory glance before continuing, "Good. I have an open-door policy. Anytime you have something you want to discuss, a question or just want to visit, my door is open. Regarding the operational area meetings, Lindsay will be sending invites to each of you with times I'd like to meet to review your respective areas. Deputy Chief Carr, your department will be first. I advise you to be prepared. I assure you, each of you, I leave no stone unturned, and that means in each of your departments as well."

The smirk left Carr's face momentarily before he turned his focus to the papers scattered in front of him.

"Fine then," Lucas continued. "Let's move on."

He distributed copies of the meeting agenda and proceeded to discuss each item in detail, inviting input from those responsible or having knowledge of each topic. Three intense, exhausting hours later, Lucas asked if anyone had any additional items for discussion. He looked at their haggard, drained faces and contained a grin. He wasn't always going to be this intense, but they didn't know that. He wanted to get his bluff in early and to start things off with them knowing he meant business.

Lucas nodded acknowledgment to each as they filed out, the cooler air from the hall a welcome respite from the stuffy conference room. Carr had studied Lucas throughout the meeting, but before he left, Carr turned and just looked at Lucas, his disdain obvious.

Lucas shook his head as he gathered papers and the electronic tablet upon which he'd taken copious notes. He still intended to work with the guy, but his patience had a limit.

AFTER HE RETURNED TO his office, Lucas gave Lindsay a lengthy list of reports and data he needed researched and retrieved. Based on what he'd learned in the meeting, he wanted to take a closer look at certain key areas—shift schedule and training being a couple. Lucas shook his head slightly as he scanned through his notes. Deputy Chief Carr had reported information regarding overtime being worked that contradicted what Lucas's own research had discovered. Lucas hadn't called him on it, but since it would have a significant impact on the budget, it was high on the list to discuss with Carr at their one-on-one meeting later in the week.

Lindsay hurried out of his office, a harried look on her face. Lucas knew he was asking for a lot, but being new to Abernathy, he had to make sure he had the facts and figures to back up the changes he would be proposing. He was digging deeper and looking at things from a different angle than this department might have done in the past, but it was necessary in order to implement alternative methods that studies had proven to be effective when applied in other departments.

Sighing, Lance glanced out the window overlooking the Station 1 driveway. The engine, battalion chief vehicle, and ambulance were all backing in at the same time, the beeps from their back-up alarms echoing in the bay.

A quick glance at the clock by his monitor showed the time to be 12:47 p.m. He was surprised it was already so late, but his stomach was reminding him he hadn't eaten since before dawn that morning. He stood, picking up the keys to his new chief's SUV and headed toward the back parking lot.

He slowed as he passed Lindsay's desk.

"I'm going to grab a quick bite then hit some of the stations this afternoon. I won't be back in the office until in the morning."

Lindsay nodded distractedly. "Very good, sir. I'll email the information or have everything you requested on your desk before I leave tonight."

Lucas turned back and smiled.

"Lindsay, you don't have to get all of that done this afternoon. You have the general idea of my focus within the department, so I'll leave it up to you to decide what needs to be done first. I have no doubt but that you'll have everything done quickly. You're doing an amazing job, and in case I haven't already said so, thank you for making sure I had what I needed to get ready for today. Call or radio if you need me."

Lindsay brightened. "Thank you, Chief. I appreciate that. I'll get as much done as I can."

Lucas nodded before he headed to the back parking lot. As he stepped outside, he felt the sun on his shoulders, accompanied by a cool breeze. The intense heat of the summer was evidently waning, and the fall was making itself known.

Lucas could see several firefighters in the bay, rolling hose and changing hose out. Hearing the good-natured banter going on made Lucas smile. He noticed Sullivan and Ennis, however, standing to the side of the battalion chief's vehicle, deep in conversation.

Lucas started toward them. He was already impressed by these two. He'd heard, and read, great things about Battalion Chief Riley Sullivan. Evidently, Sullivan had risen through the ranks quickly to be a battalion chief. He seemed reserved, but Lucas had already noticed from their brief interaction in the battalion chief's office earlier that Riley carried the air of a natural leader. Athletically built, he was currently running his fingers through his dark hair, listening with what seemed to be concern at what Jeremy Ennis was saying.

As Lucas walked toward them, he began hearing bits and pieces of what they were saying—'pattern,' 'acrid smell,' 'rake marks,' and others. They were so intent on their conversation that they didn't see Lucas until he was upon them.

"Gentlemen," Lucas said as he came to a stop. "Everything okay? Something looks pretty intense."

Riley and Jeremy exchanged glances before Jeremy turned to Lucas and said, "Sir, B-Shift just returned from a small grass fire."

A grass fire didn't usually cause this much consternation among senior officers, so Lucas waited for Jeremy to go on.

Jeremy took another glance at Riley before continuing in hushed tones. "There's something not quite right about the scene on this one, sir. I know this is my first day as fire marshal, and I assure you I'm not trying to make something of nothing, but something doesn't feel quite right."

"I called Ennis in, sir," Riley interjected. "The crews noticed something off when they arrived, and they called me in. I, in turn, called Ennis. It may not be anything, but then again . . ." Riley stopped to gauge Chief Matthews' reaction.

Lucas looked at them both thoughtfully, stroking his chin and glancing to where the other firefighters were preparing the engine for the next run.

"I hope there's nothing more to it than a standard grass fire, but I'm glad to know everyone is observant and proactive. Ennis, keep me posted if there are similar fires or if any other fires seem suspicious."

"You've got it, Chief," Jeremy affirmed with a nod as he started toward the offices.

Lucas turned to Riley. "I'd like to visit some of the stations this afternoon and meet the personnel. Why don't you and I visit them together? It will give us a chance to get to know each other, and you can perform the introductions. You're driving."

Riley gulped down his surprise. He had lots of work to do, but this was a great opportunity to get to know the new chief.

"Yes, sir. I'll let the guys know, and I'll be right there."

Lucas had already started walking across the bay toward the battalion chief's vehicle and merely waved an acknowledgment over his shoulder.

As THEY MADE THEIR way around to some of the stations, Riley was surprised at how easy Chief Matthews was to talk to and how observant he was. The Chief noticed details about the stations, the apparatus, the equipment, and even the stations' upkeep and landscaping. He talked easily with both officers and firefighters, asking questions about their families, their role in the fire department, and just general conversation. He was relatable, and Riley was glad to see that everyone seemed at ease with him. Some firefighters hung back and didn't seem interested in talking to him while others asked blunt questions about pay and a change in the length of shifts—controversial topics within the department when Bracken had been chief that had never been addressed.

"You married, Sullivan?" Lucas asked as Riley drove between Stations 4 and 6.

"Yes, sir. Maggie and I have been married nine years. Our ten-year anniversary is coming up."

Lucas glanced over and studied Riley. "Congratulations. Kids?"

Riley didn't answer right away but shifted in his seat and gripped the steering wheel tighter. "No, sir. We've lost a couple of babies, miscarriages, but we intend to keep trying."

Lucas grimaced and nodded his sympathy and understanding.

Riley cleared his throat and hurriedly asked, "And you, sir? Are you married?"

Lucas couldn't help but smile. "Yeah—Jill. We've been married for close to twenty-seven years. She's back in Fort Collins putting the house on the market and wrapping things up there. I can't wait for her to get here."

Riley smiled, knowingly. "Any kids?"

Lucas gave a light chuckle. "Twins—Jonathan and Jessica. They're sophomores in college." After a pause, Lucas added, "You know, we had trouble having kids too, but it all worked out in the end. Don't give up."

Riley nodded. It was a painful subject, and one he and Maggie agonized over.

It grew quiet between them, the silence broken only by the vehicle's tires clicking over the seams in the streets. Lucas stared out the passenger window, deep in thought.

"I'd like to meet Maggie," he said suddenly. "In fact, I'd like to meet the significant others of all the command staff. Spouses are a key factor in how well a firefighter functions—officer or not. I'll get Lindsay started on finding a location."

"Sir, if I might make a suggestion?" Riley interjected.

"Sure. Do you have somewhere in mind?" Lucas asked as Riley pulled into Station 6's parking lot and killed the engine.

"How about the Abernathy Country Club? They have a large dining room, and the food is great."

Lucas drummed his fingers on the door handle as he thought. "Sounds tempting, but I don't think the city will spring for an evening at the country club for fire command staff."

"The city won't have to," Riley replied with a grin. "But my dad will."

"Your dad?" Lucas said, turning to Riley in surprise.

"Long story, sir, but just know he's a huge proponent of the Abernathy Fire Department. He's always asking if there's anything we need or anything he can do to help. Trust me, he'd love to host your guests and their spouses. Would you like me to have him call you to discuss? No commitment either way."

Lucas pondered the idea as he opened the door and walked around to the front of the vehicle to join Riley. "Sure. Have your dad give me a call. It won't hurt to talk about it. It'd be nice to meet someone who is so supportive of the department."

"You have no idea just how supportive he is, but you're about to find out," Riley chuckled.

IT HAD BEEN A productive afternoon. He had met all the B-Shift firefighters at Stations 1, 4, and 6, receiving a warm welcome from most, if not all, the personnel at each station. Sullivan was a solid officer, and one Lucas believed could be trusted, a key component in Lucas's staff evaluations.

He and Sullivan had gotten back to Station 1 in time for Sullivan to have dinner with his crew before Lucas headed to the townhome for the evening. His phone rang on the way, and he smiled when he saw Jill's name and heard her voice.

"Lucas? Are you free?" Jill's sweet voice rang over the vehicle's speakers.

"Always for you," Lucas answered. "Just wrapping up the day and headed to the townhome. How's my girl?"

Jill laughed lightly. "I'm better now that I've heard your voice. How was your first day?"

Lucas thought back over the past twelve hours.

"It's been good . . . well, mostly good, but there's going to be some challenges."

"How was that one officer you mentioned? What was his name, Carr?"

"He's the challenge in that equation," Lucas replied with a light chuckle. "But not to worry. I've handled these kinds of situations before."

"Yes, you have, but as your wife, I don't like for you to have to."

Lucas laughed again. "I'm a big boy. No need for you to worry. All's good. How was your day?"

Jill launched into detail, putting the house on the market, how the packing was going, questions about the real estate contract and on and on. Talking to Jill, or more like listening to Jill, was a highlight today. He especially liked hearing that Jon and Jessica had made plans to come to Abernathy for his swearing in ceremony. She said Coach and Patsy were coming too as were Dan and Jessica, her parents. Lucas looked forward to seeing them all.

"What are you having for dinner?"

Jill's question brought Lucas's attention back to the present.

"I hadn't even thought about it," he replied, now feeling hungry and wondering himself.

"I left some lasagna in the refrigerator. You just need to heat it up."

Lucas shook his head. "Thank you, honey. Have I told you lately how much I love you?"

"Well, not since last night when we said good-bye."

After silence on the phone for several heartbeats, Jill said, "I wish I was there with you." The wistfulness in her voice was evident.

Lucas took a deep breath and exhaled slowly. "I wish you were too," he said softly. "More than you know."

Jill finally cleared her throat and said, "Heat your lasagna, and call me after a while."

"Yes, ma'am," Lucas chuckled. "I love you."

"Love you too, Chief."

THE PHONE WENT DARK after Jill ended the call, and he dropped it back into his shirt pocket. Lucas sighed as he sat outside the townhome in his chief's SUV that smelled of new leather and a hint of the coffee he'd gotten that morning. He took a quick glance at the emails on his phone and smiled. Lindsay had been busy. There were emails from several others too. He certainly wasn't going to lack something to do. Walking inside the townhome, he turned a few lights on as he made his way to the kitchen. Opening the refrigerator, he pulled out the plastic container with his dinner and popped it into the microwave.

Even when they were apart, Jill looked out for him. She is and had always been his strength and support. He knew she was wrapping everything up in Fort Collins, and he also knew he was being selfish, but he couldn't wait for her to be here with him.

When the microwave dinged, he pulled out the steaming lasagna, the savory aroma reminding him of family meals with everyone around the table. He smiled to himself at the different circumstances now as he took a bite and sat down at the small kitchen table. He opened his laptop and, in between bites, began reading and answering emails. His day wasn't finished yet, not by a long shot.

T HE REST OF THE week flew by in a series of morning meetings and afternoon visits to the stations.

Riley had been true to his word, and his dad, Ballard Sullivan, had called about hosting the command staff and their spouses at the country club. He couldn't have been more supportive or enthusiastic. They planned a date a month away, and Ballard said he'd get the club's contact information to Lindsay to coordinate the details.

Lucas's one-on-one meeting with Jack Weston had gone really well. Lucas had enjoyed the positive energy during the discussion involving the support service functions West oversaw. The meeting with Nate Baldwin was not quite as energetic, but it was still positive. Baldwin was more on the anxious side, but Lucas had no doubt that emergency management services was in good hands.

Lucas couldn't quite maintain the same positive feelings after the meeting with Carr. Not surprisingly, it was a difficult meeting with a test of wills. Carr had gotten especially testy when Lucas brought up the discrepancy in overtime hours that he'd found in his research versus what

Carr had reported. Lucas's research ended up being right, which only proved to make Carr more defensive and unwilling to share or discuss critical information. Lucas managed, somehow, to maintain a steady tone throughout the encounter. Carr was definitely a challenge and had shown no signs of acquiescing.

The meetings with the deputy chiefs had been informative, but Lucas realized as he talked to them separately that each knew nothing of the other two areas within the department. Lucas had encountered this issue before and termed it the 'silo' effect. Rather than working and communicating as an overall team, each area worked independently of the others.

Until Lucas started asking pointed questions, each deputy chief had seemed completely oblivious to the extent of the issue but had eventually acknowledged its existence, including Carr. All had come to realize the issue had gotten to the point where it posed a significant concern in how well they could interact should a major event occur. The issue rose rapidly to the top of Lucas's and the deputy chiefs' priority lists. Communication was key, but there didn't seem to be a lot of it going on between the deputy chiefs outside of the weekly staff meeting.

To familiarize himself with the city streets and station districts, Lucas was monitoring calls by radio, also noting the number of medical calls versus fire and other incidents. Medicals, of course, far outweighed other calls, but he'd made special note of one fire incident in particular. Something hadn't seemed quite right at the time, and that feeling had only grown after reading the dispatcher's notes he'd requested. It was a dumpster fire that came in around 2:30 a.m. the night before. It was a simple tap out, but there had been no identifiable cause and that's what bothered him. Fires were always caused by something. They didn't happen on their own.

While it had been a long, tiring, and sometimes frustrating week, it had also been a productive, refreshing, and enlightening one. Lucas could already tell he was going to enjoy working with the Abernathy Department. It had its operational issues, as did every fire department, but they were fixable. Personnel issues, that was another matter altogether, and one Lucas didn't want to dwell on as he drove home late Friday evening.

It had been a week of quiet evenings, either eating take out or snacking on a few things he'd found time to get at the store. He'd eaten a few meals at the stations in his effort to get to know the crews, and when he'd accepted the invitation, he'd made sure he'd paid into the meal kitty or taken ice cream for dessert—Bluebell, of course. Mrs. Garrett had called and invited him to dinner on Saturday evening, and he was looking forward to having longer to visit with her than when he'd gone by after his interview. A lot had happened since then.

Lucas stifled a yawn as he turned down the street to the townhome. He was hungry but didn't have the energy to use a drive through and get fast food. He'd heat some soup or something. He blinked and then blinked again. Jill's car was in the driveway. They'd talked that morning, and she hadn't said anything about coming. They'd planned for her to wrap things up in Fort Collins and be back in Abernathy later in the month. He certainly wasn't going to complain that she was here now. He pulled his SUV in behind hers and jumped out, walking quickly to the front door.

"Jill?" he called out as soon as he was through the door. He smelled food cooking as soon as he walked in. His broad smile grew even broader when a beaming Jill walked into the living room from the kitchen.

"Surprise!" Jill said with a happy laugh as Lucas crossed the small space between them and grabbed her into a fierce hug before claiming her lips in a kiss. She melted into him, kissing him back with all the yearning she'd felt being apart all week.

"I've missed you so much," Lucas said as he broke the kiss, smiled into her beautiful face, and looked earnestly into her brilliant blue eyes.

"No more than I've missed you, I can assure you," Jill said and pulled Lucas's face down for another kiss.

Holding each other for several minutes, Jill finally looked at Lucas and with a teasing grin, said, "I've made spaghetti, and if you're still hungry after that, there's chocolate cake for dessert."

Lucas shook his head. "You just being here is enough for me. You weren't supposed to be back for a few weeks. This makes me happier than you can ever know."

Jill looked up at him, placing her hands on either side of his face. "I couldn't bear hearing the loneliness in your voice when we talked, Lucas. My place is here with you. I've been working late every night, packing and getting everything else to where I can handle it from here. Coach drove a rental truck with the things we'll need to set up house here until we find the one we want to buy. He delivered it to a temporary storage unit this afternoon. The house is on the market and our Realtor, Alexandria Roman, will be showing it, so I'm here . . . with you to stay. I'm exactly where I want and need to be."

Lucas listened in amazement. "I can't believe it," he said.

"Well, believe it, Chief. I've missed you," she said softly into Lucas's shirt as she pulled him into another tight hug. "I don't ever want us to be apart again. Ever."

Lucas took a deep breath and kissed Jill's hair as she snuggled in closer. The soft scent of her perfume and the fresh scent of her favorite soap filled him with a familiar warmth.

"Me either," Lucas breathed. "I had no idea how hard it would be, but I agree. Never again. I promise."

Lucas leaned back and looked at Jill for several seconds before kissing her again tenderly. Reluctantly breaking the kiss, he stepped back and grinned at her mischievously. "But . . ."

"But what?" Jill sighed with a small, contented smile.

"The smell of that food is driving me crazy. I haven't had a decent meal all week. Can we eat? Please? I'm starving!"

Laughing, Jill gave Lucas one last squeeze followed by a playful shove. "Right this way. Table for two, sir."

LUCAS TOOK ANOTHER BITE of coconut cream pie to hide a grin. He'd barely gotten a word out since introducing Jill to Katie Garrett. They'd hit it off even better than he'd imagined. Mrs. Garrett had been excited when Lucas called and asked if he could bring Jill with him to dinner. During dinner, Lucas had been granted occasional smiles or glances from both Jill and Mrs. Garrett when they'd stopped long enough for a breath or to take a bite. Now, they were having dessert, and unaware, he chuckled aloud as he chewed the bite of creamy pie, the crust melting in his mouth.

"And just what might be so amusing, sir?" Jill asked with a slight dig into his ribs. They'd moved into the living room for dessert and coffee. Lucas and Jill had settled on a deep, soft sofa while Mrs. Garrett sat comfortably in a nearby overstuffed chair. Lucas swallowed his bite of pie with a grin.

"I'm just enjoying the two of you having such a good time even though, sometimes, it seems to be at my expense," he said, picking up his coffee and taking a savory sip. Mrs. Garrett knew how to brew good, strong coffee.

"Oh, not at your expense, dear boy," Mrs. Garrett said with the same sweet smile he remembered. "Just reminiscing about what a dear you were then and still are."

"Ah, Mrs. Garrett," Jill said, reaching over and putting her hand on Lucas's arm. "He's always been a dear. I don't think he knows how to be anything else."

Lucas felt himself blushing.

"I agree," Mrs. Garrett said softly. "Those few months you were in my class, Lucas, began what were some of the most difficult times of my life. You had no way of knowing at the time, but when Andy got sick, you were such a comfort to me.

"I don't know if you remember the day we did the exercise about what we were thankful for and writing those things on that leaf you carry in your billfold," she went on. "The one with 'firetrucks' and 'Mr. Andy'?"

Lucas nodded. Putting his empty dessert plate and cup on the coffee table, he reached in his pocket and pulled out his wallet. Opening it, he gently removed the fragile leaf from inside and ran his finger lightly over the words, one of them smudged.

Mrs. Garrett gazed at the leaf Lucas held and said in a hushed voice, "Well, that was the day after Andy told me of his diagnosis. After you told me what to write on your leaf, you placed your little hand on my shoulder and patted it gently. I nearly lost it all right then and there," she chuckled sadly. "That's where the smudge mark came from. It was a tear I couldn't stop. Do you remember any of that?"

Lucas looked into Mrs. Garrett's eyes for a long time and nodded. He remembered that day like it was yesterday. He'd forgotten plenty of other things since then, but that day was indelibly imprinted on his mind. He'd thought that smudge might have been caused by a tear but until now he hadn't known the cause.

Mrs. Garrett smiled softly as she looked at Lucas. "And, Lucas, I want you to know how much you meant to Andy. Telling him you had moved and there was no way to reach you, was hard—really hard—to do. He worried and fretted about you, saying several times he hoped wherever you were, you had someone to talk to, a friend, and an adviser.

Lucas looked back at the leaf in his hand. "I never knew," he said softly, looking at Mrs. Garrett, who was smiling at him with tears in her eyes. "Until I came to see you that day a few weeks ago, I had no idea about Mr. Andy. Leaving Abernathy that day in second grade—all I could think of was getting back here to be with you and Mr. Andy again."

Mrs. Garrett reached over and patted Lucas's arm. He placed his hand over hers, squeezing it gently.

"And here you are," she said softly. "What a fine man you've become, Lucas. I couldn't be any prouder than if you were my own son." She sat back and sniffed lightly. "You may think I'm an old crazy woman, but I believe that, somehow, Andy knows and is very pleased."

Embarrassed, Lucas looked down, afraid his own emotions might take over.

Sensing his struggle, Jill placed a hand on Lucas's knee, rubbing her thumb gently back and forth while he regained his composure. Jill watched him, love in her eyes.

"Mrs. Garrett," Jill said, "This guy has talked constantly about you and Mr. Andy and the inspiration you both were to him through some pretty dark times. It's been Lucas's dream almost as long as I've known him to come back here. He wanted to come back in a way that would make you and Mr. Andy proud of what he's done with his life from the inspiration you both gave him."

Mrs. Garrett smiled as she and Jill looked at Lucas who sat silently, staring at the leaf he still held in his hand. Sensing their gaze, he looked up, and they exchanged smiles of understanding.

"Lucas," Mrs. Garrett began, "I have absolutely no doubt, but that Andy knows and is incredibly proud of you. I wish he were here to tell you that himself, but he knows . . ." She nodded fervently. "He knows."

The silence stretched comfortably before Jill laughed lightly and wiped at an escaping tear.

"Mrs. Garrett, after everything Lucas has told me about you and Mr. Andy, I don't think I fully realized until now what a truly special relationship you share. I am so glad we've met, and I hope we can spend more time together."

Mrs. Garrett laughed while Lucas beamed his pleasure.

"Jill, my dear, that sounds absolutely delightful. I'm looking forward to it. But for now, can I get more pie for either of you?" She stood and swayed a bit, the color draining from her face as she started to reach for their plates.

Alarmed, Lucas jumped up, took her arm, and helped her sit back down.

He knelt beside her, studying her, and watched the color slowly return to her face.

"How are you feeling?" he asked gently.

"I'm fine, dear boy. I just stood and bent over too fast, but I'm fine. Not to worry."

They all stood as Jill picked up the coffee cups and carried them to the kitchen. Following Jill, Lucas walked protectively beside Mrs. Garrett, one hand on her waist while he carried a stack of plates in the other.

"We'll help with the dishes," Jill said as she set the plates on the counter.

"You'll do no such thing." Mrs. Garrett tried to shoo Jill from the sink.

Jill deftly stepped around her and began filling the sink with water. The fresh scent of dish soap floated around them as Mrs. Garrett appealed to Lucas with a look, but he only grinned and shrugged lightly.

"I've learned to just go with it," Lucas said in a stage whisper. "It's safest and easiest that way."

Jill swatted at him with a hand full of soap suds.

They talked while Jill washed and Lucas dried. Mrs. Garrett watched from a bar stool just inside the door as she drank another cup of coffee.

"You're coming to Lucas's badge pinning ceremony, aren't you?" Jill asked as Lucas dried the last plate and placed it on the stack at the end of the counter with a slight clink.

Mrs. Garrett's eyes brightened with delighted surprise. "Well, of course. I'd love to come. Just let me know when and where."

Lucas smiled and with a wink said, "I'll make sure you get a special invitation and VIP seating."

"VIP seating?" Jill asked with a teasing frown at Lucas. "You're lucky, Mrs. Garrett. I haven't even been invited yet."

Mrs. Garrett chuckled as Lucas put an arm around Jill and said, "I'll see if I can find a seat for you—somewhere."

KATIE WATCHED LUCAS AND Jill's easy banter with a smile. Lucas had found the same type of love she and Andy had shared. Andy's love was still so warm, so real—as if she could feel his arms wrapped around her, holding her close. Even after all these years, she missed him. She missed him so much.

THE MONDAY MORNING STAFF meeting had been rough—again. Lucas was excited about the vision he had for the department and was revealing his ideas for the changes a little at a time while using the same step-by-step approach as they worked to correct the operational silos. For the most part, the staff seemed enthusiastic and grasped where he was headed, except for Carr and, occasionally, Nate Baldwin. While the rest of the team eagerly embraced the ideas and worked to implement the changes, Baldwin was slow to implement any requested adaptations while Carr agreed to make them but then didn't.

Lucas had escaped to his office for a brief respite before beginning a series of afternoon meetings and then making his usual random station visits. He ran his fingers through his hair as he stared unseeing at his computer screen. He was contemplating calling Carr in for yet another one-on-one meeting when there was a knock at the door.

"Knock. Knock," a familiar voice said before Mike Bentley stuck his head in the door.

"Busy, Chief?" Bentley asked with a warm smile.

"Of course, but never too busy for you," Lucas said, standing and walking around his desk to shake Bentley's hand. "Please, have a seat." He gestured toward the two chairs at the smaller table. "It's great to see you. Can I get you some coffee?"

"No. No. I can only stay a minute. Lindsay asked me to come down to discuss some of the details for the retirement ceremony, or should I say the promotion aka badge pinning ceremony?" Bentley chuckled.

"Whichever strikes your fancy. Both, any or all are correct," Lucas replied with a smile. "How is retired life treating you? Staying busy?"

"You know, I've always heard it said that you're busier when you retire than when you're working full time. I'm not exactly sure how that works, but it's true. I don't know how I had time to work and still get everything done I'm doing now. I miss everyone, of course, but overall, it's a good change for me. I've surprised myself at how much I'm enjoying it."

And Bentley looked like he was enjoying it, Lucas thought. He looked great—well rested and happy. Retirement was really agreeing with him.

"Well, we're looking forward to celebrating your service," Lucas said with a genuine smile. "And I'm happy to say, that Mrs. Garrett is coming to the ceremony."

"I saw her this morning, and she said you'd invited her. You beat me to the punch," Bentley said with a grin. "I'd planned to ask her, but so long as she's coming, that's the important thing."

Bentley held up a hand when Lucas started to apologize.

"Nope. No worries at all. I'm just glad she's going to be there—for both of us."

"Yeah—me too," Lucas nodded with a smile.

Carr's voice drifted in from the hallway, joking loudly with some of the staff. Lucas's smile faded, replaced with a frown before he quickly smoothed it away.

"So, have you made any of those trips you talked about taking?" Lucas went on quickly.

Bentley didn't answer but leaned forward and studied Lucas.

"Carr giving you problems?"

Lucas tried to smile convincingly. "We're still trying to work things out. I'm confident we'll get there."

A sudden knock at the door interrupted Bentley's appraisal of the frustration he saw on Lucas's face.

Jeremy Ennis stuck his head in. "Chief . . . oh, my apologies, I didn't realize you had someone with you. Chief Bentley!" Jeremy said with a smile when he saw who it was. "It's good to see you, sir."

"And you too, Ennis. Congratulations on completing the requirements and getting started as fire marshal. You'll do well."

"Thank you, sir."

"Did you need something?" Lucas asked, sensing that this wasn't a social call.

"Yes, sir. You asked to be notified if there were any more suspicious or unusual fires, and we've just had another one—this one against a small shed."

"Damage?" Lucas asked.

"Minimal, but there are definite accelerant indicators. I thought you'd want to know."

"How many does this make?"

"With the one today, we're up to five."

"Okay—thank you. I'll join you in a few minutes for a full briefing."

"Yes, sir," Jeremy said with a nod to Bentley before he left.

"Trouble?" Bentley asked, his brows pinching together with concern.

"We're not quite sure. We've had some random suspicious activity but nothing major—at least so far. Ennis is on top of it. He's a good man."

"Yes, he is. You've got a good crew, but about Carr . . . if you need a listening ear . . ."

Lucas smiled and took the hand Bentley extended and shook it. "Thank you, sir. I'll keep that in mind, and I appreciate it. I don't miss the interview process, but I do miss our visits."

"I may be retired, Chief Matthews, but I'm still available to you. Never hesitate to call." Bentley gave a nod and then turned and left.

Lucas looked back at his computer and minimized the screen he'd been working in. The meeting with Carr would have to wait. He headed toward Ennis's office. These suspicious fires were becoming a major concern.

L EAVING STATION 5 THAT afternoon, Lucas turned toward Station 7 and mulled over the information Ennis had shared with him during the earlier briefing about the shed fire. Even though the fires had been in random locations, there were also definite similarities. It was becoming abundantly clear there was an arsonist at work in Abernathy. Lucas's heart sped up at the thought.

Station 7 was on the far side of town, which meant he'd be later than usual getting home from work. He'd better let Jill know his plans; plus, he wondered how her interview with the big design firm had gone that morning. He punched in the speed dial for Jill's phone.

"Hey, there!" Jill answered brightly, maybe a little too brightly, Lucas thought with a slight frown.

"Hey there, yourself." Lucas took a quick sip of coffee. "Thought I'd check in and see how your big interview went."

There was only silence.

"Jill? Are you there?" Lucas asked, looking at his phone to see if they'd been disconnected.

"I'm here," Jill finally said.

"I think I may have called at a bad time," Lucas said hesitantly. "I'll call you back later."

"No . . . wait. Sorry. I'm just so . . . so mad."

And yes, there it was. Lucas recognized the anger in her voice.

Lucas drove and listened as Jill unloaded.

"She—that Smythe woman—wanted to use my connection to you and the city to get new clients for them. Clients like the mayor, the council, the city manager. She said they're looking to grow their firm by bringing their business home. Since I'm a designer, they wanted to use me *and* you and your new job to help them kick off their new program to do that. The very nerve of that woman!"

Lucas didn't appreciate their approach either but couldn't help grinning at Jill's indignation. She continued on for what seemed like several minutes without taking a breath.

"Their offices were gorgeous but there's a lot more to a job than a fancy office, don't you agree, Lucas?" She paused, waiting for Lucas to agree.

Lucas wiped the grin off his face before he answered, afraid Jill could tell he was smiling if he didn't.

"Well, honey, I'm not a good one to ask that particular question. I do have a beautiful office to enjoy thanks to my amazingly talented interior designer wife."

"Oh, Lucas," Jill laughed.

"No, honey. You were absolutely right to walk out. You wouldn't have been happy there. I have a feeling that even with their super fancy designer offices, their standards couldn't come close to the level of work you do. Blow them off. You've got interviews with a couple more design firms. Just focus on those."

"Thank you, Lucas. You always know what to say to make me feel better. But enough about me. How's your day?"

Lucas took a deep breath and let out a sigh. "It's better now. I've talked to you and am out visiting the stations. Oh, and Bentley came by. It's always good to see him."

"Uh-huh. And . . ."

"And, what?" He knew, but he didn't want to talk about it.

"Don't you have a Monday morning staff meeting? How did that go?"

"Oh, you know. Same ole. It looks like some of them are really coming around to some of the changes and getting them implemented quickly."

"And . . . Carr? How was he today?"

Lucas pulled into the parking lot of Station 7.

"He's the same ole part of that answer and something you're not sup-posed to be worrying about. I just pulled into Seven. I'll be home around seven-thirty."

"Okay. I'll see you then. I'll have dinner ready, and we can talk more then. Love you."

Lucas grinned. "Love you too." He should have known she wouldn't let him off that easily; not when it was something she knew was weighing on his mind the way Milton Carr was.

Lucas pulled up behind Ennis's vehicle, putting his own in park. Opening the door and sliding out, he immediately smelled the pungent odor of lighter fluid. The look on Ennis's face when Lucas caught his eye, told Lucas something serious had developed. The suspicious fires were growing in scope, intensity and unfortunately, frequency. Some were minor and others larger, but the frequency was a growing concern.

The group of firefighters, their solemn faces smudged around the outline of where their masks had been, parted to make way when they saw Ennis motion Lucas over. Riley Sullivan stood with Ennis and A Shift's Battalion Chief, Tyler Forney, surveying the damage. From what Lucas saw as he approached, the burn area backed up to what used to be a white lattice fence which was now singed sticks jutting up at various angles. The fence was attached to a small wooden storage building that had also burned. Two crew members were inside the structure doing overhaul, pulling down parts of the ceiling and checking the empty space between the wall and exterior sheathing for hot spots. The acrid smell of burnt wood and rubber permeated the air already pungent with the smell of lighter fluid.

When Lucas reached Jeremy's side, he froze when he saw what everyone had been staring at. A brand new, shiny gas can sat just outside of the burn area, an envelope attached. On the envelope in broad, childlike print, the envelope read:

CHIEF MATTHEWS

Lucas's eyes grew round when he turned to Ennis, who looked worried.

"We didn't touch it, sir. We thought it best to wait for you. I'll make sure the can is safe and then detach the envelope for you. Here. Please use these when handling the envelope and whatever is inside," Jeremy said, handing Lucas a pair of evidence gloves.

Lucas nodded but put a hand on Jeremy's arm as Jeremy started toward the gas can.

"Hold up, Ennis. The note is addressed to me. I'll get it." Returning to his vehicle, Lucas retrieved his bunker gear and helmet from their storage compartment and putting them on, moved toward the burn area as Jeremy backed the group up.

Cinching the chin strap of his helmet tightly under his chin, Lucas started to take the first step toward the gas can, but Jeremy stepped to his side to block him.

"Sir, please. This is my job. I'll secure the device and retrieve the note."

Lucas put a hand on Jeremy's shoulder and with surprising strength, pulled Jeremy behind him. Pinning Jeremy in place with a look, Lucas stepped onto the crunchy black grass and walked slowly, purposefully, toward the can and envelope. The silence was intense, his labored breathing all that Lucas could hear beyond the steady crunching beneath his boots.

When he reached the can, Lucas looked all the way around it to make sure no wires were attached, or it wasn't sitting on some type of pressure device. Seeing nothing but dried grass the fire hadn't reached, Lucas pulled on the evidence gloves Ennis had given him and slowly, gently lifted the envelope, pulling it free from the can. When the last bit of tape pulled free, the can tilted precariously and then tipped backward. It was empty. Lucas and the group hovering several yards away sucked in a collective gasp.

Lucas slowly straightened and with a strained smile, turned, envelope in hand, and walked back toward the group.

"You okay, sir?" Jeremy asked, moving quickly to Lucas.

"Fine, but I don't want to have to do that again." Lucas took a deep breath, carefully pinching the corner of the envelope between his gloved thumb and finger.

"Go ahead and open the envelope, but carefully . . . very carefully. Keep as much intact as possible," Jeremy instructed; his eyes glued to the envelope.

Encumbered by the gloves, Lucas fumbled a bit, but finally managed to free the flap and then pulled out a single piece of white paper with words scrawled in the same childish writing:

GUESS WHO

Lucas and Jeremy exchanged a puzzled look as Jeremy held out two clear evidence bags. Lucas slid the envelope into one and the note into the other.

This was the sixth suspicious fire but the first gas can and note of this kind. Extensive pictures were being taken of each scene, but it was now obvious, the arsonist was enjoying this and making Lucas his target.

Leaving Ennis to secure the scene, take pictures, and collect any other evidence, Lucas drove back to the office, mulling over the obvious question in such cases. Why? What motivated an arsonist and what was the motive in this particular case? He, Ennis, and the deputy chiefs needed to meet and discuss the fires that had happened so far. They needed to look for any similarities whether in style or method. They also needed to consider the rate the fires were escalating, both in number and size, and anyway they might be able to get ahead of whoever was doing this, anticipate his next target, and stop him.

Pulling into the parking lot of the admin building, Lucas took a deep breath as he got out and walked in the back door. Headed in the direction of Lindsay's desk, he heard Carr's raised voice coming from his office.

"I told you exactly what I needed, and you screwed up. Again. Why don't you ever listen to me? I can get 200 firefighters to pay attention to the least detail, but I can't . . ."

Carr stopped mid-sentence when Lucas stepped just inside the doorway of his office.

Carr was standing, leaning over his desk, his fingertips planted on its surface, a glare accompanying the harsh words directed at a young man standing opposite of him on the other side of the desk. The young man was thin, his hair was the same light brown as Carr's but disheveled. He wore a wrinkled shirt and a pair of jeans that were beyond fashionable with their holes and tears. His tennis shoes were dirty, the laces untied.

"Is everything okay in here?" Lucas asked, looking between the two.

Carr straightened, the glare that had been directed at the young man, now directed at Lucas.

"Everything is fine, *sir.*"

Carr offered nothing further, and the young man's head ducked even lower than it had been.

Lucas took a step inside and immediately felt Carr's anger ratchet up.

Ignoring Carr, Lucas walked toward the young man, extending his hand. "I don't believe we've met. I'm Chief Matthews."

The boy's head jerked up, a panicked look on his face as his eyes flashed from Lucas to Carr.

Lucas waited patiently; his hand still extended until the young man nervously shook it then quickly withdrew his hand.

"Matthews, this is my son, Chase," Carr said.

Chase Carr wouldn't meet his eye, but Lucas nodded. "It's nice to meet you, Chase."

Chase mumbled something before shooting a quick look at his father and dashing out of the office. Lucas thought he detected the faint smell of something like cigarettes as Chase rushed past him.

Lucas looked back to Carr, who only glared defiantly back.

Lucas turned and started to the door. "We've had another arson. This time he left a note. We need to meet asap. This meeting takes priority over anything else you've got."

Walking out of the office, Lucas didn't see Carr pound a fist into his other hand and collapse into his chair.

CHASE'S MINI HATCHBACK ROARED away from the fire department's administrative building. His mom had sent him to the office with a file his dad had left at home but needed for an afternoon meeting. She had given Chase the wrong file, but *he* was the one at fault in his dad's mind, his dad always more than willing to assume the worst of him. He was almost tempted to give up trying to prove himself to his dad—but not quite yet.

CHASE'S ANGER EVAPORATED WHEN he pulled in front of the house. Casey's car was parked in the driveway. It was the first time she'd been home from college since she'd left two months ago. She was home for a long weekend, and he'd been counting the days until she got here. She wasn't just his sister; she was his ally, friend, and defender against their dad.

Chase ran through the garage. Throwing open the door to the house, he ran inside and stopped short when he got to the kitchen where Casey and their mom were preparing supper. Seeing Casey, Chase grinned from ear to ear.

Hearing him, Casey turned. "Chaser!" she exclaimed. Running around the island, she launched herself into her brother's arms. "I've missed you!"

She jumped back and tousled his hair. "How's my little bro?"

Chase laughed and grabbed her into another tight hug before stepping back. "Better now that you're here, and boy, I've missed you too!"

Grinning, Chase grabbed a bar stool and sat down. "How's college life? Ready to move back home?" he asked, reaching over and grabbing a cookie from an open tray on the island.

Casey laughed, popping a bite of the cookie Chase handed her in her mouth.

"Well . . . I have to admit I'm looking forward to some home cooking, but as far as moving back, well . . ." She paused and said in a stage whisper, "I'm having too much fun."

Brenda Carr gave her daughter a teasing glare. They laughed, all knowing it was probably true. Casey had always been a serious student, so there were no worries about her grades, but Chase could tell she *was* really happy, and he had to admit, he envied her. He wasn't happy but didn't know how to change that feeling. Now wasn't the time to worry about it. Casey was home, and they had some catching up to do.

After their mom put dinner in the oven and the salad in the refrigerator, she left on a quick errand before their dad came home from work, which meant Casey and Chase were free to do whatever they wanted. They shot some hoops on the patio in the backyard. Casey had played high school girls' basketball, and Chase had helped her practice by guarding her and trying to steal the ball while she relentlessly took shots at the hoop. Playing basketball was fun with Casey, Chase thought, but not any other time. When they'd tired of that, they adjourned to the family room, Casey draped across a chair and Chase across the sofa, both sipping soft drinks.

The peace was shattered in less than an hour when Milton Carr stormed through the door.

"Chase Carr!" he bellowed.

Casey had heard about the encounter at the office from Chase, so she was prepared to intercept her dad.

"Dad!" Casey said, throwing herself into her dad's arms. "I'm home! Are you ready to spoil me for an entire weekend?"

"How's my girl?" Carr said, grabbing Casey into a tight hug before stepping back and taking her in. "Beautiful as ever. You're not dating anyone, are you?"

"Dad . . ." Casey groused good-naturedly. "I've already got the two best guys in the world with you and Chase. Who else could I possibly need?"

"Speaking of Chase, where is your brother?"

"I'm here, Dad," Chase said, walking hesitantly into the kitchen. "Sorry about ducking out this afternoon."

"Thankfully, Chief Matthews had other things on his mind," Carr replied gruffly. "And the meeting I needed the file for didn't happen, so you're in the clear this time, but next time . . ."

"Honey, did you know you left the wrong file on top of the stack you directed me to when you called? *I'm* the one that got the wrong file but only because you . . ." Brenda began as she walked in and overheard the conversation.

"Yeah, yeah, yeah. Not now. Let's eat. I want to hear about my daughter's college life."

They sat at the table, Casey sitting across from a sullen Chase. Once everyone settled into their familiar places and the dishes were being passed, Casey kicked Chase under the table, hitting him in the knee and grinning. He rubbed his knee and grinned back. This time, he didn't care.

Having weighed the pros and cons of what he should or shouldn't do, Milton Carr finally came to a decision. It was time to put the wheels into motion.

On his way to the office the next morning, Carr made a detour and pulled into the parking lot of Station 6. He headed inside to visit Darryl McCracken whose A-Shift was coming on duty. Stepping into Six's kitchen, the familiar fire station smell of strong coffee greeted him at the door. Some firefighters were already gathered around the table while others were drifting in from the bay where they'd been prepping bunker gear and checking equipment. The station rookie was at the counter, cooking breakfast, and the smell of pancakes and sausage drifted tantalizingly in the air.

"Chief!" several exclaimed as Carr made his way through the kitchen. He stopped to greet and shake hands before pouring himself a cup of coffee and walking down the short hall to the shift commander's office.

"Milton!" Darryl McCracken exclaimed as Carr stepped inside the office. The office was small but functional. Carr took a seat in the lone guest chair after removing Darryl's jacket from the chair and laying it across a filing cabinet behind him. Darryl McCracken sat back down, the old desk chair creaking its protest. He twirled a pen in his fingers as he swiveled away from the computer to look at his long-time friend. A stickler for neatness, Carr noted that McCracken felt no such compunction. Even though the shift was just getting underway, papers and files had already been tossed haphazardly across the desk.

Stocky and powerfully built, Darryl McCracken was a hardcore fire-fighter whose handlebar mustache was legendary within the department. He was astute and always seemed to know how to work the department's political system to get exactly what he wanted. His system had worked right up until Jeremy Ennis had been selected by Chief Bracken as the new fire marshal, even though McCracken had passed the test and certification exam a full month earlier.

Knowing how deep that disappointment ran, Carr reasoned that McCracken would have a vested interest in helping him with his plan, even though Carr would make sure he kept McCracken in the dark as an unwitting participant.

"Great to see you, Carr. What brings you out our way this morning?" McCracken asked, leaning back and propping one ankle over his other knee as he reached for the coffee cup on his desk.

"Actually, I came to see you, Darryl," Carr said heavily. "I need your thoughts on a matter that's escalating, and I'm just not sure our new fire marshal can handle it."

"Oh?" McCracken said, leaning forward abruptly. "Is this about the arsons I've been hearing about?"

"Yeah. There haven't been any in your area or on your shift—yet, but they're getting bigger and happening more often. If the situation isn't resolved soon, it will be only a matter of time. The deputy chiefs are meeting to discuss the situation before the ceremony this afternoon. You trained in arson investigation, prepping for the exam. Any thoughts?" Carr went on, watching closely for McCracken's reaction.

McCracken stroked his chin thoughtfully as he glanced out the office window that overlooked the bay and the firefighters working there.

"What type of accelerants are they using?" McCracken finally asked.

"The first few were started with nothing but matches to dry grass. The last one yesterday, the guys said, was started with lighter fluid. And get this," Carr said, leaning forward conspiratorially. "There was a gas can left at the scene—brand new and empty—with a note attached to it, addressed to our illustrious new chief."

McCracken's eyes widened.

"Well, that's quite a twist."

Carr nodded solemnly, trying not to grin.

McCracken's eyes glittered shrewdly.

"You think someone's got it in for Matthews then?" he asked in low tones.

Carr shrugged noncommittally. "It's starting to look that way. And . . ." he added, leaning in even closer and lowering his voice, "it might have something to do with his past."

"His past?" McCracken said, sitting up, relishing some new gossip.

"Yeah. There are drugs in his past and that kind of activity always seems to bring out unsavory characters. Maybe some of his previous cohorts are trying to get his attention. They might even get some satisfaction from bringing him down. I don't know—but his arrival and these fires starting about the same time—a coincidence? Maybe. I don't know, but . . ."

Carr leaned back, trying to look deep in thought.

"Hmmm . . ." McCracken mulled softly, still stroking his chin. "You sure about this?"

"Read it myself. I found several newspaper articles online about it. Can't believe it wasn't uncovered in his background check, or maybe it was, and the powers that be were just determined to hire him. Who knows? I can assure you though, if they'd named me as the new chief, more than likely all this arson trouble wouldn't be happening at all. Even if there were trouble, I'd have the right people in place who could handle it," he finished, looking at McCracken pointedly. He stopped to give McCracken an opportunity to process what he *wasn't* saying.

McCracken nodded, looking at Carr thoughtfully. He'd known Milton Carr for years and trusted he wouldn't carelessly throw around such innuendos.

Carr stood and moved to the door.

"I've got to get to admin," Carr said as he turned to leave. "I'll talk to you later. If anything comes to mind about those arsons, give me a heads up."

"Count on it." McCracken followed Carr to the kitchen where breakfast was being placed on the table and firefighters were taking their seats.

"See you guys at the ceremony this afternoon," Carr said, reaching over and snagging a sausage patty.

Busily passing the pancakes and sausage around, the group chorused, "See you, Chief," as Carr gave a wave and left out the back door. McCracken pulled up a chair, joining the group at the table and began serving his own plate.

"So, guys," McCracken began, "let's get started with the latest and greatest departmental news . . ."

The townhome was utter chaos, and Lucas was enjoying every crazy minute. Jon was loudly and humorously grousing about having to sleep on the lumpy sofa while Jill, Jessica, and the other ladies were chatting as they prepared brunch. Coach and Patsy were here. They'd left Fort Collins early that morning to make the drive while Dan and Jessica, sitting across from Lucas on the sofa, had returned early from a vacation to the northwest. Meg and her family had wanted to come but weren't able to due to the kids' school activities. She called last night to congratulate Lucas, and they'd talked for over an hour.

The ladies had been in and out of the kitchen most of the morning, busily preparing the dishes, creating the delicious aromas filling the townhome. The men had tried to help but had only succeeded in being shooed out of the way. When Lucas saw the amount of food placed on the table, he was sure it was enough to feed the entire group for a month. Plates were piled high accompanied by lots of laughter and noisy banter.

Enjoying a buttery bite of a blueberry muffin, Lucas looked around the crowded room, watching everyone talking, eating, and laughing, the comforting sounds of family bubbling up around him. Jill caught his eye and beamed her brightest smile, lighting up the room for him even more than the sunlight streaming in through the windows.

Never take family for granted—your physical family or the brotherhood. Commit times with them to memory and to heart. They're priceless. Looking around, Lucas knew Mr. Andy's words were true.

He'd gone to the office earlier for an update about the ongoing arsons. It seemed the fires were no longer being set in a concentrated area. With the latest fire, it was now evident the arsonist was broadening his reach. Ennis was meticulous in preserving evidence at each scene, but nothing was adding up and the note yesterday . . . Lucas frowned.

Coach, holding a loaded plate, sat down in the chair nearest Lucas.

"Hungry, Coach?" Lucas asked with a grin as he speared a bite of his own breakfast casserole, trying to erase the unease from his mind—at least for a while.

"Something wrong, Son?" Coach asked.

"Ah—just 'chief' stuff," Lucas said with a forced grin; he knew he wouldn't fool Coach. He wiped his mouth with one of the firetruck napkins Jessica had brought. He couldn't help a grin as he looked at it.

"Trouble?" Coach asked softly, studying Lucas closely as he popped a grape in his mouth.

"Nothing I can't handle and definitely nothing for you to worry about," Lucas replied without meeting Coach's eye.

Coach studied Lucas and leaned closer. "If I remember correctly, it seems the last time you said those same words, or at least thought them, it came close to ending badly."

Sighing, Lucas set his plate aside and leaned over, putting his elbows on his knees and his face in his hands.

"Not buying it, huh?" Lucas asked, looking up at Coach, who slowly shook his head.

"Nope. Can I help?"

Lucas sighed again and sat up in the lumpy chair that matched the lumpy sofa.

"Thanks for the offer, Coach. Truly. But it really is department related. I've got an arsonist out there who is getting bolder by the day. Yesterday, he left a note addressed to Chief Matthews, taunting me as to who it is, and I have absolutely no idea. The fires are getting bigger, and I'm afraid if we don't catch whoever this is soon, there are going to be even more serious ramifications. Property is definitely in danger, and lives . . . well, that's what has me concerned most."

As Coach listened, Lucas couldn't help but notice that the lines around Coach's eyes had deepened and the bald spot on top of his head had grown, the hair around it more gray now than brown. Coach, and Patsy too, were aging, and Lucas didn't like to admit it.

"Lucas?" Jill called to him, trying to get his attention across the fray. "What time do you want us where we're supposed to be which is where?"

Lucas looked at Coach and chuckled before standing. "I think I need to start directing some traffic."

Coach nodded and gave Lucas a reassuring grin, but the concern never left his face.

The Abernathy Civic Center's event hall was a typical, large meeting space with utilitarian gray walls, dark gray patterned carpet and luminous florescent lights that were made to look like industrial chandeliers. It was the perfect neutral backdrop for any event to feature its own decor and shine. The set up for the fire department event was not elaborate and consisted of a podium, which had seen better days, an Abernathy Fire Department banner behind the podium, theater style seating and a couple of tables for the appropriately fire-themed refreshments.

Lucas and Jill sat on the front row along with Kirk Lorimar, members of the City Council, and a few department heads, all listening while the mayor made a few remarks. Police Chief Lance Harper, sat at the opposite end of the row from Lucas. Harper caught Lucas's eye and acknowledged him with a nod. Harper was a big man with a barrel chest, muscular arms, a crew cut, and piercing gray eyes that Lucas had decided he wouldn't want trained on him in an interrogation. They were getting to know each other well, working closely together on the arson investigations. Lucas had sized Harper up to be a police chief with high integrity and a no-nonsense attitude. He was always down to business and never left you wondering where you stood in his opinion. They'd hit it off immediately.

Lucas glanced behind him and beamed with pride at his family, sitting on the second row. Jessica looked over and gave him a sly wink, making Lucas grin. Across the aisle, Katie Garrett sat next to Mike Bentley. A shadow of concern had crossed Lucas's face when he'd first seen Mrs. Garrett that afternoon. She was paler and thinner than when he'd seen her just a couple of weeks ago, but she smiled brightly when he caught her eye. The woman with brunette hair on the other side of Bentley must be his wife, Lucas thought. He hadn't had the opportunity to meet her before but hoped to today.

The rest of the large room was full of firefighters, family members, and friends of those being officially recognized and pinned that day or to honor Mike Bentley for his years of service. Typically, the retiring chief would be present, but Chief Bracken had moved out of town.

Following short remarks from the Mayor, City Manager Kirk Lorimar moved to the podium and asked Lucas and Jill to join him. Lorimar then asked Lucas to raise his right hand and place his left hand on the Bible Jill held that had been a wedding gift from Coach and Patsy. As Lucas fingered the Bible's soft leather covering, he repeated the oath with a clear and confident voice, reciting each line after Lorimar.

Picking up a velvet box off the podium, Lorimar opened the lid and removed a gleaming badge with its iconic set of five crossed bugles set above the fire Maltese cross, indicating the rank of Chief. Lorimar handed the badge to Jill who took it and with a broad smile, faced Lucas and carefully pinned the badge to his starched white uniform shirt. Glowing with pride, she gently placed her hand over the badge where it was pinned over

Lucas's heart. She looked up and smiled at Lucas as he placed his hand over hers.

Fully installed as the new chief, Lucas took the podium and said a few words about the importance of each firefighter making their mission always to be better and to do better. He stressed striving to do everything that can be done in the performance of the job, before quietly adding *and then some* as he looked intently at the firefighters in the audience. He then proudly conducted the same pinning ceremony, repeating its significance for the new fire marshal, two captains and three lieutenants being recognized. Lucas smiled as he watched these firefighters share their achievement with their family just as he was with his.

Following the pinning ceremony, Mike Bentley's retirement was celebrated, giving each deputy chief an opportunity to make some remarks and give the newly retired Bentley a few good-natured jabs as well. Several retirement gifts were presented from the department and the city, including the United States and state flags that flew over City Hall on his last day of active duty, and the print of an antique fire engine, the mat surrounding the print signed by command staff. The last item presented was Bentley's fire helmet which he proudly took and tucked safely under his arm.

While Bentley's recognition and tributes continued, Lucas sat down by Jill and, taking her hand, exhaled a long breath. When she glanced up at him, he smiled and squeezed her hand gently.

A roar of approval put a punctuation mark on the comments Bentley had shared. Lucas returned to the podium after a long standing ovation in Bentley's honor with Bentley actually blushing as he returned to his seat.

Lucas shared a smile with Bentley as Lucas turned to face the large audience. "The City and the personnel of the Abernathy Fire Department are excited about the department's future while also being respectful and appreciative of our past and of those who have gone before us and served so honorably. We continue, confident in accomplishing our mission of working together to help, protect, and keep each other and the citizens of Abernathy safe."

Lucas had to pause for applause before adding, "We appreciate each of you for being here and sharing this special time with us. This concludes the official ceremony but please stay, visit, and enjoy the refreshments."

There was scattered applause as everyone stood and began talking. Jill gave Lucas a quick embrace before he was engulfed by the rest of the family.

Coach gave him a firm handshake before Patsy pulled him into a tight hug.

"We couldn't be prouder of you, Son," Coach said, his arm around Patsy and his hand resting lightly on Lucas's shoulder.

"Nor we," Dan Barkley added as he and Jill's mom, Jessica, joined the circle. "We'll miss you being in Fort Collins, but we're excited for you. You deserve this opportunity."

"Thank you, everyone," Lucas said, his eyes taking in the circle of familiar and dear faces as Jon and Jess elbowed their way through to Lucas, making everyone laugh.

"Proud of you, Dad," Jon said giving Lucas's shoulder a light shove while Jessica hugged her dad and whispered in his ear, "Best chief ever."

Lucas laughed and hugged them before they left, both turning in the direction of the refreshment table.

While Jessica only took a bottle of water before rejoining their family, Jon lingered, eyeing the sizes of the pieces of cake before finally settling on one. Picking up the plate and a fork, he was reaching for the cup of punch the smiling server was offering him when his arm was suddenly bumped by a girl who had just walked up and reached for the same cup. The server quickly handed the cup to Jon while picking up another and offering it to the girl. The girl took the offered cup and smiled coyly at Jon, who blushed.

CASEY CARR COULD ONLY smile at her luck before she and Jon were jostled closer together by others reaching for cake and punch.

"I am so sorry," Casey finally said. "I hope I didn't cause you to spill anything."

"No worries. It's just a bit of a slosh," Jon chuckled.

This girl is pretty, Jon thought, really pretty. She had short, dark curly hair that bounced when she talked and accentuated her steely blue eyes that sat above round, pink cheeks and a bright red set of lips. She was mesmerizing, and he couldn't think of a thing to say until she asked him why he was there.

"Oh, my dad is new to the department, but he's official now. How about you?"

"Oh, my dad has been with the department forever and is totally gung ho. He expects his family to be present at any occasion that has the fire department associated with it. So, even though this is my first weekend home from college, well . . . here we are . . . here I am," she said, holding her hands out playfully, one hand empty, the other holding the cup of punch.

"And I'm glad," Jon said under his breath not realizing he'd said it loud enough where she could hear until her cheeks, already rosy, turned a brighter shade of pink, and she smiled brightly.

"My name is Jon," he interjected quickly.

"Hi, Jon. My name is Casey."

"Would you like to sit down?" Jon asked, lifting his plate as he motioned to some nearby chairs.

Casey smiled and walked with Jon to the cluster of chairs where they sat down and after a few awkward minutes began talking.

CHASE STOOD NEARBY, WATCHING—AND fuming. Casey was supposed to have been getting a bottle of water for each of them before they made a quick exit. Instead, she'd sat down and was talking to this guy. Chase knew who he was and knew Dad would not be happy about Casey talking to Chief Matthews' son. Besides, Casey was only home for a short while, and she was supposed to be spending that time with him.

L ucas smiled, shook hands, and acknowledged the many professional greetings and congratulations from city management and fire department personnel. The only exception, Lucas noted with a small smile to himself, was, of course, Milton Carr, who seemed to be working hard to avoid him but was spending a lot of time with council members. Shaking another hand, Lucas felt a light touch on his arm and turned to see Katie Garrett at his side, looking up at him with the same sweet look she always had for him. Pride shone in her eyes, and she clasped his hand in both of hers.

Lucas turned to give her his full attention. Her hands were like ice, and he clasped them even tighter in his own.

"Lucas, seeing you today, in charge and in your element, I just want to say again how incredibly proud of you I am. I know Andy would say the same and be so happy and proud at how you're following in his footsteps." She paused and, pulling her hand gently from Lucas, reached into her purse. "And because of that, I want you to have this."

She handed a small box to Lucas, her hands trembling. He took the box and carefully removed the lid. Inside, on a soft cloud of cotton was a firefighter's badge that gleamed as the bright lights touched it. Lucas's eyes grew wide as they looked to hers.

"It was Andy's," she said softly. "I've saved it all these years, knowing it must have a special purpose. When you showed up on my doorstep and told me you'd become a firefighter because of Andy's influence, I knew its purpose is to be with you. I want you to have it, and I know without a doubt Andy would want you to have it too."

The words Lucas so desperately wanted to say stuck in his throat. He could only nod, tears in his eyes, as he looked at Mrs. Garrett. He clutched the badge in his hand, its cool metal against his warm palm as he hugged her tightly.

"I will treasure this always, Mrs. Garrett," he finally managed. "I will carry it with me every day just as I carry Mr. Andy's spirit with me." Sniffing, Lucas stopped and wiped at his eyes. "You have no idea how much this means to me. Thank you—thank you so much."

Mrs. Garrett touched her cool fingers to Lucas's cheek and smiled up at him.

"Thank *you*, Lucas. Seeing you again, seeing what a success you've made of yourself as a person, as a firefighter, and now as a chief in the fire service, you bring everything full circle. I—no—*we're* so very proud of you."

Katie wiped at her own cheeks before smiling and taking a step away from Lucas.

"Now go on," she said with a slight sniff. "I've monopolized too much of your time. You have others wanting to congratulate you."

She took Lucas's hands and squeezing them, stood on tiptoe and kissed his cheek. She smiled up at him before turning to join Mike Bentley who had been receiving his own well wishes and congratulations. Bentley, along with his wife, were waiting patiently for Mrs. Garrett. Lucas was glad to have had the opportunity to meet Amy Bentley after she'd made her way through the crowd to congratulate him. Lucas watched as Bentley put a protective arm around his wife, who he'd entrusted to hold his helmet, and around Mrs. Garrett, as he steered them toward the door.

Lucas looked down at Mr. Andy's badge and wrapped his fingers tightly around it before slipping it into his pocket. He would carry it with him as a reminder of the type of firefighter and leader Mr. Andy had inspired him to be. Jill stepped to his side, handing him a plate with a large piece of cake and a cup of punch on it. A minute or so later, Lucas shifted the plate to his other hand and pulled the badge from his pocket to look at it again. Smiling, he slipped it back into his pocket, and with a fond look at the retreating forms of Mrs. Garrett and Bentley, he turned his attention to those who had been waiting to talk to him.

"Don't you know who that guy is?" Chase hissed urgently as he walked to the parking lot beside Casey, the crisp winter wind tugging at their hair.

"Jon. His name is Jon," Casey said with a dreamy smile. "Last names didn't come up."

"Well, his name is Jon Matthews—you know, *Matthews*, as in the new Chief Matthews' son," Chase said tersely. "Don't you get it? Dad is going to be furious. He hates Chief Matthews. Dad thinks that *he* should have gotten the chief's job instead. You'd better listen to me. I'm telling you—don't talk to that guy again."

Chase's voice had gotten considerably louder, so Casey stopped and turned to face her brother who'd come to a stop beside her. Pushing some of her dark curls aside, Casey said, "I didn't know about any of that, but if it's true, then I'm not going to tell Dad anything." She looked at Chase with a dare in her eye. "So, if Dad finds out I'm going out with Jon tomorrow night, I'll know exactly who he heard it from."

Chase grabbed Casey's upper arm in a tight grip. "Hold on. We're supposed to be going to the movies tomorrow night. Remember? Mom has made plans for a big family dinner tonight, so tomorrow night is our only chance before you go back to school."

Casey looked at Chase with a bit of unease as she pulled her arm out of his grasp. "We can hang out tonight after dinner, Chase. I promise. I never thought I'd meet someone like Jon while I was home, so I've got to seize the moment as they say. Come on. We can stay up as late as we want tonight and do whatever you want. How does that sound?"

They'd reached Casey's car. She'd opened the door and jumped in with a bright smile before Chase had an opportunity to reply. Rigid with anger, he stood at the passenger door, fuming. First the chief and now his son were causing a lot of trouble for him and for his family. A *lot* of trouble.

L UCAS SETTLED INTO HIS seat at the head of the conference room table while the others filed in and took their seats. It had thankfully been a quiet weekend with no suspicious fires. Maybe the arsonist was bored and had decided to move on. While that would be nice, it wasn't likely.

It had been a great family weekend. After a large, celebratory family dinner Friday evening at a restaurant Lindsay had recommended, everyone gathered back at the townhome for coffee, dessert, and talking—lots of talking, accompanied by lots of laughter. Lucas felt refreshed. He'd needed that family time.

Coach and Patsy, along with Jill's parents, had stayed until Saturday afternoon before driving back to Fort Collins. The rest of the weekend had been quiet, hanging out with Jon and Jessica, at least most of the time. Jon had a date Saturday night with a girl named Casey he'd met at the promotion ceremony. Lucas wasn't familiar with the names of staff family members yet, so he wasn't sure whose daughter she might be. Jon had only been gone a couple of hours before he'd returned to spend the rest of the evening with the family.

"What are you doing home so soon?" Jill had asked when Jon walked in and flopped down beside Jessica on the sofa.

"Eh, she's not really my type," Jon replied, grabbing a hand full of popcorn from Jessica's bowl. "Since Jess and I have to head back tomorrow, I decided I'd rather spend the time with the fam."

Lucas and Jill had exchanged a pleased smile, hearing Jon's explanation. Lucas put his arm around Jill, who scooted closer as they'd all settled in to watch a movie. It had been a wonderful family weekend. Now, it was back to work.

Looking at the meeting agenda he held, Lucas's pleasant thoughts about the weekend were soon interrupted by Milton Carr who huffed into the conference room and planted himself defiantly in the chair at the other end of the table. His dour looks joined the guarded expressions of other officers around the table.

"Good morning, everyone," Lucas began, looking from face to face, trying to catch someone's eye. Jeremy and Elise returned his look, both with questioning glances around the table at the others.

Grumbled good mornings accompanied the dour looks as Lucas passed out the meeting's agenda. Standing, Lucas walked around the table to push the conference room door closed.

"I'll give you a few minutes to take a look at the agenda and last meeting's accompanying notes," Lucas began as he returned to his chair and eased into it.

"We don't need a few minutes," Carr blurted out with a fierce look at Lucas. "We've got things to do—a lot of things that you have added to our already heavy workload. We need time to work—not waste time in meetings or—parties. *We* don't have the leisure of being out of the office most afternoons. *We* have work to do."

Heads popped up, eyes wide as nervous looks darted to Lucas and then to Carr.

"Sir, I . . ." West began. "I have that information you requested."

Lucas leaned back in his chair, holding Carr's glare, while he casually twirled a pen between his fingers.

"Thanks, West. We'll get to that in a minute, but it looks like we have another matter to discuss first."

"Mr. Carr," Lucas began, straightening in his chair.

Milton Carr visibly bristled at Lucas's omission of his title.

"It seems *we* have a bit of a problem here. You used the term 'we' several times. Who exactly is included in that 'we?'" Lucas asked never taking his eyes from Carr.

Carr looked around the faces at the table who were looking back at him, their eyes wide.

Lucas noted curiosity on their faces. They were evidently not knowingly part of Carr's collective 'we.'

"Well, sir," Carr began in a defiant tone. "Several members of the staff are concerned about the workload you . . ."

"Once again, Mr. Carr, who *specifically* are you speaking of?" Lucas interjected.

West looked from Lucas to Carr before saying, "Milton, you seem to be implicating the staff at this table in your statement. As I've already told you, I, personally, do not agree with you. I have no problem with my workload or with how Chief Matthews spends his time. I see positive results from the changes he's asked to be implemented. And as far as his time out of the office, he's typically in the stations with the crews when he's not at City Hall attending meetings. And actually, he *is* the Chief. How he spends his time is his business. Not ours."

Still defiant, Carr shifted in his seat then looked to Nate Baldwin.

Nate shook his head, looking at Carr. "Milton, I told you—I'm not with you on this. I agree with West that Matthews has us headed in the right direction. The workload is what it is for command staff. We are responsible for a lot of lives, so in my opinion, you can never work too hard."

Working to maintain a calm, disinterested look, Lucas appreciated what West and Nate had just said. Carr had been trying to incite grievances against him with the officers, but it obviously wasn't working. Lucas had had some very productive discussions with both West and Nate about their divisions. There had been some give and take on all sides before coming to mutually agreeable resolutions that were better for having been vetted with thorough discussion. Both men were in the process of making the changes and adaptations and were getting positive feedback from firefighters as a result.

Elise Stephens sat quietly, her eyes wide and face white with strain as she looked between those speaking. Anger plain on his face, Jeremy Ennis was on the edge of his seat, his mouth open and about to speak, but Lucas caught Jeremy's eye and gave a small shake of his head. Ennis took a deep breath and sat back.

Several long, tense seconds ticked by, the silence broken only by cars passing on the street outside and the murmur of voices from the other side of the closed door. Lucas leaned forward in his chair; his look riveted on Milton Carr.

"Deputy Chief Carr," he began in measured tones. "Is there anything else you'd like to say?"

"Evidently, not at this time," Carr bit out, his eyes darting like daggers around the table.

"I thought not," Lucas said evenly. He rarely got angry—really angry—but right now, he was close. He'd been more than patient with Carr, but his patience was about at its end. The insubordination must stop, not just for his and Carr's sakes, but more importantly, for the department.

Standing, Lucas's eyes still on Carr, he said, "Deputy Chief Carr, please join me in my office and bring your things with you." Turning to the others he added, "I'll be back in just a few minutes."

Carr's eyes went wide as he sat without moving. The eyes of the others were round with surprise as they looked between Chief Matthews and Deputy Chief Carr. Exchanged glances reflected the same question: Was Carr about to be dismissed?

Lucas walked to the conference room door and opened it, waiting for Carr who still hadn't moved.

"Now, Mr. Carr," Lucas said flatly, waiting by the open door.

Carr took one more, quick look around the table before gathering his things and standing slowly. He brushed by Lucas on his way out the door, which Lucas pulled closed behind him.

Following Carr down the hall and into his office, Lucas also closed the office door behind them with a soft click.

Lucas moved to stand in front of Carr, waiting, his body rigid, until Carr finally raised his eyes and looked at him.

"I won't bother asking you to take a seat. This won't take long," Lucas began. "Deputy Chief Carr, let me reiterate once again that I fully understand your disappointment at not being named chief, but that decision has been made, and the department is moving forward. It will be up to you whether you move forward with it or not. What you just did in there was highly inappropriate and a full act of insubordination. It will not happen again. What I am saying to you now is a verbal reprimand which will be placed in your personnel file. Any other behavior by you that constitutes insubordination will result in a written reprimand. In the event of another instance, the next step will be termination. Do I make myself clear?"

Carr seethed, his eyes narrowed as he glared at Lucas. His fingers gripped the folders in his hand tightly, his knuckles white.

Lucas waited, his stance widening, his fisted hands had moved to his hips.

"I repeat, Deputy Chief Carr. Do I make myself clear?"

"Perfectly. Sir," Carr finally spat out through clenched teeth.

Lucas went on. "You will not return to the staff meeting. You will submit your update to me via email, copying Lindsay no later than noon today."

Lucas took a deep breath and stepped back, trying to relax his stiff posture.

"From what I've seen of your division and other work responsibilities, Deputy Chief Carr, you are a fine officer, but when it comes to working with others, especially those at a higher command level, you are seriously lacking. I am going to have HR contact you with relevant training classes, which you will complete within two weeks. I will have the results sent directly to me for assessment. Right now, I suggest you leave for an hour or two. Take that time to determine if you wish to continue with the Abernathy Fire Department and if so, how you want to conduct yourself going forward."

Carr's heavy breathing was loud and raspy, the sound hanging thickly in the air.

"Is that all, sir?" Carr asked with a hardened glare.

"For now. Yes. You are dismissed."

Stepping away from Lucas, Carr threw the office door open and stormed out.

Lucas took a deep breath and rolled his eyes heavenward before following Carr into the hallway.

Opening the door to the conference room, Lucas walked in and resumed his seat at the head of the table, everyone's eyes wide with anticipation.

"Deputy Chief Carr will not be joining us for the remainder of the meeting. Now, where were we?"

Consulting the agenda, he turned to Jack West. "West, we're looking forward to those new apparatus. When will you be headed to Minnesota for their final inspection? Has Pierce given you an estimated delivery date?"

West cleared his throat as his face lit up. It always did, Lucas had come to realize, when West talked about fire engines, trucks and other apparatus for which he was responsible.

"The trip to Minnesota is scheduled for the end of November—right after Thanksgiving. I'm taking Brendan and Garfield with me. Pending what we find, Pierce has projected completion and delivery by mid-January."

"End of November in Wisconsin?" Baldwin said with a chuckle. "It is gonna be cold. Glad my name wasn't on that list."

Nate gave an exaggerated shudder. The tense atmosphere dissipated as the group laughed at the usually stoic Nate's theatrics. Lucas laughed along with them. This is what a staff meeting should be like.

THE MEETING ENDED UP being a very productive one. Lucas was pleased with the overall progress and the way the team was coming together with the frustrating exception of Carr. Lucas had watched Carr interact with others, both the admin staff and firefighters in the stations. With them, he was likable, funny, and seemed to be a popular officer. He certainly hadn't shared that side of him with Lucas. Hopefully, the verbal reprimand would bring Carr to his senses, and he'd get on board with the rest of the team.

The group filed out of the conference room one by one while Lucas finished writing some notes from the last discussion, so he was surprised to look up and see Jeremy still sitting at the conference table, studying him.

"Ennis? Something to add to your report?" Lucas asked as he began gathering the papers in front of him.

"No, sir. I was wondering . . ." Jeremy paused, looking uncertain.

Lucas stopped what he was doing to give Jeremy his full attention. "Wondering what? Remember my open-door policy. You can share what's on your mind."

Jeremy cleared his throat. "Well, sir. Okay then. I was wondering why. Why do you let Carr talk to you the way he does? You're the chief, and he has been nothing but rude and disrespectful to you," Jeremy's voice rising with indignation.

Lucas could tell he surprised Jeremy when he simply smiled.

"Ennis, I appreciate your enthusiasm and your support, but your question is not an easy one. I always try to give every man as much opportunity to come around as possible or the reverse—as much rope as necessary to hang themselves. Deputy Chief Carr came dangerously close to the latter today. I hope when he comes back to the office this afternoon, he'll have a new attitude."

Lucas paused and studied Jeremy, seemingly hesitant before coming to a decision to go on. "And . . . my approach to Carr, well, it also goes along with that phrase you've heard me use."

"The 'and then some' phrase?" Jeremy asked, cocking his head with the question.

"That's the one," Lucas confirmed. "The full phrase is, 'Give it all you've got . . . and then some.' And the rest is, 'And then let God handle it.'"

Jeremy sat back, surprised. "I thought it just meant give it a little more than your best effort."

"Well, it does that too, but for me, it has a lot more meaning," Lucas said. "Plus, it's a great reminder. We can, and should, put forth every possible best effort, but ultimately, the end result is up to God."

Jeremy nodded thoughtfully.

Lucas smiled, seeing Jeremy's contemplative frown.

"I certainly appreciate that, sir," Jeremy finally said, looking at Lucas with an understanding smile as he gathered his own folders and papers. "I like it. I like it a lot, and you're right, it *is* a great reminder. I appreciate you sharing it with me, but still, what you're doing has to be hard. I admire your restraint. I know I'm new to admin and maybe that gives me a different perspective, but I just don't trust Carr."

Lucas smiled as he looked at Jeremy. "I respect that, and I can't say that he has my complete trust, but as my mentor, Andy Garrett, told me, *trust but verify*. And believe me, I'm verifying everything Carr tells me and reports on. I'm considering it a good learning exercise for me. It's helping me get familiar with the department faster than I might otherwise."

"Well, thanks for answering my question, Chief. It was probably impertinent, but I just had to ask—for my own sake. I can see that the department is improving, things are tightening up, and the overall direction is certainly positive. I'm personally excited about what's happening, and those I've talked to are as well."

Lucas allowed a small smile. "Thank you, Ennis. I'm glad to hear it."

Jeremy had just stood and was picking up his folders and coffee mug, when there was a soft knock on the open door, causing him and Lucas to look up at the same time.

"Excuse me," Rachel, the front desk assistant said, sticking her head in the door, "but Fire Marshal Ennis, you have a visitor."

No sooner had he been announced than Officer Cade Marshall appeared in the doorway.

"Cade," Jeremy said, looking from Cade, who'd taken a few steps into the conference room, to Lucas who had stood and glanced at Jeremy questioningly.

"Chief Matthews," Jeremy began, "this is Officer Cade Marshall, Campus Resource Officer Coordinator for the local Tri-County area."

Lucas smiled brightly and stepped closer, extending his hand to Cade.

Cade grinned at Jeremy before looking to Lucas and shaking his hand.

"And even though Jeremy probably won't admit it," Cade said with a mischievous grin, "he and I are friends—have been for a long time."

"Is that right?" Lucas asked, looking at Jeremy, who glared at Cade.

"Yes, sir," Jeremy said finally looking back to Lucas. "Actually, since middle school, but you'll soon come to see why I try not to claim him."

Lucas chuckled, and Cade laughed, slapping Jeremy on the back.

"What are you doing here?" Jeremy asked.

Cade clasped his hands over his heart as if deeply offended.

"Mr. Fire Marshal, we have a meeting as you might recall. Arrangements for the upcoming holiday basketball tournament?"

Jeremy's face reddened slightly.

"Oh right. Of course. But sorry—I actually didn't remember . . ."

Cade and Lucas chuckled, seeing the embarrassment on Jeremy's face.

"So, you're a campus resource officer?" Lucas interjected, turning to Cade.

"Yes, sir. Well, I have been a resource officer previously and still love doing it, but currently, I'm coordinating CROs for the Tri-Counties, so I'm not actually on campus much right now. That's about to change for a few weeks while we get ready for the holiday basketball tournament. It's Abernathy's turn to host this year."

"You see, Chief," Jeremy said, giving Cade a good-natured punch on the arm. "What Officer Marshall here isn't telling you is that he began the Tri-County CRO program. He's getting to combine that with his love of basketball for the holiday basketball tournament, so he's a happy camper right now."

"I see. I see," Lucas said, joining them in the doorway. "I have a very high respect for CROs, Officer Marshall. I owe my life—quite literally—to one."

Jeremy and Cade exchanged a surprised look as Lucas preceded them into the hallway.

"Now tell me about this tournament. You mentioned it's during the holidays?"

"Yes, sir," Cade began, excitement in his voice as they followed Lucas down the hall. "It's a high school basketball tournament held the week between Christmas and New Year's. It's a prestigious tournament, invitation only. Varsity high school teams from surrounding counties are typically invited along with a few prominent teams from outside the state. It's quite a tradition, and the games are always sell-outs. It's . . ."

"You get him started, and you can't get him to stop," Jeremy said, shaking his head.

"Ah, come on, Jeremy," Cade said, pinning Jeremy with a teasing look. "You know you and Allie have fun when you go."

Lucas looked at his watch. He was hungry and no wonder—it was half past noon.

"You guys hungry?" Lucas asked, briefly halting the good-natured bickering.

They looked at each other and then back to Lucas.

"Well, now that you mention it . . ." Cade said eagerly.

"Chief, fair warning. Cade is *always* hungry."

"A man after my own heart then. Where shall we go? I'm still learning places in town, but I bet you guys know a great place for burgers."

"Max's," Jeremy and Cade said at the same time, as they all laughed.

"Max's it is then," Lucas said, putting a hand on each of their shoulders and guiding them out the door with a quick nod to Lindsay, who was shaking her head.

CARR HIT THE BAR on the back door of the office as he stormed out. He'd gathered his keys and nothing else. Did Matthews think he was putting him in his place by pulling rank with a verbal warning? Carr slammed his SUV door closed and gunned the engine as he screeched out of the parking lot.

The streets of Abernathy flew by in a blur. He had no idea where he was going. He just needed to get away from that office. He gripped the steering wheel tighter as he glanced over and saw the package he'd picked up from the post office that morning on the seat. The specialty parts he'd ordered for his '65 Chevy had finally come in. Brenda didn't know about that post office box or about the parts he secretly ordered, but what she didn't know wouldn't hurt her. With a grim smile and another glance at the package, he turned around. He'd go to his shop.

Pulling into the driveway, he noticed Brenda's and Chase's cars were gone. Brenda was probably running errands while Chase was still at school and basketball practice. Good. He wanted to be alone.

He took out his ring of keys, selected the one to the shop, slid it into the lock, and turned it. The door swung open on well-oiled hinges. He stepped inside, flipping on the florescent lights one after another, which buzzed into the silence as they came on. The Chevy truck sitting in the middle of the shop was definitely a work in progress. His rolling stool and back board were at the head of the truck while the broom he'd used to sweep out last night leaned against the space at the back where the tailgate would eventually be. Light blue shop rags were clipped neatly to parts of the engine to protect against dust.

Since he would have to go back to the office, he couldn't get grease on his uniform. He satisfied himself with running his hand along the rubbery smoothness of the workbench top and, after pulling his stool beneath him, sat down and placed the package on the workbench. Retrieving a box cutter from the drawer, he sliced through the shipping tape and began carefully unwrapping each part, placing them side by side in front of him. His goal was to make every part of the truck's restoration authentic, and the cost of these particular parts had been exorbitant.

"Milton, what are you doing home?"

He jumped before quickly placing the parts back in the box, pushing it aside before he forced himself to turn around.

He couldn't meet the questioning look in Brenda's eyes—for so many reasons. He just shrugged in response to her question before he turned back toward the work bench and began to finger some of the tools he'd left out the night before.

Brenda walked to him and placed a hand on his shoulder.

"Something's happened. Tell me."

"I shot my mouth off in a meeting and got a verbal reprimand," Carr stated flatly. Standing, he walked over to the truck and ran his hand along the fender beside where the engine block would be placed.

"Oh, Milton," Brenda said, her voice betraying the disappointment in him he knew she'd feel.

"I know. I know. You warned me but how was I to know a guy with a supposed 'open door policy' wouldn't be able to take a few comments. He doesn't mind dishing out judgment on others. Who knew he couldn't take a bit himself? If there's a next time, he said it'd be a written reprimand, and then if there's another one, I'd be done."

Silence hung in the air, the buzzing of the florescent lights was joined by a large fly that had flown in the open door and was being a nuisance.

Milton Carr loved his job. He had a family, but the fire service was his life and had been for over twenty years. Here he was, on the verge of blowing it all—the years of risk and work, the respect he'd gained and the advancements he'd earned. All because someone higher up, who didn't understand the fire department, gave Matthews, an outsider, the job that should have rightfully been his.

Brenda came and stood beside him, placing her hand over his where it rested on the fender. He jerked his hand away but didn't move.

Unsure of what to say or do, Brenda just looked at him. Finally, she ventured, "I'm glad you still have a chance to prove your abilities. But Milton, you've got to get hold of yourself."

Milton stared at the far end of the shop and nodded reluctantly.

"If you weren't let go, what are you doing home now?" she asked as she moved to the door.

Carr sighed. "Matthews told me to get away from the office for a couple of hours. Clear my head and think about if I want to remain with the Abernathy Department and how I will conduct myself going forward."

"And have you decided . . . what you want?"

Carr's eyes flew to Brenda's in surprise.

"You know what I want."

"Do I? More importantly, do *you*? The chief's job is out of reach—for now—but you must still be with the department to be promoted. Think hard, Milton, and pull back on your verbal sparring with Matthews. It's not getting you closer to your goal, but further away. Promise me you'll try."

Milton looked at Brenda, her eyes silently pleading.

"I will—at least I'll try."

"I know you'll give it everything you've got, Milton."

He turned away from her and sat back down on his stool.

"I'll fix us some lunch. You hungry?" Brenda asked.

Milton shrugged.

"Great," Brenda said, forcing a false brightness into her voice. "There's some stew left from the other night, and I'll mix up some cornbread. It will be just a bit. I'll let you know when it's ready."

Milton didn't respond.

Troubled, Brenda turned and looked at Milton over her shoulder as she stopped at the doorway. She was worried—about him, about his future—about their family's future.

CHASE STOOD JUST OUTSIDE the shop door, listening. There was a chill in the air, but where he stood was in the sun. He was supposed to be at school but hadn't gone back after leaving campus for lunch. He only had a couple of afternoon classes and supposedly basketball practice. His dad still believed he'd made the team.

He went back to listening to his parents' exchange. His dad was close to being fired? Things were worse than Chase had thought. That new chief was making things hard, not just on his dad, but on their family. The new chief's son, Jon, had ghosted Casey after one date and that date had even ended early. Casey had returned home that evening disappointed, and Chase thought even a little embarrassed that the guy had ended their date after only an hour or so. Chase didn't understand his sister. She still talked about Jon and hoped he'd call. Chase hoped he didn't.

He leaned against the cold metal wall of the shop and listened to his mom pleading with his dad to keep himself under control. Chase shook his head. It just wasn't right that Matthews and his family could continue to cause so much trouble for his family. Things hadn't been great before, but they were definitely worse now.

He heard his mom getting close to the shop door where he was standing. He moved as quickly and quietly as he could onto the driveway and back down the block where he'd parked his car, out of sight of the house until he'd determined if the coast was clear, which as it turned out, it wasn't.

Climbing into his car, Chase grabbed a cigarette and a lighter from where he stashed them inside the console. Lighting and deeply inhaling the smoke, Chase puffed out a large cloud while he rested his elbow on the car door, the cigarette dangling outside the window. Yep, Chase thought as he took another puff, his eyes narrowing, things were taking a turn for the worse.

LUCAS TOOK ANOTHER BITE of his first Max burger. It was as good as the two eating across from him had claimed it would be. He'd have to bring the family here when the kids were back in town.

Lucas wasn't just enjoying a great burger; he was also enjoying the time with these two guys whose longtime friendship was obvious from their good-natured banter. Max's was packed, and the hum of conversation hovered over the juke box, which played nonstop in the corner.

True to Ennis's prediction, Cade was very enthusiastic about the holiday tournament coming in a couple of months. With the ongoing arson threats, Lucas was impressed they were planning the safety logistics this far in advance. The goal was for the arson situation to be resolved before the holidays, but they were wise to plan now for all safety contingencies.

"With three games scheduled to be played at the high school gym per day, we're going to need a lot of uniformed officer support rotating in and out as well as firefighters on-site, staged, and ready for both medical and fire incidents," Cade was saying as Lucas and Jeremy nodded agreement.

"Sully!" Jeremy called out and waved, seeing Riley enter the dining area and head toward the takeout counter.

Riley smiled and, walking over, greeted everyone, shaking Lucas's hand and slapping Ennis and Marshall on the back.

"Join us, Sullivan," Lucas said, gesturing to the fourth chair at their table.

"I don't want to interrupt your discussion," Riley said, looking uncertain. "I was going to pick up something to go."

"We're just talking about the holiday tournament," Jeremy said, pointing to the extra chair. "Sit down, Sully."

"Never use the word 'just' in front of the words 'holiday tournament' in my presence," Cade said as he dipped a French fry in ketchup and put in his mouth.

"Cade, I want to make sure you know this is our new chief," Riley said, motioning toward Lucas with a look that said behave yourself.

Lucas laughed as he picked up a fry from his own basket.

"No worries, Sullivan. We're having a productive discussion about the tournament."

"Okay. Well, good, but you should be warned that if you start Cade talking about the tournament, it's going to be hard to shut him up, and believe me, he's hard enough to shut up no matter what." Riley motioned the server over and gave his order without looking at a menu.

"So, I take it you come here often too?" Lucas asked as Riley took a sip of the soft drink the waiter had quickly placed in front of him.

"We've hung out here since high school," Riley said, looking at his friends with a smile.

"So," Lucas began and nodded with mock enlightenment. "You guys have known each other since then."

"Actually, since middle school if you want the ugly truth of it all," Jeremy added with a grin, wiping his mouth with a paper napkin. "The three of us have actually been best friends since then. For better or for worse."

Riley and Cade nodded solemnly before glancing at each other and grinning.

"We're just not sure whether there's more better or more worse," Cade interjected, causing everyone to laugh.

General talk was followed by additional discussion about safety measures and personnel needed for the tournament as they finished their burgers and then ice cream sundaes. They were enjoying the last few bites of ice cream when Jeremy's radio suddenly went off, followed immediately by Lucas's, calling out apparatus from three stations.

"Engine 1, Engine 2, Engine 4, Truck 4, Med 1, Battalion Chief 303. Structure fire. Mobile home 11404 Turbine Lane, Oasis Park. Caller reports heavy smoke and flames. Time Out 1:52."

THESE TYPES OF CALLS were coming much too frequently. With grim glances around the table, they rose as one and headed toward the door. Lucas hurriedly stuffed the receipt for their meal into his pocket as they reached the parking lot.

"Sullivan, you're off duty but your station is one of the ones on the call. If you'd like, you can follow us over. You may observe something those working the fire won't have time to see. The more eyes with experience we have on scene the better," Lucas said as he reached the chief's SUV. Sully hurried past him with a nod, followed quickly by Jeremy, moving to his own car. Cade waved, allowing them all to pass as he stopped at the side of his campus patrol car.

Kicking on their lights and sirens, Lucas and Jeremy led the way out of the parking lot, pulling into the mobile home park a few minutes later behind Engine 4. The other equipment had arrived just ahead of them, each maneuvering into position.

The trailer home, fully engulfed with flames, was surrounded by tall, dry grass, and weeds. The roar of the flames was punctuated with periodic loud pops from the trailer's glass windows bursting. Curious mobile home park residents were being moved away from the fire area by police officers arriving on the scene.

Engine 1 was maneuvering closest, its hose in the process of being laid, while the other apparatus were being deployed under the command of C-Shift's Battalion Chief Carl Chastain.

Lucas parked his vehicle near the fire ground while Jeremy parked directly behind him. Riley parked a further distance away and ran to catch up with them as they moved toward the fire. Sirens announced the arrival of additional police vehicles, including Chief Harper, who came and stood next to Lucas and the others, as dark smoke and flecks of embers swirled in the air around them. The smoke was dimming the afternoon's bright sunshine, giving the surrounding area the feel of late dusk.

Lucas watched in frustration as precious minutes ticked by while fire-fighters tried to locate the fire hydrant nearest to the trailer. When it was finally found, it was covered by tall grass and debris. Firefighters began clearing the area around the hydrant but then visibly hesitated. One lifted something, holding it up and looked in Lucas's direction. Lucas's heart skipped a beat when he saw it was a shiny new gas can the firefighter was holding in his gloved hand. A white sheet of paper was attached to the can, flapping in the whirl of the dense smoke and soot.

Pulling on his evidence gloves, Jeremy hurried toward the firefighter. Taking the can, he turned and walked back to Lucas.

As Jeremy approached their group, Lucas's focus returned to the fire-fighters securing the hose to the hydrant. When the water began to flow, the amount and pressure were regulated and monitored by the driver as it flowed through the truck's pump system. Firefighters picked up the charging hoses as they expanded with the water's pressure. When the firefighters opened the hose nozzles, water poured onto the flames, generating loud hisses as steam rose above the smoke and evaporated into the bright afternoon sunshine. The billowing dark smoke began dissipating in a matter of minutes as the fire was methodically brought under control.

Lucas watched the entire process with an experienced eye, noting how command managed the situation and how each crew successfully executed their responsibilities to bring the situation under control quickly. He made a mental note to create a plan for all fire hydrant locations to be identified and cleared of any grass and debris on a regular schedule.

Fighting this fire had been a good, solid effort, but as he turned to where Jeremy, Police Chief Harper, and a couple of police investigators were examining the gas can, he couldn't help but dread hearing what they'd found. Chief Harper had emailed just that morning, letting Lucas know in light of the amount of ongoing suspicious fires, he'd requested dispatch to notify him of all fire activity. Lucas was glad to have him here.

When Lucas turned and started toward the group, Jeremy rose slowly from where he and the others crouched around a plastic cloth on the ground, the gas can in the middle.

Lucas slipped on the evidence gloves Jeremy held out to him before taking the note that had been attached to the can. Once again, the envelope was addressed to "CHIEF MATTHEWS" in the same scrawling print.

Taking the envelope, Lucas pulled out a single sheet of white paper.

ME AGAIN.
MISS ME?

"Any ideas?" Lucas asked, handing the note back to Jeremy, who slipped it into an evidence bag and then slipped the envelope into a separate one.

Chief Harper rose and walked over to Lucas, taking him by the arm and pulling him to the side.

"Lucas, these notes continuing to be addressed to you specifically are a serious concern. I know we've talked about this before, but do you have any idea of someone who might have it out for you . . . who would want to intimidate you for any reason?"

Stroking his chin, Lucas thought but shook his head. "The only person who has an issue with me is a firefighter—Deputy Chief Carr—and as plainly as he's made his feelings known, his record is impeccable. He's responsible for hiring and training most of these guys. He wouldn't keep putting their lives at risk. No, I can't think of anyone who would hold this kind of a grudge."

Chief Harper studied Lucas intently. "Keep thinking. If anyone comes to mind—even a remote possibility—inform me personally and immediately. At the escalation rate in the size of these fires, we need to follow every single lead quickly—even ones you think may seem far-fetched or unlikely. In the meantime, I'm going to do some discreet checking into Carr. I agree it's hard to imagine him doing anything like this, but we still need to check it out. In the meantime, Lucas, be careful. Whoever is doing this is most likely capable of doing just about anything. Be on your guard."

Lucas looked at Harper somberly and gave a single nod as they moved back to the group.

Lucas stopped beside Riley, who was watching firefighters performing overhaul, moving debris side to side, checking for hot spots and placing water where they spotted embers. Having donned his bunker gear, including helmet and mask, Jeremy moved toward the smoldering pile of debris.

He waded into the pile, eyeing the blackened remains, looking for any indication of the use of an accelerant. After a methodical sweep through the debris, he ended up where the trailer's kitchen had been located against the one wall still standing and moved closer. Despite the afternoon sunshine, the smoke filtering up from the debris made it difficult to see clearly. Pulling out his flashlight and moving closer, Jeremy spotlighted the remaining wall and saw what he'd been hoping not to find—a burn pattern indicative of the use of an accelerant. The area had broken swirls of charred white above the blackened remains of the stove, its door hanging open. The scorched enamel kitchen sink had dropped inside the burned-out cabinets and was resting at a precarious angle. Jeremy pulled his camera from the pack he had over his shoulder and took carefully detailed pictures of the entire area, including the wall and swirl patterns.

The mobile home park manager had informed them the trailer was currently unoccupied but was being used for storage. Charred ashes were all that remained of the interior with a leg of a chair, twisted remnants of an aluminum table, and the singed springs of a mattress the only distinguishable items.

Besides Lucas and a couple of police investigators still on scene, the others were gone by the time Jeremy returned. Lucas paced anxiously, waiting to hear what had been found, if anything.

"Find anything, Ennis?" Lucas asked as Jeremy walked up and pulled off his mask, hood, and helmet. He wiped a gloved hand across his sweaty forehead.

"I believe so, sir. Definitely looks like an accelerant was used in the kitchen area. I've taken quite a few photos and will get those to the forensic folks, so they can confirm. I also took some samples from the ashes in the area to run labs for accelerant content."

Lucas nodded. "Good work. Keep me posted. I want to know just as soon as you hear something."

"You've got it, Chief. And sir, we're going to get this guy. Never fear."

Lucas gave Jeremy a dispirited smile and clapped him on the back before walking back to his vehicle.

Climbing in, Lucas started the engine while checking his messages. Jill had called.

Lucas dialed and couldn't help but smile when Jill answered after a couple of rings with, "Good afternoon, Chief Matthews. How's my guy?"

Lucas chuckled. "Always better after hearing from my gal. Everything okay?"

"Oh, Lucas!" Jill exclaimed. "I found it—the perfect house. When can you look at it with me?"

Lucas could hear the excitement in Jill's voice. He wanted to say he could meet her right away, but he had the afternoon's scheduled meeting with HR about Carr. Seeing the house would have to wait until after work.

"Honey," Lucas groaned, "I'm so sorry. I've got a personnel meeting this afternoon that I absolutely cannot miss. Can we schedule a look late this afternoon—say 6:00 or 6:30?"

"Uh-oh—personnel. The same issue?" Jill asked, reading between the lines of what Lucas wasn't saying.

"I'm going to have to work on my delivery," Lucas quipped as he pulled into the admin parking lot. "You saw right through that one. Yes, the same issue."

Jill sighed. "Oh, Lucas. I hate this for you. If I ever meet this guy, I'll . . ."

Lucas smothered a smile and asked, "You'll do what exactly . . . ?"

"Oh, I don't know, but what I do know is that I'm getting *really* tired of this guy giving my husband such a hard time."

Lucas smiled into the phone as he walked into the building and down the hall toward his office. He stopped beside Lindsay's desk.

"Well, you're going to meet him Saturday night. I'll let the guy know he'd better be on his best behavior." Lucas chuckled as Lindsay looked up from her computer. "I've gotta run, honey. Schedule that showing for after 6:00, and text me the address. I'll be there. And I love you."

"Love you too. Be looking for the text. Did I mention it was the perfect house? Love you."

The smile the conversation brought quickly faded when Lucas noticed Lindsay's serious expression.

"Mr. Lorimar called. He said to let you know he heard about the trailer fire on the news. He didn't want to talk to you while you were on scene but asked that you call him when you checked in."

Lucas ran one hand down his face before pinching the bridge of his nose.

"Thanks, Lindsay. Would you please call Mr. Lorimar and let him know I'm headed to city hall to see him in person. I have another meeting right after, so I'm not sure when I'll be back."

"Yes, sir. Of course."

Lucas wasn't sure which meeting he dreaded more. Sighing, he braced himself as he turned and walked back out the door.

Lucas's mind was already in the meeting with Kirk Lorimar. He was mentally reviewing the arson investigation progress along with the progress of different initiatives within the department itself when he heard the screech of brakes and the sickening sound of metal crunching against metal. It jarred him back to the traffic light where he was stopped. In the middle of the intersection in front of him, a large pickup, a Ford F150, and a Honda CR-V SUV, had collided, evidently violently for both to be so mangled. The front of the Honda was crumpled into the engine of the large pick up. A bit of black smoke drifted up from the engine of the Honda while a lone tire's rim cover rolled off to one side. Car doors banged as occupants of other vehicles stopped at the light were leaving their vehicles and hurrying toward the wreck.

Lucas slammed his SUV into park and jumped out. With no time for anything more, he quickly grabbed his traffic safety vest, thrusting his arms through its arm holes before stuffing several protective gloves into his shirt pocket. Reaching back inside the vehicle, he pulled out his radio, rapidly lifting its strap over his head.

Screams were coming from one of the involved vehicles as Lucas walked toward them, radioing, "Dispatch, this is 303. Vehicular accident, Dixon and Marsh. Potential injuries, unknown number of victims. Request PD and Fire."

Dispatch acknowledged his message with tones immediately sounding over his radio.

Hearing the screams, Lucas walked determinedly toward the accident. He hadn't had time to grab any additional protective gear, but what he had would have to do. Time was of the essence. The plume of black smoke from the Honda's engine was growing larger, and the screams were becoming hysterical. Seeing his uniform, the others who had approached moved aside to allow Lucas access to the vehicles.

Pinpointing the source of the screams, Lucas moved to the pickup. Stepping up on the foot rail, he hoisted himself up to where he could see inside. A middle-aged woman, screaming for help, was pinned behind the steering wheel. Fine powder from the deployed air bags floated in the air. She was bleeding from the cuts and scrapes across her face and arms caused by shards of window glass. Her eyes darted around the window opening, and upon seeing Lucas, she began screaming even more frantically.

Lucas smiled gently and reaching inside, patted as much of her shoulder as he could reach.

"Ma'am, everything is going to be fine. Please calm down. I'm here to help you, and others are on their way and will be here soon. Can you tell me where any pain is located?"

"Well, where do you think? Look at me!" the woman blurted out, holding up her arms and glaring at Lucas. "I hurt all over. That stupid girl ran the light and crashed into me. Get me out of here!" she said as she began to pound the steering wheel.

"Ma'am, I need to check the other vehicle for victims. Please calm down. Help to get you out is on the way. Take some deep breaths for me. Can you do that please?"

With another glare, the woman stopped pounding the steering wheel and reluctantly began breathing. After a few breaths, Lucas could see her physically relaxing.

"You're doing great. Just keep going," Lucas said as he eased out of the pickup's cab and down off the foot rail.

Side stepping a large puddle of antifreeze that was rapidly growing, Lucas took a few steps over, sidled up to the SUV, and hoisted himself up to the driver's door. When he looked inside, blood was everywhere. A young woman was lying across the console, her legs pinned beneath the steering wheel, causing her to dangle against the seat belt at an awkward angle. She had long golden-brown hair which hung over the side of her face, already bright red with blood. Lucas leaned inside, careful of the glass still in the window, managing to get close enough to see the blood was coming from a large gash across her forehead. She wasn't moving.

Lucas stepped down and tried to open the passenger door, and after several hard yanks, it reluctantly screeched open. Angling himself inside, he carefully moved to where he could see the young woman better. She was unconscious, but when he put a finger to her throat, he felt a slow but reassuringly persistent pulse. The gash was bleeding profusely, and even though the paramedics would arrive at any minute, the blood flow needed to be staunched immediately.

Reaching into his pocket for the protective gloves he'd grabbed, he pulled each one on with a quick snap. Without time to think about any additional protection for his own safety, Lucas squeezed inside, and balancing precariously on the edge of the seat, he carefully pressed the two folds of skin together where her forehead had been cut and began applying pressure. Seeing a scarf on the floorboard, he picked it up and placed it on the wound, continuing to apply steady pressure. The scarf was saturated with blood almost immediately, but Lucas held on.

From the angle where he sat, he couldn't see out, but he heard the engine and ambulance pull up, their sirens squelching almost simultaneously, their diesel engines reverberating. It was a familiar and comforting sound. Quickly, two heads popped into the side window, their eyes going wide at seeing him.

"Chief!" Carlton, a young firefighter with blond hair, exclaimed. Lucas had just met him a few days earlier. As Carlton moved inside the open door, he set the 'ambulance in a bag' on the pavement.

"Head wound," Lucas said calmly. "Her legs are pinned."

Eyeing the interior of the Honda and seeing the situation, Carlton said, "Copy that," and was gone. A few minutes later Lucas heard the jaws of life roar to life and within minutes could see the firefighters working to separate the two vehicles, so they could extricate Lucas's patient. He hadn't heard any more screaming from the other vehicle, so he figured others were working to free that victim as well.

Once the vehicles were separated, the driver's door was quickly removed and the steering wheel lifted with a hydraulic ram so the young woman's legs could be freed. The paramedics moved in and stabilized her with a neck board. Lucas maneuvered out of the vehicle as they pulled her out, keeping his hand on the head wound. Stepping to the side, he released his hold to make way for the paramedic to take over. The girl was pretty and looked to be in her mid-twenties. She reminded Lucas a lot of Jessica.

"Take good care of her," Lucas said as he looked up at Carlton.

"Yes, sir. We will. Thank you, Chief," Carlton said, eyeing Lucas with obvious respect. Lucas nodded and then looked down. His white uniform shirt and black pants were heavily splotched with deep red blood stains from just below his badge to his pant pockets.

Dan, the engine driver, handed him some wipes with a grimace. "These might help a little," he said, eyeing Lucas's uniform.

Lucas half-heartedly dabbed at some of the bigger spots before shaking his head. "I'm afraid you're right. And I don't have a spare shirt or pants with me. They're back at the office. Oh well, it can't be helped. I'm already late for a meeting at city hall. Hopefully, the city manager will understand."

"I think he will, sir. Thanks for the assist. She's lost a lot of blood." Dan nodded toward the ambulance where Carlton was overseeing the young lady's stretcher being loaded.

Lucas nodded and looked down.

"Just glad I was here," he finally said as he looked up. Giving up on his uniform, he took the extra wipes Dan offered him to finish cleaning his hands.

"What about the other victim?" Lucas asked. "How is she?"

Dan chuckled. "Oh, she's fine. More upset about her truck than anything else. She only had a few superficial cuts and scrapes. She was really lucky. I hope she realizes that."

Finishing wiping his hands, Lucas nodded, watching the ambulances pull away. "I hope so, too. Let me know about the other victim, if you would."

"Of course, sir, and thanks again. I don't think I've ever seen a chief in action."

"Well, Dan," Lucas began with a slight grimace, "this is a do as I say, not as I do situation. I violated protocol in a number of ways just now, so you guys don't follow suit. I'd hate to have to write anyone up, and I guess, technically, I should write myself up, but it was a gut call. I was on scene when the accident happened. There was no time for full protective gear, but again, this is not how we operate. Are we clear?"

Dan nodded solemnly. "Yes, sir. Of course." And with a grin, quickly added, "It was still impressive to see a chief in action though."

Lucas couldn't help but grin. "All in a day's work. I'm here to serve," he said, before adding, ". . . and then some."

Lucas opened the glass door to the city manager's office area and stopped at the receptionist's desk.

"Good afternoon, Chief," the receptionist began but stopped abruptly, seeing the dark spots on Lucas's uniform. She looked up at him, a question in her eyes.

Lucas looked down and grimaced. "I'm afraid it's blood. My apologies. Worked a traffic accident on the way here."

The receptionist nodded hesitantly and motioned down the hall. "Mr. Lorimar is expecting you. Go right in."

Lucas nodded and forced a smile as he walked down the short hall to the city manager's office. Even though Kirk Lorimar had just asked Lucas to call him, Lucas had decided to come in person, so it wasn't good to keep the city manager waiting.

Lucas self-consciously pulled his shirt away from him, careful not to touch the blood spots, even though they were pretty much dry. Reaching the door at the end of the hall, Lucas knocked lightly and stepped inside.

Lucas had only been in the city manager's office a couple of times, once when he interviewed for the position and once after he'd been hired to meet Abernathy's mayor. It was a second-floor corner office overlooking the downtown city square. The square was a park, its trees starting to turn bright reds and oranges with the cooler fall temperatures. Benches dotted the park with plenty of people enjoying the beautiful afternoon. Kirk Lorimar's office was not pretentious with a slightly larger than typical desk with an old-fashioned ink well and pen sitting at the front and center; the desk currently covered with a scattering of folders and papers. A corresponding credenza and some bookshelves were behind the desk, containing a variety of books and a series of three-ring binders with a city department's name on a label for each binder. On the remaining wall, a replica of the City's logo was hung, a conference table and four chairs beneath. A clear glass pitcher and four clear glasses sat on a tray in the middle of the conference table.

"Chief! Come in," Kirk Lorimar said, rising and coming around his desk to shake Lucas's hand. He stopped abruptly, seeing Lucas. "What on earth happened? Are you okay?"

Lucas gave a grim smile in response to Kirk Lorimar's question.

"I apologize for being late and for the condition of my uniform. A traffic accident occurred on my way here. I assisted one of the victims," Lucas said, looking down self-consciously at his stained uniform.

"I had an extra uniform shirt back at the office but knew I was already late and didn't want to keep you waiting any longer. The wound was a head wound, and they always bleed a lot."

Lorimar nodded incredulously. "Chief, can't say I've ever had a department head in my office with blood all over his uniform, but I'm glad you were able to help. I trust the victim is going to be okay?"

"I don't know, sir. She was taken to the hospital still unconscious. I've been asked to be notified of her condition."

Kirk nodded again, stroking his chin. "Thank you, Chief. I appreciate you coming down. I actually expected a phone call, but it's even better you're here in person. I think you remember Council Member Lucille Dower?" Lorimar stepped to the side to reveal the lone council member who, unbeknownst to Lucas, had opposed his selection as chief.

Lucille Dower was an intimidating figure. Her gray hair was fashioned into a tidy bun on top of her head, while her steel gray eyes glittered with malice, or maybe it was appraisal, from behind round, black-framed glasses. She wore a dark blue suit, a contrast to her fair complexion which was marked only by a few lines about her mouth and at the corner of her eyes. Fingers on both hands were elegantly manicured and held rings of varying sizes and stones. Her imperious look hadn't phased Lucas during the interview process, but there was no doubt she was a combative figure who felt no compunction at sharing her thoughts, opinions, and ideas on a wide variety of topics.

Lucille eyed Lucas critically from head to foot, taking in his uniform and its condition before returning her gaze back to his face, her eyebrow cocked.

Lucas kept the same forced smile as he nodded and moved to shake the hand of the council woman whose last name, he thought to himself, fit her perfectly. "Council Member Dower, how nice to see you."

"Chief Matthews," she began with no pleasantries, "the Council is concerned with these arsons. They seem to be getting out of control. What are you doing about them, or are you too busy with other things?" she asked, her gaze once again dropping to the red stains on his uniform. "We need to know if we've hired the right man to handle a big job."

Lucas's eyebrows shot up as he looked to Kirk, who shrugged slightly and looked at Lucas apologetically.

"Well, Chief?" Lucille asked again. "We hired you to protect the public, not allow arsonists to run rampant across the city."

"Council Member Dower, I appreciate your concern," Lucas said with sincerity. "I assure you all appropriate resources are working diligently to determine the arsonist or arsonists and to put a stop to all of this. We are making progress and are as anxious, if not more so, than anyone else to bring this situation to a final resolution."

Lucille eyed Lucas with a stare Lucas was sure could freeze water.

Turning to Kirk, she said, "Kirk, the citizens of Abernathy are getting nervous. Get this fixed."

"Yes, Ma'am," Kirk replied with a vigorous nod. "Chief Matthews is here to brief me on recent events. I will place it on the agenda for discussion during Tuesday's executive session, but I'd like to wait until the next meeting to discuss anything in open session."

Lucille nodded and stood. She moved to the door and turning back to face them, said, "Very well. Thank you for your time, Mr. Lorimar. Chief."

Turning to Lorimar after she'd left, Lucas said, "You wished to see me, sir?"

"Lucas, sorry about that. Didn't mean to ambush you, and especially after . . ." He motioned to Lucas's uniform. "She came in while you were on your way, or else I would have given you a heads up."

Lucas nodded as he sank into one of the guest chairs across from Lorimar.

"Executive session, sir? I'm not sure we have enough to satisfy everyone's concerns right now."

"What *do* you have?" Kirk asked, leaning back in his chair.

"Fire along with PD are making a thorough investigation of every scene. We're obtaining all security camera footage in the vicinity of each incident and finding new gas cans—empty—at each scene. The last two have had notes attached—addressed to me."

"Addressed to you?" Lorimar asked, leaning forward and putting his elbows on top of some of the papers on his desk. "What do the notes say?"

"The envelopes are addressed to Chief Matthews while the note inside doesn't say anything specific—just 'Guess who.' That kind of stuff."

"You say Harper knows about all of this?" Kirk asked.

"Yes, sir. We were both at the scene of the trailer fire this afternoon."

"And what does Harper say about these notes?"

Lucas hesitated. He didn't want to say anything that would make his new boss think he couldn't handle the situation, but he also wanted to be upfront about the caution Harper had asked him to take.

"There's more to it, isn't there, Lucas?"

"Well. Sir. No. Not a lot really. Chief Harper has just asked if there's anyone who might want to intimidate or taunt me this way."

"And is there?" Kirk asked, watching Lucas.

Once again, Lucas hesitated before taking a deep breath and saying, "To be perfectly honest, sir, I am having insubordination issues with an officer on my command staff. But because he is a part of command and a senior officer who knows better, I just can't believe he would willingly put firefighters' lives at risk responding to these fires. But other than that, no one else comes to mind."

"And what else does Chief Harper have to say about this?"

Lucas frowned slightly and cocked his head to the side. The air was cool in the office, and his stiffening shirt grew more uncomfortable by the minute.

"Well, sir, he's asked me to be on my guard and to notify him immediately if anyone else comes to mind. I've given him the name of the officer and, of course, will cooperate with PD in every way."

Lucas hurriedly went on, "We're also taking photos of onlookers for any recurring faces. It's a fact that most arsonists come back either to see the results of what they've done or to watch firefighters work."

"I don't like the sound of someone taunting you, Chief," Lorimar said. "I trust you'll let Harper or me know if something comes up and you need assistance. It sounds like you and Harper are covering all your bases. However, I would strongly discourage you from sharing more than just the basic information with council, even in executive session. If they ask anything further, I'll just say that due to security and safety considerations, all discussion will be suspended pending more information."

"Thank you, Kirk. I appreciate that," Lucas said, standing and moving toward the door.

"Go get cleaned up, Chief," Kirk said, motioning to Lucas's shirt. "And for all of our sakes, get to the bottom of this arson business—quickly."

I T HAD BEEN A day, and Lucas was reaching his limit. From the encounter with Carr that morning and another arson to the car accident and meeting with Lorimar and then with HR about Carr late that afternoon, he was just about spent. Having followed his GPS to the address Jill had texted him, he put the SUV in park in front of the house Jill wanted him to see. He closed his eyes and took a few deep breaths. He'd showered at Station 1 and pulled on the spare uniform he kept in his office. Jill would have had a fit to see the amount of blood on his other uniform, so he was glad he'd decided to send it to the department's special laundering service for cleaning. He'd watched Lindsay mark the bag as biohazard before it'd been sent off. Dan, the young firefighter at the accident scene, had called and said the young lady with the head wound was going to be kept at the hospital overnight for observation, but she was awake, coherent, and had suffered no internal injuries.

Lucas slowly expelled a deep breath and opened his eyes to take a long look at the house Jill was so excited about. It was an attractive single-story brick home, situated on a slight rise and surrounded by mature trees whose leaves were bursting with rich, autumn colors. As he started up the sidewalk, the front door flew open, and a beaming Jill stepped onto the porch. Feeling himself smile in return, he hurried up the steps and pulled her into a quick hug and longer kiss.

"Lucas, the Realtor is here," Jill said with a smile and a quick glance over her shoulder.

Lucas tried to look repentant but didn't quite succeed as Jill grinned and grabbed his hand, dragging him into the foyer.

"Lucas, this is Tucker Delaford, the Realtor."

"Delaford," Lucas said with a grin, shaking the man's hand.

"Chief," the young man said nervously, his cheeks growing a light pink.

Jill looked between the two and, turning to Delaford said, "Oh no. You're . . ."

"Captain, B-Shift at Station 5," he answered with a quick look at Lucas.

Lucas laughed. "No pressure, Delaford. Seriously. We'd love to see the house."

Delaford seemed to relax and began the tour, explaining the features of which Lucas was sure Jill was already aware. It *was* a beautiful house, Lucas had to admit. Walking through its rooms with Jill, he already felt at home. There were things Jill mentioned she'd like to change, such as new hardwood floors, painting the entire house, and adding some built-in bookshelves to the rooms she'd selected for his office and her own. The house was empty, but as they walked through with Jill pointing out the changes she'd like to make and where their furniture could be placed, she brought it to life. Lucas could easily see them living there.

The late afternoon light was waning as they completed the tour. Standing on the back deck overlooking a backyard that opened into a large, wooded area, Lucas looked at Jill, who was studying him anxiously.

"Well?" she whispered breathlessly after Delaford stepped inside to give them some privacy. "What do you think?"

"No, what do you think?" Lucas asked, pulling her close so he could see her face in the ebbing light. The lights from the kitchen and breakfast nook area brightened a portion of the deck, the paned patterns of light creating a soft glow on their faces.

She was smiling and happiness lit her eyes, making them sparkle even brighter than usual.

"Lucas, I love it. It feels like home. I know it's not the house we built in Fort Collins, but it's close. It's so close. What do you think? Do *you* like it?"

Lucas pulled her closer, saying softly, "Yes—I do. I love it. It's in our price range with even some extra for new hardwood floors, carpet, paint—those special things you'll do to make it uniquely ours. I say let's do it."

Jill squealed and pulled him into a tight embrace. "I knew you'd love it!"

"Any word on the Fort Collins house?" Lucas asked, keeping his arms around her.

"There were several showings over the weekend, and Alexandria believes we'll have at least two, maybe three offers from those. She'll know more in the next few days." Jill put her head on Lucas's chest. "I think we're going to love Abernathy, Chief."

Lucas was quiet, holding Jill tightly in his arms. With everything going on, he couldn't relax and think of enjoying life in Abernathy—not until things were resolved. Lucas hoped beyond hope she was right, but that happiness seemed like a long time away.

Lucas and Jill enjoyed a quiet dinner and an evening at home, talking and then watching some light and silly reruns on the streaming service. As they switched off the service, the evening news was coming on. The opening shot was of a reporter standing in front of the burned-out trailer home. The banner along the bottom read, "Abernathy Arsons Continue Unabated." Lucas quickly hit the remote and the screen went black. Jill looked at him, worry in her eyes.

He glanced over and tried to smile. "I deal with it all day. I don't want to have to hear the news version at night."

Smiling softly, Jill leaned close and brushed a strand of Lucas's hair from his forehead then cupped her hand to his cheek. "And you don't have to. When you're home, this is your safe haven away from it all."

Lucas rested his forehead against Jill's. "You're my haven," he said, right before he kissed her.

Later that evening, the identity of the arson and his taunts swirled in Lucas's mind as he drifted into a restless sleep. He sensed the answer to the question was within his reach, but every time he tried to grab hold of it, his fingers came up with nothing but air. As his fingers flailed, his chest tightened, and he started gasping for air. He was drowning, and every time he fought to take a breath, he choked. Familiar faces—faces from the past—hovered over him, their features wavering across his vision as he struggled to breathe. The faces—four of them—laughed, then frowned as Lucas felt something being forced down his throat, and then there was more water, causing him to choke again. He tried to fight them as he gasped for air, but he was being held down. The more he struggled, the more the faces laughed, a haunting, taunting laugh. Lucas fought to wake up—he had to wake up—but even as he struggled, he felt himself being pulled down into blackness.

"Lucas, wake up! Lucas, can you hear me?"

Jill frantically shook Lucas as his thrashing and moaning continued.

Keeping a hand on his arm, Jill reached over Lucas's writhing body to switch the lamp beside the bed on.

Lucas's eyes were open, but he didn't seem able to see or hear her or even be aware of where he was.

Jill tightened her grasp on Lucas's arm but was surprised when he suddenly relaxed and his body went limp. She quickly glanced at his face in time to see his eyes slide closed.

As frightening as his jerking and thrashing had been when they woke her, his sudden stillness now was even more frightening.

Putting her hand gently to his cheek, Jill looked into his face. "Lucas," she said softly. She waited and then said his name again, a little louder. After another several seconds with no response, Jill said it again, more urgency in her tone, "Lucas!"

He moaned several times before his eyelids eventually fluttered open. The vacant, disoriented look in his eyes scared Jill, but she continued to lean over him, saying his name and stroking his hair soothingly. After several minutes of his eyes darting back and forth in confusion, Jill finally saw recognition register when his eyes came to rest on her, a puzzled then anxious look crossing his face.

"What? What is it? What's going on?" Lucas asked groggily as he sat up. Clearing his throat, he ran a hand over his face, stubbly with its overnight growth.

"You were having a bad dream," Jill said, putting a hand on his arm and rubbing her thumb soothingly over his damp skin.

"Dream?" Lucas straightened and turned, putting his bare feet on the floor and his head in his hands. "Yeah. I think I remember. Sorry to wake you."

"There's nothing to apologize for so long as you're okay."

Jill eyed Lucas with concern before standing and walking to the bathroom. She returned with a thick bath towel and handed it to Lucas. He bunched the towel and buried his face in it, wiping his face and then running it over his sweat-soaked hair.

Jill sat on the edge of the bed, her arm draped protectively across Lucas's strong, bare shoulders. Shoulders that were carrying so much weight.

Holding the towel tightly, Lucas tried to smile and, lifting it slightly said, "Thanks, Hon, and don't worry. I'm okay. It was just a dream."

"Are you sure that's all it was? You were thrashing almost uncontrollably and moaning. I couldn't wake you, and then you just . . ."

"I just what?" Lucas asked, turning his reddened eyes to Jill.

"You just went limp. I had to say your name several times before you woke up."

Lucas nodded; memories of the dream were flooding back. That night—so many years ago—when those high school bullies forced him into a Fentanyl overdose, he'd fought them with everything he'd had, but it hadn't been enough. He'd almost died that night. He hadn't had that nightmare in years, but now, here it was back to taunt him when he was already stressed and worried. Maybe, he thought, the stress and worry were what brought it back. He shook his head and stood, Jill watching him anxiously.

"Was it the same nightmare?" she asked softly.

Lucas nodded, one hand resting at his waist, the other clasping the towel tightly.

"It's been a long time since you've had that dream. Do you want to talk about it?"

He looked down at her and forced a smile. He took a strand of her blond hair between his fingers and gave it a gentle pull.

"No. I'm fine. Don't worry. Go back to bed. There are still a couple of hours before the alarm goes off."

"I don't want to go back to bed without you," Jill pleaded, her eyes round with worry. "If you're going to stay up, then so am I. Even if it's just to sit with you."

Lucas smiled and sat down beside Jill with a sigh. His mind was spinning, and his heart was still racing from the unexpected rush of adrenaline the dream had produced. He knew he wouldn't be able to sleep, but he didn't want Jill to stay up because of him.

"Well, let's try to go back to sleep then," he said. Taking the towel, he spread it over the sweat-drenched sheets and reached to turn the lamp off. Jill nodded, and lying back down, she placed a protective arm across Lucas as he eased down beside her.

She couldn't sleep and knew Lucas wasn't either. Her head resting on his shoulder, she looked up at him. He lay staring at the ceiling. She was worried about him. Lucas was stronger than anyone she'd ever known, and he'd been through more than anyone should ever have to, but this job was spiraling more and more out of his control. It was no fault of his, but he bore the responsibility, and it was weighing heavily on him.

When Lucas finally did fall asleep, it was a fitful sleep filled with bad dreams—different dreams this time. One dream in particular was of roaring fires and a taunting laugh that didn't stop until he jerked awake the next morning.

When he opened his eyes, it took a few seconds for his eyes to focus. The first bit of morning light started to peep through the window blinds. It was the inky time between full dark and when the sun rose over the horizon. He lay still for a few seconds, his body aching. He was more tired now than when he'd gone to bed.

Lucas glanced at Jill's quietly sleeping form and brushed a bit of hair back from her face before he stood and walked to the shower. It was a new day.

Lucas remained seated, taking a deep breath and then a drink of watered-down iced tea from the plastic cup he'd picked up to go with his untouched dinner. Members of the city council stood up from the conference table, gathering their official meeting portfolios and with a few nods and glances in Lucas's direction, filed out, heading toward council chambers for the monthly public meeting.

Lucas's report on the arson investigation and the back-and-forth discussion during executive session had just concluded after an hour. It had been intense with question after question, each more heated than the last. Lucas stole a quick glance at Jeremy Ennis who'd sat quietly at his side throughout the meeting. He'd asked Jeremy to sit in just in case he needed additional information about the investigation, but Lucas had been able to answer each question directed at him. Without divulging important security information, he and Chief Harper had both assured Council their departments were working together diligently to narrow the search and identify the arsonist.

"Impressive," Jeremy said, turning and looking at Lucas.

Lucas quirked an eyebrow at Jeremy who quickly cleared his throat.

"Uh, sorry, sir. Well done," Jeremy corrected.

Lucas chuckled lightly. Clapping Jeremy on the back he said, "Thanks, Ennis. You're good to go. I'll see you in the morning. I've got to stay for the public session."

Jeremy looked surprised. "Sir, I'll be glad to stay . . ."

"Thanks, but no. Head on home."

"Okay then. See you, Chief, and good luck." Jeremy stood and walked to the door. He stepped into the hallway with a quick glance over his shoulder at Lucas.

Lucas fought a small grin at Ennis's concern and tiredly pinched the bridge of his nose before standing. With last night's nightmares, he hadn't gotten much sleep. After a quick meeting with Carr that morning, that unsurprisingly didn't go well, and the afternoon's preparation for tonight's meeting, followed by the intensity of the meeting itself, he was exhausted. The agenda for the public meeting looked innocuous, so he hoped it would be a quick one.

"Chief, Ennis was right. That was impressive. I'm not sure Council is accustomed to their probing and parrying being deflected so effectively," Police Chief Harper said. "Their bark is a lot worse than their bite. Trust me. I speak from experience, but you did well. I've been where you are right now," Chief Harper added, standing from where he sat across the table from Lucas. "You're still new, so they're each trying to get their bluff in on you. And if this is ever opened up in public session, you'll really see them posturing then."

Chief Harper grinned, little humor accompanying the smile. "I wish I could say when the rubber meets the road, they'll back you. Lorimar is a good man and typically supports his team, but council members are more concerned with how they'll look politically than backing city staff. Let's hope we get this situation resolved quickly, or else we both might be looking for a job."

Lucas nodded, stifling a yawn. Gathering his files, he followed Chief Harper into the hallway that led to the public Council chambers where he could hear the low rumble of voices. Erasing the tired smile he felt, he replaced it with a serious but pleasant expression as he followed Chief Harper into the gallery area to take his seat. He nearly stopped in his tracks when he saw that almost every seat in the room was filled, a dramatic increase from the usual monthly meeting attendance. The faces looking his way did not look happy.

Lucas took a fortifying breath as the meeting was called to order. He should have had Ennis stay. After the pledge of allegiance and opening comments were given, the floor was opened for public comments as was the custom at each Council meeting. In her allotted three minutes, the first citizen to speak, a middle-aged woman, asked about the growing number of fires, expressed concern for her and her property's safety, and asked exactly what the fire department was doing to address the situation.

Just as the woman began to speak, Jeremy Ennis eased into the seat next to Lucas.

"Couldn't abandon you, Chief," Jeremy whispered.

JILL HEARD LUCAS'S KEY turn in the lock. She'd been dozing, a warm throw over her, as she waited for him to get home. Hearing the door click closed behind him, she was now wide awake.

When Lucas turned and saw Jill, she pushed the throw aside and walked quickly to him, pulling him tightly to her. She sensed the tension in him begin to relax as he put his arms around her. They stood silently holding each other for several contented minutes. The light jazz playing in the background that she'd turned on after watching the council meeting was a soothing antidote to the tumult that she'd seen during the public comments.

"Lucas . . ." Jill began.

"No. We're good. Don't say anything—please," Lucas said, leaning back and looking into her eyes.

"Lucas, you did wonderfully—so calm and in control, so reassuring. I am very proud of you," Jill said, reaching up and stroking Lucas's cheek.

"But the way those people talked to you . . . the meeting, it was . . . the way they . . ." Jill spluttered. "I want them to know how hard you're working, how much this weighs on you, and then for them to say the things they did . . ."

"Shh . . ." Lucas soothed as he put his hands on either side of her head, pulling her back to him. "This is what I need right now."

After several quiet moments, Jill stepped away from Lucas, and putting her hands on her hips said, "How can you be so calm? I was ready to march down there and give those people a piece of my mind!"

Lucas chuckled lightly. "Oh no you don't. I love every piece of you, so please don't give anything away."

"Lucas, I'm being serious."

"And so am I. Come here."

Lucas took her hands and pulled her down beside him on the sofa. He turned to her, his face drawn and serious.

"They're angry, but their anger comes from fear. No one knows when or where this arsonist is going to strike next, and it has everyone on edge. Yes—the meeting was as bad as it looked, and I hope not to have to go through another one like it again, but I've got the support of you and the family and the support of others in both fire and police. We're all dedicated to resolving this situation as quickly as possible. And we will, so you are not to worry. Okay?"

Jill couldn't help the hint of tears that threatened as she felt Lucas's finger below her chin, tipping her face up to look at him. His kind, brown eyes were studying her earnestly, his other hand resting gently on her shoulder.

"Okay?" he asked again softly.

Jill sniffed, nodded, and attempted to match the smile Lucas was trying to offer.

"My concern is for you, Lucas. This move . . . this job—it wasn't supposed to be like this."

"I know. I know," Lucas said. "But I am the fire chief which means I'm the one they're going to direct their anger and frustration toward. So, think about it this way. Once the case is solved. I'll be the one they love."

He looked at Jill with a teasing glint in his eye, coaxing a small grin from her before he pulled her into his arms. But being a new chief and having an arsonist taunt him with notes at the fires . . . Frankly, he had to agree with Jill. He'd been thinking the same thing himself. This job wasn't supposed to be like this.

J ILL WOKE UP LATE that night, sensing something was off. When she rolled over, Lucas's side of the bed was empty, the sheets barely disturbed. She sat up and saw a light in the hallway. Getting up, she wrapped her arms around herself against the chill and walked barefoot down the narrow hall to the room Lucas was using as a study. He sat at the desk, completely still, his back to her, one cheek resting against a fisted hand. She walked up quietly behind him and, looking over his shoulder, saw fire scene photos and notes scattered across the desktop.

Putting her hands on his shoulders, her head against his, she asked softly, "Is something wrong?"

Startled, Lucas jumped and turned to face her as she straightened. His face was drawn and lined with exhaustion. He looked so tired. It hurt Jill to see him so troubled.

He smiled sheepishly. "I hope I didn't wake you."

"No, you didn't. Something didn't feel right, and I realized you were gone." She took the hand he offered her and nodded toward the pictures on the desk. "Your mind won't let you rest, will it? You *are* worried."

"Ah, nothing for you to fret about though. I just got to thinking about some of the comments made at the council meeting and thought they might help put some pieces together if I looked at this again," he said and gestured toward the desk. "But you go on back to bed."

"Not without you. I want to help."

Lucas smiled and pulling her hand to him, kissed her palm. "You already help just by being here."

He sighed and took one more look at the photos before standing and pulling the chain, turning off the desk lamp.

"Come on. Let's go to bed," Lucas said, putting his arm around Jill as they made their way back to their room. Climbing into bed, Jill pulled the sheet over both of them as she snuggled up to Lucas and he put an arm around her, pulling her to him.

As Jill's breathing slowed and evened, Lucas lay awake, going over the day, the council meeting—everything. Who was this arsonist and why was he taunting him? They had to catch a break—and soon.

IT HAD BEEN A long day, and Milton Carr was ready to get out of the office. Matthews had been unusually withdrawn and quiet that morning and left before lunch for his daily visits to the stations. Carr had to smile to himself. He'd known all along Matthews couldn't handle the responsibilities of the job. It was far too big for him. It was only a matter of time until everything came together, Carr thought, and Kirk Lorimar would come crawling to him, asking him to take the position.

He took a quick glance at his phone to check the time. It was 5:20. He'd run into Chris Franks with city maintenance earlier that day as they were both filling up with gas at the City's service center. Chris had told him there was a basketball game tonight at 6:00. Chris's second son, Kit, was the same age as Chase and a forward on the varsity basketball team. The game was news to Milton. Chase hadn't told him about it, and who knew why? Milton shook his head. Casey had always been a good kid— good grades, participated in school activities, and excelled at everything. But Chase . . . well, he was a totally different story. No matter, Milton thought as he stood. He'd do the parent thing and go to the game. Besides, it'd be interesting to see how Chase got along with the coach and his teammates.

Carr picked up his jacket, swinging it on as he turned off his office lights. He'd just wrapped up the training schedule for the incoming recruits along with the results of the 48/96 shift schedule change survey and emailed both reports to Matthews. Matthews was a stickler for accuracy and promptness as Carr had found out the hard way after being late with reports a couple of times. But right now, it was after 5:00, and he was going to his son's basketball game.

The gym's parking lot was filling quickly as Carr pulled into a spot. He nodded to a few people as he walked across the lot and into the frenzy of the gym's activity. The continuous thump of bouncing basketballs and the hum of the crowd permeated the lively atmosphere as he joined the crowd streaming through the doors. The unmistakable aroma of popcorn smelled wonderful and was a reminder he hadn't eaten. He wandered over to the concession stand and, after waiting his turn in line, bought a box of popcorn and a Diet Coke. As he casually munched on the popcorn, he walked into the gym, took a seat on the home team side, and exchanged greetings with a few other parents he knew.

The gym had been renovated about two years ago; the hardwood floor shone beneath the bright lights. The black and gold school colors surrounded the Abernathy Bobcat logo, emblazoned on the floor at center court. Two state-of-the-art electronic scoreboards, one at each end of the court, retractable bleachers with memory foam seats, and a powerful public address system along with countless other upgrades from the old gym had been included throughout the gym complex. It was a well-loved and well-used facility.

Abernathy and the opposing team were on the court warming up. Carr looked around as he tossed a few more kernels of popcorn in his mouth, his gaze roaming across the players, as he looked for Chase, but he saw no sign of him. Carr frowned, but maybe, he thought, Chase might still be in the locker room for some reason.

The teams returned to their respective locker rooms for the last-minute coach's pep talk before re-entering the gym a few minutes later to enthusiastic cheers. The Abernathy Bobcats were escorted in by seven little boys between the ages of five and seven, known as the Little Dribblers. They were an Abernathy tradition and a crowd favorite. It was a tremendous honor to be selected as a Little Dribbler. They dribbled the ball and passed it to one another at center court while the high school teams did their last-minute warm-ups at either end. The gym had filled to capacity, and the air inside was electric with anticipation. With this being the season's first game, supporters for both teams were out in force.

As the teams gathered at opposite ends of the court, Carr scanned the row of Abernathy players lined up, hands over their hearts, listening as the Abernathy jazz band played the national anthem. Still no Chase. Carr's eyes cut back and forth across the players, the bench, and then the row of coaches standing alongside the team in case Chase was standing with them. But Chase was nowhere on the Abernathy side of the court.

Losing his appetite as a suspicion began to take hold, Carr set the unfinished bucket of popcorn and the Diet Coke beneath his seat and stepped across a few people to get to the nearest aisle. Slowly maneuvering his way down the steps to the floor, he made his way to the table where Brad Cox, a friend and the head high school scorekeeper, sat doing last minute adjustments to his list.

"Brad Cox!" Carr almost shouted over the noise as he came up behind him. Carr got as close as he could without stepping over the line behind which the score-keeping table sat. "Brad Cox!" a little louder this time.

Brad Cox lifted one side of his headphones and turned around, hearing his name. Spotting Milton Carr, he broke into a big smile. Taking the headphones off and laying them on the table beside the microphone, he stood and walked toward Milton Carr, his hand extended.

"Milton Carr, what on earth are you doing here tonight? I hope it's nothing fire related—especially not after the recent slew of arsons."

Carr shook his head. "No way I'd miss the first game. And I thought my son might be playing tonight. He's hinted around but hasn't come right out and said. He's kinda quiet that way." Carr didn't want to come right out and ask if Chase was on the team's roster.

A puzzled frown crossed Cox's face. "Your son's name is Chase—right?"

"That's right," Carr said as he stuck his hands nonchalantly in his jacket pockets and tried to look unconcerned. Cox turned and thumbed through some papers on the table once and then again, a second time.

"Milton, so sorry. I'm not exactly sure how to tell you, but Chase isn't on the team—any team—varsity or otherwise. I'd say he might be a sub for tonight, but I don't see his name listed anywhere. Sorry."

The buzzer sounded, bringing players to center court and preventing any further conversation. Brad gave Milton an apologetic wave before resuming his seat at the scorer's table and putting his headphones on.

Carr glared at his shoes for several seconds before turning and walking past the bleachers full of people, past the concession stands, and past the latecomers, streaming toward the gym and hoping to get a seat. Carr's temper rose with each step. Chase had better have a good, a *really* good, explanation.

CHASE LEANED BACK IN his chair, putting one foot on his desk, crossing his other leg over it at the ankle. He balanced a plate of chips and bowl of queso in one hand as he finagled the dials on the stereo. He had just cranked up the sound in his headphones, his head bobbing with the rhythm, when his chair was yanked backward, sending him and his food flying.

Surprised, his heart racing, Chase's eyes flew open to see his father towering over him, face beet red, and his eyes flashing dangerously. Fury radiated from him like a furnace out of control.

Reaching down, Milton Carr ripped the headphones from his son's head and threw them across the room.

"Did you forget something tonight, Son?" biting sarcasm saturating the question.

Chase sat up and blinked several times, his mind racing, a complete blank. What was happening tonight? His mother's monthly book club meeting was tonight, and his dad didn't have any work-related meetings, at least not that Chase knew or remembered. What was . . .

The color drained from Chase's face as it came to him, and he swallowed—hard. The first basketball game of the season . . .

"Ah. So you do remember," his father said, crossing his arms across his chest as he glared down at his son.

"Dad, please, I can explain . . ." Chase pleaded as he tried to stand, his dad only moving closer.

"I'm listening."

Chase gulped as he got to his feet. Who was he fooling? He couldn't explain. He hadn't tried out as he'd told his dad, and then he'd lied about making the team.

Chase blinked and then looked down without saying a word.

"Yeah. Just as I thought." Carr's eyes narrowed as he took another step closer. "Did you even try out?"

Chase, still looking down, shook his head slowly.

"So, it was all a lie. Every last bit of it."

Carr ran his fingers through his hair before moving to sit on the edge of the bed, pushing a stack of dirty clothes aside.

"Why, Son? Why all the lies?"

Surprised at what was a deceptively calm response, Chase looked at his father for several seconds, the tinny sound of music still playing from the headphones across the room.

"I'm no good at basketball, Dad. I don't like it. I never wanted to try out. Trying out was your idea—not mine." Chase looked down and picked at some of the queso that had landed on the T-shirt he was wearing.

"And the lies?"

"I didn't know how to tell you. I knew you'd be mad." Chase sniffed.

"Mad? I'm a whole lot more than mad. Being mad is just a very small part of it. Would you like to know the rest?"

His father's voice was rising at an alarming rate. "How about what it felt like walking into that gym looking for you on the court, telling Brad Cox you were on the team, and then him checking multiple lists only for him to have to tell me that my own son wasn't on a team—*any* team."

Chase cringed. He knew better than anyone how much his dad hated to be embarrassed, even inside the family, and this was worse because it had been at the gym and in front of a friend and anyone else who might have overheard.

"Dad, I'm sorr—"

"Save it. I don't care to hear an empty apology. I don't trust you anymore, Chase. I can't. My son lied to me, which means you don't respect me either."

"I do, sir, I do—"

Carr put a hand up, stopping Chase. Carr leaned over and put his elbows on his knees, his head in his hands. It was a lull before the inevitable storm Chase knew was coming.

"I don't want to hear it," Carr said. "And honestly, I don't even want to hear your voice. To help you understand better the seriousness of what you've done, from this point forward, and until I say otherwise, you are grounded. Hand over your car keys."

Carr stuck his hand out, waiting.

Chase's eyes rounded in horror. His heart was racing. He had to have that car. More importantly, his dad couldn't gain access to what was in the trunk.

"What? No car?!" Chase finally managed to splutter. "I need a car to get to school."

"Your mother or I will drive you to school and pick you up until further notice—or you can walk."

"Dad, no. That's not even reasonable. I'm a junior. How's it going to look if my mother drops me off and picks me up in front of everyone? And . . . and it's a little far to walk."

"Guess you should have thought of that before you lied. Keys."

His father's hand remained outstretched. Chase reluctantly picked the keys up from the desk. Clutching them tightly, he slowly turned to his dad, trying one more time.

"Please, sir. I really need my car . . ."

Carr stood quickly and, before Chase could react, snatched the keys out of Chase's hand.

"Next, when your mother or I pick you up from school, you will come home, to this room, and do any homework you have. There will be no music, no videos, no TV, no phone, no video games. No nothing. Are you getting the picture?"

Chase's eyes rounded in disbelief.

"When you are finished with homework, there will be chores. You can start with raking the leaves—front yard and back. When your mother and I feel like the lesson has been learned, we'll talk about modifying the punishment. But don't expect that anytime soon." Carr held up a warning hand, silencing Chase. "Maybe not until summer."

Now Chase was angry and opened his mouth to protest, but his father held up a hand once again, stopping him.

"I want the stereo off. I'll take the headphones and your phone. You'll clean up this mess, and I'm not just talking about the food. I'm talking about everything." Carr scuffed a shirt and pair of jeans lying on the floor with the toe of his shoe with a withering look at Chase. "I am deeply disappointed in you, Chase. More than that, I'm ashamed you're my son."

Chase took a step back. There it was. He'd always thought deep down his dad felt that way, but to hear him say it out loud—and to his face—was a gut punch. Chase lifted his chin defiantly, determined to keep his father from seeing how deeply the words had cut. He thrust the headphones and phone into his father's outstretched hand. With one last look, first around the room and then at Chase, his father turned and walked out the door, slamming it closed behind him.

Chase fumed as a few minutes later, he slowly began picking up scattered chips and dabbing half-heartedly at clumps of queso. He tossed clothes, whether clean or dirty, into scattered piles, shoving his shoes into a mismatched lump on the closet floor. He eventually lay down on his bed, his mind and thoughts racing. An hour or two later, he began hearing muffled voices through the door. His mom must be home. Maybe . . . he thought . . . he could enlist her aid at least to get his car back. More importantly, he had to get the keys away from his dad—even if just for a few minutes.

Jeremy blinked his tired eyes several times as he combed through the ashes of a small grass fire that had originated in a neighborhood trash dumpster and spread several feet in either direction. The fire had just been extinguished. Puffs of smoke and glowing embers were still easily visible through the ashes, its acrid smell permeating the frosty morning air. Jeremy's rubber boots crunched the dead grass surrounding the burn area as he stepped carefully around the edges, snapping pictures.

The floodlights from the engine illuminated the surrounding area while the firefighters rolled the hose after disconnecting it from the hydrant a few houses down the street. The fire engine's diesel motor reverberated through the quiet residential neighborhood as its emergency lights swept the nearby houses in orbs of red and blue. The neighbors who had heard the siren, seen the lights, and come out of their homes had already disbursed, but not before Jeremy snapped several pictures of them while he waited for the all clear for him to start his work.

This fire had most of the hallmarks of the arsonist but was smaller in scope than the last few had been. One of things he'd noted in his investigation was how the fires were growing progressively larger in size and in the structure or material. This fire broke that pattern. It was also odd there was no gas can as there had been at previous fires. What if they were dealing with two arsonists now?

"You about done, Ennis?" the station lieutenant asked as he stepped inside the flood lit burn space.

Jeremy straightened and looked around, turning in a tight circle, taking in the entire burn area, with occasional glances around the perimeter, checking for remaining spectators. An arsonist would want to hang around as long as possible.

Jeremy shifted the air tank on his back to where it was more comfortable before taking the few steps to close the distance to where the lieutenant was waiting.

"Yeah, I'm done. I think we can wrap this one up. Thanks, Josh."

The lieutenant nodded and gave the signal to his crew to douse the floodlight as the engine's rumble grew louder in preparation of leaving.

Jeremy walked to his vehicle, returning his tool kit to the SUV before shutting the compartment door lid firmly. Getting in, he put the SUV in gear, turning up the heat as he pulled onto the residential street and toward home. At least he could get a few hours of sleep before work the next day. As he turned the corner, he didn't see the shadowed figure that stepped in between two of the nearby houses and disappeared into the darkness.

THE DAYS FOLLOWING THE council meeting were a blur of activity. Meetings were necessary as were the briefings from Ennis and the police detectives on the continuation of the arson investigations. But Lucas gained his sense of balance, a reconnection with the mission—what it was really about—from his visits to the stations.

Thursday afternoon he pulled up to Station 6 just as Deputy Chief Carr was pulling away. Carr didn't acknowledge Lucas as their vehicles passed in the station's drive. He'd been his usual non-cooperative self at Monday's staff meeting, and Lucas hadn't seen much of him Tuesday, but Wednesday, there was a marked difference in Carr's demeanor. Carr had been in a foul mood and tighter lipped than usual since Wednesday. He seemed deeply troubled. Lucas had hoped that they might at least be able to establish some kind of a relationship where they would feel comfortable talking. That possibility seemed like a long shot at best, but Lucas would keep trying.

Lucas hadn't been able to get away from the office until late afternoon, but he was determined to visit at least one station before heading home.

Jill had called earlier and said the Realtor was supposed to have an update that afternoon. He was looking forward to finding out how close they were to finalizing the loan, so they could start preparing to move.

In spite of the cool fall temperatures, Lucas had a couple of gallons of Bluebell ice cream with him. A Texas firefighter's love for Bluebell ice cream was a universal thing and spanned all four seasons. Parking and grabbing the grocery bags, Lucas walked around to the back bay area where three firefighters were putting equipment back into the storage areas on the engine. The ambulance's back doors were open, and a paramedic was inside and, from what Lucas could see, was restocking supplies. The unmistakable smell of meat being grilled drifted over the fence of the station's back patio enclosure.

"Good afternoon, gentlemen," Lucas said, stopping just inside the bay door.

Lucas noticed furtive glances between the firefighters as he walked toward them.

"Hello, Chief," one firefighter said, wiping his hand on a rag before shaking Lucas's hand. "What brings you to Six?"

"Oh, just thought I'd drop by. I brought dessert." Lucas grinned and held up the grocery bags.

"Well, you've certainly got our number, Chief," another firefighter said with a broad grin, the others nodding agreement.

Lucas smiled and began walking toward the door into the station as they slowly resumed their work. Lucas frowned slightly as he noticed more glances exchanged between them and then a look toward him.

Opening the station door, he heard voices. Making his way down the narrow hall from the bay, he stepped inside the kitchen doorway. It was a busy spot with a couple of firefighters at the counter chopping peppers and onions while another was standing over a pot on the stove. Their chatter stopped immediately when he was noticed.

"Chief!" the firefighter at the stove said nervously. "We were . . . We were . . ."

"Looks like you're cooking dinner, Campbell," Lucas replied. "And it smells great."

A firefighter carrying a large platter of sizzling meat opened the back door, catching the door with one heel, stopping just inside when he saw Lucas.

"Chief!" he said, handing the platter to one of the firefighters near the counter.

Lucas eyed them as they all shifted nervously.

"What's up with you guys?" Lucas asked, setting the grocery bags on the kitchen island. "You all look like cats on a hot roof as does the group in the bay."

Silence met his inquiry as they continued to shuffle, not meeting his eye.

"Milton, I thought you'd left," said Darryl McCracken as he bounced into the kitchen, coming to a sudden stop, the grin sliding from his face when he saw Lucas.

"Oh, Chief. Welcome," McCracken laughed embarrassedly, sending a nervous look around the room. "I'm sorry, sir. Deputy Chief Carr was just . . ." he began as he walked over to shake Lucas's hand.

"Yes. I passed him on my way in. Does he drop by Six often?" Lucas asked as McCracken shot another quick look around the circle of nervous faces.

"Uh—occasionally. I'm sure he visits all of the stations regularly just as do you," McCracken said with a smug huff.

"Yes. I see." Lucas nodded, and he truly did see. He wasn't sure what was going on with Carr this week, but Lucas had given Carr more credit for being above the high school behavior Lucas suddenly suspected was happening. It looked like Carr was escalating the situation between them without Lucas being the wiser for it, and Lucas didn't like it. He didn't like it one bit.

"We weren't expecting you, sir," McCracken went on. "Can you join us for dinner? Lindale has grilled up some fajitas. Not to brag, but he's the best in the department on the grill."

Lucas eyed McCracken and the group in the kitchen along with those coming in from the bay. Whatever Carr's purpose had been in being here, something had set them all on edge, and that wasn't good for them or their mindset for work. Lucas had lost his appetite, but dinner was the perfect time for a meaningful conversation. Lucas recognized the opportunity, and he wasn't going to miss it.

"I'd love to join you. Those fajitas smell great," Lucas said, pulling the ice cream out of the grocery bags. Opening the freezer door of A-Shift's refrigerator, he placed them inside. "Ice cream should top dinner off perfectly. Now, what can I do to help?"

Exchanging glances, everyone chuckled as Campbell handed Lucas the spoon and instructed him to stir the beans cooking on the stove.

"So, Lindale is pretty good on the grill?" Lucas asked over his shoulder.

"He *thinks* he's good," Campbell interjected as he pulled plates from the cabinet and set them on the island.

"Yeah, but we bust his ego down to size when we have to," Connor Bland, the paramedic who had been loading supplies in the ambulance, added with a chuckle.

Lindale shrugged nonchalantly as he moved the heaping platter of meat to the island. "If anyone wants to take over the grill, you'll get no complaint from me. It'd be kinda nice to be on the other side of the critical barrage for a change."

"We'll let the Chief decide," McCracken said as he tossed a corn chip in his mouth and grinned deviously.

Lucas looked over his shoulder at the faces, waiting for his response, some friendly, some hesitant.

"All right then, gentlemen," Lucas said with a light chuckle. "You've got a deal, but first, let's just have a nice, friendly dinner—and no trying to influence the judge either. I'll render my verdict then."

Lucas intentionally turned back to the stove, not waiting to see their reaction. This should be an interesting dinner.

L ucas drove away from Station 6 two hours later. Jill had been texting throughout his time at the station, but he'd only been able to give cursory replies and hadn't known how long he'd be.

He'd been right to be suspicious of Carr's being at Station 6 earlier. The fajitas had been some of the best Lucas had ever tasted, but he hadn't eaten much. He'd been more intent on his main purpose in staying for dinner. The conversation around the table had been lighthearted and the typical good-natured banter—at first. There had been numerous questions about the arsons and the ongoing investigation, which Lucas answered with as much as he could share, but when Lucas gently tried to steer the conversation toward more specific departmental topics, it was slight at first, but he detected an undercurrent of hesitation and resistance.

The more specific Lucas became, the quieter the group grew. He asked for their thoughts about the training schedule, about the proposed 48/96 shift change, about the vacation request process—all things Lucas was really interested in knowing, but each topic resided in Deputy Chief Carr's purview. The more specific Lucas grew, the more often McCracken stepped in and deftly steered the conversation toward more mundane, non-departmental topics. Lucas watched the group closely and saw the furtive glances being exchanged when they thought he wasn't looking. Every fiber in Lucas's body told him something was going on, and it wasn't good. He'd find out, though, of that there was no question.

Darkness was falling as Lucas drove to the townhome through Abernathy's quiet streets. It would be interesting to see how tomorrow night's command dinner at the Abernathy Country Club would go. There was nothing he could do about his suspicions until Monday, but that wasn't going to stop him from putting some ideas together on how he could respond. He was deep in thought when he pulled into the driveway behind Jill's car.

Opening the door, he stepped inside and smelled something delicious. He hadn't been able to eat much before, but now he allowed himself to feel hungry.

Jill stepped out of the kitchen as he slid his jacket off and hung it on the hook she had placed just inside the door for that purpose.

"What smells so good?" Lucas asked as he glanced at the few pieces of mail on the entry table.

When Jill didn't respond, Lucas looked up and grimaced.

He was in trouble. He'd sent her a quick text, letting her know he was going to be delayed but not for how long. And then, he'd been too distracted to call and let her know he was on his way home, and Jill was angry.

"I thought you were going to be home an hour ago," Jill said. What she intended as a glare was countered by her lips trembling.

"Jill, what is it?" Lucas asked, crossing the room quickly and putting his hands on her arms. "What's happened?"

She immediately burst into tears.

"The house . . . We may not get the house . . . The Realtor said . . . The mortgage company called . . ."

Lucas put an arm around her and led her to the couch. His arm remained firmly around Jill's shoulders until her tears slowed. Handing her a tissue, he waited patiently until she looked up with a sheepish grin.

"Just what you needed after the week you've had. A weepy wife," she said with a roll of her eyes and an unhappy shrug.

"I always need my wife—weepy or not," Lucas said, squeezing Jill's shoulder. "Now tell me. What's happened."

Jill sniffed a time or two and then said, "Delaford, the Realtor, called and said the mortgage company has had a delay in processing our loan for the house since it's contingent on selling our other house. In the meantime, there's been another offer on the house here. If they can't get the paperwork for our loan processed in time, we may . . . we may lose the house."

Surprised at this sudden turn, Lucas looked into Jill's eyes, seeing anxiety and uncertainty there that were so unlike her. He was dealing with a lot, but right now, Jill needed him and needed some reassurance and that took priority over everything else. Pulling on reserves from somewhere deep inside, Lucas suppressed a sigh and gave a slight grin instead.

"I've heard things like this happen all the time when buying and selling houses. I don't think we have anything to worry about. I tell you what. I'll call Delaford tomorrow and see how things are laying out here, and why don't you call Alexandria in Fort Collins and see where things stand on those offers that were made. We'll convene a Matthews war council once we talk to them and have a few more concrete facts. Let's not panic quite yet. It's going to work out. I just know it will, and we're going to be moving into that awesome house before you know it."

He tilted his head and raised his eyebrows, grinning a bit wider.

Jill sat back, crossing her arms in front of her with a humph.

"Lucas Matthews, with all that's going on right now, with all that's been happening, how on earth can you sit there, smiling and saying it's all going to work out? How? I love you for it, but how do you do it? I'm about at my wits end and I'm not front and center of an arson investigation or having to pacify an anxious city council and public, not to mention managing an entire fire department that's on edge or an insubordinate officer, or . . . everything else."

She shook her head. "I'm not sure you're human sometimes—super-human maybe—but not human."

Lucas chuckled and gently yanked a strand of blond hair that had fallen into Jill's face.

"Well, for a superhuman, I'm super hungry. What smells so good?"

"I thought you were having dinner at one of the stations."

"Well, I sorta did, but it was more business than a meal for me, so I'm starving."

Jill sniffed and stood, pulling Lucas up beside her.

"Your basic meatloaf and sides."

Jill moved toward the kitchen with Lucas in tow.

"My favorite!" Lucas said with a slight tug on Jill's hand.

Jill turned, shaking her head. "We both know it's not your favorite, but . . ."

"But having anything with you is my favorite," Lucas interjected, pulling Jill close for a quick kiss. "Now, bring it on before this superhuman passes out from hunger."

With Jill sleeping soundly beside him, Lucas lay in bed later that night unable to sleep, his thoughts spinning restlessly. He looked at her familiar, beautiful face and marveled again at how they'd found each other after years apart, never knowing if they'd see each other again. He was beyond grateful that they had, and for their wonderful life, and the two amazing kids they shared.

Absentmindedly fingering a strand of Jill's hair between his fingers, Lucas's thoughts, as they were constantly doing, returned to department issues and events in Abernathy. Things were intense, getting bigger, and starting to feel like they were closing in. No matter how calm and in control he looked on the outside, his insides were churning with anxiety. He needed help and some guidance. While he was definitely not superhuman, he knew a superior power who would help him. Lucas slid quietly from bed and knelt beside it, clasping his hands in prayer, pouring his heart out, laying all of his worries and concerns at the feet of the One who would provide the wisdom, help, and guidance he so desperately needed.

MILTON CARR GRUNTED AS he shrugged on his jacket Saturday evening. A jacket was bad enough. Thank goodness he didn't have to wear a tie too.

Brenda came up behind him, and putting her hands on his shoulders, smiled into the mirror as she caught his eye.

"Just as handsome as the day I married you," she said with a light kiss to Milton's cheek. Milton's frown remained entrenched on his face despite Brenda's attempt to coax him into smiling.

"Milton, you can't keep brooding and go tonight with that scowl on your face. You've done what you thought was right by Chase. He lied to you . . . to us . . . and that can't go unpunished."

Carr's glance locked with Brenda's eyes in the mirror.

"He's doing chores around the house, and he even swept out your shop this afternoon," Brenda went on, attempting to placate her husband. "And for what it's worth, I think it was a smart move to return his phone, disabling or enabling the calls he can make and receive. I feel better, knowing he has a way to communicate if needed. You know, for safety . . ."

Carr never acknowledged what Brenda said but silently moved to the dresser and picked up his wallet and car keys, dropping them both into his pant pockets before walking to the door.

"Milton, you can't keep fuming over it—especially tonight. You're too grumpy for it not to be noticed, and you certainly don't want that."

Brenda moved to stand in front of him, took his jacket lapels in her hands, and looked earnestly into his eyes.

"You've talked to McCracken and started the ball rolling with the rumors that will undermine Matthews, but you can't call attention to yourself tonight. Instead of looking like the grim reaper, you need to fly under the radar, and let your plan unfold subtly. You've managed it quite effectively so far, putting McCracken's insatiable desire for gossip to use. He'll never know how you're really using him to oust Matthews."

At the mention of their plans for Matthews, Carr couldn't help but smile. He had narrowly missed Matthews' arrival at Six yesterday, but he'd already successfully set the rumor mill into motion with what he'd been sharing, bits and pieces at a time with McCracken about Matthews' background. The rumors were already spreading quickly. Carr allowed a small smile. Matthews didn't stand a chance. And besides, the rumors were true—mostly.

Even though Carr was making progress on the Matthews' front, he was bothered by Chase's lying more than he wanted to admit. For now, Carr's immediate focus had to be on getting Matthews removed before he became any more entrenched in the department. After Matthews was gone and Carr was chief, then he'd figure out what to do about Chase. Except for school, Chase was where they could keep an eye on him, but was that enough? Was there more they could or should be doing? Probably, but Chase was under control, and Carr had other things on his mind . . .

Brenda cleared her throat, breaking his train of thought.

"We're going to be late if we don't get a move on. Zip me up, please dear."

Milton turned and zipped Brenda's dress as she observed his scowling face in the mirror.

Turning to the dresser, Brenda picked up a necklace. "I'm looking forward to meeting Matthews' wife. What's her name . . . Jill? Have you met her?"

"No," Milton mumbled as he walked to the door.

"I wonder what she's like . . . if she's anything like her husband," Brenda mused as she picked up her small handbag and followed him into the hallway.

Milton looked at her over his shoulder. "We've got to put our time to good use tonight. You get as much information about her as you can but also share as much of the rumors with the other wives as you can without being obvious. I'll do the same with the guys. Between us, I bet we can get the word out there plus come up with more to use against them."

"Just remember," Brenda added as Milton helped her on with her coat. "We need to be subtle in how we go about it. You haven't been too subtle with your feelings at the office, so we have to be careful going forward."

"Well, there's no doubt he's got a good idea how I feel about him, and I'm not going to pretend I'm any other way but the way I am. That's always been good enough—at least until this guy showed up," Milton groused as he retrieved the car keys from the entry table.

Opening the door and allowing Brenda to move ahead of him, Milton turned back inside and shouted, "Chase, we'll be back in a few hours."

There was no response.

"Chase!"

Still no response. With a roll of his eyes, Milton retraced his steps down the hallway and to the door of Chase's bedroom. Chase lay sprawled across his bed, hands behind his head, staring at the ceiling. Arms crossed over his chest, Carr waited for Chase to acknowledge he was there. While he waited, Carr noticed that Chase's room looked much better than it had in months—no clothes on the floor, the bed was made, and almost everything was in its place. Looking back at Chase and still not getting a response, Milton walked over and kicked one of Chase's feet hanging over the edge of the bed.

Chase rolled his head to one side and glared at his father.

Narrowing his eyes, Milton said, "Your mother and I are leaving."

"So?" Chase replied and looked back to the ceiling.

"So . . . we'll be back in a few hours. Your mother left supper for you in the oven. What are you going to do while we're gone?"

Chase's head popped up.

"Are you're actually asking?" Chase snorted. "There's not much I can do now is there? Have fun at your fancy party."

"It's a work thing—a dinner—not a party," Milton retorted and turned toward the door. Without turning to look at his son he added, "Behave, Chase. I mean it."

"Sure, Dad," Chase said sarcastically. Under his breath he added, "Whatever."

Milton joined Brenda on the porch before they walked to the car. After they got in, Brenda glanced at her husband.

"Everything okay with Chase?"

"As much as it ever is."

CHASE WAITED UNTIL HE heard his parents drive away before sitting up. He thought they'd never leave. After sitting in the silence for several minutes, he stood and walked to the kitchen. Opening the oven, he pulled out the plate his mom had left for him. After he gingerly removed the foil, he pulled a fork from the drawer and plunged it into the mashed potatoes, taking a big bite. Setting the plate on the counter, he grabbed a glass from the cabinet and the pitcher of tea from the refrigerator and poured himself a full glass.

Taking a seat at the bar, Chase continued to eat while he sat deep in thought. After the longest five days of his life, his dad had modified the original punishment that morning and returned Chase's phone but with new restrictions. He had use of the phone but only for emergencies; all internet, games, and other features had been disabled. He could call his parents and his sister but no one else.

He'd called Casey last night, but she was studying for a test and hadn't been able to talk long. She brought up Jon Matthews—again. She was still bothered he hadn't called her. She really liked him and was sure he'd call her even though she had to admit Jon hadn't said he would when Chase pressed her on it. Casey said she'd texted the guy several times, but he'd never replied.

Chase hoped that loser didn't call. Chase didn't need some jerk taking up his sister's time when she was home. Jon Matthews must take after his dad. In fact, the entire Matthews family was making life miserable for his family, him included. With a quick glance to the door leading to the garage, Chase ate quickly. He knew where his dad had hidden the keys to his hatchback, and there was work to do.

J ILL STARED OUT THE window as they drove to the country club. Lucas glanced over and then took another look. Jill looked absolutely stunning. They were both getting older, but, in his eyes, Jill was somehow managing to escape the touch of time. Her blond hair was a bit shorter now, but her eyes were the same brilliant blue and her face still held its captivating grace and charm. As he'd helped her on with her coat, he'd noticed the dress she was wearing beneath was light blue, and it complimented her in all the right places and ways. Its soft fabric fell in attractive folds, reaching just below her knee, and its blue enhanced the brilliant blue of her eyes, which were framed with fans of long, delicate lashes. A diamond drop necklace and diamond earrings, his Christmas gifts to her a couple of years ago, completed her look, and it was breathtaking.

As for him, the dress code at the club, according to Sullivan, required a jacket for men but no tie, so Lucas was wearing a black jacket, pants, and a black and white checked shirt.

"In case I haven't mentioned it, you look absolutely gorgeous," Lucas said, reaching over and taking Jill's hand.

Jill turned and smiled at Lucas. "You might have mentioned that a time or two. And, as for you, well let me see . . ." She pretended to eye Lucas closely before saying, "You'll do."

Lucas's eyes widened as he looked from the road back to Jill. "I tell you that you look gorgeous, and all I get is 'you'll do?' Seriously?"

Jill's light laugh sparkled in the air between them. She squeezed Lucas's fingers.

"Lucas, if we weren't headed to a fancy dinner, I'd grab you and kiss you senseless," she said, laughing. "Don't you know by now? I think—I've *always* thought—you're the best of everything all rolled into one incredible guy, and *I'm* the lucky one married to him."

She leaned over and kissed Lucas before they both laughed as she rubbed the lipstick away she'd left on his cheek.

"You forget," Lucas said, glancing at Jill, his eyes soft and warm. "I know you too well. There's something on your mind. We've got calls into both Realtors, and we can call the mortgage company Monday morning. The house deal is going to work out. Please don't worry."

Jill sighed and removed her hand from Lucas's grasp.

"It's not the house—at least not entirely. It's . . . well . . . it's . . ." She didn't finish; simply turned and looked back out the window again.

"It's what?" Lucas asked softly.

"I had two more job interviews this week," Jill finally said. "Both liked my portfolio but neither one was hiring. I've talked to every interior design firm within thirty miles, and . . ." Jill shrugged and sighed dejectedly. "I never dreamed I'd have trouble finding a job. I know we don't really have to have my income, but it's just something I enjoy. You know . . ."

Lucas grinned. "Oh yeah, how well I know. I've been through enough remodels for ten husbands," he said, laughing.

Jill swatted his arm and couldn't help but grin.

"You're right, and that's why I need a job remodeling *other* people's houses to keep me from remodeling ours all of the time."

"This is quite the serious matter then," Lucas said, feigning concern. "But I have an idea."

"An idea?" Jill asked. Her eyebrows rose with intrigue.

"It's really simple. Start your own interior design business. Since you'll be working for yourself, you can work only with the clients you truly want to work with and only do the jobs you know you'll enjoy. It's the perfect solution."

From the look on Jill's face, Lucas could tell she thought he'd lost his mind.

"Lucas . . . I . . . I can't start my own business!" Jill spluttered, taken by surprise. "I've never handled the business side before, and besides that, where am I going to find clients who aren't already working with these other firms? I don't want to end up costing us money."

"You won't. In fact, I think you're going to have more business than you can handle. Tonight is the perfect opportunity to network. You'll be meeting the wives of the other staff members. You can just mention that since you're new in town, you're opening your own design firm and seeing if they need a designer or know of someone who might. Networking is a powerful tool, and you never know what innocent comments in conversation will spark some interest."

A small grin began to play about Jill's lips before it bloomed into a wide smile.

"You think I can do it?" Jill asked, turning in the seat to face Lucas. "You really think I can do this?"

"I have no doubt—not one. You're going to be a design force to contend with in Abernathy. You were too good for those snooty ladies at Shipley, Smythe, and Saalfeld and those other firms. They didn't recognize how fortunate they would have been to have you. I say, 'Look out, Abernathy. Jill Matthews is in town.'"

Jill laughed, a relieved happy laugh, before leaning over and kissing Lucas on the cheek, once again smoothing away lipstick with her thumb.

"Thank you for having faith in me and for being so smart," she said, still leaning close. "You give me the confidence in myself I wouldn't have otherwise."

Lucas put his free hand on Jill's cheek and pulled her close for a quick kiss.

"I don't know about the smart part, but you've given me confidence in myself many times when I didn't have it otherwise," he said softly after releasing her lips. "It's about time I returned the favor."

LUCAS PULLED INTO THE sweeping drive that led to the front of the Abernathy Country Club. Coming to a stop at the valet stand, he started to open the door, but one valet opened his door while another opened Jill's and offered his hand to assist her out.

Lucas came around the back of the car after taking his claim ticket and stole another quick, appreciative glance at his wife who was smiling and chatting with the valet. He gave a quick nod to the valet and took Jill's hand, pulling her close as they approached the front door.

"Quite the place, huh?" Lucas said with a low whistle as they walked across the drive. "Somewhere this poor foster kid never thought he'd be—that's for sure," he said as they approached the front door.

"And look at you now, Chief Matthews! This is going to be fun."

Lucas quirked an eyebrow. "Fun?"

"Well," Jill said, giving his fingers a squeeze, "let's say . . . interesting."

"That sounds more like it," Lucas agreed as the doorman opened the massive front doors, the club's logo, etched in glass, inset in each. The doorman motioned them inside.

As they entered the lobby, Jill's eyes lit up as she took in the room's ambiance. The walls of the opulent room were a warm, honey paneling. A large, round wooden table, polished to a glossy shine, sat in the center of the black and white checked marble floor. The table held an over-sized vase filled with an enormous display of fall flowers. A sparkling chandelier hung above the table, casting it all in a soft light. Jill had just started toward a large landscape painting to get a closer look when Lucas spotted Riley and Jeremy.

Riley and Jeremy saw Lucas and Jill about the same time and started toward them. Riley was holding the hand of an attractive blonde Lucas knew, from Riley's descriptions, must be his wife. Jeremy was saying something to Riley as they approached and was holding the hand of a woman who must be his wife, a charming young lady whose face held the glow of an expectant mother. When Lucas had spent some one-on-one time with Riley and Jeremy, each man had talked extensively and proudly about his spouse. With his first glimpse of them as couples, Lucas could see that each man was crazy about his wife.

Riley and Jeremy were dressed similarly to Lucas with jackets and open-collar shirts. Lucas had asked Lindsay to relay the dress code to the rest of the staff and their spouses who were attending. Lucas wanted this dinner to be a relaxed opportunity outside of the office to meet each other's spouses and visit and not a stiff or formal occasion. Their wives looked lovely, each dressed in a similar style to what Jill was wearing.

"Chief," Sullivan said, extending his hand as they drew closer. "Welcome. May I introduce my wife, Maggie. Maggie, this is Chief Matthews and his wife."

"And this is my wife, Allie, and the little Ennis to be," Jeremy said proudly with a small gesture to Allie and the round baby bump.

"It's a pleasure to meet you," Lucas said, shaking each of their hands. "I've heard a lot of great things about both of you," Lucas added, his eyes going first to Sullivan and then to Ennis with a grin. "And may I present my wife, Jill. Jill, this is Battalion Chief Riley Sullivan, his wife, Maggie, and Fire Marshal Jeremy Ennis and his wife, Allie."

"I've been so excited to meet everyone tonight," Jill said with a bright smile as she shook their hands. "Lucas has mentioned everyone at one time or another, but it's so nice to put faces and names together."

"Uh-oh," Jeremy said, turning to Riley with an exaggerated grimace. "That means the Chief has been talking about us. I hope it's been good."

"Well . . . mostly good," Jill hedged teasingly.

Everyone chuckled.

"But he didn't tell me you two are expecting. Congratulations! When are you due, and do you know what it is? Sorry—I don't want to pry. Are you sharing that information?" Jill asked.

"No holding anything back in this household. Jeremy is shouting it from the rooftops," Allie said with a fond look and soft punch to Jeremy's arm. "It's a boy, and his name is going to be Jeremy Charles, but we're going to call him J. C. We're naming him after Jeremy and Jeremy's dad."

Jill and Maggie exchanged smiles as Allie went on.

"He's due in just a little over four months. I know I need to get busy on the nursery, but I just can't decide on a theme."

"I've offered my help," Maggie interjected, "but I'm more of a graphic artist so that doesn't translate well into designing a nursery."

"Well, if you'd like, I'd love to help," Jill said, exchanging a smile with Lucas. "It just so happens I'm an interior designer and opening my own business here in Abernathy."

Jill's face lit up with a sudden thought. "And if you're agreeable, I'd love to design your nursery—in exchange for some photos I can use to advertise my business. You know, show people what my work looks like. You'd only pay for materials—no design fee. What do you think?"

Allie's eyes widened with excitement as she looked at Jeremy. "What do you think, Jer? Is that okay?"

Jeremy grinned. "I think it's great, so long as it's okay with you. I'd actually be very grateful," Jeremy added, turning to Jill. "It will take a load off Allie. She tends to overdo, and the time is getting closer every day."

"You worry too much, Jeremy Ennis," Allie said with a laugh. "Thank you, Mrs. Matthews. That would be such a relief, and to have a professional designer! This is better than I ever imagined."

"I suggest we all sit down and talk ideas," Jill said, including Maggie in the discussion, "but I do have one stipulation to working with you."

Maggie and Allie exchanged a puzzled look.

"You have to call me Jill since I don't answer to Mrs. Matthews. Otherwise, we might have a communication problem."

"Then Jill it is," Allie said, Maggie echoing the agreement as they all laughed.

"Now, Maggie," Jill said, looping her arms through Maggie's and Allie's, "tell me what kind of graphic design work you do."

Shaking his head, Lucas looked first at Riley and then at Jeremy.

"We seem to be off to a great start, gentlemen," Lucas said with a grin.

"I don't know, sir," Riley said, feigning concern. "I'm not sure Jill knows what she's gotten herself into with those two."

"Don't you worry, my boy," Lucas said, clapping Riley on the back, "Jill can hold her own. Now, where will our group be?"

"My father reserved the smaller dining room to give the group a chance to visit more comfortably. It's right down this hall."

Riley gestured toward a hallway just off the main lobby, and the group started in that direction.

"Very thoughtful of him. Are we the first to arrive?" Lucas asked.

"Yes, sir. We wanted to make sure we were here to meet you, so we all rode up together," Riley replied. "It also gave me a chance to visit some with my sister who is too busy for her brother these days."

"Oh, you're one to talk," Allie retorted, laughing and popping out of the conversation about Maggie's graphic design. "I think we're all too busy for our own good."

"Can't argue with that," Riley said with a shake of his head.

"Well, you two being related explains some things," Lucas said, eyeing the group.

"Sir, just by marriage," Riley quickly interjected, exchanging a sudden concerned look with Jeremy.

"It doesn't and won't interfere with our job duties," Jeremy quickly added.

"Never thought it would. It just goes to the whole point of having this dinner and getting to know the officers more than seeing them on the job. You guys know how it is when you work shift duty, you know each other's families and all of their goings on. This will help me to know those in my command a bit better and put pieces together I wouldn't have known otherwise."

As they entered the dining room, Lucas took it in with an approving eye. The room was the perfect size. The dining tables were set in a square to encourage the flow of conversation. The spacious area where he stood was just inside the doorway and large enough for the entire group to visit and mingle with drinks before sitting down to eat. The drinks for the evening were to be iced tea, sparkling cider, or cranberry juice. There would be no alcohol since some of the officers would be going back on duty after dinner.

Lucas smiled appreciatively. Sullivan had volunteered to make all of the evening's arrangements on his days off, which had proven to be a tremendous help. Lucas needed Lindsay to work on other projects, and with Riley's familiarity with the Club, it had worked out wonderfully.

"My compliments. Well done, Sullivan. This will work perfectly," Lucas said with a nod.

"Thank you, sir. I'm glad you're pleased." Riley smiled. "Don't get too carried away just yet. The evening is young, but hopefully, all will go off without a hitch."

"If Riley planned it, I assure you, Chief Matthews, it will go smoothly," Maggie said, laughing and slipping her arm through Riley's. "He planned his marriage proposal along with a party to celebrate afterward here at the club, and all on New Year's Eve. Everything was absolutely perfect. He even managed to make it a complete surprise. It was an amazing evening."

Lucas nodded, smiling. He was already learning a lot about the men he worked with, and the evening was just beginning.

Turning to Jill, Lucas asked, "Shall we greet our guests?"

With a nod to the two young couples, Lucas placed his hand on the small of Jill's back and guided her back to the main lobby where they greeted the others who were beginning to arrive.

Milton and Brenda Carr were among the last to come through the door. Lucas was curious how Carr would behave tonight. Lucas squeezed Jill's hand and, without looking at her, nodded slightly in the Carrs' direction when they entered. Jill smiled sweetly and greeted them just as she had the others. Brenda Carr was all smiles as she cooed compliments which Jill appeared to take in stride. Lucas had to suppress a smile when he noticed the firm line of Jill's lips, which he knew betrayed the dislike she was trying to hide. When the last couple had arrived, he and Jill followed them into the dining room.

"So that's him?" Jill asked in a whisper as they followed the Carrs from a distance.

"That's him," Lucas confirmed. "He's being halfway civil tonight, but I'm sure that's due to your charm," he said, looking down and smiling at Jill. "I might need to take you with me to the office from now on."

"Oh no you don't." She laughed. "I've got a new business now. Remember? I'm afraid you are on your own," but then she seemed to catch herself.

Pulling Lucas to a stop beside her, Jill made a face.

Lucas frowned. "What's wrong?"

"I just realized how that sounded. I didn't mean it. You are not on your own, Lucas, and never will be. I am here and always on your side."

Touched at Jill's fervor, Lucas with a quick touch to her cheek said softly, "I know . . . I know."

Taking a fortifying breath, he then looked to the dining room's open door and said, "Well then, shall we enter the fray?"

"Yes. Together," Jill replied with a firm nod.

L
UCAS SIPPED HIS ICED tea and looked around the table at those gathered as Jill and Maggie Sullivan talked animatedly about design. He was glad Jill had found someone who shared such a passionate interest. While the gentle hum of conversation continued, Lucas took the opportunity to look at the faces he had already come to know well in the time he'd been with the department. Most were married and were here with their spouses while those single were here with their significant others. He appreciated the quality of staff he'd inherited from the previous chief. Even Carr, with his condescending behavior and rebellious attitude, had his strong points.

After nervously clearing his throat, Lucas stood and raised his glass. The conversation in the room faded quickly, replaced by soft music and the clinking of plates and dinner glasses as salads were placed in front of each guest and beverages were refilled by the staff with quiet efficiency.

"Thank you for coming tonight," Lucas began after taking a deep breath. He knew he wasn't a strong public speaker, but he was working on it. "I appreciate this opportunity to visit with each of you and learn more about you and your family and give everyone an opportunity to interact outside of work. A special thank you to Battalion Chief Sullivan who handled all of the evening's arrangements, and another special thank you to Riley's dad, Ballard Sullivan, who sponsored our meal here tonight."

"Sully," several said, raising their glasses with teasing smirks.

Riley waved them off with a laugh.

"As we enjoy our meal," Lucas continued, "I'd like for each staff member to share a little something about himself or herself—something others probably don't know about you. It can be something about you personally or about your family. It can be serious, or it can be fun. It's totally up to you. Mr. Ennis, why don't you start us off."

Lucas sat down and lifted a fork to spear a leaf of lettuce, looking at Jeremy and waiting to hear what he would say. Lucas noticed Jeremy and Riley exchanged a significant look before Jeremy grinned.

"Well, sir, there's not much that Sully doesn't know about me, but I don't think anyone else knows that I always carry a lucky rabbit's foot with me. My grandfather gave it to me, and I can assure you, it really works."

"Ah, come on, Ennis," Nate Baldwin said with a chuckle as he tore a roll in two and began buttering one side. "How do you know it works?"

Jeremy's face grew serious. "I know because the one fire I didn't have it with me, I nearly died. When a friend made sure I got it back in the hospital, that's when I woke up, and the docs knew I was going to make it."

A low murmur of surprise went around the table.

"Was that the big loft fire several years back?" West asked as others looked at Jeremy expectantly.

Jeremy nodded firmly. "I'm telling ya, it works. Now, who's next?"

"I'll go," Tyler Forney, A Shift's battalion chief, spoke up.

"Chastain bit his dog's nose once. Even drew blood," Forney said with a taunting grin at Chastain.

"That was only because he bit me first!" Chastain shot back before quickly turning red and shooting a horrified look around the table. Everyone erupted into laughter at the same time.

"Well, he did," Chastain said again, laughing himself.

After the laughter quietened, there were several minutes of silence as everyone ate.

The silence was broken when Elise Stephens said softly, "I nearly died from drugs. I survived and decided I wanted to do something positive with my life. That's when I got clean, finished college, and entered the academy. I'm thankful to be alive, clean, and here with all of you."

"Elise, we're proud of you and glad you're here too," Carr rushed to say as everyone nodded agreement.

Lucas nodded appreciatively as well but noticed several turn and look at him questioningly. It was as if they were expecting him to say something in response to Elise's comment but what were they expecting him to say? Something about Elise or about drugs? Lucas wasn't sure but Jill had also noticed and looked at him just as puzzled. He gave a small shrug and returned his attention to what was being said.

By the time they'd gotten through the salad and the main course's entree of filet mignon followed by large pieces of a triple-layered chocolate cake with ice cream for dessert, everyone had shared at least one thing with the group. Some had shared several things, causing the group to laugh and give them an especially hard time.

Jill had everyone wiping tears of laughter with her rendition of Lucas singing in the shower. He and Jill had talked beforehand about what they were going to share, but Lucas knew he still turned beet red. "Trust me," Jill had said still laughing, "you don't want to wake up hearing *that* in the morning."

Lucas just grinned and shook his head before he paid her back, eliciting a round of laughter, telling the story of Jill finding out she was expecting twins. "As a paramedic," Lucas said, "I thought I was going to have to bring out the defibrillator—for both me *and* her."

This is what Lucas missed about working shift duty in the stations—the camaraderie and the fun banter. But tonight—this was actually even better with the spouses here, sharing stories as well.

As the stories eventually died down and the evening was drawing to a close, Lucas rose to thank everyone for coming. He had just started speaking when Jeremy's radio went off, followed immediately by his own, then several others.

A round of groans accompanied everyone standing simultaneously. Lucas turned to Riley.

"Mr. Sullivan, could I impose upon you to take Jill home for me please?" Lucas asked, Jeremy quickly appearing at his side, Allie in tow.

Riley had taken half a shift off to make sure all was set for the dinner tonight, so he wasn't due back at the station until later.

"Of course. Of course. Not to worry, Chief, Jeremy. I'll get them home and will be there as soon as I can," Riley said hurriedly with a quick glance between them.

"Honey, I'm so sorry. I'll see you at home," Lucas said as he turned to Jill, adding a quick kiss to her cheek.

A worried look in her eyes, Jill squeezed Lucas's hands and nodded stiffly. "Be safe. Please."

Lucas gave a small smile, releasing her hands and turning to Jeremy.

"We'd better hit it, Mr. Ennis," Lucas said as they took off down the hallway in a controlled jog.

RILEY PULLED UP AT the scene to see the last of the flames being tapped out at what had been a small, wooden frame house. From the diminishing glow of the flames, Riley could see Chief Matthews standing just outside the fire ground. Chief Harper was at his side, both looking intently at what was left of the home. Jeremy was nowhere in sight but had probably already started his investigation.

As Riley got out of his truck and approached, he noted numerous police cruisers along with the fire engine and truck that had been dispatched. The flashes from all of the red and blue emergency lights were creating a strobe effect against the houses of the neighborhood. Riley made his way over to Kenneth Burkett, Station 1's out of class battalion chief for the half day Riley had taken off.

"Sullivan," Burkett said as Riley came to a stop beside him.

"What have we got?" Riley asked, pulling his helmet's chin strap tight and latching it beneath his chin.

"Single story. Wooden structure. Owner said it was a rental unit, vacated just last week."

"Has Ennis spotted anything out of place or unusual?" Riley asked as he zipped the front of his bunker coat closed.

"He's just started his investigation. Over there," Burkett said, motioning to the furthest corner of the lot where a few remaining blackened pieces of the house jutted out of the ashes at precarious angles. Even though the whole area was brightly lit with spotlights, from where Riley stood, he could see the beam of Jeremy's flashlight moving among the ashes with occasional flashes from his camera.

"I'll let you finish things up here, Burkett. Looks like it's well in hand. Thanks."

Burkett nodded as Riley clapped him on the back and moved to where Chief Matthews and Chief Harper were standing, their focus on Jeremy and the police investigator who had joined him.

Riley was sorry to have missed being here to handle most of the incident but was glad he'd been able to be of service to the chief and his wife. The drive taking Mrs. Matthews home had been a quiet, solemn one. He, Maggie, and Allie had exchanged concerned looks as the silence stretched on. He could tell Mrs. Matthews was worried. Riley was worried about Allie and her fretting over the stress Jeremy was experiencing thanks to this arsonist. The acts of this one foolhardy person caused ripple effects far beyond his unknown original intent, whatever that might be.

"They're going to figure this out and catch whoever is doing this. It's just a matter of time," Riley had said, catching Mrs. Matthews' eye in the rear-view mirror.

"Yeah, and when they do, I'm giving him a piece of my mind," Allie said from between clinched teeth.

"Now, sis, you know Jeremy doesn't want you worrying about this. He may be a new fire marshal, but it helps to be fresh out of training too.

He's learned the latest and greatest techniques, and you know Jeremy is giving it his all."

"Everyone is," Mrs. Matthews spoke up from the back seat for the first time. "Lucas has said many times how hard everyone is working. It's just frustrating not knowing what this person's motivation is and why he keeps taunting Lucas. We haven't been in town long enough to make enemies. It's all a bit unnerving."

Mrs. Matthews' statement stuck in Riley's mind. It was a valid point. Who would know Lucas well enough to consider him an enemy. They'd been thinking it was someone set to embarrass a new chief but an enemy, something more personal, could put a whole new spin on things.

"SULLIVAN. DID YOU GET my wife home okay?" Lucas asked with a quick glance to Riley when he walked up.

"Yes, sir. Delivered directly to your door."

Lucas nodded curtly without taking his eyes from where Jeremy and the police investigator were working.

Lucas cleared his throat and then glanced over at Riley, looking a bit sheepish.

"My apologies. I should be saying thank you instead," Lucas corrected himself before turning, hearing Jeremy calling his and Chief Harper's names.

They walked quickly to where Jeremy and the police investigator were standing, and Riley saw Lucas physically stiffen. Jeremy was holding up a gas can that had been a shiny red and gold—just like all of the others. The only difference, this one was now singed black.

"Anything attached to it?" Lucas asked as he and Chief Harper stopped a few feet from Jeremy.

Jeremy held the burned can out where they could see it better.

"No, sir. Looks like the arsonist got this one a little too close. Any note that might have been attached or any fingerprints, DNA, etc. is long since gone—burned. Sorry, sir."

Lucas ran his fingers through his hair before fisting his hand and putting it back at his waist.

"Anything else unusual turn up so far?" Lucas pressed on, hoping for something new—anything that would lead them to the person doing this and keeping everyone on edge.

"Not yet, sir," Jeremy replied, placing the can inside a transparent evidence bag and sealing it securely. "We'll run this through the lab to see if anything helpful turns up. In the meantime, we'll be going through everything here with a fine-toothed comb. I'll keep you posted."

"Thank you, Ennis. I know you will," Lucas said and joined Chief Harper as they walked toward their vehicles.

"Any thoughts, Lance?" Lucas asked as they came to a stop beside the police chief's cruiser. He looked as solemn as Lucas felt. He shook his head slowly before raising his eyes to Lucas's own.

"We're doing everything we can to get to the bottom of this, but Lucas, I don't like it. These fires are growing in size and property value. We'll catch a break, and this person, whoever it is, will make a mistake. They always do. It's only a matter of time. I just hope it's soon."

L UCAS PULLED INTO HIS spot at the admin building and quickly walked inside, the cold wind biting at him. Winter was starting to descend with its frigid temperatures and cutting winds. Shivering slightly as he stopped at Lindsay's desk and checked in, he then walked in the direction of Jeremy's office. He was anxious to see if Ennis had learned anything new since his update over the phone yesterday afternoon. As he approached, Lucas heard the low tones of Ennis's voice followed by the voice of another.

As he drew closer, Lucas heard Jeremy say, "You may have something, Sully. We've been thinking it's someone out to embarrass Chief Matthews, but this might be an actual grudge. It's certainly something to consider."

"But who?" Riley responded. "The Chief has only been in Abernathy a few months. Who would have it out for him so bad and make it so public too?" Riley's voice trailed off, and there was silence in the room as Lucas stepped to the door.

"Good morning," he said, waving them both back into their chairs as they'd started to rise. He walked in and eased into the second guest chair.

Jeremy's office reflected a true firefighter from the firefighting prints on the walls, all with white mats and black frames, to the bookshelf behind his desk where his helmet held the place of honor on the top shelf. Angled where he could see them, were framed pictures of both Jeremy and Allie and then, just Allie on Jeremy's desk.

"I heard a bit of what you were saying. You've got something to point to a new theory?" Lucas asked, taking a drink of coffee from the travel mug he'd brought from home.

Riley and Jeremy exchanged a quick, uncomfortable glance.

"Sir, we don't mean to imply that . . ." Riley quickly began.

"There's nothing to apologize for, Sullivan. All angles need to be examined, no matter what they are. So, you guys are thinking a grudge scenario?" Lucas asked, looking first at Riley then at Jeremy.

"It's certainly possible, sir," Jeremy said, leaning forward. "Do you know of anyone who has something against you that would drive them to set these fires?"

"No. Jill and I have talked about it too. I've gone over a potential list of people but just can't think of anyone who would go to these lengths."

"Good morning, all!" Milton Carr's voice boomed from down the hallway. "Where's our illustrious leader this morning? Across at One having ice cream?" he said loudly, followed by his own raucous laughter.

The three exchanged looks, their eyes growing wide, heads cocking to the side.

"Are you sure no one comes to mind, sir?" Jeremy asked, looking Lucas in the eye. "No one?"

"He's a sworn officer. He wouldn't . . ." Lucas said, unable to finish the sentence.

"There is one thing they taught us at the police academy, sir," Jeremy said looking solemnly at Lucas. "Anything is possible—*anything*."

Lucas looked from Jeremy to Riley and back to Jeremy. Sitting back, Lucas shook his head as if trying to think more clearly. Could it really be possible that Milton Carr, a fire department veteran of twenty plus years and a sworn officer, could be the serial arsonist, motivated by hatred of *him*?

Lucas shook his head, thinking back. He had been in a similar situation before, and this was all too familiar. The memories always hovered nearby. History could not be repeating itself. It just couldn't.

Lucas didn't linger over agenda items during Monday morning's staff meeting. Reports were given and information noted quickly. Lucas saw puzzled looks exchanged at the fast clip he was moving through the agenda. Each deputy chief, including Carr, gave his reports, and Lucas asked only the most necessary follow-up questions. Lucas watched Carr closely and couldn't detect even the slightest hint of discomfort or deception.

West brought up the arson investigation as Lucas was wrapping up the meeting. Lucas had purposefully left it off the agenda and asked Jeremy not to volunteer any information unless Lucas asked for it specifically—which he hadn't. Carr's attention was immediately snagged.

"Is there any new information about the arsons after the latest fire Saturday night?" West asked offhandedly as he stacked his files.

Carr's head popped up, looking first to West and then, narrowing his eyes, sliding a glance toward Lucas.

Jeremy waited for Lucas to give him an indication he wanted him to say something, but Lucas simply stood.

"We'll have more on that later," Lucas said with a quick nod in the general direction of the group before he walked out the door, leaving everyone looking at each other across the table.

"A bit touchy today, isn't he?" Carr asked with a smirk.

"Deputy Chief Carr," Jeremy addressed Carr, staring him down with a thinly veiled glare. "With all due respect, sir, I believe Chief Matthews has a lot on his mind right now. We are his support staff and should do everything we can to support him—whether certain ones of us like it or not."

Carr jumped to his feet. "Why you—I ought to—"

Jeremy stood and straightened to his full height, his eyes blazing. "You ought to what, sir?"

Carr's eyes narrowed to slits; his hands clinched into fists at his side as his face turned a deep shade of red.

Jeremy met his glare head on without flinching.

The room went deathly quiet as the others looked anxiously between them.

"Captain Stephens, Channel 8 is . . ." Lindsay began as she stepped inside the door but stopped mid-sentence, seeing Carr and Ennis squaring off across the table.

"Looks like you get a reprieve, Ennis," Carr sneered. "It might not work out so well for you next time," he said, grabbing his papers and heading toward the door.

"Nor for you, Chief," Jeremy said, lifting his chin defiantly.

Carr stiffened, about to say something, but refrained. He stormed from the conference room as Lindsay, wide-eyed, quickly stepped out of his way.

"But Chief—" Jeremy tried to interject before Lucas could go any further.

"There's no 'but Chief' in this conversation, Ennis. I appreciate you defending me, but I'll handle this without things coming to blows. I should have already put a stop to Carr's insubordination. I'd just hoped to win him over, but that's evidently not going to happen. If anything, your action might have proven to be the catalyst I needed to take the necessary action. Sometimes relationships seem complicated, and then sometimes it takes something simple to make them clear."

"Chief, I'm sorry if I caused any problems," Jeremy said, somber faced. "I just respect you and know the pressure you're under and what you're trying to handle. Then, hearing Carr mouthing off again and again—sorry, I guess I just reached my limit."

Lucas smiled and clapped Jeremy on the shoulder. "Thank you, Ennis. I appreciate your support, but you've got an arson investigation to handle. I suggest you get to it."

"Yes, sir." Jeremy gave a quick nod and was gone.

Lucas closed the door behind Jeremy and slowly walked around his desk and sank into the chair. He sighed, dropping his head into his hands and running his fingers through his hair.

"Lord, I prayed for help, but that wasn't exactly what I thought you might have in mind," Lucas prayed silently and smiled faintly. "But Lord, you know best, and I still need that help."

Lucas straightened and took another deep, cleansing breath. He had his report to prepare for the council meeting tomorrow night. He had just opened the document on his computer and found where he'd left off when his desk phone buzzed.

"Yes, Lindsay," he answered brusquely, still typing.

"Chief," Lindsay said, her voice wary, "you have a visitor up front."

"Did you get a name?"

"He just said to tell you Cap was here—that you'd know."

Lucas stopped typing and broke into a huge smile.

"Yes—yes, I do know. Send him back right away."

Lucas shook his head, still smiling, and looked toward the ceiling. "Thank you. That's exactly what I needed."

L ucas sat back and just soaked it in. He had no idea what Cap was currently talking about, nor did he care. He just knew Cap Cory Rio was here, in his office, sitting across from him. This was the balm Lucas needed so desperately for his weary spirit and mind. Lucas had spent many hours with Cap both in his official capacity as the Fort Collins Fire Department Chaplain but also as close friends, talking, sorting through issues, and hypothesizing how best to settle conflicts.

Oh, how Lucas had missed bouncing things off him, especially the past few weeks. Lucas had had no idea, until this very minute with Cap sitting in front of him, how much he'd missed—and needed—this. Abernathy's chaplain, Guy Johnson, had been out of the office when Lucas started and would continue to be out indefinitely with complications from what should have been a routine surgery. Even if Johnson had been in the office, Lucas didn't share the history and comfortable relationship he had with Cap.

"You haven't heard a word I've said," Cap accused, his gruff tone undercut by the teasing twinkle in his eyes. Cap was in his mid-fifties Lucas guessed. He was tall with a slender build, and while his black hair had been generously streaked with gray ever since Lucas had known him, the lines at the corners of his eyes and around his mouth had become more pronounced. What hadn't changed, though, were his eyes, one blue and one green. They always seemed prone to twinkle with amusement, but Lucas had also seen them shimmer with tears of compassion when talking with victims experiencing a loss.

"Sorry, Cap," Lucas said, leaning forward and putting his elbows on his desk. "It's just so good to see you. I had no idea until Lindsay told me you were here just how badly I needed a friendly face and some strong, listening ears, but the Lord knew and sent the best."

Cap nodded from behind the rim of his coffee cup. "I can't explain it, but I just got a feeling when your name came up the other day."

"My name came up?" Lucas's eyebrows rose with surprise.

"Word gets around—you know—when serial arson is involved. There have been some news reports and just talk in general. You've always been a fine officer and can handle more pressure than anyone I've ever met, but what you've got in front of you takes things to a whole new level. So, tell me, Lucas, how are you—really?"

Lucas stared at Cap for several long, silent seconds. He wanted to tell Cap everything—unload it all, but Lucas also knew his role as chief meant shouldering more than anyone and quietly carrying on. But on the other hand, Cap was here, Lucas believed, because the Lord knew he needed someone he could really talk to, someone who understood the fire department and knew what Lucas's responsibilities entailed.

"Well, Lucas?" Cap asked, leaning forward, never taking his eyes from Lucas as he set his coffee cup on the desk between them. "You know you can tell me anything and everything. Whatever it is you need to share. That's why I'm here."

Lucas nodded solemnly. "Yes, sir. I know. I'm just trying to decide where to begin and how much time you have."

"I have as much time as you need. Start at the beginning."

Lucas took a deep breath and did just that, starting with Deputy Chief Carr's resentment and the resulting insubordination, which Lucas acknowledged, with chagrin, he had yet to fully address. Lucas told Cap about the arsons and the taunting notes left on the gas cans, calling him out specifically. He talked about the city council and how they, as well as the public, were growing more impatient and anxious by the day. It was understandable, but he had nothing concrete to tell them.

Lucas talked until he was talked out. He looked at Cap and took a swallow of his Dr. Pepper whose ice had long since melted.

"It's a mess, isn't it?" Lucas stated more than asked, sighing heavily.

Even if this was Cap, Lucas was typically not so open. He'd confided much more than he'd intended, exposing what he considered to be failures on his part. It was a relief to get everything out there, but being so open also made him nervous.

Cap sat quietly. He hadn't said a word during Lucas's entire oration. He'd simply sat and listened, studying Lucas thoughtfully.

Lucas grinned ruefully and shook his head. "I had no idea this chief business was so—"

"Messy?" Cap supplied.

"That's a good word for it, but I was thinking political. I thought I'd be making sure the department ran at its most efficient level while ensuring the safety and wellbeing of the department's personnel. None of what I'm dealing with fits within those parameters."

Lucas paused and, looking down, absentmindedly fingered some papers on his desk. "You know . . . maybe I wasn't cut out to be a chief."

Cap's mouth opened and then closed.

Lucas leaned back sharply in his chair. "Is that . . . is that what you're really thinking but don't want to tell me?" A pained look crossed his usually stoic face.

Cap shook his head. "Lucas, I wish the chiefs I knew had half—just half—of what you've got. You're an outstanding leader, and I don't want you to ever think otherwise. I wouldn't have driven all this way to talk to you if I didn't think you had the right stuff to see this through.

"Yes, you've been thrown some curve balls here that most chiefs will never encounter in their entire careers. Unfortunately, your curve balls are high risk and have high visibility, but Lucas, you're strong, both mentally and physically. You're also smart, and I don't mean just book and common-sense smart—you're people smart. These situations are tough ones. Absolutely. But I know you. You're tougher. I know what you came through growing up. The only things different from then to now are the people. I have every confidence you'll handle this—all of it—and handle it well. Don't ever, *ever* doubt yourself. I don't."

Lucas ran his hand down his face, holding it there before looking up. "Sorry, Cap. I guess the pressure has built more than I realized. Your being here and shoring me up means more than I can say."

Cap studied Lucas for several minutes then looked over and pointed at the plaque hanging by the closed door of Lucas's office.

"I see you remember."

Lucas glanced at the plaque and then to Cap Rio with a small, knowing smile.

"Of course I remember. It came from you, so you know how important it is to me. It's what I live by and what I'm attempting to pass on to this department."

Looking at the plaque, Cap nodded and said softly, "Give it all you've got . . . *and then some.* And then, let God handle it."

Lucas nodded solemnly. "Wise advice from a wise man."

Cap chuckled lightly. "I'm not sure about the wise part, but I do believe that's the right path to follow. I bet you've got work to do. Let's talk more over dinner tonight if you're available. I'm buying."

"Cap, you and I both know there's no way you're buying dinner, so let's just get that settled right here and now," Lucas said as he smiled tiredly.

Cap gave Lucas a long, appraising look then chuckled as he stood and lifted his jacket off the chair next to him. "I've got a hotel room, so I'll go check in. Just let me know when and where."

Lucas nodded as his phone rang. The ID said Kirk Lorimar. He swiped to answer and held up a finger, indicating for Cap to wait.

Lucas nodded silently while Kirk Lorimar talked on the other end of the line.

"Yes, sir. I am fully aware and have a draft ready for tomorrow night. Would you like me to discuss it in executive session or in the public meeting?"

Lucas listened, jotting down a few notes.

"Yes, sir. That sounds great. I will send it over in the morning for your review before submitting it for the executive session agenda. Yes, sir. Thank you. I'll see you tomorrow." Lucas tapped his phone and sat it on the desk face down.

"Rain check for dinner?" Cap asked, standing.

"No, sir. I'm just about finished with the report he's asking about. I'll have it to him plenty early in the morning. He was just giving me a heads up about Council Member Dower. My name seems to be coming up a lot with her."

Cap put a hand on Lucas's shoulder, giving him a quick pat as Lucas walked with him to the office door. They walked into the hallway, Lucas stopping at Lindsay's desk as Cap continued to the door to leave. Before opening the door, Cap glanced back at Lucas, who was talking to his assistant. That boy had more steel in him than anyone he'd ever known, but Cap frowned. Even steel had a breaking point.

L UCAS ARRIVED AT THE office the next day feeling better and more optimistic than he'd felt in weeks. The visit and the advice Cap had shared with him over dinner last night had been just what he'd needed. They'd enjoyed a nice breakfast before Cap headed back to Fort Collins. Lucas felt like he was ready to tackle whatever lay in store for him today.

"Good morning, Lindsay," Lucas said, stopping at her desk and picking up the mail.

"Good morning, sir. How are you this morning?"

"I am great. Thanks."

"These are for you, sir," Lindsay said, handing a stack of printouts to him. "This is the information you requested to complete your report for the evening's council meeting."

"Excellent. Thank you. And this is for you." Lucas handed her a sheet of paper and grinned.

"Would you please type this up for me? Make it look all official and then make copies. I'll need enough for everyone that attends the Monday morning meeting."

Lindsay nodded, quickly reading what was on the paper. She looked up at Lucas and smiled.

Lucas grinned in response. "I know it's a strange time for this with Thanksgiving this week, but I also know there's no time like the present. We'll have a quick meeting if you would please send an invite to the group."

Thirty minutes later, the staff was assembled in the conference room, looking confused, when Lucas walked in and shut the door behind him.

"Good morning, everyone," Lucas said with a bright smile. "This won't take but a minute. Starting today, each of you will be taking turns and joining me to cook lunch for each shift until we work our way through all of the stations and prepare a meal for each shift. Here is the schedule. The crews have been sent the list of supplies. They're doing the shopping. We're doing the cooking."

Surprised looks and raised eyebrows were on each face as copies of the schedule passed around the table.

"I know everyone is busy, as am I, but it's important we spend time with the crews, and eating lunch is something we all have in common. We'll be fixing a lunch favorite at most stations—tacos—which won't take long to prepare or serve. We start today. Chief Carr, you're with me at Six. You and I will also be meeting immediately after—1:30, back at the office."

"Sir, I can't possibly. I already have meetings scheduled—" Carr tried to object.

"Reschedule," Lucas cut him off. "I'll see you at Six at eleven o'clock. Questions? No? Good. That's it. Thanks."

Lucas stood and walked out without an opportunity for comments or questions.

Jeremy was trying to suppress a grin but couldn't stop it from spreading when Elise Stephens laughed, then tried to disguise it as a cough. West and Baldwin were shaking their heads but smiling when Jeremy looked around the table.

"I like it," Nate Baldwin said. "A bit unconventional. But I like it."

"Well, I don't," Carr said hotly. "He may have time to play around at the stations, but the crews don't, and neither do we."

"Come on, Carr," West said, irritated. "There's nothing wrong with this, and you know it. Cut Matthews some slack. He's doing his best under difficult circumstances. The crews need to see us out and about during all this arson business. Until that's solved and put to rest, I think it's best we show unity and support each other. And besides—I love tacos," Nate added, laughing.

"Always our favorite lunch time meal when I was at Five," Jeremy agreed. "I can't wait until it's my turn. When they shop, I hope they load up with extras."

Everyone walked out, comparing schedules, leaving Carr at the table alone and seething. Matthews had done it again, and Carr didn't like that he hadn't thought of doing something like this first.

Curious, the crew at Station 6 gathered just outside the kitchen and watched as Chief Matthews and Deputy Chief Carr began preparing lunch.

"We're here to cook, but we're not mind readers," Lucas said, turning to the watching crew with a grin. "Where are the skillets, pans, utensils? You know . . . all the stuff you cook with?"

The stainless-steel island in the middle of the kitchen was piled high with the food the grocery shopping team had just returned from buying, following the list sent over that morning. Not having to prepare a meal was a treat, but for two of the chiefs to be cooking for them, *that* was something extraordinary.

The group laughed as Campbell stepped into the kitchen and opened a couple of cabinet doors, pulling some pans out and then opening the drawer holding the cooking utensils.

"Excellent. Thank you," Lucas said as he grabbed the largest skillet. Stepping to the stove, he turned on one of the gas burners and set the skillet onto the burner to heat. He then opened three packages of hamburger meat, breaking each into smaller pieces and dropping them into the pan. The meat began sizzling immediately.

"Carr, we're going to need those onions sooner rather than later," Lucas said with a wicked grin aimed at Carr who was chopping onions and wiping tears. "I'll make note for the list tomorrow to get *chopped* onions," Lucas added with a grin.

Lucas noticed the crew nodding and exchanging smirks as they watched. They were enjoying this. Exactly what he'd hoped.

While Lucas was preparing other items, Carr picked up the first avocado to make guacamole.

Carr turned the avocado in one hand, eyeing it closely. Lindale asked with a tease, "Can we help you with that, Chief Carr? You're not looking too sure about how to attack it."

Carr shot Lindale and the crew gathered around him a dark look as they waited, chuckling, to see what Carr would do. Lucas glanced over his shoulder to see what would happen as well.

Carr grunted then took the paring knife and cut the avocado neatly in two. He scooped each half into the waiting bowl, doing the same with the remaining avocados, before adding salsa, jalapenos and onions to the mix.

"Any questions, gentlemen?" Carr asked as he proudly set the bowl on the table along with three big bags of chips.

"Impressive, Chief. Impressive," Lindale said with a nod and a smirk.

Chuckling, Lucas added taco seasoning and chopped onion to the cooked meat, saving a few onions for those who wanted to put some on top. Lucas then dumped the shredded lettuce into a bowl and tore open the extra-large bag of cheese. Sidestepping each other as they worked around the stove, Carr pulled the warmed taco shells from the oven while Lucas removed the skillet from the burner. They placed them on the stainless-steel kitchen island where they lined everything else up and added plates. The crew had inched closer as the meal came together.

"Smells pretty good I have to admit," Darryl McCracken said, elbowing his way through those watching, a smug look on his face as he glanced at Carr. "Didn't know chiefs could cook."

"Never forget we're firefighters first. We know our way around the kitchen—and a taco or two," Lucas replied with a pleased grin as he added a spoon to the meat for serving. "I think it's ready. Anybody hungry?"

Heads nodded as the one nearest the plates moved forward.

"Glad you're hungry, but hold up. First things first. Let's ask the blessing please."

Lucas bowed his head and after a couple of seconds glanced around without raising his head to see the others had joined him.

"Lord, thank you for the food we're about to eat," Lucas began. "Thank you for our jobs and for the skills you've given each of us. Please show us how to best use those skills to help those who need us. Keep everyone here safe and bless this food. Amen."

A rumble of amens immediately followed as the line surged forward. After plates were filled, everyone took a seat around the large rectangular table with the station logo embossed in the center. Station 6's nickname was the Dawg House, the logo aptly depicting a fierce bulldog emerging from a fire station bay door.

Lucas watched from his seat at the head of the table as stacks of tacos were quickly devoured. Carr's guacamole and the chips were passed around until both were completely gone. Lucas was glad he'd asked for a few extra supplies as the food disappeared quickly. The banter around the table was relaxed, and when boxes of Girl Scout cookies appeared, the banter turned on Lucas.

"Cookies?" one firefighter feigned outrage as he reached for his third and fourth cookies. "We thought you were a Bluebell man, Chief."

Lucas laughed as he plucked a couple of cookies from the box being passed. "Never look a gift cookie in the mouth is my motto, but never fear, the Bluebell will return."

After a third box of cookies had been emptied, the meal was deemed a total success.

"Great job, Chief," Campbell said, leaning back and patting his stomach. "Do you do encores?"

"You never know—maybe. The problem is—how do you top tacos?" Lucas asked, leaning back and taking one of the toothpicks offered. "And you know, the good news for Chief Carr and me?" Lucas asked as he leaned forward and shared a conspiratorial look around the table. "We don't have to do the dishes."

Everyone groaned in unison.

"Ah—come on, Chief," some ribbed him good-naturedly.

"We kept it pretty basic, didn't we, Carr?" Lucas asked, sliding a look across the table at Carr, who had obviously been enjoying the meal and the banter but who dropped his smile as soon as Lucas addressed him.

"Sure, Chief. Whatever you say," Carr retorted flatly.

"Well, I say I'm outta here," Lucas said, ignoring Carr's sullen attitude as he stood and picked up his plate.

Lucas set his plate in the sink then turned back to the group. "Seriously. You guys good on the dishes? Don't want to be labeled a shirker—especially when it comes to dish duty. I don't want it getting back to my wife."

The crew laughed again as Lucas watched McCracken and Carr exchange another glance that appeared to be filled with hidden meaning.

"No worries, Chief. We've got this. We just appreciate you and Chief

Carr coming out and cooking. The tacos were great but the opportunity to visit with you was even better. We haven't had that opportunity lately," Lindale said, standing and piling plates into a tall stack. Several nodded their agreement as Lindale carried the dishes to the sink.

Firefighter Bartlett spoke up as Lucas turned to leave. "Sir, if I may ask. Are we any closer to catching this arsonist?" He looked sheepishly around the table. "My wife is worried since we don't know where or when he's going to strike next."

Lucas looked around the table, the others looking at him and nodding agreement. Seeing the same concern on each face, Lucas sat back down and took a deep breath.

"Let me assure all of you. We're going to catch whoever is doing this. Ennis and the police investigators are working together, assimilating leads that are coming in every day. This arsonist is clever but not perfect, so it's only a matter of time. I personally don't think it will be long. You've probably heard about the gas cans found at each site. Those are being scoured for any clues to direct us to who bought them. I assure you. Every possible angle is being covered."

"Hey, Chief Carr, you keep a supply of gas cans, don't you, since you work on old cars?" Campbell asked casually. "You might know which ones can be found at what stores. Right?"

Lucas shot a pointed look at Carr, who quickly averted eye contact. Carr had repeatedly declined Lucas's invitations for the one-on-one lunches Lucas had been having with the other officers, getting to know them better. Lucas hadn't had that opportunity with Carr to find this out.

Carr's face turned red at the question.

Lucas's breath hitched. Could Sullivan and Ennis be onto something after all?

"You think *I'm* the arsonist?" Carr snapped.

Nervous laughter had begun before McCracken shot to his feet. "Come on, guys. Ridiculous hypothesizing, and you know it. Chief Carr's no arsonist any more than you and I are unless you call almost burning taco shells arson."

Lucas stood amid the heavy silence that followed McCracken's comment and cleared his throat.

"Okay, guys. Now, I've really gotta go. Appreciate each of you, and thanks for sharing lunch. Chief Carr, 1:30."

Carr barely nodded in Lucas's direction.

As Lucas left, variations of thank you went around the table, and everyone moved toward the kitchen or bay area to go back to work.

McCracken sidled up to Carr as Carr leaned against the kitchen cabinet, sipping iced tea and watching everyone work.

"Milton, lunch was nice, but what was that all about. Was there more to it?"

Deep in thought, Carr shook his head.

"I wish I knew, but one thing I do know for sure. He's clever, *and* he's stubborn." Turning to McCracken, Carr added, "but then, so am I."

Tнis was not going well—again. Lucas stood, moved in front of his desk, and began pacing as Carr sat motionless in one of the guest chairs, staring, or rather glaring, straight ahead.

Lucas stopped and eased back to sit on the edge of his desk.

"Milton," he began in a conciliatory tone, "it's the Monday before Thanksgiving. We have a lot to be thankful for, but we've also got a lot of major concerns right now, catching that arsonist being top of mind. Though I would be well within bounds to write you up for your behavior, both seen and behind the scenes, I'm going to hold off. You see, no matter how much you tend to disappoint me with the professional choices you're making, I still hold out hope that we might be able to work together. I'd like you to be a part of the strong team we've got here. But right now, you are playing on your team of one, and let me assure you, that's a losing team. Think about it over the holidays. I understand you have the rest of the week off, so enjoy the time with your family."

Lucas sighed when Carr didn't respond, look at him, or even bat an eye.

A sudden thought occurred to Lucas. "Carr, how's your son? What's his name—Chase?"

Carr flinched and frowned. The first real emotion he'd exhibited while sitting there.

"What does my son have to do with anything?"

"Well, nothing official. Just thought I'd ask. Do you and he share an interest in working on old vehicles?"

Carr shifted nervously before responding. "We don't have much in common, sir."

Lucas's back straightened from where he sat on the edge of the desk. It was the first time Carr had sounded—vulnerable.

"And your daughter," Lucas went on, "I understand she's away at college. Is she coming home for the holidays?"

"She got home Friday evening."

Lucas noted Carr seemed more at ease when his daughter was mentioned than he did with his son. Lucas was trying to make general conversation and gauge Carr's family life. Carr had seemed on edge more than usual the last few weeks. Lucas was aware how life at home could affect you more than you realize.

Lucas studied Carr's stony face, his rigid posture, and his tense demeanor. Lucas thought they'd made some progress as they'd worked on lunch together just a short time ago, but that progress seemed to have evaporated. Sullivan's and Ennis's comments about Carr holding a grudge ran through Lucas's mind again. Carr didn't like him, possibly even hated him, for getting the job he'd wanted so desperately. Lucas still couldn't believe, though, that Carr would abandon the oath he'd taken when he became a firefighter. But again, men do desperate things when they feel driven to it.

Lucas heaved a big sigh and stood, looking down at Carr, who kept his eyes straight ahead.

"All right, Carr. That's all. You have the lunch schedule. I think you and I are set to cook for Four next week when you're back. Enjoy your time off."

Lucas stepped behind the desk and resumed his seat as Carr stood and stalked out the door without a parting word. Lucas made a few notes in the personnel file he'd started for Carr apart from HR's official file. Sliding it into a desk drawer, he turned the key. It might come to nothing, but Lucas was determined to keep trying to get through to Carr.

Lucas glanced out the office window overlooking the drive and bay area of Station 1. The bright sunshine wasn't dispelling the arctic front that had blown through earlier, and with the colder temperatures, the bay doors were staying closed. Lucas looked back to his computer and almost groaned at the number of emails that had arrived in just a short while. He glanced at the time on the monitor and then at his calendar to check the time before his next meeting, which would be followed by the afternoon's station visits.

A soft knock came at the door, and Lucas looked up. Elise Stephens, the public information officer, stood in the doorway, iPad in hand, an apologetic look on her face.

"Chief, I'm so sorry to bother you."

"No bother at all, Elise. Come on in. Have a seat." Lucas gestured to one of the open guest chairs.

"That's okay. I'll just take a minute of your time."

"No worries. Please have a seat. I have a question I've been meaning to ask you."

A reluctant look crossed Elise's face as she tentatively sat on the edge of the guest chair Carr had just vacated. Elise fascinated Lucas with how such a demure, unassuming person could transform instantly into a tough, no-nonsense persona once the TV cameras were on and the media began peppering her with questions. Besides her work in front of the camera, she was also a force on social media and other communication mediums, continually putting the Abernathy Fire Department in a positive light. She was very good at her job.

"Yes, sir?" Elise asked, still looking a bit hesitant.

"Ennis may have already asked this, but are you getting any unusual questions from reporters or anyone else about the arson investigation? Anything that might make you think the asker knows more than he's letting on? That he may be probing to see how much *we* know?"

"Interesting question, Chief. Ennis and I, of course, have talked, and he's shared only certain things with me for response to specific questions I've received from reporters but not in that particular light." She paused, thinking, and then shook her head.

"No, sir. I don't believe so, at least nothing stands out right now. I'll be more cognizant of that possibility at the next press briefing."

"That would be great. Thank you, Elise. And I just wanted to say thank you and commend you on the job you're doing with the media about these arsons. We've all been so involved with the investigation as well as day-to-day operations that I apologize I haven't been available more or said anything. But you field the media's questions deftly and with a poise and charm I'm sure drives them crazy when they can't rattle you."

Lucas smiled and Elise relaxed and smiled in response, her green eyes brightening.

"Thank you, sir. That means a lot to me. Really—thank you."

"Credit where credit's due I say. Now, were you needing to see me about something before I hijacked the conversation?"

"Yes, sir," Elise responded, now all business. "With the holidays coming, we work with PD to decorate the kids' Safety Town. The fire department then serves cookies and hot chocolate while holiday music plays over the speakers. Visitors have a chance to stroll through the park and enjoy the lights. It's open on Friday and Saturday nights each weekend between Thanksgiving and Christmas. It's a lot of fun for families, and children in particular really enjoy coming out. In the past, the admin staff and their families have volunteered to work a couple of nights each weekend. I wanted to see if you were good with continuing that tradition."

Lucas picked up a pen and twirled it with his fingers as he cocked an eyebrow. "You are aware that the first weekend after Thanksgiving is in just a few days?"

"Yes, sir, and I apologize for not asking until now, but wires got crossed between me and my counterpart at PD. I won't bother you with the details. All of the other weekends are covered, but we need four people from admin to work this Friday and Saturday night. Deputy Chief Baldwin and his wife have signed up to work both nights, but no one else seems to be available. Would you . . ."

Lucas shook his head with a quick sigh of relief. This kind of problem he could handle all day long.

Elise's eyes grew large as Lucas shook his head.

"Elise, I tell you what. Tell Baldwin he's won a get out of jail free card. My family will take both shifts. It sounds kind of fun and will kick the Christmas season off right. My kids got in last Friday and are already getting a bit stir crazy, so this will be a great family activity. Whether they realize it or not," he added with a chuckle.

"That's great. Thank you, sir!" Elise relaxed, making some entries onto her iPad and stood to leave.

"Stephens."

Elise stopped abruptly, hearing the Chief's tone.

"Make sure and get those wires uncrossed without delay. This situation isn't an emergency, but the mindset can creep into other areas if we're not careful. Last minute is not how this department operates. Are we clear?"

Her cheeks reddening, Elise said, "Yes, Chief. Very clear. Thank you."

Elise spun and left quickly, leaving Lucas turning to his computer screen and clicking the mouse once again to return to his emails. Before he had the opportunity to get started, the radio on his desk went off. The only times it had gone off lately were when there was a suspicious fire. He groaned to himself, but then, hearing the dispatcher, his heart skipped a beat. The call was a medical emergency, and the address was Mrs. Garrett's address on Meandering Lane. He had left instructions with dispatch to be notified any time they received a 9-1-1 call for that address.

Throwing on his jacket, Lucas hurriedly left the office, turning several heads at his pace and the serious intent on his face. Jumping into his SUV, Lucas slammed it into gear and pulled out of the parking lot, his lights and siren screaming.

Lucas pulled up at Mrs. Garrett's house the same time as Station 2's engine and ambulance. All sirens squelched, one after another, the equipment's red and blue emergency lights continuing to spin. Lucas started up the walk on the heels of the paramedics and engine crew who looked at each other in surprise, seeing the chief and noting his anxiety.

Entering the now familiar living room, Lucas spotted Mrs. Garrett sitting on the sofa but trying to stand.

He rushed over, and kneeling at her side, gently pushed her back down onto the cushions.

"Oh, dear," she said feebly, seeing the paramedics and engine crew coming through the front door. "I didn't mean to cause such a row."

"You've done no such thing. You know the guys will take good care of you. I'll get out of their way, but I wanted you to know I'm here." Lucas patted Mrs. Garrett's hand and stepped out of the way, staying close enough to hear and see everything.

Mrs. Garrett's eyes followed his movements with a fond look that tore at his heart. He knew she'd been having some issues lately. He prayed she'd be okay.

Lucas watched as the paramedics worked, taking her vitals and asking the appropriate questions. She told them she'd felt lightheaded and that her heart had started beating rapidly. Lucas looked over the nearest paramedic's shoulder at the iPad where he was recording her blood pressure and pulse rate. Both were low. Too low.

They placed oxygen tubes in her nose, gently placing the strap over her head. Lucas smiled reassuringly as she sought his eyes.

"Mrs. Garrett," a sandy-haired paramedic with Carpenter, Paramedic/ Firefighter, stitched on his navy-blue uniform shirt, said in a soothing voice. "Your blood pressure is a little low. We'd like to take you to the hospital to have everything checked out."

They were interrupted when the front door opened, and Mike Bentley stepped inside.

"I heard the call on my scanner," he offered by way of a quick explanation as he moved to stand by Lucas. "How is she?" he asked with a smile to Mrs. Garrett.

The two paramedics looked between Lucas and Bentley, curiosity evident on their faces.

"Are you okay with us taking you to the hospital?" Franklin asked again, looking back to Mrs. Garrett, pulling her attention back to him.

She looked between Lucas and Bentley, who both nodded their reassurance.

"Yes—that will be fine." She gave a weak smile as they lifted her gently onto the gurney and covered her with blankets, securing her in with straps.

"We're right behind you," Lucas assured her, patting the blue blanket where her hand should be. "No need to worry. This is just precautionary."

"I'll lock up the house and be there in two shakes," Bentley said with a firm nod. "Matthews here is right. Don't worry. Just relax, and let these guys take care of you. I'm pretty sure they know what they're doing."

Mrs. Garrett managed a smile, one that made it to her eyes this time. "Oh, I know they do. They've learned from the best, who also learned from the best."

When Bentley turned away, clearing his throat, Lucas realized just how much Mrs. Garrett meant to him as well. Evidently, Lucas wasn't the only one she and Mr. Andy had influenced and helped.

After arriving at the emergency room, Lucas and Bentley ended up having to wait nearly two hours for any kind of word from the ER doctors. In that time, Bentley had called Trenton Maine, Mrs. Garrett's brother, who also lived in Abernathy. When he arrived, Lucas could tell Trenton must have been a large man in his prime. While still imposing, he had gotten a bit smaller with age, his salt and pepper hair was mostly gray and his kind eyes were a lot like Mrs. Garrett's. From Trenton's anxious demeanor, it was obvious how much he cared about his sister.

"How is she? Any word?" Trenton asked in a rush when he hurriedly walked through the emergency room's automatic doors. The waiting room was mostly empty with only a few scattered people sitting in the hard plastic chairs.

Lucas followed as Mike Bentley stood and walked over to greet Trenton when he came across the room.

"They're still evaluating her and running some tests," Bentley replied, shaking Trenton's hand. "The doctors should be out any time." Seeing Lucas standing to the side, Bentley waved him forward.

"Trenton, I'd like for you to meet Chief Lucas Matthews. He's—"

Trenton took a step toward Lucas, extending his hand. "So, I finally get to meet Lucas Matthews," he said, a large smile spreading across his drawn face.

Lucas took the proffered hand and smiled in return.

"You know my name?"

Trenton chuckled lightly. "My boy, you have no idea how happy you've made my sister. You're a favorite topic of conversation when we're together. She brags on you all of the time. Since she told me about you and that you'd moved to Abernathy, she's smiled more than she has since Andy . . . well . . . you know."

Lucas fought down a sudden catch in his throat. "Yes, sir. I do—or at least I do now. I didn't until a few months ago. It's still kind of fresh for me."

Trenton, studying Lucas thoughtfully, placed a firm hand on his shoulder and squeezed it, his eyes reflecting his sympathy and understanding.

The moment was broken when the doors from the examination room area swung open, and Dr. Turner strode toward their group.

"Is there a relative of Mrs. Garrett's here?" the doctor asked, looking between the three men.

"I'm her brother," Trenton spoke up. "How is she?"

"She's resting comfortably. As you probably know, she has had congestive heart failure for some time, and it is progressing. The condition of her heart is deteriorating, and at her age, there is nothing I can recommend that will alleviate the progression. We can continue to make her comfortable, and she's free to return home. With monitoring, she can continue to enjoy a limited lifestyle."

"Does she need someone with her?" Bentley asked, taking a step closer.

Looking to Trenton for confirmation to share the information, he nodded. "With appropriate monitoring, she can continue to live in her own home for as long as she'd like. If she would prefer to move to an assisted facility, I can make some recommendations."

"I'll talk to her, but I can almost guarantee she's going to want to stay at home." Trenton sighed sadly. "Can I see her?"

"Of course. This way." The doctor started to step away, but Bentley cleared his throat.

"And us? Are we allowed to see her too?"

"They're like family," Trenton said in response to the inquiring look from the doctor.

"Please, gentlemen, this way." The doctor tapped his badge to a monitor beside the door, and the doors popped open, allowing them inside. Lucas had been in emergency and examination rooms like this hundreds of times as a paramedic, but this was his first time to experience it as part of the family.

Coming to Room 9, a large sign above the door indicating the number, the three followed the doctor inside.

Mrs. Garrett, looking small and frail, lay in the bed, her eyes closed, the sheet rising and falling gently with her shallow breathing. The breathing tubes were still in place, her mouth slightly open.

"Katie," Trenton said softly, stepping to the side of the bed and gently taking her hand.

"Trenton!" she said, trying to sit up when she saw him. "Oh my, I've made way too much of a fuss. I'm so sorry to have bothered you."

Trenton gently pushed her shoulder back into the pillow.

"You're never a bother, Sis. How are you feeling?"

"Oh, I'm fine. I shouldn't have rushed to call 9-1-1. I just . . . uh . . ."

Her eyelids fluttered and then closed as she trailed off, seeming to lose her train of thought. The doctor looked to the panels on the wall above and behind the bed and then motioned to the three of them to step outside.

Bentley and Lucas exchanged a concerned look. They had seen what the doctor saw on the panels.

"I'd like to keep her overnight. Her oxygen levels keep dipping, and we'd like to make sure they're leveled out before releasing her."

Trenton nodded agreement, his brows furrowed with worry.

"Whatever you think is best, Doctor. I'll call my wife, and either she or I will stay with her."

"I'll stay," Lucas spoke up before he could think better of it. There was a mountain of work back at the office, and he still needed to get to at least one of the stations today, but this was by far more important.

Trenton's eyes rounded in surprise but then he smiled at Lucas, understanding.

"Of course, Lucas, and thank you. Stephanie and I will be back in a couple of hours to relieve you." Trenton stepped back inside the room and leaned over, patting Katie on the shoulder and speaking softly to her.

Lucas overheard him saying, "Katie, you're going to be spending the night here but not to worry. They just want to get some things leveled out before they send you home. Lucas is going to be keeping you company for a while, so you two will have some time to visit. Stephanie and I will be back in an hour or two. Okay?"

Lucas could see Mrs. Garrett slowly nodding her head as she listened.

"You sure you've got the time, Chief?" Bentley asked, eyeing Lucas with concern. "I know you've got your hands full right now."

Lucas sighed, putting his hands on his waist and looking down.

"You're right. I do have a lot on my plate, Bentley, but nothing right now is more important than Mrs. Garrett. I owe her a lot. There's no way I can repay her, but maybe I can do a little something by sitting with her, and I'm more than happy to do it."

Bentley nodded as he cast a glance into the examination room where Trenton was still talking to Katie.

"I'll check with Trenton in the morning, and if she's still here, I'll be back to do the same," Bentley said and looked at Lucas.

"You're a good man, Lucas Matthews. I can see why Andy and Katie saw so much and invested so much in you. From my perspective, their investment was well made."

Lucas looked down, his cheeks reddening with embarrassment at the praise.

"Thanks, Chief, but Mrs. Garrett—Mr. Andy—they're both pretty special. I'm just proud—and fortunate—to have been even a small part of their lives."

Bentley shook his head, placing his hand on Lucas's shoulder. "My boy, you have been and are a lot more than a small part. Don't ever forget that."

Trenton stepped out of the exam room and, with a look at both of them, pulled out his phone.

"Matthews, what's your number?"

Lucas pulled out his own phone while relaying his number to Trenton, storing Trenton's number in his own phone's contacts.

"We appreciate this," Trenton said, shaking Lucas's hand firmly.

THIRTY MINUTES LATER, LUCAS found himself in the hospital room where Mrs. Garrett had just been moved, sitting at her bedside and holding her hand. Lucas had texted the room number when he'd gotten it to both Bentley and Trenton. Lucas had also called Jill to let her know what had happened and that he'd probably be late for dinner, if he was there at all. He promised to keep her updated and to give Mrs. Garrett Jill's best.

Lucas sighed as he settled in. So many thoughts, so many memories came to mind as he watched Mrs. Garrett's sweet face as she slept. After his dad's death, his mom had never been the same, and Mrs. Garrett had given him the attention and boost of confidence he'd needed so desperately when he showed up to her second-grade class. It wasn't so much what he'd learned in her class, as how she'd made him feel—noticed, important, and smart—things he hadn't felt for a long time. Between her and Mr. Andy, Lucas wasn't sure if he would have made it to adulthood without their support, encouragement, and attention.

Mrs. Garrett had been asleep since they'd brought her to her room, and Lucas eventually pulled his eyes from her to look around. It was a typical hospital room with its linoleum floor, sink, and mirror, the bed in front of the wall filled with monitors and screens. The window overlooked the roof of the connecting wing of the hospital. The lights in the room were dimmed with only the small florescent light on the wall behind the bed on and turned to a lower setting. The blinds on the window were mostly closed, blocking the last few rays of afternoon sunlight before they dipped below the horizon. The door to the hallway was only slightly open after Lucas had pushed it almost closed, trying to cushion the noise from the nurse's station just outside. The small opening left only a small triangle of light on the room's floor from the bright florescent lights in the hall.

Lucas watched Mrs. Garrett closely as she began to move her arms and legs restlessly beneath the sheet and thin blanket the nurse had placed over her. Glancing between her and the readings on the monitors, Lucas's concern was growing that she wasn't showing more signs of improvement.

"Could I have some water, dear?"

Lucas's eyes went to her pale face as he smiled and stood. Retrieving a plastic cup of water from the rolling table near the bed, he held its straw to her lips.

She took a few small sips and after swallowing, her eyes drifted closed once again.

He pulled the chair closer to her bedside and settled into it. He must have drifted off to sleep, because when he came to himself, he realized Mrs. Garrett was awake, her eyes bright and twinkling, studying him with a smile. He was glad to see her looking so much better. He took the hand she held out to him, its dry softness warm in his own as he wrapped his fingers gently around hers.

"Andy, I've missed you. I've missed you so much," she said, looking at Lucas earnestly and squeezing his hand. "I'm glad you're here with me now. Please don't leave me again. Promise me you won't. Please."

Lucas shifted nervously in his chair. The room was dim, and he knew she couldn't see him clearly. He wasn't sure if he should let her know he wasn't Mr. Andy or just go along to put her mind at ease. With his free hand, he reached into his pocket where he kept Mr. Andy's badge. When he fingered its edges, he had his answer.

Lucas leaned a bit closer. "I promise," he said softly and squeezed her fingers gently.

Mrs. Garrett smiled, squeezing his fingers in response before closing her eyes and falling back to sleep. Lucas placed his other hand on top of the one he still held and patted it softly. He sniffed as a stray tear escaped from the corner of his eye. The door to the hallway suddenly opened wide, and Lucas blinked at the hallway's bright light spilling into the room. Trenton and a striking, older woman, who must be his wife, stepped quietly inside.

J ON AND JESSICA WERE doing an amazing job and having a blast, interacting with children and parents, who had come to Safety Town to enjoy Christmas lights and music along with the hot chocolate and cookies Lucas and Jill were serving up. It was a merry atmosphere that belied the underlying tension in Abernathy.

Lucas looked up and smiled at the squeals of delight Jon was eliciting from children jumping up and down in a circle around him as he blew the air horn on the antique fire engine on display.

"Do it again! Do it again!" several yelled as their smiling parents pulled them away.

Jon waved and laughed as a new group of children eagerly took their place.

Safety Town looked amazing. Lucas was proud of the work Elise had pulled off and was glad he'd volunteered his family to work these first two nights. Every building, miniature car, and traffic light was decked out in Christmas lights, including a fire engine that sat on one of the side streets, making a great photo op. Christmas carols belted out from speakers positioned around the park. The atmosphere was lighthearted, fun, and festive. The crowd was large but not overwhelming, and the police officers on duty were keeping anyone who attempted to be extra jovial under control.

Thanksgiving had been quiet but good with Coach and Patsy driving down for the day. Jill's parents were out of the country, but they'd phoned in on a video call and gotten to talk to everyone. He was glad he and Jill had decided to have the holiday here in spite of the ongoing unease.

Lucas smiled as he opened a new package of cookies and handed them to Jill. He needed some holiday festivities to take his mind off work and off of his concern for Mrs. Garrett. She'd gone home from the hospital the next day and had known him by name when he'd stopped by the hospital the next morning. He'd never forget those few minutes when she'd thought he was Mr. Andy. That meant more to him than he could adequately put into words.

"Dad . . . Dad!" Jessica called from across the drive where Jon stood by the antique engine.

Lucas looked up and smiled when he saw Cade Marshall. Cade was holding the hand of one little boy who looked just like him and the hand of a young woman who was holding the hand of a second little boy, also the image of Cade.

"This guy says he knows you," Jessica said with a teasing smile. "He is requesting permission to approach the Chief."

Lucas rolled his eyes and laughed. "Permission granted."

Cade and his wife shepherded the two boys forward, the boys' eyes growing wide at the number of cookies on the table in front of them.

"Dad?!" they asked one after the other, looking up at Cade, their eyes pleading.

Cade cocked an eyebrow at Lucas after getting the nod of approval from his wife.

While the boys claimed their cookies, Lucas extended his hand. "Cade Marshall, great to see you. This must be the family."

"Yes, sir. It is. This is my wife, Emily, and these are our boys: Adam here is the oldest, and Eric is just a year younger. They keep us busy."

Emily smiled distractedly at Lucas and Jill and briefly looked up from wiping chocolate from both boys' mouths.

Lucas chuckled. "It's nice to meet you. Marshall, I hate to tell you, but it looks like you've got two boys on your hands that are all boy. Things are only going to get rowdier from here. I guarantee it."

Lucas pointed to Jon, who was on the first step of the antique engine, regaling the children around him with what must be a Christmas story. "That's my son, Jon; you met my daughter, Jessica; and this is my lovely bride, Jill."

Cade and Emily smiled in the direction of Jon and Jessica. They were about to say something when Jeremy and Allie Ennis and Riley and Maggie Sullivan walked up.

"Okay, now explain to me why no one signed up to work this weekend, but you all decided to come out anyway?" Lucas threw open his arms in question, a perplexed look on his face. "I'm not complaining, mind you, because we're having a blast. I'm just curious."

"Well, sir," Riley began with a grin at Maggie. "It seems that Safety Town is the new Abernathy hot spot, and we don't want to miss out. You know—FOMO?"

"FOMO?" Lucas's eyebrows furrowed in confusion. "What the heck is FOMO?"

"Fear of missing out, Chief," Cade Marshall replied with a chuckle.

"I get the latest lingo at the high school, and I pass the knowledge on to these two lunkheads, so they can try to sound cool."

"I believe we've been called lunkheads by the chief lunkhead," Jeremy said with a punch to Cade's arm.

Maggie rolled her eyes. "They never stop. They're all three worse than kids."

"Hey, don't insult my boys," Emily Marshall said with mock horror before everyone dissolved into laughter.

With all of the greetings, slaps on the back and general laughter, the place somehow managed to get even louder than the carols playing over the speakers. Lucas found himself laughing and joking with them when he caught Jill watching him, a pleased smile on her face. He'd needed this, and she knew it. In fact, the whole family needed this, and what a fun time they were having!

"Chief, how'd you get roped into working the first weekend and for both nights?" Jeremy asked, taking a quick sip of hot chocolate.

"I did it the good old-fashioned way. I volunteered. You might try it sometime, Ennis."

"Whoa ho," Cade said, slapping Jeremy on the back as Jeremy's face turned red.

"Did you not volunteer to work, Jeremy Ennis?" Allie asked, a teasing accusation on her face. She turned to him and put her hands on her waist, which had gotten a bit rounder since the last time Lucas had seen her. Jill was having a wonderful time working on the designs for their nursery. Between the Ennis's nursery, gearing up to open her own business, and the holidays, Jill was staying busy.

"I did, Al. I did. I promise," Jeremy rushed to assure Allie. "My weekend is in two weeks. You are more than welcome to come out and help."

Smiling, Allie looked at Jeremy and nodded. "I just might do that, Jeremy Ennis. It looks like fun," she said with a quick look around before turning to answer a question Jill had just asked while drawing Emily into the conversation.

"Thanks for trying to get me in trouble, Chief." Jeremy sent an eye roll in Allie's direction.

"My pleasure, Ennis. Trouble loves company, and I could use the company right now."

"No closer to catching the arsonist, I take it?" Cade asked, releasing the boys into Jessica's care with an appreciative smile.

"Ennis is piecing some clues together, but there's still a way to go before we can pin anything down. We'll get there. Sometimes these things just take a little longer, and then suddenly, everything drops into place. It's just a matter of time."

Jeremy popped a cookie in his mouth just as his eyes got big and he mouthed an "uh-oh" around it.

Lucas glanced where Jeremy was looking, and his heart sank a bit. Milton Carr and his family had just stepped onto the landing outside the doorway. Looking across the grounds, Carr was talking to his wife with a smug look, which quickly faded when he turned and saw Lucas and the group around him. Carr's eyes narrowed when he met Lucas's gaze. He gave a small nod of acknowledgment before turning back toward the grounds.

Carr's wife looked over her shoulder, giving the group a small smile, as Carr said something into her ear. The boy fidgeting nervously near them Lucas recognized as Carr's son, Chase. The dark-headed girl must be the daughter Carr mentioned was home for the holidays.

The girl seemed bored as she glanced around but suddenly brightened when she turned and saw Jon. Without hesitation, she headed straight for him. Lucas's gaze went to Jon, whose smile disappeared quickly, replaced by a wary look. Lucas watched as the girl walked up, stood close, very close, to Jon, and started talking. He was replying, reluctantly.

Lucas started to move in their direction with a pretense of needing Jon's help with something but stopped and smiled when Jessica stepped up and took Jon's arm. She was motioning to something behind the engine, and Lucas caught the words, "We need your help," as she pulled him away. A crestfallen look on her face, the dark-haired girl stood there for a few seconds before she walked slowly back to her family.

After a few minutes, Lucas casually walked over and stood by Jessica, who had just taken a group of children to Jon to hear his Christmas story.

"Hey, Dad," Jessica said, patting the last little one on the head.

"Just curious. What was all that about?" Lucas asked, indicating the Carr family, who was moving away.

"Oh, that's the girl Jon took out the weekend of your badge ceremony. Remember?"

Lucas nodded. "The one he came back early from their date?"

Jessica laughed and nodded. "That's the one. She hasn't left him alone since—texting, leaving messages—you know. I just thought I'd run some interference. She's relentless, and Jon's too nice to tell her outright he's not interested, but maybe she's getting the message. I hope so—for his sake."

Lucas gave Jessica a quick hug. "Keep up the good work, Kiddo."

Jessica smiled and gave him a smart salute before turning to the next group.

Lucas walked back toward Jill unable to hide a smile.

"What are you grinning about?" Jill asked as he stopped beside her.

"Our kids. They're amazing, you know?" Lucas moved back to the cookie table, Jill behind him.

"Oh, I do know. You'll have to tell me what sparked that thought out of the blue, but right now, we've got cookies and hot chocolate to get to the masses."

Lucas chuckled and glanced back over his shoulder to see Jon and Jessica back in their original spots by the antique engine. The smile was back on Jon's face, and for that, Lucas was thankful to Jon's sister. Lucas smiled to himself as he opened another package of cookies.

"Chief, we're going to give you and the Mrs. a break and take in the sights," Ennis said, walking back up to the table. "I've observed closely, so I think I might be able to handle cookie and hot chocolate duty in a couple of weeks."

"You guys stay out of trouble," Lucas called after them with a chuckle as the group waved farewell.

Lucas watched them as they walked away. Running to catch up, Adam, the older of Cade's boys squealed when Cade snatched him up and tossed him gently into the air, earning another squeal. The smaller one, not to be out done, squealed his turn when Cade tossed him in the air then over to Jeremy who caught him and started carrying him under one arm much to the boy's delight.

"That's what I want for the entire department—that kind of camaraderie." Lucas indicated the group with a nod.

Jill watched the group approach an intersection with its miniature stoplight flashing as they crossed.

"They've been friends for years, so they've got a head start, but if anyone can create that kind of atmosphere, you can, Lucas. And don't give up either. You're at a bit of a disadvantage right now, but you'll get there."

"Oh, you think so, do you, Mrs. Matthews?" Lucas leaned in and gave Jill a quick kiss on the cheek.

"No—I don't think so. I know so." Jill smiled at him before turning back to the cookie table and a whole new group of hungry Christmas visitors. Lucas looked around, taking in the atmosphere, the twinkling lights, people talking and children laughing—everyone having a good time. Lucas breathed deeply, infused with a fresh sense of purpose and confidence.

"Who needs cookies?" Lucas asked and then laughed as little hands eagerly shot in the air.

BOTH REALTORS HAD WARNED them that things moved slowly over the Christmas holidays. Most people were not in the mood for buying or selling houses, and they weren't to expect any movement on either house until after the Christmas and New Year holidays. Jill didn't quite understand that. She was ready to buy *and* sell a house now.

The townhome was nice enough, but not being able to decorate for the holidays was not appealing. Thanksgiving hadn't been too bad. It had been a bit cramped with Jon and Jessica at home for a week, but as she'd told them, they were making special memories. The kids had gone back to school after church yesterday, and she missed them and the rowdiness they brought to the house. It had made her heart happy to see Lucas smiling and more relaxed. She attributed some of that to the kids being home but a lot of it to Deputy Chief Carr being on vacation and out of the office the past week. He'd be returning this week though.

Jill glanced down at her GPS and then turned into what at one time had been Abernathy's old downtown district but had recently been reno-vated into a chic, destination-style location. It was delightful. Christmas decorations infused the space with a festive feeling even in the daylight. Jill could only imagine what it would look like after dark when the Christmas lights were on. She'd have to bring Lucas down to see it. Jill glanced to either side of the brick-paved main street and the charming old-fashioned style storefronts. She saw the neon sign of the Electronix Doc's location Maggie had mentioned in one of their conversations. Riley had purchased the repair and service store a little over a year ago from his mentor. Business was thriving, keeping Riley busy even on his days off from the station.

Jill spotted the cafe where she was to meet Maggie and Allie for lunch. They'd invited Emily to join them, but she was filling in for a pre-school teacher at the boys' school and asked for a rain check. Finding a parking space was a bit challenging, but Jill luckily found a spot not far from the cafe after circling a few times.

Stepping out of her car and into the brisk wind, she pulled her coat and scarf tighter and walked past a few storefronts toward the cafe. An empty window caught her eye, and she stopped to read the sign hanging in the window by a single piece of tape. The space was for rent. Jill's eyes went wide. She grabbed a notepad and pen from her purse and quickly wrote down the name of the leasing agent and phone number. The rent might be too steep, but it certainly wouldn't hurt to check it out.

"Jill!" Allie called and waved to her as soon as she stepped into the warmth of the bistro. The whitewashed walls and distressed white furnishings were straight out of a designer magazine. Allie sat at a table next to the wall on the right side of the cafe. Glancing around to take it all in, Jill made her way through the maze of tables filled with diners, unbuttoning her coat and loosening her scarf as she walked. The diner was packed with Christmas shoppers and those off from work, enjoying the holiday atmosphere.

"I hope you haven't been waiting long," Jill said, sloughing her coat and scarf onto the back of the extra chair and taking a seat.

"Oh no. I've just been here a few minutes. Maggie texted, and she's running a few minutes late. She told me what to order for her, so we'll all get our food at the same time."

Jill nodded as she perused the menu and made her selection. Laying the menu down beside the antique plate and linen napkin set at her place, she and Allie exchanged comfortable smiles.

The waitress approached, and after giving their orders, they settled back in their chairs.

"Have you had a chance to look at the suggestions I emailed over and decided what theme you'd like to use?"

Allie scrunched her face into a playful frown as she fingered the delicate dainty cut glass goblet in her fingers.

"Please don't give up on me, but I just can't make up my mind. Jeremy says it's baby brain. That's why I wanted to get the two of you together, so you can tell me which theme to go with."

Jill laughed as Allie looked up and waved. Maggie hurried toward them, an apologetic look already on her face.

"I'm so, so sorry. I got a last-minute call, and it's one I'd been waiting for. I hope I haven't thrown us too late."

"We just gave the waitress our order, so all's good," Allie hurried to assure her.

Looking between them, Jill said, "Well ladies, it looks like we've got some deciding to do. Are you ready?" With a chuckle, Jill reached down and pulled out her iPad, opening it to the pictures of coordinated fabrics, accessories and furnishings for the three themes Allie said she had been considering.

"Oh, these are good. Really good," Maggie breathed appreciatively, studying the pictures. "I don't blame you for not being able to decide, Al."

They talked about each of the themes. The first was motorized vehicles of all kinds. As a former mechanic, Jeremy's dad had made the request, saying that since this was his first grandson, he should have his suggestion at least considered. The second theme was giraffes. It was a favorite of Allie's and not just because her mother had suggested it, but because it had been the theme of her own nursery when she was a baby. And then there was Jeremy's request for a fire truck theme. It was hard to argue against any of them, yet one needed to be selected today. The pros and cons of each were weighed as if this was an earth-shattering decision, which to Allie it had become.

The three went through the photos and had just finished with the third theme when their food arrived. Taking a sweet potato chip from her plate and chewing it thoughtfully, Jill was about to put her iPad away while they ate when a message flashed across of an incoming call. The name on the caller ID was Alexandria Roman, the Fort Collins Realtor. As badly as Jill wanted to take the call, Allie was a client so, right now, she needed to focus on Allie and her nursery selections. With the delays and Allie being unable to make up her mind, everything needed to be ordered quickly, so it would arrive in time for installation before Allie's due date.

After they'd finished their meal of homemade soup, sandwich, and chips, they discussed the different themes while enjoying small tea cakes and hot tea, sparkling water for Allie, while Allie contemplated each theme.

"Okay, okay," Allie finally sighed dramatically. "We're going with fire trucks. No, wait—giraffes—or maybe the vehicle theme. They're all just so cute. Oh, I don't know," Allie fretted and put her elbows on the table and her chin in her hands.

Looking between Jill and Maggie, Allie cut her eyes to Jill. "This is all your fault, you know," Allie said, picking up the remaining bite of a tea cake from her plate and taking a nibble.

"My fault?" Jill asked, surprised.

"Well, of course it is," Allie replied with a tease. "Everything you're showing us is just so cute. You could have tried at least a little to make one more appealing than the others. They're all precious."

"I'm afraid she's right," Maggie added, setting her teacup back into its saucer. "I've seen the nurseries of several friends having babies and what you've done for Allie outshines all of them combined. I think you're going to have your hands full of work when people see Allie's nursery—whichever theme she *finally* picks."

"I appreciate that, Maggie—thank you. I hope to be overrun with business soon," Jill smiled as she took a sip of tea.

"That's great, but it doesn't help me any!" Allie said irritably, rubbing her hand over her extended stomach, a frown on her face. "Oh, hey—I'm sorry. You've both been such wonderful help. I'm just a bit out of sorts right now. I can't seem to think."

Jill put her hand on Allie's arm. "It's perfectly understandable. You're just weeks away from having your first baby, and it can all be overwhelming." Jill smiled warmly and squeezed Allie's arm. "And if it helps, I've discovered that your first instinct is usually the right one."

Allie raised her head and blinked away tears that had suddenly threatened.

"Really? Well, okay then," she said, brightening. Scanning back through photos of the components for each theme, Allie suddenly smiled. Looking first at Maggie and then at Jill, Allie pointed to one and said, "Fire trucks it is. I tried to hold out for something different, but this is Jeremy's son, so his dad deserves to have the say in his nursery. I can't wait to tell Jeremy a decision has been made. I have a feeling he'll be pleased."

Jill and Maggie exchanged relieved smiles.

"Yes, he will," Maggie quickly assured Allie. "But then again, he would be pleased with anything you picked."

Allie blushed and took a drink of her sparkling water while Jill nodded her agreement, putting her iPad and notes away.

"I've got the room's dimensions, so I'll get everything ordered this afternoon, including the paint. Do I need to hire a painter, or will Jeremy be painting the room?" Jill asked, zipping her small briefcase closed.

"Jeremy Ennis will be painting the room. I'm doing this part," Allie said emphatically, motioning to her midsection, "Jeremy can help with the painting."

Jill and Maggie exchanged another knowing smile as each took a sip of their tea to hide their grins.

JILL GRIMACED. AFTER ALLIE decided on her theme, Jill had been on the phone ordering nursery furniture and accessories and didn't hear the call beep in. She had been clarifying delivery times with the manufacturer's representative she'd been working with for years. When she got off the phone, she saw the message, indicating Alexandria Roman had called. Jill eagerly listened to the message, which just asked Jill to call back at her earliest convenience.

Jill called back immediately. Alexandria's phone rang three times before it went to voice mail. Jill left a brief message and huffed in frustration after hanging up.

The dining room table had somehow turned into a mess with scattered notes, photos and binders all pertaining to Allie's nursery. Jill was in the process of ordering materials for the curtains and the bed's duster when her phone rang, Alexandria Roman's name on the ID.

"Mrs. Matthews," Alexandria said smoothly when Jill answered, "I'm glad to have caught you."

"I'm glad to hear from you, Alexandria. Do you have good news for us?"

"I believe I do. Your home here in Fort Collins has garnered quite a bit of attention. Your reputation as an interior designer spurred a lot of foot traffic. Currently, there are three serious buyers, who are all so serious they started a bidding war among themselves."

Jill held her breath. She hoped she knew what this meant.

"I'm happy to tell you the bids are now final, and the lowest offer is several thousand dollars higher than your asking price."

"Really?" Jill breathed in sharply.

"Yes, ma'am. I'd like to email all three offers to you and let you and Mr. Matthews take a look. You can then let me know which one you decide on. Congratulations. This doesn't happen often, but when it does, it sure is exciting."

"Yes—thank you. This *is* exciting. My husband is rather busy with work right now, but we'll get back to you as soon as possible."

"The buyers are anxious to get an answer, so they'll know how to proceed, so the sooner the better."

"I understand. Thank you so much."

"It's my pleasure, Mrs. Matthews. It's a win/win for you and the successful bidder. Be looking for my email and let me know what you decide."

"Thank you, Alexandria. I certainly will."

Lucas was driving back to admin. He'd stayed later at Station 8 than he'd intended, but he and the station crew were having a really good conversation. It was the kind of conversation he'd hoped would develop when he'd started visiting the stations. The crews were getting to know him just as he was getting to know them. He wanted them to feel comfortable with him, so when they did, they'd be more comfortable with the changes he was implementing or at least comfortable enough to ask questions.

The poll Carr had conducted on making shift change showed 87% in favor of switching to the 48 on and 96 off shift rotation versus staying with the 24 on and 48 off rotation that had been the norm in the department for decades. The change would be a big switch, but it would help not only internally, but externally with recruitment. It was a heavily discussed topic over lunch.

West made tacos with him today. They'd developed a pretty good routine, incorporating a bit of showmanship which brought some laughter and created a relaxed atmosphere. Lucas chuckled to himself. He wasn't going to want another taco for a long time after he made it through every shift at each station.

He looked down when his phone rang the tone for Jill. He punched the speaker that put the call on the SUV speakers.

"Hey, Hon. What's going on?" Lucas asked as he plucked his Dr. Pepper out of the cup holder and took a drink.

"Lucas!"

That was all Lucas understood. Jill was excited and talked so fast he couldn't understand her.

"Jill, honey. Whoa. Slow down. What's going on?"

Jill laughed and took a deep breath.

"Sorry, but this is such good news, and I'm excited! I heard from Alexandria Roman, the Realtor in Fort Collins this afternoon."

"And . . ." Lucas prompted.

"And evidently, there was a bidding war for our house, Lucas! We have three offers to consider, and all well above our asking price."

Lucas's eyebrows rose in surprise as he absorbed the news. It was almost too good to be true.

"Now Jill, are you sure you understood her right? I mean it'd be great to get one over asking, but all three?"

"I'm absolutely sure. As soon as the email was in my inbox, I opened it and read each attachment. Lucas, the lowest is $15,000 over asking!" She couldn't contain her excitement.

"Are there contingencies attached to any of them?" Lucas had to be sure.

"One just asked that we change some landscaping around the pool, but other than that—no. Nothing."

Lucas nodded to himself, deep in thought, drumming his fingers on the steering wheel as he drove.

"Lucas? What do you think? Should we just go with the highest offer? The sooner we move on this, the sooner we can let the Realtor here know and head off that other buyer."

Lucas pulled into the admin parking lot as he waved to the firefighters working in the bay next door.

"No. Don't do anything just yet. Let me look at them when I get home tonight."

His statement was met with silence.

"Jill?"

"Do you think me incapable of reading an email or is it that you just don't trust me? We can give the word now and get a full day into the process instead of waiting for you to look at them tonight."

Lucas took a cautious breath before saying anything. He knew Jill was tired of the townhome and anxious to have their own place, but the dollars were too big for both of them not to review them. But . . .

Lucas's radio went off. Dispatch was reporting a structure fire, possibly suspicious.

"Jill, honey, I'm so sorry," Lucas began as he flipped on the siren and lights. "I just got a—"

"I heard. I heard. I'll talk to you later."

The phone went black. That timing couldn't have been worse.

L UCAS TURNED ONTO THE street right after the truck and engine from Station 1. A second engine from Station 2 along with the battalion chief's vehicle were already on the scene.

The house was large and looked abandoned. Black smoke billowed from the windows as they cracked and exploded from the intense heat generated by flames already visible. Even before Lucas got out of his vehicle, he could hear the roar. Visibility was quickly growing difficult with thick smoke hovering low. It covered the scene, engulfing not just the structure but the apparatus and firefighters trying to lay hose and deploy. Making it even more hazardous, the yard surrounding the house was overgrown. The tall grass, extremely dry, acted like kindling, whooshing instantly into flames as sparks swirled in the smoke and hot air before landing on the grass.

Lucas sat in his SUV, listening to the radio traffic, as he watched Riley take command, directing each apparatus where they would be most effective. Riley had just started talking to someone who was evidently connected with the property as the interior search about to take place was quickly canceled. All occupants must be accounted for.

Onlookers were gathering, and Lucas hoped Jeremy would arrive soon to capture pictures in case this fire turned out to be suspicious.

Just as Lucas stepped out of his vehicle and slipped the radio strap over his shoulder, the radio went off again. It was another structure fire just a couple of blocks over. A coincidence? Maybe. Maybe not.

He quickly checked with Riley, and seeing the situation was in hand, jumped in his vehicle and made a U-turn in the middle of the street. Lucas passed Jeremy as he was pulling up. Lucas signaled he was on his way to the second fire and, with a quick wave, drove the two short blocks to its location. A group of young people huddled on the sidewalk across the street as an engine and truck from Station 4 maneuvered into place. Firefighters hooked a hose line to the nearest hydrant while others donned their breathing apparatus, hoods, and masks, readying to enter the house.

Lucas moved to stand by Tom Harrow, the officer in command from Station 4, and observed as the firefighters worked the scene. After a quick interior attack, the fire was tapped out, and the scene was brought under control. Hose lines covered the front yard, excess water emptying onto the street and running into the gutter.

As the activity gradually slowed, Lucas took the opportunity and glanced at the crowd of gathered onlookers. Discreetly taking his phone from his jacket pocket, he snapped several photos, a small section of the crowd at a time to capture faces most effectively. Snapping a couple of shots, he thought he saw a familiar face in the frame. When he took his phone down to get a better look, that face was gone, but in the brief glimpse he'd gotten, it had looked like Chase Carr.

Frowning, Lucas looked up in time to see Jeremy park and get out of his SUV. Even with the smoke swirling between them, Lucas could see the look on Ennis's face, and it did not bode well.

"Chief." Jeremy stopped a few feet from Lucas and turned to look at the burnt structure and the firefighters putting out hot spots.

"Anything turn up at the other fire?" Lucas asked, taking a drink from a bottle of water he'd gotten from the canteen unit.

"I'm afraid so. I told PD I'd be back after I took a look here, but it looks like the arsonist is escalating things. That other house looked abandoned, but it was actually a rental and occupied. The people weren't at home, but they lost everything. They arrived right before I left and were understandably distraught. The Care Team was called and were on their way when I left. They'll help them find shelter, clothing, and supplies, but this is the first time the arsonist has displaced a family."

"Well, this makes two," Lucas said, tossing his thumb in the direction of the second burning house. "The people over there are university students sharing the house." Lucas nodded in the direction of a group of five young ladies who seemed dazed. He turned back to Jeremy. "Were there any new clues at the first house?"

Jeremy indicated his SUV with his chin. "Yes, sir. You're not going to like it."

Lucas gave Jeremy a questioning look before they turned and walked to the SUV. Jeremy opened the tailgate and pulled out a carefully labeled plastic bag holding the now familiar shiny red and gold gas can along with a note in a separate bag that read:

GIVE UP, MATTHEWS.
MOVE ON.

Taking a deep breath, Lucas closed his eyes. He took his helmet off and ran his fingers agitatedly through his hair. He would not be bullied—not ever again. He'd had enough of it growing up, and he didn't take well to being threatened now.

"Ennis, I want this person—whoever the hell it is. Do you understand me? I want him caught and caught now. I want you on this 24/7. I'll talk to Chief Harper and ask that his investigators do the same. This. Has. Got. To. Stop."

Jeremy, his eyes wide, nodded and, swallowing hard, took a step back. "Yes, sir. I'm on it."

"Talk to these people," Lucas said, jerking his thumb in the direction of the students. "See if they saw or heard anything or if there is anything like this around here." Lucas held up the plastic bag containing the gas can.

Jeremy nodded and quickly started toward the group who were talking to a member of the Care Team who had just arrived.

Lucas ran his hand down his face, pinching the bridge of his nose and shaking his head. They were missing something, but what? He started to set the bag with the gas can back into Jeremy's SUV when his radio went off again. The call was another structure fire. This one was on a street in the neighboring subdivision. Where the two homes already burning were smaller and older, that neighborhood had larger and newer homes.

Lucas shook his head and exchanged a somber look with Jeremy, who had stopped and turned around. Lucas headed toward his vehicle, loose gravel from the street scattering under his boots as he walked quickly to his SUV. He hoped not, but it looked like this could be a long night.

S ITTING ON A STOOL by the scanner, Jill sighed and put her head in her hands. Four. There had been four major structure fires in one day. The last one had come in about three hours ago, and she hoped it was the last. Unable to listen any longer, she turned off the scanner. She hadn't talked to Lucas since she'd snapped at him earlier that afternoon, and she felt terrible. He already had enough on his mind before and now . . . They had to catch a break sooner or later.

"Please, Lord, let this end soon," she prayed.

The front door suddenly opened, and Lucas walked in, closing the door wearily behind him. He looked up, saw Jill, and tried to smile, but Jill saw the worry and tiredness weighing on him. His face was spotted with soot marks, and his usually pristine white uniform shirt was gray with dark spots of soot and ash.

"Hey," he said with effort as he sank into the sofa, his head hanging with exhaustion. "I'm sorry I didn't call. I . . ."

Jill walked quickly over and sat down close to him. She put her hand on his shoulder, waiting until he looked up.

"Lucas, I was listening on the scanner. I am so sorry."

He smiled and pulled her hand into his and squeezed her fingers.

"Jill, I have no idea who's behind this. The frequency of these fires is increasing, and they're getting bigger. No lives lost—yet—thankfully, but now, there is major property loss. It has become even more abundantly clear that this fanatic, whoever it is, wants me out of Abernathy and evidently doesn't care what it takes to make that happen."

Lucas turned to her and looked at her with fervency despite his tiredness. "Promise me, Jill. Promise me that you'll be extra vigilant. Be extra careful and always keep an eye on your surroundings. Don't ever let yourself be caught alone in a strange place. I don't know what this person's plans are, but I'm concerned now for your safety and . . . for mine as well," he said, his voice trailing off.

Jill pulled back with alarm. "Lucas, you're scaring me."

"Good. I want you to be scared if that causes you to be more aware and cautious. This arsonist wants me out of Abernathy. The notes found at the last few fires have made that extremely clear. Ennis and the PD investigators are making encouraging headway, but this is far from over. So, do I have your word—you'll be extra careful and extra vigilant, and you'll let me know if you see anything unusual or out of place."

Jill nodded hesitantly. "Of course, Lucas. You have my word, but you must promise me the same. That you'll be careful and not put yourself in any undue danger. Please. I couldn't stand it if anything happened to you." Jill couldn't stop the tears that spilled over.

Putting his hands to either side of Jill's face, Lucas brushed the tears away and then pulled her close. "Sorry—I know I smell smoky."

"I don't care, Lucas. Just hold me and promise me everything will be all right." Jill squeezed him tighter as he did the same.

"I promise, Jill. As much as I'm able, I promise. We may need to talk about celebrating Christmas back in Fort Collins with Coach and Patsy, but we can discuss that later after we see how things go the next few days. I'm not sure I want Jon and Jess here either, but we'll play that by ear too."

Lucas leaned back and gave Jill a light kiss before standing. "I'll get a quick shower, and then let's take a look at those offers."

Jill sat up straight. "Lucas, you're exhausted and besides, shouldn't we wait until we see how things go. We may not want to commit to a house in Abernathy."

Lucas stopped and slowly turned to face Jill. "We. Are. Not. Leaving. When I was young, I was forced to move from one foster home to another all while constantly being picked on and bullied. As you well know, I was threatened and bullied in high school and even almost killed. I will not. I repeat. I will not be forced out from here. This is my mountain, Jill, and I choose to stay and fight. No one will drive me out. As powerful a hold as those memories still have on me, I'm fighting them and this arsonist with everything I've got. I will not give up until this person is brought to justice, and we are happily settled here."

Jill could see the steely resolve in his brown eyes, unwavering—strong and resolute.

Jill tilted her chin up with her own resolve. "I'll have some supper for you when you get out of the shower, and then we'll look at the offers—together. Because you're my mountain, Lucas, and when you fight, I fight."

THE NEXT DAY DAWNED clear and cold. It was good to see the sun after a smoke-filled Monday afternoon and evening. Tuesday was city council meeting day, and Lucas knew he would be on the hot seat. Kirk Lorimar knew it too. It would be no ordinary city council session. The regular executive session was canceled with everything focused on the public session.

Lucas and Chief Harper spent the day with Jeremy and the police investigators, going over the information they had in preparation for the questions and inquiries that were to come. Even though he wasn't hungry, Lucas had forced down a deli sandwich, knowing he'd need something to sustain him through the evening, but just the thought of food had made him queasy.

Lance Harper sat across the conference table, studying Lucas, thoughtfully chewing a bite of his own sandwich.

"Are you sure you're ready for this?" Harper asked. "It's going to be rough."

Lucas set his drink on the table and looked up.

"I'm ready. I'll lay out what we have, minus the confidential details, of course, but yeah, I'm ready." Lucas sounded more confident than he felt.

"You're not a very good liar, Matthews," Chief Harper said as he wadded up the paper from his sandwich and tossed it in the trash can near the door. "You'd be a fool to say you're ready and really believe it. And Matthews, you're definitely not a fool."

They were in the small conference room in the fire department's admin offices, the whiteboard, the walls, and the table filled with pictures, evidence, and stacks of reports, everything short of the physical gas cans that had been found at each scene. Photos of the cans corresponded to an index card with the date it was found, the note attached and any forensics that had been generated. They'd cleared a small space on the table for their notepads and where they'd eaten lunch.

Lucas sat back in the conference chair, rocking back and forth, deep in thought, absentmindedly playing with threads from worn spots on the chair arms. Chief Harper waited, studying Lucas, not envying the spot Lucas was currently in. Finally, Chief Harper cleared his throat, breaking Lucas from his reverie and causing him to look up.

Looking Lucas directly in the eye, Chief Harper said with a measured, weighted tone, "I've been in similar situations such as this, and when people are scared for their family's safety and the security of their property and aren't seeing the results they want to see from authorities, they don't like it. Trust me, it can get ugly. I'll have your back and support you in every way I can, but remember, when the public gets up in arms, politicians like the illustrious members of this city council go into self-preservation mode. They want to be perceived as supporting their constituents and will do that by any means necessary, including leaving staff hung out to dry. Keeping votes becomes their only goal."

Lucas listened, feeling confident in the work they'd done and in his own abilities, but also keenly aware he was way out on that limb Harper was talking about, and it could buckle beneath him any second.

"Thank you, Lance. I appreciate that. I really do, but we've got a good game plan backed up by solid investigations by both fire and police. Once it's laid out, the public and the council will understand."

Chief Harper stood and sighed, shaking his head slightly. "Matthews, I sincerely hope you're right, but you have no idea what's about to be thrown at you."

It turned out to be just as bad as Harper predicted.

After he'd given the report containing the details he and Harper had agreed would be appropriate to share, Lucas spent the next hour and a half at the podium responding to questions from Council members who were spurred on by citizen comments made during the public forum. Comments and questions from the public had been heated and brutal. Some of the remarks were directed at Council members while others were directed at the fire and police departments.

Incited by the charged atmosphere in the chambers, Council members began to take their frustration out on Lucas directly. From the dais, Kirk Lorimar looked at Lucas sympathetically but was only able to interject and try to deflect when there was a break between speakers. Lorimar attempted to rein in comments when several Council members began making disparaging comments about Lucas's inability to catch the arsonist and the job he was doing generally. As each Council member spoke, the rhetoric grew more and more heated while Lucas silently absorbed most of the vehemence and anger.

He stood resolutely at the podium, fielding questions when asked or standing stone-faced as Council members stated their thoughts. It was time to wrap up this portion of the agenda, but one Council member hadn't spoken. Council Member Dower. It had become generally known she had opposed Lucas's selection as fire chief. Lucas took a deep breath and braced himself when he saw her moving the microphone closer to speak.

The packed chambers were warm, the air was stale, and the crowd was restless. Lucas felt a bit lightheaded and regretted not eating more when he'd had the chance. He gripped the smooth edges of the podium but not too tightly, hoping to look more relaxed than he felt. He'd just about exhausted his reserve of patience and understanding after being pummeled repeatedly by Council members and the public, managing somehow to retain a calm demeanor. The Council members were frustrated, Lucas knew, but they'd also conspicuously pandered to their constituents just as Harper had forewarned him they'd do.

As the room quietened in expectation, Council Member Dower took a long look at Lucas and cleared her throat.

"We have all heard comments made tonight from both the public and from my fellow Council members. We have also heard from Chief Matthews and Chief Harper, regarding the work they are doing to catch the person setting these fires. I agree this is an alarming situation.

"I've heard multiple innuendos and caustic comments directed at Chief Matthews tonight, both personal and professional. I've marveled at his quiet, but confident responses. Most of you know by now I opposed Chief Matthew's appointment as Abernathy's fire chief. The reasons seemed valid to me at the time, but they have long since been eclipsed by what I've seen and come to learn about this public servant standing before us.

"Speaking for myself, I didn't know what firefighters do day in and day out. I know the joke is they cook, eat, watch TV, and sleep."

A light chuckle went around the room. Council Member Dower didn't smile.

"But you see, I've come to see and to appreciate, from a very personal perspective, a little more of what a firefighter does and what the right work ethic and mentality should mean to this community. A few weeks ago, my granddaughter, Amy, was involved in a serious car accident. She was injured and had to be taken to the hospital. When that accident happened, I was in our city manager's office, waiting to see Chief Matthews. He was late."

Council Member Dower paused and slowly looked around the room, her eyes coming to rest on Lucas. His eyes widened as understanding dawned. Looking back at the crowd, Council Member Dower went on, her voice thick with emotion.

"When Chief Matthews arrived, his shirt and pants were stained with blood—my granddaughter's blood."

The silence that suddenly filled the room was deafening. All heads on the Council's dais, turned to Mrs. Dower.

"You see," she continued, "on his way to city hall, he'd witnessed that accident. He didn't wait for the paramedics, although they arrived quickly. He stepped in and helped her without medical equipment or supplies. He staunched the flow of blood from her head wound with his own hands. Afterward, when he arrived at the meeting, he was apologetic for his appearance but ready to discuss my concerns. That, my fellow Abernathy citizens, is the exact kind of person we want, and need, as our fire chief. Chief Matthews, you have my sincerest thanks and appreciation for the help you gave my granddaughter."

Looking back to the room, she added, "I have come to believe in Chief Matthews and know that he has as much of a chance of catching this arsonist as any of the other men interviewed for the job would. Rest assured, the arsonist will be caught, and I pray it's before anyone gets hurt. Afterward, Abernathy will be that much better off having a fire chief of Chief Matthews' caliber. Please keep us updated as you have been doing, Chief, but the topic has been covered adequately for this evening. Mr. Mayor, I move we close this item on the agenda and move on to the next."

Council Member Jenkins quickly seconded the motion.

Mayor Tompkins rapped the gavel once sharply, and looking at Lucas with a brief nod said, "Chief Matthews, you may take your seat."

Lucas stepped stiffly from the podium. Stunned at how quickly things had just turned, he sank into his seat as the meeting moved on to more mundane matters. As he tried to keep his focus on what was being said, the words from Council Member Dower played repeatedly in his mind. He'd reacted at that accident as any paramedic would, but after the verbal beating he'd just experienced, her support tonight lifted his spirit and renewed his faith in others. Most importantly in this moment, it reminded him of his motivation for why he'd chosen this career—helping others.

Watching from the laptop in his shop, Milton Carr switched off the closed-circuit broadcast of the council meeting and swore beneath his breath. The meeting had been going well with Matthews taking the verbal berating he so well deserved. What a disappointment Council Member Dower had turned out to be! She had been solidly behind Carr as fire chief during the search process and then tonight—what was that pathetic little speech she gave? Matthews always seemed to be in the right place at the right time, but his luck was about to run out.

Carr realized now, more than ever, there was no one else he could really count on but himself. Darryl McCracken had done a great job while being an unwitting accomplice, spreading the rumors from the newspaper article Carr had shared with him, but even McCracken had backed off. Carr had snorted his derision when McCracken commented that Matthews was making a positive impression on him as well as the crew. The more time Matthews spent at the station, McCracken had said, the better they got to know him, and they liked him as a leader and just a nice guy to hang out with.

Dower might have propped Matthews up tonight, but it was temporary. Carr was ready to rid himself and the department of Matthews once and for all.

Thankfully, it had been a quiet night. Quiet as far as no new fires, Lucas thought, as he lay down in bed and sighed a long, deep, exhausted sigh. Fireworks from the council meeting had been enough.

Jill reached over and put a hand on his arm. Her touch was tender and gentle, and he could feel her protectiveness without her saying a word.

"You okay?" she asked softly.

"I'm fine. Even better now."

"It hurt me watching the way they talked to you tonight. You don't deserve that, Lucas. Do they not know that firefighters hate fires, they don't start them?"

"They're just scared," Lucas replied, staring tiredly at the ceiling. "I don't like that kind of reaction either, but I can understand it too."

Lucas rolled his head to the side and looked at Jill in the bedroom's dim light. She was propped up on one elbow looking down at him with such love in her eyes, it helped ease the tension away. He reached up and pushed a strand of hair behind one ear before he took her hand in his, gently weaving his fingers with hers.

"No matter how the day goes, no matter how many fires there are or how many good citizens want a piece of me, you, Jill Matthews, are my rock. You keep me grounded and make me feel like I can handle anything as long as you're by my side."

"And I'll always be there, Lucas. But please, catch this guy—whoever it is—so we can get on with our life."

"Yes, ma'am," Lucas teased lightly. "First, we've got business to discuss."

He sat up in bed and pulled Jill up beside him, putting an arm around her and drawing her close.

"Did you hear back from the Fort Collins Realtor after we selected the offer we wanted to accept?"

Jill turned to look at him.

"Lucas, we are not going to discuss that right now. You need to get some sleep—you look exhausted."

He *was* exhausted, but he meant what he'd said the other night. They were staying in Abernathy. It was best to keep their plans moving forward, and those plans included buying the house Jill already loved so much.

Lucas reached over and switched on the light. Jill's brows furrowed with even more worry when she got a good look at Lucas's face and eyes in the light. He looked more tired and haggard than she'd ever seen him.

"Jill, either you give me the latest, or I'll have to get up and check the emails. I saw them come through today but haven't had a chance to read them."

Jill knew he wouldn't let it go and sighed indulgently.

"I called Alexandria first thing this morning and let her know which offer we approved. She called a little after noon and said the couple who'd made that offer was thrilled, so she's drawing up all the final paperwork. She followed up with an email, confirming everything."

Lucas nodded. "I saw one from her and hoped it was good news."

"I then called and emailed Tucker Delaford and gave him all the particulars. Alexandria is supposed to be sending him everything to document the contingency being satisfied, so we can finalize the offer and contract on the house here. He said it would take a couple of days but would keep us posted. With the contingency settled, it all looks good. The house should be ours within days."

Lucas smiled sleepily. He was listening but began nodding slower and slower until his head drooped and his eyes drifted closed.

Jill smiled softly, watching him. She reached up and lovingly placed her hand against his cheek. She woke him enough to help him slide down and onto his side. He was in a deep sleep within seconds.

With a light kiss to his lips, Jill whispered softly into his ear, "I love you, Lucas Matthews."

Fire Admin was decked out for Christmas. There was a Christmas tree in the lobby and colorful garlands with blinking LED lights strung throughout the office. The roof of each fire station was outlined in alternating red and white Christmas lights. A fire Maltese cross in lights with the station number in the middle hung in prominence at each station as well.

Most of the stations had decorated for Christmas, some more than others. While most had put up a tree in either the kitchen or recliner room, others had added more, giving each station a distinct personality and a reflection of the crews working there. The community was showering every station with sweets, cookies, and treats of all kinds. The generous and giving nature of the Christmas season was in full swing. The spirit within the department seemed to be lifting as well. Only a couple of minor fires had been noted since Thanksgiving. Even those didn't have the hallmarks of the arsonist. It was a festive time of year. Lucas just wished he felt more festive.

The first two weeks of December rushed past. It was only a few days until Jon and Jessica would be out for Christmas break and well past time to tell them they were going to Coach and Patsy's for the holidays and not coming to Abernathy. He had to admit, he and Jill had been procrastinating in telling them. There would be a 'discussion,' and it would be hard to hold the line since he and Jill wanted them home just as much as he knew they'd want to be here. Things were just too precarious right now, never knowing when or where the arsonist would strike next. Just because it had been quiet for a few days didn't mean it would stay that way—not until the arsonist was caught.

It was after five o'clock, and most of the office staff had left for the day. Lucas had gotten back early from Station 7 and was at his computer catching up on emails. It was quiet, and the early dark of winter had already settled outside his office window. There was a threat of light snow. He'd turned off the overhead florescent lights in his office and was working by the glow of the lamp on his desk. It was a soft light and seemed calm compared to the frenetic buzzing of the florescent lights.

He was waiting to talk to Ennis about the latest on the investigation, but Ennis was at police headquarters, so the update would probably have to wait until morning.

"Chief," Lindsay said with a light knock.

Lucas looked up from his computer. Lindsay was standing just inside his door. The florescent lighting from the hall illuminated one side of her, leaving the other in shadow.

"I'm headed home for the day, Chief, unless you need anything else."

"No. Thanks, Lindsay. I think we're set—at least I hope so. Have a good evening." Lucas smiled and then looked back at his monitor.

"Thank you, sir, and you too," Lindsay responded but didn't move. She stood quietly, looking at Lucas.

Lucas glanced up, sensing her still standing there. He leaned back in his chair when he saw the troubled look on her face.

"Is there something wrong, Lindsay?" Lucas had noticed that the usually bubbly Lindsay had become subdued and quiet lately.

"Sir, I . . ." Lindsay faltered and then came to a stop.

Lucas leaned forward in his chair and gestured to one of the guest chairs across from him. "Have a seat and tell me what's on your mind."

Lindsay hesitated before blushing with embarrassment and uncertainty. She took a hesitant step but then stopped with Lucas's kind but concerned gaze focused on her, his eyebrows raised in question.

Lindsay inwardly flinched. She should have left when he'd said good night. Why hadn't she just turned and walked out the door before getting herself into this awkward situation? She wanted—no she needed—to talk to him and find out if the rumors she'd been hearing about him were true. But with him looking at her with such obvious concern, if he wasn't aware of the rumors, and he didn't seem to be, she just couldn't hurt him by telling him.

He was trying so hard and bringing much needed and positive change to the department. It was taking some of the staff a while to get on board, but most were there or getting there quickly, at least she thought they were. From what she'd been hearing and the whispers going around, the department seemed split in their opinions.

As for her, she had no doubts about the Chief. He was a good man and a great chief, which made the rumors even more confusing. They directly contradicted the person she knew, or thought she knew, him to be. She'd worked closely with him, and he was always thoughtful and kind. The only exceptions were some of his dealings with Milton Carr. But Carr was grossly disrespectful, so who could blame Chief Matthews in those instances? And then there were these arsons that had everyone on edge. The weight of it all rested on his shoulders, but right here, right now, he was willing to take time and talk to her. That spoke volumes about him.

"Lindsay? Is something wrong?"

The Chief's question brought her back to herself. She mentally shook her head and, forcing a smile, took a step back toward the door.

"No—sorry, Chief. Everything is fine. Sorry to bother you. I'll see you in the morning."

She turned, but before leaving, she saw the look of confusion, and maybe even disappointment cross his face. She hoped, if it should ever come to it, he would know he could count on her.

When he walked in the townhome door later that night, Jill had her back to him and was leaning against the side of the sofa with her head down. One arm was draped across her middle while she held the phone to her ear in her other hand. She was deep in conversation, and from the little bit he'd caught as he came through the door, she was talking to the twins. When she heard the door open, her head popped up, she turned, looked at him with a hesitant smile, pointed to the phone, and mouthed, "the kids," followed by an eye roll.

"Jon, Jess, hold on. Your father just walked in the door. Let me put you on speaker."

Lucas raised his eyebrows in question, but Jill just grimaced and put the phone on speaker. She walked around the sofa, and she and Lucas sat down, facing each other, their knees touching, Jill holding the phone between them.

"Dad?" Jessica's voice came through. "We're coming home for Christmas. There's no need for further discussion."

Lucas opened his mouth to respond, but before he could, Jon spoke up. "You were probably just about to say something like, 'Now, kids,' but sorry, Jess is right. We're coming to Abernathy. Period. End of discussion."

"Now, listen you two. You have no idea how hard it is for your mother and me to say no to you on this. We want you both here more than you know, but things are just too . . ."

Lucas hesitated as Jill shook her head vigorously.

"What?" he mouthed.

Jill put the phone on mute. "I haven't told them what's going on—the danger you're concerned about . . . you know, everything. I thought you'd know best how much or how little to tell them."

"Hello? Hello?" Jon and Jessica were both saying over the phone's speaker.

"Do you guys have us on mute?" Jessica asked. "I might remind you this is supposed to be a family discussion."

Lucas and Jill looked at each other, shaking their heads, grinning slightly, before Jill reluctantly took the phone off mute.

"Sorry, kids," Lucas began. "There's just a lot going on right now. Your mother and I want to be honest with you, but we don't want you to worry either."

The silence that fell with that statement was quickly broken by Jon and Jessica both speaking at the same time.

"One at a time. One at a time," Jill said with a light chuckle.

"What's going on?" Jon asked. "Jess and I want, need, and deserve to know. You guys are the parents, and we respect that, but we *are* a family after all. So, spill the beans. What's up?"

Jessica added, "I agree. What Jon said."

Lucas sighed, and with a nod from Jill told them about the arsons, about the notes threatening him to leave Abernathy, about the city council meetings, about his insubordinate deputy chief, and on and on until he'd told them everything he'd hoped to keep from them, so they wouldn't worry. Once he got started, he couldn't stop.

When Lucas finished, there was silence on the other end of the phone. After the silence stretched on for a while, Lucas looked to Jill and shrugged.

"Did I lose you guys?" Lucas asked tentatively.

With that inquiry, the dam broke. Jon and Jessica were both talking at once, and from what Lucas and Jill could make out, they were not happy. That was putting it mildly.

"Don't let me catch this Carr guy alone in a dark alley," Jon said after a short break in his and Jessica's rantings. "I won't be held accountable for what I'd like to do."

Lucas chuckled. "Sorry, Son. You're going to have to get in line behind your mother. She's said the same thing."

They all laughed before a heavy silence fell again.

"Kids, I think you can understand now why we're asking that you go to Coach and Patsy's. They're looking forward to you spending Christmas break with them. Your mother and I will be with you there for a few days over Christmas, but this . . ." Lucas had to stop to clear a sudden catch in his throat. "This is best."

Jill reached out and took Lucas's hand, squeezing it as a stray tear slid down her cheek. Lucas grimaced at the pain that he and this situation were causing his family.

Desperate to change the subject, Lucas asked with a falsely bright voice, "So, on to a hopefully happier note. How are the grades looking this semester?"

Mutual groans from Jon and Jessica made Lucas and Jill laugh.

"Dad . . ." Jessica began. They could already hear a tease in her voice. "My grades are outstanding as usual, but as for Jon, well, you know."

"Hey, let me speak for myself," Jon said with false indignation.

The conversation and teasing continued for another thirty minutes until Jill said, "Kids, your dad's had a long day, and I bet he needs some dinner. We'll talk to you in the next day or so. Coach and Patsy are expecting you this weekend, and we'll be up soon and can't wait to see you then. Love you!"

A round of *I love you's* was said before the call ended.

Lucas and Jill sat across from each other, looking silently into the other's eyes.

"I think that went pretty well after the initial surprise, don't you?" Jill said and stood suddenly before walking to the kitchen.

Lucas could hear the whoosh of the refrigerator door opening and the metallic clink of a pan being placed on the stove and then silence. He got up and walked to the kitchen where he saw Jill bent over, one hand on the tiny island, her other arm cradling her stomach, doing her best to stifle the sobs she couldn't stop. Lucas walked over, silently took her in his arms, and held her tightly, whispering soothing nothings in her ear until the sobs eased.

"Jill," Lucas said softly. "Please. I want you to listen to me. Leave tomorrow and go to Coach and Patsy's. That way you'll be there when the kids arrive. I know you're needing them right now, and if I know them, they're needing you too. I'll feel much better knowing my family is out of harm's way. I'll be there for Christmas, and we can all be together then. Okay?"

Jill had started shaking her head when Lucas said he wanted her to leave the next day. She stepped back and, wiping her cheeks, said, "Your fight, Lucas Matthews, is my fight. Remember? I'm staying. I just needed a minute."

Lucas opened his mouth to object, but Jill held up a hand, stopping him.

"End of discussion," she said with a swipe at a tear. "Now, I've got dinner to make."

Lucas hoped she'd insist on staying. He *needed* her to stay.

Cʜʀɪsᴛᴍᴀs Eᴠᴇ ᴡᴀs ɪɴ three days. The atmosphere at the Fire Administration offices should have been festive and cheerful with the Christmas lights and decorations. Instead, it was somber and anxious with 12 taunting notes and 15 unsolved arsons hanging over their heads and the constant threat of more.

The morning's staff meeting had been short and sweet. A couple of command officers were taking Thursday and Friday off for Christmas, and Carr was already out, taking the entire week, so there wasn't much regular business to report. Lucas planned to drive to Fort Collins Christmas Eve morning and back at the end of Christmas Day. He wouldn't be comfortable being away any longer. He was still trying to get Jill to leave and join the twins at Coach and Patsy's, but she was stubborn, insisting on staying, and he was glad.

Swallowing down the last bite of a quick lunch, Lucas grabbed a fresh cup of coffee to warm him up and joined Jeremy in the conference room reserved for the arson investigation. It was a small conference room out of the main hallway with no windows, but it did come with a lock on the door. With so many arsons, the amount of evidence had almost outgrown the size of the conference room.

"Afternoon, Chief," Ennis said, from one end of the conference table, looking up from a stack of notes he was sifting through.

"Ennis," Lucas responded as he walked to the table where the notes left at each scene had been carefully compiled. In chronological order, each note had been secured in a clear, sealed bag after being dusted for fingerprints and after the paper and ink had been analyzed. The paper was plain, white copy paper and the ink was from a wide-tipped Sharpie; both could be bought anywhere. The handwriting varied between the notes, but the handwriting expert called in from Dallas had verified it was the same person writing each one. After the notes were sealed inside their respective protective bags, they were tagged with the date, time, and address of the incident. For a new fire marshal, Ennis was doing an admirable job. He was thorough and detailed, and going the extra mile to make sure no stone was left unturned.

The notes at the scenes had quickly progressed from a tease to taunting to threatening with the threats directed personally at Lucas. The arsonist was specific. Whoever it was wanted Lucas gone. Who, besides Carr, could have developed such hatred for him so quickly? Lucas's thoughts went back, again, to middle school and the bullies who had haunted him throughout high school. Their dislike had happened just as quickly, and there was still, all these years later, no clear answer as to why. He just seemed mysteriously to draw unwarranted animosity, Lucas thought darkly to himself. The same nightmare was still haunting him, but at least it wasn't every night. He was tired enough without losing more sleep.

Holding the hot coffee cup to warm his hand and taking occasional sips, Lucas scanned the notes as he walked slowly along the table. He had to admit, it was a bit unnerving to see it all together and laid out so plainly.

"PD investigators are on their way, sir," Jeremy said, walking up to stand beside Lucas, his gaze falling across the sealed notes as well. "Not a pretty sight, is it?"

"No, Ennis, it's not. I'm ready to put this to rest. I know you are too."

Jeremy let out a low whistle. "You've got that right, sir. I was supposed to have a nursery painted last weekend but with four arsons in one night, there just wasn't time to process all the evidence and do that too. Allie is anxious to have the painting done, but she also knows this is a priority."

Lucas and Jeremy moved together to the map of Abernathy tacked to the wall where Jeremy began pinning the location of the four new fires with a small tag that gave the date and address alongside each known and suspected arson already tagged. When they'd begun, the fires had been spread across Abernathy with no rhyme or reason, except that, in each instance, the property was either abandoned, empty, or in the middle of a vacant lot where it seemed the arsonist took care not to cause collateral damage. But after the first four or five fires, the pattern had narrowed to a more condensed area. The properties were increasing in value, and four fires now had involved displacement of families or renters. Lucas was holding his breath that until they caught this person, there'd be no human injuries or casualties.

Lucas turned and looked at Jeremy. "I know this is taking its toll on everyone. We're going to catch a break soon. With this many fires, the arsonist is going to make a mistake. The law of averages is on our side. If we could figure out why he's pinpointed me, that would help narrow the suspect pool."

"We have a pool now, sir?" Jeremy asked, cocking an eyebrow. "I thought we had a pool of one—Carr."

Lucas shook his head. "I know we're watching him, but I still can't believe someone with his number of years in the service would turn into an arsonist in spite of how bitter he's become."

"Whether it's Carr or someone else, it's certainly not your fault he's intent on a vendetta. This is fire department business, and we brothers stick together, sir."

Lucas gave Jeremy a wan smile. "Thanks, Ennis. You should get a bonus for cheer leading."

Jeremy looked up and greeted the two investigators from the police department as they walked in. With a nod to Lucas, they moved to the table to join Jeremy while Lucas walked to the wall where pictures of onlookers at each fire had been hung, by date and location. There were no repeats as far as Lucas could tell, but with several of the fires at night, several faces were shadowed and indistinguishable.

Most of the conference chairs had been moved against the wall beneath the pictures to create more space around the table. To get closer, so he could study each picture in more detail, Lucas maneuvered his way in and around the chairs, glancing from one picture to the next and then back again until he knew for certain. There seemed to be the same dark figure in each picture. The figure in each picture was the same height and, from some of the better angles, seemed to be of the same build. The figure always wore a bulky dark jacket with a hood, his face shielded from the light and always at the periphery, folded into as much shadow as possible.

Lucas went photo by photo, from first to last, one more time just to be certain. Nodding, he was sure.

"Ennis, come take a look at this."

Lucas began with the first fire and pointed to the same dark figure in each photo. Jeremy's eyes grew wide as he went down the row with Lucas pointing out the same figure in each one.

"How did we not see this before?" Jeremy asked, shaking his head and running his fingers through his hair. "It's so plain now that you see it."

"It's like one of those pictures where there are two different images captured in the same photo. What you see depends on the angle you look at it."

Excited, Jeremy turned to the two police investigators. "Guys, come look at this."

As Lucas stepped aside to allow Jeremy and the PD investigators closer access to the photos, his phone buzzed. He looked down to see Mike Bentley's name on the caller ID. He grimaced. Lucas always appreciated Bentley's calls, but he couldn't stop at such a critical juncture.

His phone stopped buzzing, and the note popped up indicating a recent call, but Bentley didn't leave a message. Lucas joined Ennis and the police investigators as they began making date and time stamp notations to go back and check the doorbell and security cameras in those neighborhoods again and look at them more closely. Keys on the three laptops belonging to Ennis and the PD investigators began tapping lightly as they entered the time stamp information and address requests to pull up the security camera footage already on file.

Lucas paced, anxiously watching, when his phone buzzed. Bentley's name popped up on the caller ID again. Lucas frowned. He was about to take the call when Bentley hung up too quickly for him to answer.

A couple of minutes later, Lucas had moved to lean over Jeremy's shoulder to watch the start of one of the videos when Lindsay came to the door of the conference room. "Chief, you have an important call. It's Deputy Chief Bentley."

Lucas's heart skipped a beat as he straightened. He'd tried to ignore the feeling after Bentley's second call but now he knew. Something was wrong.

He excused himself and walked quickly to his office, closing the door behind him. Lindsay immediately transferred the call, and Lucas picked it up mid ring.

"Bentley? Lucas Matthews here."

"Lucas," Bentley began but then stopped. Bentley had never called him by his first name before.

"Lucas, I'm so sorry to have to tell you but Katie—Mrs. Garrett—"

Lucas didn't hear anything else before dropping into his chair. His head in his hand, he cradled the phone in his other hand as tears welled. The sudden roaring in his ears made Bentley's voice sound as if it were coming from far away. A wave of dizziness had him grabbing onto the edge of his desk. When the roaring in his ears gradually dulled, he heard Bentley's voice and insistent inquiry.

"Lucas? Are you there?"

Lucas opened his eyes and said gruffly, "Yes, Mike. I'm here. Would you please repeat what you were saying? I'm sorry—I didn't—I couldn't—"

"Of course. I understand. I had lunch plans with Katie today. It was our tradition to have a little pre-Christmas lunch, and today was the day. I went by for her, but there was no answer. I called for a well check, but she was already gone. It must have just happened because she was dressed and sitting on the sofa. It looked like she was waiting for me." Bentley's voice caught. "And you know? She was holding a picture of Andy. I've never seen two people love each other the way they did." After a pause, Bentley added, "I've notified Trenton. He's taking care of the arrangements, but I wanted to call and tell you personally."

Lucas cleared his throat. The dizzy spell had passed and the roar in his ears was lessening.

"Thank you, Mike. I appreciate it. I guess after that recent episode, we knew it could be any time but it's . . . you're never . . . you're just never ready."

"No. You're not. Katie was a dear, sweet friend, and, Andy, well, they didn't come any better. I'll have to tell you about mine and Andy's relationship someday. I wasted so much time resenting him. I'd give anything to have that time back, but that's a story for another time."

"It sounds like a story I'd like to hear. Knowing both of you, I can't imagine either of you resenting the other."

"Oh, but I did him, and how I regret those times! But anyway," Bentley hurriedly went on, "Trenton will be getting in touch with you about Katie's service."

"I would appreciate that. You know I'll be there. It's hard to put into words—to express just how much she and Mr. Andy have meant to me."

"Well, you'll want to work on that because Katie asked for you specifically to say a few words at her service. She said it would mean a lot to her—and Andy. She mentioned just the other day that she was going to talk to you about it. She'd already made a note in her funeral plans. She was very organized, you know."

Lucas didn't know what to say. He knew how much she and Mr. Andy meant to him, but knowing, right until the end, how much *he'd* meant to them, both of them, was almost more than he could take in right now.

"I'm honored, Mike. I'll . . . I'll do my best."

Bentley chuckled lightly. "Lucas, I think your best will be perfect. You do both of them credit. I'll be in touch soon."

Ending the call, Lucas leaned back and closed his eyes, thinking back to second grade and what it had been like being with Mrs. Garrett and Mr. Andy. He remembered smiling a lot when he was with them and then how devastated he'd been when he and his mom had moved.

Lucas reached into his pocket and pulled out Mr. Andy's badge and gripped it tightly, feeling its edges in the palm of his hand. It shone brightly beneath the office lights just as it had on Mr. Andy's shirt when he'd sat across from Lucas eating lunch in the school cafeteria.

Lucas rubbed his eyes. Somehow, despite everything going on, he'd find the right words to express what Mrs. Garrett meant to him and how much she'd impacted his life. She and Mr. Andy had always been his inspiration. He owed them both his best.

After hanging up with Bentley, Lucas lingered, gathering his thoughts, willing himself to focus. The doorbell to the office lobby chimed once, and Lucas could hear soft voices from the hallway. He heard Lindsay's phone ring, and her cheerful voice answering before falling in volume as she talked. In spite of everything continuing as it always had, his world had shifted. Mrs. Garrett and the path she and Mr. Andy had set him on all those years ago was still there, but it, too, had shifted to where he was today. The closeness the three of them had shared was undeniable.

Standing, he sighed. Wiping a hand over his face and bracing his shoulders, he was reaching for the door handle when his phone buzzed. Pulling it out of his pocket, he saw Jill's picture and name pop up. She seemed to have a way of sensing when he needed her. He eased down into one of the guest chairs in front of his desk and put his elbows on his knees, his head in one hand.

"Hello?" Lucas answered, his voice a bit thick.

"Lucas, I just wanted to—" Jill began but stopped. "What's wrong?"

"Katie—Mrs. Garrett—she . . ."

"Oh no, Lucas, I'm so sorry."

"Bentley just called." Lucas paused and sighed. "It looks like her heart just played out on her."

"Is there anything I can do? Anything you need?" Jill asked, her voice soft.

"No, Hon. Not right now, but thank you. I may need your help putting some remarks together. Bentley said Mrs. Garrett asked that I say a few words at her service. I know how I feel and what I want to say, but I just want to do her and Mr. Andy justice for how much they did for me."

Jill was silent for a while before saying, "It's quite an honor to be asked. The perfect words will come, but really, you just being the person you are is a testament to them. That alone says more than mere words will ever be able to say. Always remember that."

"You always know what I need to hear—thank you. But you called me," Lucas said, clearing his throat.

"Oh, that's right I did, didn't I? No worries. I was just calling to say hi. That's all."

"That's all? You never call just to say hi."

"Well, this time, something told me you just needed a call."

OR THE FIRST TIME since the arsons had begun, Lucas's hopes were rising. After spending the remainder of the afternoon with Ennis and the two police investigators, they'd agreed there had been a crack in the case.

After spotting the elusive hooded figure in multiple scene photos, security cameras of neighbors had picked up additional details of the figure. The time stamps proved helpful by providing a more concise time frame for footage of cars parked on nearby streets. That search had been successful. Even though its plates were never legible, a similar vehicle had been spotted near multiple fire scenes. It would take time to retrieve the requested security film footage and double-check everything, but it was beginning to look like they were close to a breakthrough. Maybe they'd be arson-free by the new year. Until then, the danger was still very real.

Lucas regretted not visiting at least one of the stations that afternoon, but right now, catching this arsonist took priority. Shivering inside his jacket, Lucas punched up the heater in the SUV and turned the radio volume down a bit. Since it had been dark for over an hour, he took a few minutes as he drove home to look at some of the Christmas decorations. Most were traditional Christmas lights, but some were clever scenes with animated characters as well as large blow ups of Santa, elves, and reindeer. "It would be great if Santa delivered an arsonist all wrapped up with a nice bow," Lucas thought. His breath hitched with anticipation, thinking about the progress made today. Even though he was almost home, he reached over and punched the heater up another notch or two. He just couldn't seem to get warm these days.

The street with their townhome was seriously lacking in Christmas spirit. The townhome homeowners, or renters, weren't too enthusiastic about Christmas, but over the last couple of weeks, a house every so often had started sporting Christmas lights. Lucas hoped next Christmas would be a lot different for his family. They typically went all out for Christmas, but with everything in storage, he and Jill would have to get by until they got to Coach and Patsy's. He was sure their house would be fully decked out.

Lucas rubbed one eye and sighed tiredly as he turned the corner and onto their street. When he got close, he slowed and leaned forward, straining to see through the windshield. Jill's SUV was in the drive, as usual, but parked behind her vehicle was Jon's truck and parked parallel in front of the house was Coach and Patsy's SUV.

Lucas gripped the steering wheel tightly, blinking rapidly. He should be irritated. He'd told the twins to stay in Fort Collins with Coach and Patsy for their safety. They obviously hadn't listened, and now, Coach and Patsy were here too. Lucas shook his head and couldn't help but grin as he parked behind Coach and Patsy's vehicle.

The door of his SUV had barely slammed shut when Lucas looked up to see the front door open and his family spilling onto the front porch. Before he knew it, they surrounded him, patting him on the back or reaching for a hug. Jessica, Lucas noticed, hung on tightly and for the longest.

"Let him breathe, Jess," Jon groused before reaching for Lucas himself and hugging him tightly. "The cavalry's arrived, Dad!"

Lucas laughed. This felt so good. Putting his arms around Patsy and Jill's shoulders, he steered the laughing group back inside.

Thankful someone had started a fire in the fireplace, Lucas claimed a chair close to its heat as the flames popped and crackled. Everyone settled in wherever they could in the small living room. Coach and Patsy, she in the chair and Coach on the chair's arm, sat across from Lucas, concerned looks on their faces. Lucas gave them a reassuring smile as he reached over and took Patsy's warm hand, she squeezing his tightly. Before he could say anything, there was an insistent knock at the door.

"Now who could that be?" Lucas asked with a frown. No one else got up to answer, so he rose, noticing knowing looks among the others. Lucas understood why when he opened the door and Meg flew into his arms, grabbing him in a tight hug. Her family tumbled in behind her, ushered in by a gust of frigid air carrying a snowflake or two. Justin, Meg's husband, smiled and pumped Lucas's hand, Meg's arms still tightly around Lucas.

"Did I miss the surprise?" Meg asked, giving Lucas a kiss on the cheek.

Everyone laughed. Justin took Meg's coat, and Lucas sat back down by the fire, taking the cup of hot coffee Jill handed him as she handed others to Coach and Patsy.

"This *is* the surprise," Patsy said, gesturing to the group.

"Ah—I love being a surprise," Meg said with a wink at Lucas as she gathered her youngest in her lap.

"Is anyone going to explain this . . . surprise?" Lucas asked, gesturing to the circle.

"With everything going on, you don't think we'd leave you here to go through it alone do you, Dad?" Jon asked, trying to sound stern.

"We were thrilled to have Jon and Jess with us for the holidays," Coach interjected. "But when they told us why you wanted them in Fort Collins instead of here, we hatched the plan for all of us to be together. We thought you might need a few friendly faces."

"And you are so right. I can't tell you what a lift it is seeing all of you. But I do have a question for my lovely wife. Where, dear, are we going to put everybody? A hotel is not the place to be on Christmas."

"We totally agree," Patsy added. "That's why we've rented a roomy Airbnb not ten minutes from here. There's plenty of room for all of us," Patsy gestured in the direction of Coach and Meg and her family, "while you, Jill, and the twins stay here."

"Appreciate the sacrifice being made, Dad. Guess who will be sleeping on this old thing," Jon said, giving a cushion on the lumpy sofa a good punch.

"Sacrifice duly noted and appreciated, Son," Lucas said, giving Jon a playful shove.

"Your Realtor firefighter, Delaford, was very helpful in finding the place for us," Jill said with a bright smile. "It's all set and ready for Christmas."

"It looks amazing!" Jessica piped up, her eyes shining. "We got here this morning and have been decorating for Christmas all day. We'll spend Christmas Eve there, and then we'll open presents and eat Christmas dinner there too. Mom and Patsy are cooking."

"I'm helping with Christmas dinner, too!" Meg piped up.

Lucas groaned, and she threw a pillow at him, making everyone laugh.

Lucas shook his head. "It seems like there was a whole lot of planning going on without my knowing. I'm not sure what to think about this being put together so easily. I had no idea."

"And that's why they call it a surprise, Dad!" Jon said with an exaggerated eye roll, making everyone laugh again. "But enough of that. I'm hungry," Jon went on. "What's for dinner, Mom?"

JILL CRAWLED INTO BED and snuggled close to Lucas. Sighing contentedly, she put an arm around him as he pulled her closer.

"Are the kids all settled in?" Lucas asked, reaching over and turning the lamp off.

Jill smiled. "They are. Jon's still complaining about the sofa, but he'll get over it."

Lucas chuckled. "You're amazing, Jill Matthews. Did you know that? Having everyone here for Christmas is absolutely perfect."

Jill laughed softly. "Don't thank me. Thank your kids and Coach and Patsy. They spearheaded the action, and I'm sure glad they did."

"I'm glad too," Lucas murmured.

Jill looked up at Lucas and stroked his cheek softly. "Lucas, I'm so sorry about Katie Garrett. She was such a dear. I know how much she meant to you."

"Yeah," Lucas said softly. "She did. It was the memory and the thoughts of her and Mr. Andy that kept me going through all those foster home years. I don't think I could have made it through all of that without the strength they gave me from afar." Lucas took a deep breath and let it out slowly. "So much time lost. I should have come sooner."

"You came when you could. You got to see her again, and she got to realize the impact she and Andy had on you. Even after so many years, you're here and carrying their legacy forward. Isn't that what counts?"

"I suppose," Lucas mused, almost to himself. "I just wish—I just wish there'd been more time—with Mr. Andy and with Mrs. Garrett. Time goes by so quickly. It's hard to appreciate the moment. But right now, there's one thing I know for certain."

"And what's that?" Jill asked, studying his earnest expression.

"We are going to enjoy and appreciate every single minute of this Christmas with all these crazy people we love. Right?"

"Yes, we are. It's going to be one of the best Christmases ever."

Lucas looked into Jill's eyes, his face sobering and said, "And then, we'll see what the new year holds."

"A new year *always* holds bright promise," Jill said, kissing Lucas lightly.

Her head on his shoulder, she fell asleep quickly. Her soft and steady breathing was comforting. Lucas stared at the ceiling, gently stroking Jill's silky hair as his mind searched relentlessly for the elusive answers to questions he didn't even know how to put into words.

THE DAYS OFF AT Christmas had been wonderful but woefully short. Even though the time with Allie and the family had been fun, the week between Christmas and New Year was still a regular work week.

The regular Monday morning staff meeting had been short. The agenda had been brief as Chief Matthews seemed anxious to get through the meeting quickly. He seemed a bit preoccupied. Who could blame him, Jeremy thought, with as much as the Chief had on his mind and now, the passing of a close friend. When it rained it poured, and Chief Matthews was getting a monsoon these days.

Jeremy ran his hands down his face before rubbing his bleary eyes. After staring at them for so long, the figures in the photos hanging on the conference room wall in front of him were blurring together. Jeremy paced the short length of the conference table, shaking his head trying to clear it.

Cade was supposed to come by in about an hour to discuss finalizing the security and safety protocols for the holiday tournament that was starting tomorrow, but right now, Jeremy needed something to revive him. He could smell the coffee even before he reached the break room. He lifted the pot and started to pour a cup but then changed his mind. Setting the pot back on the burner, he walked over to the vending machines, humming in the corner. He punched in his soft drink selection after feeding the dollar bill into the slot. When nothing happened, he gave the machine a solid thump on the front panel and grinned when he heard the can thundering down the chute. Retrieving the chilled can, Jeremy popped the top open, and took a long, carbonated drink.

"Somebody let you out of your cell, Ennis?"

Jeremy jumped and turned quickly to see Riley in the doorway, grinning.

Jeremy held the cold Coke can aloft. "I am not working in a cell, but I am working hard if I say so myself. I was just in need of refreshment."

"Well, you can say you're working hard all you want, but I'm inclined to believe you since the only time I see you out and about is when there's a fire."

"Life of a fire marshal with multiple unexplained fires," Jeremy said more sharply than he'd intended.

The grin disappeared from Riley's face. "Sorry, Jer. I know you're under a lot of pressure. Anything new showing up?"

Jeremy shook his head in response.

"No new fires this past week so I've had more time to comb through what we already have. Pieces are coming together, a little bit at a time, and several pieces of evidence are at the forensics lab for analysis. The notes are no help—all mundane. The paper and marker can be bought just about anywhere. As far as the gas cans, we've got multiple leads on those, but with a key computer system down that tracks sales at a major retailer plus holiday time off for employees working the day we've pinpointed the arsonist bought several, we're stuck in the proverbial holding pattern for now. The lab's taking way too long in my opinion."

"It seems like there ought to be something to speed up the lab," Riley said with surprise. "They could be sitting on something crucial."

"They probably are. Both Chief Matthews and Chief Harper are applying as much pressure as possible. The closer we look at what we've got, the more we're discovering. One small break could blow this thing wide open. It will happen. I'm feeling it."

Jeremy slapped Riley on the back as he walked past him, headed to his office. Riley followed close behind.

"Jeremy," Lindsay said, stepping to the door as Jeremy and Riley filed into his office. "Cade Marshall to see you. He's in the lobby."

"Thank you, Lindsay. Would you mind bringing him back?"

"Happy to. I'll be right back."

"Guess that's my cue to leave," Riley said, moving to the door about the time Cade bounded up, talking enthusiastically to Lindsay about the tournament.

"You should come out. It's going to be great!" Cade was saying as Lindsay ushered him through the doorway.

"Actually, my husband and I are planning to come one night. His former high school team, the Brenton Bandits, is going to be playing, but we're not quite sure when."

"I've got the schedule memorized at this point, so I can tell you the Bandits play the third game Thursday night at 8 p.m. but get there early. Ticket sales for this year's tournament are far and above what they've been the last few years."

"Good to know. Appreciate it, Officer Marshall." Lindsay smiled at the three before leaving.

"Hey, guys!" Cade turned his attention to Jeremy and Riley, who were shaking their heads.

"What's with you two?" Cade asked, plopping into one of Jeremy's guest chairs with a thud.

"Nothing . . . nothing," Riley said, stepping to the door. "I'll leave you two to talk. Just try to get some work done while you're at it."

Jeremy waved him off. "Speaking of work, don't you have a shift to be running, Battalion Chief Sullivan?"

Riley laughed and gave them a quick wave as he left. They briefly heard the ladder truck's diesel engine in the bay before the exterior door closed behind Riley.

"So, is what you said true, Cade, or are you just trying to spur ticket sales?" Jeremy asked, sitting down in his desk chair and swiveling to face Cade.

"What? Not me," Cade said, raising his eyebrows in mock indignation, but then grew thoughtful quickly. "I'm actually being very serious. Ticket sales are way up. The majority of high schools invited this year are all state contenders in their different divisions and have enthusiastic and large followings. It should be an intense, but fun three days."

Jeremy nodded somberly as he set his Coke can on his desk and turned it with his fingers. "We'd better be on our A game then, hadn't we? I don't want what's been happening in Abernathy to affect the tournament."

"Neither do I," Cade agreed, all joviality gone. "Let's go over everything one more time."

L ucas took a seat on one of the folding chairs already set up beneath the awning next to Katie Garrett's grave site. He was early—very early—for the service, but the funeral home had already completed their arrangements. An attendant was standing nearby at a discreet distance.

The day was bright and sunny but bitterly cold, with only a slight breeze floating silently through the bare tree branches overhead. Lucas pulled his heavy coat closer around the dress uniform he wore. It was even colder in the shade of the small tent's awning.

Mrs. Garrett had requested a graveside service, and Lucas had known exactly where to come. He'd been to Mr. Andy's grave several times since moving to Abernathy. The first time he'd come, it had been to pay his respects and say the thank you and goodbye he'd never gotten to say. It was so peaceful and quiet here, that he'd returned several times over the past months. It was a good place to gather his thoughts amid the ongoing chaos.

Now, as when he'd been here previously, he considered the actions he'd taken and, in some instances, *not* taken as chief. All he'd ever wanted to do was serve, and through that service help people while improving the job for his fellow firefighters. Chief was a title—a rank—and one he'd felt he'd earned through hard work, dedication, and experience. None of that seemed to matter in Abernathy. He'd always known he'd have to prove himself, but what he hadn't imagined was a fellow officer pushing back and an arsonist targeting him—bullying him—trying to get him to leave.

Lucas leaned forward and put his elbows on his knees, resting his head in his hands and closing his eyes. The quiet settled over him. His racing mind slowed, and peace gradually came over him.

Believe in yourself, Lucas. Trust your instincts. Let me guide you, and know I'm with you—always.

Lucas's head popped up. He looked around quickly, but saw no one except the funeral home attendant, pacing slowly beside the hearse. Lucas shook his head slightly. That voice had been so plain. He looked up and squinted into the bright sunshine and breathed in deeply. No—he knew where that voice had come from. It was the ultimate and true source of the strength that had sustained him through the years. He took a deep breath and closed his eyes. He once again felt the reassurance he'd momentarily lost—the reassurance that he'd have the inner strength and guidance he needed—no matter what the future might hold.

He looked over to the headstone where Mr. Andy's name was engraved and where soon Mrs. Garrett's would be. The inscription beneath their names read, "In Love—Forever."

He'd worried about what he would say today. He wanted to honor Mrs. Garrett the way she deserved to be honored by someone whose life she'd touched and changed forever in a few short months. And now, he knew exactly what to say.

JILL WATCHED LUCAS AS he talked with Mike Bentley and some other men she didn't recognize. Evidently, Lucas was just meeting them since Bentley looked to be performing introductions. Jill buried her chin inside the wool scarf she wore beneath her heavy overcoat and wrapped her arms more tightly around her. The air was frigid despite the bright sun.

The chairs beneath the awning were filling as was the standing room in the areas on either side of the tent. Katie Garrett's service was going to be attended above her expectation. Jill watched as more men who looked to be firefighters joined the group where Lucas stood. The crowd continued to grow, and Jill knew some of these, like Lucas, must be former students, all a testament to Katie's influence and inspiration. Jill saw those who must be Mrs. Garrett's family fill the first two rows. Lucas had mentioned she had a brother. He, his wife, their two sons, and their families were a nice-looking group.

Jill sat in the back row of the folding chairs where Lucas had asked her to save a seat for him. She smiled at him as he walked over.

He sat beside her and pointed toward the group of men he'd been talking to and turned to her with a smile. "After Mr. Andy's death, Mrs. Garrett became an advocate for firefighters fighting cancer. And would you believe some of those guys over there were at Station 2 when Mrs. Garrett's class went there on a field trip in second grade? Some even remembered that little boy who stuck to Mr. Andy's side the entire time." Lucas shook his head with a shaky grin and looked down.

Understanding the depth of emotion betrayed in that unsteady smile, Jill simply covered Lucas's hand with her gloved one.

The large crowd, already hushed, quietened even further when the minister took his place before them and opened the service with a prayer. One of Mrs. Garrett's nephews read her obituary, adding a few of his own thoughts and special memories of his aunt. Her other nephew spoke next, recalling some poignant memories of his Aunt Katie. Bentley read a selection from the Bible, and then it was Lucas's turn to speak.

Patting Jill's hand, Lucas stood, removed his overcoat, and handed it to Jill.

"It's so cold, Lucas. Don't you—" she whispered.

"No. I'm fine. The uniform will do her more honor," he replied softly.

Lucas walked to the front, the dry, brown grass crunching beneath his shiny black dress shoes. Jill was anxious to hear what Lucas would say. He'd mentioned needing help putting his talk together, but he'd only mentioned it once and never brought it up again. Mrs. Garrett's loss was extremely personal, and Jill knew what Lucas wanted to say was very important to him. She was confident what he said now would be perfect.

As Lucas took a spot near the casket, the breeze grew a bit stronger, causing the flowers on the casket to flutter and the awning of the tent to flap quietly. The caws of some jays flying past were carried on the breeze, leaving an even more serene silence in their wake.

Lucas cleared his throat and looked at both those seated in front of him, beneath the tent's awning and those standing at the sides. He glanced behind him at the oak casket, its polished brass handles and wood gleaming. The spray of delicate flowers on top, light pink roses, yellow daisies, and baby's breath symbolized perfectly the sweet essence of Katie Garrett.

"Mrs. Garrett was my second-grade teacher," Lucas began, his voice soft. "I had the privilege of being in her class for only a few months, but she, being the amazing person she was, changed the trajectory of my life forever in that time."

A sad smile on his face, Lucas reached into his jacket pocket and pulled out a piece of red paper. It was leaf shaped, and as he unfolded it, writing became visible on one side.

"This leaf was part of a bulletin board in Mrs. Garrett's classroom," Lucas said as he held it up. "She asked us to name the two things we were most thankful for, and then she wrote them on our leaves. When it came my turn, I said Mr. Andy and firetrucks, which she wrote on this leaf." He paused. "One of the words she wrote, I soon realized, was blurred by a tear. I didn't understand why she was so sad that day, but after I moved back to Abernathy, she explained."

Lucas held up the leaf once again. "The day we did this was the day after she'd learned of Mr. Andy's cancer diagnosis. In the middle of her fear for Mr. Andy and what their future might bring, she was there for her students, giving us something positive to hold onto. And I did. I've held onto this little leaf all these years. I've pulled it out many times as a reminder of her and what she inspired in me.

"Mrs. Garrett told me recently that she made it through the darkest and most difficult time of her life after Mr. Andy passed by drawing on the depth of the love they shared. She never stopped loving him as the engraving on their marker says, 'In Love—Forever,'" Lucas said with a gesture toward the marker.

"She said that in her grief, she'd felt like withdrawing, but instead, she embraced the fire service Mr. Andy loved so much. She became an advocate for firefighters and worked to create cancer awareness. She worked alongside her brother, Trenton, to help numerous firefighters dealing with cancer, she continued to teach school, and the list goes on, so I think it's fitting for us to say she loved fiercely and served mightily.

"From the size of the group here today, I'm sure it's safe to say that Mrs. Garrett's impact on lives—students, firefighters, friends, and family—continues. We all probably have or are examples of how she influenced and inspired those around her. As for me, thanks to Mr. Andy's influence, the fire service was my goal since second grade, and because of Mrs. Garrett's inspiration and encouragement to believe in myself, I made it through some difficult times and ultimately achieved my own goal to serve."

Mindful that those listening were fully aware of the recent events in Abernathy, Lucas continued, "We all have faced, will face, or are facing difficult times. We can look at Mrs. Garrett's life as our continuing inspiration and know that we, too, can find the strength, desire, and heart to make it through whatever trials we face. Hold on to that and have confidence that you'll have what you need when you need it most."

Lucas smiled and held up the little red leaf once again. Looking at it before looking back to those gathered on the frigid afternoon, he concluded, "Mrs. Garrett once told me I was Mr. Andy's legacy. I consider that a tremendous honor and a privilege, and I will carry it forward to the very best of my ability. I'll always be thankful for Mr. Andy and for firetrucks, but today—today—I'm *especially* thankful for Mrs. Garrett because she not only believed in me and encouraged me, but she also taught me the true potential for service that lives in all of us. Mrs. Garrett was the spark of inspiration that brought that potential to a blaze in my life, just as she's been the spark that brought potential to a blaze in a variety of ways in the lives of those here today. I think she would be pleased."

Lucas and Jill, along with Mike and Amy Bentley, had been invited by Trenton to join his family for lunch at their home after the service. It had been a nice opportunity to talk to Trenton and his wife, Stephanie, and to meet their two sons, Katie's nephews. It was a quiet but very gracious gathering, and they had been warmly welcomed. Lucas felt as if he had made a tremendous new advocate and friend in Trenton.

Jill hadn't said much since the service, but right before she got out of the SUV at home, she'd put a hand to his cheek and looked him deeply in the eyes for several seconds, her own eyes shining with tears.

"Lucas Matthews, sometimes I'm just in awe of you, and today is one of those times. What you said at the service today was perfect—absolutely perfect in every way. You wanted to give Katie the honor she deserved, and you did that and more. I know Katie would be—*is*—so proud."

Those words were ringing in Lucas's ears as he pulled into the admin parking lot early that afternoon. The place was practically deserted. Both the engine and truck were gone as was the battalion chief's vehicle. The only vehicle in the main parking lot was the fire marshal's Ennis drove and an SUV Lucas thought belonged to Riley Sullivan. Glancing at the dashboard clock with a frown, he read 2:03. Where was everyone at this time of the afternoon?

The cold wind had picked up even more since that morning, and he hurried inside. Where the offices were typically humming with voices and activity, they were now eerily quiet. No one was here, and that did not bode well.

Lucas walked to his office, slipping off his coat and uniform jacket, tossing them on the back of one of the guest chairs. He sat down slowly in his desk chair, glancing at the door several times, expecting someone—anyone—to pass by or speak.

He had just turned on his computer when he heard voices down the hall.

"He needs to know what's going on," Lucas heard Jeremy say, urgency in his voice. "I saw him pull in. We've got to tell him and now."

Alarmed, Lucas then heard Riley agree in hushed tones, "I agree, but are we the ones to tell him? It seems like this is something that should come from one of the deputy chiefs, not from those further down the command chain."

Lucas stood and walked to his office door. Stepping just outside, he saw Ennis and Sullivan standing a short distance down the hallway.

"Gentlemen, I suggest if you know what's going on and where everyone is, you share it with me—now."

Flinching, Jeremy and Riley exchanged a worried look and walked down the hall, following Lucas into his office. Lucas moved to stand behind his desk where he waited, his hands fisted on his hips, and his heart beginning to race.

"You tell him, Riley. I'm too angry," Jeremy said and began pacing.

Riley reluctantly began, and as he talked, the color drained from Lucas's face. He reached for the edge of his desk, gripping it so hard his knuckles turned white. He was angry. No. He was livid. Absolutely livid.

The afternoon sunlight was spilling into the room, but all Lucas could see was red. He could feel his pulse pounding in his ears.

"Who?" Lucas gritted out when Riley paused. "Who is spreading these lies?"

Riley glanced at Jeremy, who had stopped pacing and was running one hand down his face. Raising his head, he gave Riley a small, solemn nod.

Riley took a quick breath before saying, "Sir, we believe it started with Deputy Chief Carr."

"You believe, or you know?" Lucas asked, looking sharply between the two. "I need to know for certain."

"It's Deputy Chief Carr, sir. For certain," Jeremy confirmed. "We did some checking on our own when we started hearing the rumors and learned that Deputy Chief Carr has been at Six several times over the past month or two, talking to Captain McCracken in private each time. McCracken is a known gossip, and he took it from there. That's when the rumors started circulating. From what we've heard, it seems Carr thought if he could get rid of you, he would get your job and then name McCracken fire marshal in my place," Jeremy added.

"I see," Lucas said stiffly.

"They've made sure the entire department has heard at least one version or another of the rumors. A few of the guys are concerned, while a few others think it's too far in the past to matter, while others—the majority, I might add—don't believe it at all. Most are blowing it off, but coupled with these ongoing arsons, it's creating some anxiety and uncertainty throughout the department." Riley stopped briefly before adding, "Carr is taking advantage of it all to stir everyone up, sir, and . . . hold a vote of no confidence."

Riley looked uneasily from Lucas to Jeremy.

The clock on Lucas's desk chopped off several harsh, fraught seconds. A phone rang, unanswered somewhere.

"When does this vote of no confidence take place?" Lucas bit out as he straightened to his full height.

Several more seconds ticked by before Riley reluctantly answered. "It's happening right now, sir. Carr told everyone to report to the civic center."

Lucas rubbed the back of his neck with one hand, jamming his other hand into his pant pocket as he stared down at his desk. His look was fierce. He couldn't remember ever being this angry before. Ever. He wasn't just angry at Carr or at the situation, he was angry with himself. He should have addressed Carr's insubordination once and for all a long time ago. But now, he *had* to address the situation, and best to do it with everyone gathered. That way everyone would hear the same thing at the same time.

He had naively assumed his reputation with the Fort Collins Fire Department, the commendations he'd received, and the improvements already being seen and felt in the Abernathy Department would all count for something. But in the light of one man's ambition and deep-seated bitterness and frustration, something had been brought forward from Lucas's past and distorted into something that didn't even resemble the truth. Lies were being used against him, tarnishing his reputation both personally and professionally.

A thousand thoughts ran through his mind, but the one that snagged was the timely words of advice from Mr. Andy, *You'll never go wrong by doing right.*

It would be hard, but Lucas knew the right thing to do. He took a long, deep breath and exhaled slowly as Riley and Jeremy stood by waiting uncertainly. Lucas picked up the keys to the chief's vehicle and walked around the desk.

"I'm headed to the civic center. Would you gentlemen care to come with me?" Lucas asked, looking between the two.

"We'd be honored, sir," Riley said as Jeremy nodded emphatically.

Lucas paused as he reached the door. Turning, he looked at the two of them.

"Thank you—thank you both. I appreciate your honesty and loyalty. I've mentioned my story several times in passing, but that's just it—it's *my* story. I never thought there would be a reason the whole thing would ever need to be told—especially under these circumstances—but now, it looks like it does."

Lucas threw on his uniform jacket, grabbed his heavy coat, and walked resolutely out the door.

T HE EVENT HALL IN the Abernathy Civic Center was jammed with firefighters, all three shifts, as well as support staff. Lindsay wasn't sure how Deputy Chief Carr had managed to get everyone out of the stations, but doing it right now, as Chief Matthews attended a funeral, was an especially low move on Deputy Chief Carr's part. It was also dangerous to gather an entire branch of emergency services at any time as it could potentially lengthen response time on any calls, but it was most especially dangerous with an arsonist on the loose.

The room was crowded; the hastily assembled rows of stiff, uncomfortable chairs were jammed close together without much leg room between rows. The air in the room was hot and dry. The palpable tension and uncertainty made it even hotter. The smell of food from an event earlier in the day lingered in the air.

Lindsay sat in the front row, along with the other administrative assistants, who looked as confused and upset as she felt. Deputy Chief Carr stood behind the podium and with an air of self-importance, was carefully laying out what were basically unsubstantiated claims and insinuations against Chief Matthews. On the heels of his comments, Carr said the matter warranted a vote of no confidence in the Chief, a move Lindsay could tell took not only her but everyone by surprise if the low murmurs and nervous shuffling throughout the room were any indication. Carr, unrelenting in his efforts, persisted, until it became evident that he was pushing for an immediate vote.

Lindsay listened, her anger building. She didn't want anything to do with this. She felt as if she, the other administrative assistants, and probably the rest of the department, had been tricked into coming if the rumblings she'd heard as everyone filed into the room were an indication. Most everyone had been as oblivious to why they had been called here as she had been.

On the other hand, Lindsay thought she needed to stay, so she would know what Carr said and be able to tell Chief Matthews exactly what had happened. Lindsay knew from working with Chief Matthews that what Carr was saying wasn't true. It couldn't be true in spite of how loudly Carr was railing. She and most of the rest of the department had heard rumors circulating but had not seen this coming—especially a step of this severity.

Deputy Chief Carr was speaking passionately, expounding on the defamatory information he'd accumulated on Chief Matthews. Carr was in the middle of assuring everyone that they, the rank and file of the Abernathy Fire Department, could take the important first step toward Chief Matthews' removal by holding a vote of no confidence today when he suddenly stopped mid-sentence. Carr's eyes grew wide, when something caught his eye in the back of the room.

Everyone turned in unison to see what had snagged Carr's attention and sucked in a collective gasp, followed immediately by deathly silence.

Still in his dress uniform, its brass buttons gleaming under the bright lights, Chief Lucas Matthews stood just inside the door, surveying the room as several breathless heartbeats passed. Slowly, purposefully, he walked up the center aisle, glancing from side to side, noting the familiar faces on each row. Most were reluctant to meet his gaze, and others avoided eye contact altogether. As he approached the front of the room, his focus shifted from the firefighters to the lone figure of Deputy Chief Carr, who seemed rooted to the floor behind the podium, his mouth gaping awkwardly.

Reaching the end of the aisle, Lucas stopped and, looking Carr in the eye, said, "Please, Deputy Chief, go on. You were saying?" Lucas casually stepped to the side and sat in an empty chair on the front row while Riley and Jeremy, who had followed him through the back door, moved to stand against the back wall. Lucas's casualness was forced; his insides were roiling as he fought to keep himself and his temper intact.

Carr's face turned red and beads of perspiration broke out on his forehead and upper lip as he bristled, fumbling with his notes on the podium.

"I'm finished, sir," Carr mumbled, crunching the papers together and quickly taking a seat on the far side of the row from Lucas.

The silence hung heavy and thick. The only sound was the powerful north wind of an approaching cold front hurtling against the outside doors. No one stirred. The anxiety in the room was like a living, breathing being.

Lucas waited, feeling the tension in the room building as hundreds of eyes bored into his back. On the drive over, he'd gotten his initial anger under control, but being here now and seeing what Carr was putting these good people through made him angry all over again. Everyone was here, and he needed to refute the lies that had been told. He was their leader, and they deserved to know the truth, but that truth meant telling a very personal story; one he thought he'd put behind him long ago. He hadn't tried to hide it; he'd dealt with it in his nightmares and moved on. But now, he was compelled to set the record straight.

Lucas took a deep breath and closed his eyes briefly before standing and moving to the podium. As he looked at the group, he slowly surveyed the apprehensive faces staring back at him. He knew these faces now along with most of the stories behind each one. He'd made a point of learning about each one's desire to become a firefighter, his reasons, and the importance of what the job meant to him. They were giving him their best, and he wanted to give them his reassurance, honesty, and clarity in return.

Lucas placed one hand casually on the podium, its trembling barely noticeable while he pushed his other hand into his pants pocket to take hold of Mr. Andy's badge.

Clearing his throat, Lucas began, "I understand you have heard some things about my past—rumors being spread about me. From everything I've heard, what you have been told is false and might be considered borderline slander."

Lucas stopped and looked pointedly at Deputy Chief Carr, who attempted to look defiant but only succeeded in looking like he'd been caught red handed.

Lucas chuckled humorlessly. "I have heard outrageous stories. Stories such as I dealt drugs in high school. I've also heard that I was arrested, put on trial, and managed somehow to turn the tables on my dealers, getting them convicted while I got off scot-free. I've even heard that I was so addicted to drugs that I overdosed and nearly died." He paused and looked across the group once more, adding, "I can assure you while some of the facts individually may be correct, the overall narrative is not."

Deputy Chief Carr, his head down, shifted nervously in his seat.

Lucas went on. "While I don't like having to share my personal story under these types of circumstances, I want to share it with you now because you deserve for me to be completely honest and transparent."

Lucas took a deep breath, exhaling slowly before beginning.

"My father was in the Army. He died in a base training accident when I was in first grade. Afterward, my mom and I moved continually, only in one place for a few months at a time. One of the places we landed was here in Abernathy where I met a firefighter named Andy Garrett. His wife, Katie Garrett, was my second-grade teacher. In fact, her funeral was just a few hours ago. That's where I was when this assembly was called.

"Andy inspired me and planted the seed of a dream in me to become a firefighter—just like him. Those few months in Abernathy were the best I'd ever had, but my mom and I moved again, and shortly after that move, my mom died. It was at that time I was placed in the foster care system and went from one placement to another. Let me assure you, being a foster kid is not a fun experience.

"When I started another new school—a middle school—I was bullied by three boys, who for some reason, found pleasure in making my life miserable. They did me a favor, though, because through one of their beatings, I was introduced to a permanent foster family, which changed my life. They gave me a real home about the time I entered high school, but unfortunately, the bullying continued. Those same three bullies decided I was going to help them place Fentanyl in the drinking water of an opposing football team. When I refused, they forced the drug down my throat instead and left me to die on the field house floor."

Lucas looked down and paused for several heartbeats. He could hear throats clearing and an uneasy rustling move across the room. He tapped his fingers lightly on the podium and finally looked up.

"And you know, they very nearly succeeded. If not for an amazing campus resource officer, I wouldn't be here. I spent several days in the hospital, and it took a while to get my strength back and my life to return to normal. When it came time for their trial, I was asked to testify against them. They were sentenced to life with eligibility for parole at age seventy-five."

Lucas straightened to his full height and, individually meeting the eye of as many firefighters as he could, said, "I promise each of you as I stand here and look at you, that those drugs were the only drugs that have ever entered my system, and they were forced on me most unwillingly. I have never dealt drugs and have never had the desire to take them."

Lucas took a deep breath and continued in a slightly lighter tone. "You've heard that saying, 'the rest of the story,' and, well, this is mine. Those few months I lived here in Abernathy set the direction of my life. Firefighter Andy Garrett, whose picture hangs in the TV room at Two, and his wife, Katie, my second grade teacher, not only gave me the dream of becoming a firefighter, but also planted in me the essential seed of believing in myself—the belief that I could, and would, achieve what I set my heart on doing.

"Because Andy shared his love of the fire service with me, it was my dream from that point on to become a firefighter. It was also my dream to come back to Abernathy as an officer and surprise him and Mrs. Garrett. I wanted to make them proud of me and of what they'd inspired in me. When I returned, I learned that Andy had died from work-related cancer just a few months after my mom and I had moved. I never even knew he was sick. He made sure the times we were together were always good for me—a little second grade kid he'd just met. To me, as that little kid and still today as a Chief, that is what being a firefighter means—looking out for others and for each other."

Stepping behind the beat-up old podium, Lucas subtly took hold of its worn top, suddenly feeling lightheaded. Willing the room to stop tilting, he forced himself to go on. "I'm sure most of you have heard of the Back of the Bay effort. It's training—pushing yourself and another, not individually, but together, to motivate and encourage each other to become the best version of ourselves we can be. Back of the Bay is about having standards, accountability, culture—and the brotherhood.

"It's about encouraging a brother, being the brother you said you'd be, and being a part of something bigger than yourself. I hope you'll remember that and know that I'm here, not only leading you, but beside you, pushing and encouraging each of you as you push and encourage me. We are stronger together—not driven apart."

Lucas paused and took a deep breath.

"Well, I've said my piece and provided you with the facts. I entrust this vote into your hands. I will accept the consequences either way. I have faith in you and in the brotherhood. But take it quickly and get back to your stations and to the service and protection of the City of Abernathy and its citizens."

LUCAS WALKED UP THE aisle, retracing his steps out of the room. He didn't stop until he went through the back door and into the biting cold north wind outside. The sudden cold felt good and helped to clear his lightheadedness. His cheeks were hot, and his heart was racing, but he felt at peace about what he had shared and how he'd shared it. He had succeeded in speaking from the heart and not from anger. If the vote went against him, so be it. He'd given it his very best.

The door banged open behind him as Riley and Jeremy hurried out. They stopped short, seeing him, questioning looks on their faces.

"You all right, Chief?" Jeremy asked hesitantly.

Lucas tried to smile and respond but nothing came out. He was spent.

"Chief, that's the most inspiring speech I've ever heard in my life," Riley said earnestly. "If that doesn't touch every last person in there, I don't know them like I thought I did."

"Thanks, Sullivan. Thanks, Ennis," Lucas finally managed to say. "You both need to get back in there and cast your vote. Who knows, yours may be the only two I get." Lucas managed a weak smile. "I'm headed back to the office. I'd appreciate an update."

Riley and Jeremy exchanged a puzzled look.

"Sir, we don't want to . . ." Riley began, gesturing to the closed door behind him.

Lucas put a hand on each of their shoulders and steered them toward the door.

"No. Please. Go. I'll see you at the office later."

Lucas turned and walked away as Riley and Jeremy watched. They saw him climb into his vehicle and, after a few minutes, drive away, maneuvering the chief's SUV through the parking lot crowded with fire apparatus from across the city. Exchanging a look, they walked inside, determined to defend Chief Matthews with everything they had.

Lucas pulled into the empty admin parking lot for the second time that day. His instruction had been for all personnel to get back to their stations quickly, but he had no way of knowing how long the meeting at the civic center would last. He just knew he had work to do and needed something to occupy his mind. The bitter north wind cut through him as he hurried inside. The wind was getting stronger, causing the flags outside the building to snap sharply.

Christmas lights in the hall continued to blink merrily even though the offices were dark and empty. The hall was quiet and in places dim where some of the automatic lights had shut off due to lack of activity. He walked past Lindsay's empty desk. He'd seen her in the front row when he'd stood and faced everyone. She'd had a pained and sympathetic look on her face, but after he'd spoken, he'd caught her smiling, which was gratifying. He hated the difficulty and distress Carr had caused for the department.

As he sat at his desk, there was one thing Lucas needed to do before anything else. He pulled a small key from his pocket and sliding it into the lock in the left-hand desk drawer, he gently turned the key. Opening the drawer, he reached inside and pulled out the personnel file he'd started for Milton Carr. He quickly thumbed through hard copies he'd made of the memos and emails which were also saved on his computer. He always wanted hard copies on hand if needed. He opened a blank document on his computer and began typing, detailing the events of the day. Either he, depending on the vote being held right now, or Kirk Lorimar would dismiss Carr. There was no way someone so divisive, conniving, manipulative, and self-serving could remain and be an effective leader after today.

Lucas was just finishing the details of what he'd heard and witnessed at the civic center along with a general outline of what he'd shared when his radio went off. With the offices so quiet, Lucas jumped reflexively. He could hear the tones going off in the empty bay at Station 1 next door, their echoes bouncing off the cinder block walls. Jumping up, he grabbed his radio along with his jacket and started toward the back door and his vehicle.

Zipping his coat, he instinctively began to walk faster until his steps faltered when he heard the address—the Abernathy High School gymnasium. His mind jumped immediately to the holiday tournament in progress. The gym, as well as the parking lot, would be packed with people and cars, coming and going.

Lucas jumped into the SUV and started the engine. Turning up the heater, he rubbed his hands together for warmth as he listened closely as the first apparatus arrived on scene, confirming a structure fire with flames and heavy smoke showing. The next call was for a two, and then finally a three-alarm fire, the highest alarm possible. Lucas slammed the SUV into gear, squealing his tires out of the parking lot, as he flipped on his lights and siren and flew down Abernathy's streets to the high school. If this was the work of the arsonist—he couldn't finish that thought. He just had to get there.

Tones continued to sound across the radio. It seemed like almost every apparatus was being dispatched. Radio traffic was heavy, everyone aware a large structure was involved with the potential need for mass casualty operations. Lucas had to admit; it was providential that the entire department was at the civic center, which was only a couple of blocks from the high school. That proximity made their arrival much faster than it would have been if apparatus and crews had had to come from across the city. Sending a quick prayer heavenward, Lucas gripped the steering wheel tighter as he sped to the gym.

W HEN HE TURNED THE corner and could see the gym, Lucas blinked and then swallowed hard. What he saw was worse than he'd imagined. He slowed, cutting his siren but leaving his lights on, as a police officer motioned him through a barricade, holding up a section of perimeter tape being installed to keep onlookers out. Lucas parked his vehicle a distance from the active fire ground but close enough to access it quickly.

Billows of black smoke were roiling at the headwall near the roof line of the gym with occasional flames licking out angrily. Heavy flames were visible lower, smoke pouring from every crevice and opening in the structure. Three banks of doors across the front of the gym stood open with a constant stream of people materializing, bringing with them heavy clouds of black smoke.

The parking lot was full of people flowing around parked cars or people in their cars trying to leave while fire apparatus maneuvered against the flow, attempting to get close to the structure. People filed past, their faces black from smoke, some crying, some screaming with fright, and some searching, yelling out names of family or friends.

While keeping an eye on the different fire apparatus making their way closer to the gym, Lucas opened his gear's storage compartment at the back of the SUV. Pulling on his bunker gear, he quickly zipped up the front of his jacket before lifting the radio strap over his head. He hefted his air pack over his other shoulder and pulled on his helmet. He slammed the door closed and started toward the middle of the parking lot where it looked like Battalion Chief Forney was managing to set up a command area.

As Lucas made his way toward Forney, side stepping the throngs of people flowing past him, he studied the gym, analyzing it for best access and attack. It sat at the back of a large parking lot with another sizable parking area on the Delta, or right side, a cafeteria was on the Bravo, or left side, with a small, connected classroom wing just beyond. The smaller parking lot was filled with school buses while the larger parking lot he was crossing was filled to capacity with cars jammed wherever a space was large enough. Cars trying to leave the parking lot were creating congestion, their horns honking frantically as people tried to leave but were blocked by approaching fire apparatus or were being turned around by police not allowing vehicles to leave should this be a crime scene. It looked and sounded like something from an apocalyptic movie.

The air was thick with smoke, making it difficult to see as well as to breathe. Sparks were darting about like fireflies, whipped by the strong winds. The possibility these sparks might catch surrounding areas on fire was an additional worry. The wailing of sirens filled the air as fire and police units continued to arrive. Officers hurried through the crowd, trying to help those who needed assistance, taking them to the triage area paramedics were hastily setting up at the back of the parking lot. Frightened screams and shouts of panic continued to be heard over the roar of the flames and the diesel engines of the fire apparatus.

Finally reaching the command area, Lucas came to a stop by Forney who was radioing deployment commands one quickly after another. They acknowledged each other with a brief nod as Lucas heard Riley's and Carl Chastain's voices responding over the radio. Lucas could tell by the commands Forney was issuing that he had prioritized victim evacuation over fire suppression. Firefighters were deployed inside and were clearing the structure; people were flowing rapidly from the building.

With fire suppression the next priority, Forney was already preparing for that phase by deploying units on all three accessible sides of the structure for fastest approach. Lucas was thankful to have all three battalion chiefs on scene. Effective deployment was crucial, and the full parking lot and the crowd surging from the gym were making it slow and difficult. Forney was adjusting personnel and equipment quickly as the fluid situation demanded.

Lucas studied the fire ground and nodded to himself. Forney was commanding the situation exactly as he would have. A stray frustrating doubt flashed through Lucas's mind. Would Forney have the same level of confidence in him if the roles were reversed? Lucas's mind raced on, and he couldn't help wondering about the results from the vote of confidence. *Did* he have the confidence of the department's personnel? Finding himself in the situation of leading a group of men he wasn't sure had confidence in him was totally foreign to him, and he couldn't help but wonder if that were the case, especially with a massive incident to work.

When there was a brief lull in radio traffic, Forney stepped toward Lucas, and looking Lucas in the eye said, "Sir, per ICS, I'm designating you Safety Officer."

Lucas swallowed hard and nodded curtly. "Copy that, Forney."

When Forney stepped away, lifting his radio to transmit additional orders, Lucas took a deep breath. If Forney still had enough confidence in him to designate him as Safety Officer on an incident this size, it was a good sign. As Safety Officer, Lucas had free reign to do whatever he deemed necessary on the fireground overall as the situation evolved and developed. Or, Lucas thought, maybe it was just a show of respect, but also a way to keep Lucas out of the way?

Frustration surged through Lucas. He had never doubted himself or been doubted by others as a firefighter or as a fire officer, and now, not knowing what those in his command thought of him seemed surreal. But, this situation was reality at its harshest, and it needed his full professional attention.

Lucas nodded to paramedics and EMT's as they passed, shepherding those needing medical assistance toward the triage area. All in all, everything was moving quickly, being deployed and set up rapidly.

Lucas watched the scene and listened closely to the radio traffic, pacing agitatedly as he splashed through water already covering the ground. If there was the least hope of saving any part of the gym complex, they needed to get this under control quickly.

Flames were leaping from every opening and the roar and snaps of the fire were growing louder and louder. A group of officers hurried up, Riley and Jeremy included, awaiting additional deployment orders from Forney, the seriousness of the situation evident on every face.

As Forney began relaying his change in deployment orders, Lucas straightened, hearing something familiar, and quickly turned toward the gym. He'd heard that sound before at another structure fire—metal groaning a few minutes before the second floor of an abandoned office building had collapsed on two firefighters—two friends.

"Forney, call for an emergency evacuation—NOW!" Lucas yelled toward Forney over the din. "Signal for evacuation. Get everyone out of the building."

Forney turned to Lucas, surprised, but quickly issued the order over the radio, repeating it twice as an alternating air horn and siren blared from every apparatus, adding to the cacophony of noise. Firefighters began pouring out of the building, carrying hose and bringing more smoke with them.

Lucas heard it right before it happened. There was another loud groan and then a screech of metal as the gym's roof collapsed with a thunderous crash, sending a large cloud of smoke and dust into the air, huge flames swelling into the sky. Forney turned and looked at Lucas in amazement.

"Is everyone accounted for?" Lucas asked quickly.

"PAR. I need a PAR," Forney hastily radioed as the officers who'd approached scattered, radioing their teams.

One by one the reports came in as the officers returned to the command area, gathering near Forney.

Forney turned to Lucas. "I don't know how you knew that collapse was about to happen, but everyone is accounted for. The PAR is complete. Thank you, sir."

Lucas nodded grimly. "Experience, Forney. I've heard that warning sound before."

Forney nodded, a lingering look of appreciation on his face before he turned from Lucas and back to those gathering around him.

Unfortunately, the structure was now too far gone to go safely inside, so personnel and apparatus needed to be redirected. The priority now was to make sure everyone known to have been inside had been evacuated and were accounted for and then save as much of the building as possible.

"We're going defensive," Forney said, looking at the group.

As Forney was completing the assignments, a breathless figure, his face darkened with soot, ashes in his hair and covering a police uniform, suddenly appeared at the edge of the circle. His eyes were wide as he frantically scanned the circle of firefighters.

"Riley!" the ash-covered figure yelled into the din when he spotted him.

Hearing Riley's name, both Riley and Jeremy turned. As Lucas watched, they broke away from the circle and moved quickly toward the unrecognizable figure who was bent double, gasping for air. Lucas started toward him as well and, as he grew closer, realized it was Cade Marshall.

Breathless, Cade spluttered, "I . . . I couldn't reach them. They . . . the mascot dribblers for Abernathy's team were waiting in the locker room . . . until after . . . after the warm-ups, and now . . . I couldn't . . . I couldn't get to the locker room. Please . . . you gotta try to reach them."

Riley took hold of Cade's arm to get his attention. "How many, Cade? How many are there?"

Cade, still trying to catch his breath, managed, "Four, maybe five, but four . . . four for sure."

Lucas looked toward the building. Cade had given him a cursory tour of the gym complex when they'd first started talking about security for the tournament. The locker rooms and several small classrooms were separated from the gym by a wide, connecting corridor. That corridor and the locker rooms might still be intact and navigable.

Cracks, another loud crash, and a sudden roar caused frenzied screams from those who had exited the gym and were now watching from behind the safety perimeter. The large group of onlookers gasped and shrank back, shadows from the flames dancing across their frightened faces. Police officers worked to keep everyone outside the cordoned area as the black and yellow tape marking the boundary popped in the cold wind.

At the sound of the crash, all heads turned toward the building. Another part of the roof had caved in and tall plumes of smoke and fire were shooting through the new hole, adding to the black cloud of smoke enveloping the entire area. The ladder truck immediately began adjusting its extended ladder toward the new threat as Riley and Jeremy turned their attention back to Cade who had disappeared.

Scanning the area frantically, Jeremy yelled and pointed. "There! He's headed back to the gym!"

Lucas looked to where Jeremy was pointing and saw Cade running toward a small door situated at the far left of the main doors of the gym. That door led to the corridor between the gym and locker room. Firefighters were swarming the area, putting water on as much of the building as possible. Cade managed to side-step them and disappeared inside.

Riley and Jeremy had already pulled on their hoods and were putting on their helmets, preparing to follow Cade, when Forney motioned them back to the group. Lucas watched as Riley and Jeremy looked at each other, their eyes widening, looking frantically from Forney to the gym.

Understanding the quickly intensifying situation, Lucas stepped to Forney's side as the other officers moved away to implement their assignments. "Forney, attach me, Ennis, and Sullivan to the Rapid Intervention Team that's standing by, designate it as activated for Officer Marshall, and change the designation to Rescue. We'll include a standard search with an expanded mission scope for the four potential victims on the Bravo side."

"Copy that, sir," Forney agreed with a quick nod. He quickly gave the necessary orders to Captain Calhoun, the RIT team officer.

"Chief Matthews, you are designated rescue. Captain Calhoun, you are now entry control. Switch communications to TAC 4."

"Copy that," came in quick succession from Lucas and Calhoun over the radio.

"Forney, protect Bravo side as long as you can. Have paramedics standing by. Those boys have been in there for a while."

"Copy that, Chief."

Riley stepped toward the gym, anxious to get started while Lucas hastily scanned the growing crowd. He lifted his air pack onto his shoulders and pushed his arms through the straps, pulling them tight. Pulling his hood on, Lucas turned to Jeremy, saying, "Ennis, you're coming with me and Sullivan, but just as soon as we're done, I want you scanning this crowd and taking pictures—a lot of pictures. I have a feeling our arsonist is out there, watching all of this, and I want him. But right now, let's get to Marshall and the others."

"Yes, sir," Jeremy said, cutting an anxious look toward the growing crowd.

Reaching for his mask, Lucas fit it firmly to his face before slipping his helmet on. Cinching the chin strap tight, Sullivan and Ennis were completing the same procedure. Each took tools the Rapid Intervention Team handed them and moved toward the doorway where Cade had disappeared.

The air pack felt heavy on Lucas's back, but the mask and hood felt familiar. Even though Lucas worked out regularly, entering the dark, smoke-filled interior was a bit intimidating, considering the number of years that had passed since he'd done it. It felt even stranger to be entering a burning structure without a charged hose, but time was of the essence. Feeling another bout of lightheadedness, he fought to slow his breathing to a more normal rate.

Riley took the lead as they entered, followed closely by Lucas and

Jeremy, who closed the exterior door behind them to cut off the flow path feeding oxygen to the fire. Lucas, carrying the tag line rope, tied it to the exterior door and gave Riley a nod to move forward.

Thankfully, Riley was familiar with the layout of the building and moved directly toward a doorway Lucas wouldn't have known was there. The space immediately grew smaller, and Lucas realized they'd left the large corridor and entered a smaller hallway into the locker room. An orange glow visible ahead let them know they were approaching the end of the hall—and the fire.

The space opened up as they entered the locker room, and in the dense haze, their flashlights played across a figure on the floor. Riley pulled on the figure's shoulder, and Cade rolled over, looking up at them, coughing and bleary-eyed. When he saw them, Cade scooted back a short distance, revealing two little boys curled beneath him. Both the boys and Cade were coughing and gasping for air. Unable to speak, Cade held up three fingers and pointed further into the room that was shadowed but quickly growing brighter from encroaching flames.

Lucas handed one of the boys to Jeremy, and Cade picked up the other. Jeremy, wrapping an arm around Cade, half carried, half dragged him as the four slowly started back the way they had just come, following the tag line rope Lucas had unrolled. Lucas and Riley turned and moved forward.

A few steps further and they saw the fire beginning to lick through the wall in front of them, quickly turning it into a bright wall of orange flames. Two other walls of the locker room had holes burning through them, the fire greedily and quickly increasing their size. The heat in the room had increased significantly, and Lucas could feel sweat trickling down his back and face, stinging as it got into his eyes.

Sweeping his flashlight across the floor as they navigated around a long set of lockers, Riley suddenly stopped. He pointed to the right where two figures together and a third a short distance away lay prone on the floor, their little bodies illuminated by the beams from the flashlights and the flickering shadows of the flames. Riley stopped and picked up first one, then the second, little boy. Breathing heavily, Lucas stepped around Riley and moved to the third figure. Picking him up, he cradled the boy in his arms and made his way back to where Riley waited, holding a boy on each shoulder. Lucas picked up the tag line rope and led the way out, Riley following, as they quickly retraced their steps through the narrow hallway, the smoke having lowered significantly; visibility practically nonexistent.

Opening the door, they stepped outside, handing the unconscious boys to waiting paramedics. Dizzy, Lucas eased off his mask, helmet, and hood and walked slowly behind Riley to the command area. Stopping at the back of a nearby engine, he kept his back to the group, his head down, bracing himself with one hand and waited until the dizziness slowly passed. He didn't know what was causing these spells, but he was ready for them to stop.

Taking deep breaths, he turned back to the command area where Riley was talking to Forney and getting his next assignment. Jeremy was nowhere to be seen. Lucas slipped off his air pack and leaned it against the tire of the engine. After his brief conversation with Forney, Riley was in the process of changing his air tank out for a fresh one, when Jeremy hurried up.

"Paramedics say Cade's got some pretty bad smoke inhalation, but he's going to be fine. The boys are a bit more problematic as they're smaller and took in more smoke, but the paramedics are getting them all ready to transport them to the hospital. The boys' parents were already waiting at triage, so they'll be with them."

"We'd never have known those boys were there if not for Cade," Riley said as he hoisted his air pack back on. "With so many people . . ." His voice trailed off. "I just hope we've found everyone."

"The teams made a pretty thorough sweep of the gym area before the roof collapse but with the size of this crowd, it will be a matter of time before we know everyone is accounted for on scene or transported to the hospital," Lucas said as he put his helmet back on.

Turning to Jeremy, Lucas asked, "Photos?"

"It took a while at triage, but I'm off to take more now," Jeremy patted his bunker coat pocket containing the camera. "And I've talked to the school's security officer, who will be pulling camera footage. He wasn't sure how soon they'd be able to get it to us with all of this," Jeremy gestured around them. "But he did say it would be as fast as they could."

"Good. If this is the work of the arsonist, this will be our best chance to get some conclusive evidence," Lucas said, his lips set in a grim line.

Another wave of dizziness swept over him, and he reached out to steady himself with a hand against the back of the engine.

Jeremy stepped close and took Lucas's arm. "Chief, you all right?"

"I'm fine, Ennis. Thanks." Lucas felt hot despite the frigid late-afternoon air. He pulled uncomfortably at his bunker coat and wiped a hand across his sweaty forehead.

Jeremy studied him for a few seconds longer, glancing at Riley who was frowning as he looked at Lucas with concern.

His head clearing slightly, Lucas turned to Jeremy as Riley stepped away. "Check in with Forney. It looks like things are getting under control, but he may need some additional manpower, but Ennis—only after photos."

Jeremy nodded and, pulling the camera from his pocket headed discreetly toward the onlookers.

Lucas watched as the firefighters he'd come to know over the last several months worked the scene professionally and easily in tandem. Did they realize just how well they worked together? How did they see *him*? Did they see him as a part of their team or as someone they didn't have confidence in to lead them? Had he shown them *he* was the man to lead them? Had he done . . . enough?

Lucas stayed with Forney at the command center and watched as the situation gradually came under control. It was close to midnight when the last of the flames were extinguished and the confirmation came that everyone who had been in the gym was accounted for and safe. A miracle Lucas was very thankful for. The mop-up operation was well underway and would continue during the night with several units assigned to stay until morning to make sure all hot spots or anything that re-ignited would be tapped out.

Lucas stared across the smoldering pile of rubble where the high school gym had stood just hours before and shook his head. An occasional crash could be heard from somewhere within the debris when something else gave way. Now that the winds had calmed, acrid smoke floated in the air and hovered before slowly dissipating. They had been lucky that in spite of the wind, no other structures had caught fire, but what a waste this was. What a disheartening night.

It was a terrible loss at the hands of a sick mind. What possible motivation would make someone cause such destruction to school property that would affect the lives of so many students. It would be at least a couple of years before a new gym could be rebuilt and operational. What would that mean to those in high school now or those in youth programs who wouldn't have its use. Lucas shook his head at what this loss meant for the entire community. Jeremy hadn't found anything that linked this fire to the arsonist—at least not yet, and Lucas sincerely hoped they wouldn't. Maybe this was just a tragic and untimely accident.

"Chief," Forney said, coming up behind Lucas. "Looks like everything is under control. It took a while, but I think we're there."

"Job well done, Forney," Lucas said, putting a hand on Forney's shoulder, partly to steady himself and partly as a gesture of commendation. "That was quite the operation."

"Thank you, Chief. That's the largest fire I've commanded. It was certainly a challenge, but I have to say, the recent changes implemented made a notable difference in the ease of communication and operations flow. Having all three battalion chiefs on scene was something that's never happened before, but the communications system worked well."

Forney surveyed the rubble and shook his head sadly. "The loss of property is certainly regrettable, especially for the students. I'm just thankful there were only slight injuries and no fatalities in all of this. There's a blessing to be found no matter the circumstances, I suppose."

Forney paused and looked at Lucas with a tired smile. "It's times like these, that you give it your all . . . and then some. I think we can all say we did that tonight, can't we? Good night, sir." Forney nodded and stepped away.

Lucas brightened at what Forney had said. Maybe he was having an impact after all. As he turned to leave, the thought Forney left with him went through his mind. "There's a blessing to be found no matter the circumstances." That was a good way to end such a sad and bleak night. It was always best to look at things in a positive light. With the confidence vote still hanging over him, Lucas wondered if it was possible to spin a vote of no confidence by those in your command into something positive. Taking a deep breath, he removed his helmet and ran his fingers through his hair. He shook his head as he retrieved his air pack and hoisted it onto his shoulder before tucking his helmet under his arm.

Lucas started toward his vehicle. As he made his way across the parking lot, still filled with cars, he nodded his acknowledgments to those securing the area as well as those who would be there through the night checking hot spots. His steps slowed the closer he got to his SUV, and it became difficult to walk, his legs growing heavy. He saw Jill waiting beside his vehicle. How long had she been waiting? he wondered. She looked worried but smiled and waved when she saw him coming.

Lucas tried to wave in return, but just like his legs, his arm felt heavy too. Jill's image blurred, and he blinked several times, trying to clear his vision as darkness crept in at the edges. There was a sudden roaring in his ears as the darkness grew thicker, finally engulfing him as Lucas's legs buckled beneath him. He never knew when he hit the ground.

JILL SAW LUCAS COLLAPSE, and in that moment, everything began to move in slow motion. She watched his white helmet roll to the side with a muted clatter, his air pack falling from his shoulder, hitting the ground with a thud that reverberated like an explosion through her. Her vision narrowed, and all Jill could see was Lucas on the ground, not moving. She wanted to scream, and for a brief instant, she couldn't move, but in the next heartbeat, she was running to him. Running like she'd never run before.

J ILL SAT, ROCKING GENTLY in the hospital room's lone guest chair, her arms clasped tightly around her. Lucas hadn't woken since he collapsed hours ago. They'd just taken him for more tests, and now she was sitting alone in the empty room. The chair's plastic creaked beneath her as she continued to rock. The beeps and hums from the monitors that had been attached to Lucas were silent for now until they brought him back. The doctors weren't sure, or at least weren't telling her, what they thought might be wrong. They didn't seem overly concerned. They just kept running tests.

Jon and Jessica had called a little after midnight, and for the first time ever, she hadn't answered their call. She was terrified and upset and didn't want to scare them too until she had more to tell them. Even though she would have welcomed family being with her, she also didn't want to scare Coach and Patsy and raise an alarm without having more information. She didn't feel alone though. One of the nurses had told her at some point during the night that there was a large number of firefighters in the waiting room, and they'd asked that Jill be notified they were there in case she needed anything—anything at all. It was a comfort to know they were there.

She stood and began nervously pacing the width of the hospital room, back and forth, back and forth. Noise from the hall filtered in through the open door as nurses, doctors, and orderlies moved up and down the hall, talking as they tended other patients and made their rounds. The room seemed large without the hospital bed, the floor around where the bed had sat was littered with strips of paper and small bits of the plastic packaging the nurses had used to attach IV, monitors and tubes to Lucas when they'd brought him upstairs from the emergency room. That empty space where Lucas's hospital bed had been reflected what her heart was feeling without him near, she thought. Empty.

She swiped at a stray tear and was just about to sit back down when Jon and Jessica suddenly appeared in the doorway, rushing in and grabbing their mother up into a fierce hug.

"Mom! We tried to call . . . We saw on the news . . ." They both started talking at the same time as the three stood in the middle of the room, holding onto each other tightly.

Jill tried to stop them, but the pent-up sobs and tears escaped, and she began to shake with their force. The twins exchanged a terrified look over their mother's head, never having seen their mother like this.

"Mom, we're here," Jon said soothingly. "It's okay. We're here."

Jill stopped and took a deep breath. Pulling back, she looked at their two young, frightened faces through watery eyes. She put a hand to their cheeks, still cold from the brisk wind blowing outside, and did her best to smile.

"I'm so sorry, kids," she said, brushing the tears away with a sniff. "It's just been a long night. What time is it?" Jill glanced at the window, and even though the blinds were shut, a tiny bit of light was beginning to come through.

"It's a little after 7:00," Jessica said, rubbing her mother's back.

"And what are you two doing here when you're supposed to be at school?" Jill asked, blowing her nose into a crumpled tissue.

Jon looked at her with a quirk in his brow. "Seriously, Mom. The Abernathy High School gym burning was big news last night and when you or Dad didn't answer your phones? Well, we hit the road as soon as we could. We called the fire department's emergency number to try and reach Dad. All they would tell us is that the Fire Chief had had a medical emergency, so we figured the hospital would be the best place to start. When we told them we were the Chief's kids at the desk downstairs, they gave us this room number. There were a lot of firefighters down there too, and when they heard us ask about Dad, they came over to talk to us. They're all concerned too."

"Mom?" Jessica asked hesitantly, glancing at the space where the hospital bed was supposed to be. "Where *is* Dad?"

Jill wiped her cheeks and, taking one of their hands in each of her own, said, "Your father collapsed last night at the gym's fire scene and hasn't woken since. They brought him here immediately and while they don't think he's in any danger, they're not sure what caused the collapse. They've been running all kinds of tests and have taken him to run more. They should be bringing him back any minute."

Jon and Jessica exchanged a look of uncertainty. Alarm on their faces.

Jill sighed, looking at them, as she wiped her nose with the fresh tissue Jessica handed to her. "This is why I didn't answer your call last night. I wasn't sure what to tell you. I'm still not sure. I didn't want to frighten you without knowing more."

"Oh, Mom," Jon reached out to hug his mother just as an orderly came to the door wheeling Lucas's bed back into the room. The orderly was followed by a nurse who quickly re-attached the IV bag, monitors, and oxygen with efficient snaps and clicks. With a nod to Jill, she turned and left as quickly as she'd come.

Jon and Jessica looked from their dad's pale face and still figure to their mother, who had stepped to the other side of the bed and taken Lucas's hand.

"Forgive me for not answering your call last night, but I'm glad—*so* glad—you're here now. I—we—need you," Jill said, looking up from Lucas to Jon and Jessica.

"Is there anything we can do?" Jessica asked tentatively, taking her dad's other hand.

Jill sniffed and stood up straight. "Yes. Would you both stay here with your dad? I need to call Coach and Patsy. They will have seen the news too."

"Of course, Mom, whatever we can do. You know that. Is there anything else?" Jon asked, uncharacteristically subdued upon seeing his dad.

"No, dear. I wish there were, but all we can do is wait . . . and pray."

L UCAS FELT AS IF he were waking from a deep sleep—a very deep sleep—filled with frightening dreams. Everything was foggy as snatches of memory floated through his mind. There was a room of faces, all looking at him expectantly, but he wasn't sure why he was there or what he was supposed to say. The faces dissolved into black smoke and large flames roaring out of control. When he looked down, he saw three small figures lying on the ground before they were quickly replaced by bright sunshine. He was standing by a casket with more people looking at him expectantly. Who'd died, he wondered, and what were they wanting from him? As his mind wandered and the images drifted from one to another, Lucas fought to grasp onto something—anything—familiar.

He soon became aware of low sounds and murmurs—voices, ebbing louder at first then softer. Some of the voices sounded familiar while others did not.

He wasn't sure how long he hovered between images, going from one to the next and back again, before he realized he'd been floating slowly up through the darkness, rising until he reached the surface.

His eyes fluttered open, and he blinked several times, unsure of where he was. The unfamiliar room was dim with a few odd hums and beeps coming from somewhere.

"Dad?!"

Lucas looked to where the voice had come from and saw Jon's young face, lined with worry, hovering over him.

"Oh, Dad. You're awake," Jon said in a rush. "You had us worried. Hold on . . . let me get Mom. She's downstairs, and Jess is right outside."

Jon disappeared, and Lucas took the opportunity to look around. He realized he was in a hospital bed in a hospital room. But how? What had happened?

Struggling to sit up, Lucas realized he had an IV in one hand and air tubes in his nose with other various wires hooked up to him. What was going on? Jon rushed back into the room followed by Jessica, and as they moved to Lucas's bedside, Jill hurried in. All three looked worried but had relieved smiles, their eyes shining with what Lucas realized were tears.

"Lucas!" Jill said, rushing over and taking his hand. She gave him a quick kiss on the cheek before stepping back to study him closely. Turning quickly to Jon, she said, "Would you run down to the nurse's station and ask them to page Dr. Brant. Tell them Chief Matthews is awake."

Jon nodded and was quickly gone.

Placing a hand on Lucas's arm, she asked, "How are you, dear? How are you feeling?"

"I'm a bit confused," Lucas confessed with a frown. "Why am I here? What happened, and what are Jon and Jess doing here?"

"You collapsed at a fire scene Wednesday night, Lucas," Jill replied gravely as Jon hurried back into the room.

"Neither one of you guys were answering your phones, and when we saw the fire on the news, we hit the road, and here we are," Jessica added.

Lucas's eyes darted between the three, frowning further with confusion. "I collapsed at a fire scene?" he asked. "What fire scene?"

Jill leaned back, looking at him with concern. "You don't remember?"

Jon glanced quickly at his mom before saying cautiously, "The gym at the high school burned night before last, Dad. It was a total loss. And the story goes that you rescued some kids."

"That was real?" Lucas asked, shaking his head before lying back on the pillow. "I thought it was all a dream."

He lay there thinking for several minutes, his family watching anxiously. But if that was real, he thought, then . . .

That was when everything came rushing back—Mrs. Garrett's funeral, the no confidence vote, the high school gym fire. He closed his eyes and sighed. "I remember now."

Lucas opened his mouth to say more but was interrupted by a young man in a doctor's coat entering the room with a nurse on his heels. The doctor looked way too young to be a doctor, but his confident air and the respect the nurse's demeanor implied gave Lucas a quick, positive impression. Stepping past Jon and Jessica, the doctor and nurse stopped near one side of the bed, the doctor studying Lucas while the nurse looked at monitors on the wall behind him.

"Good afternoon, Chief Matthews. I got the word you were awake. I'm Dr. Brant, your attending physician." The doctor nodded at something the nurse pointed out, typing a note on the iPad he was carrying with him.

Turning back to Lucas, Dr. Brant said, "I must say you're much improved from how you were when you came in a couple of days ago."

"Days?" Lucas asked, looking at his family questioningly.

"Lucas, honey, it's Friday afternoon," Jill said. "You've been out since Wednesday night."

Dr. Brant cleared his throat, his face growing serious as he checked the monitors behind Lucas and made some quick notes on his iPad. Satisfied, he looked at Lucas, giving him his full attention.

"Chief Matthews, I understand you've been under a little stress lately," Dr. Brant began.

"Well, yes. It comes with the job," Lucas replied hesitantly. He thought he knew what was coming and didn't want to have this conversation in front of Jon and Jessica. He looked to Jill, silently imploring her to understand what he couldn't say out loud.

Understanding, Jill said, "Kids, why don't you go and grab something to eat and give your dad and me time to visit with the doctor." She stood and tried to shepherd them toward the door.

"We're staying," Jon said, looking between his parents defiantly. "We want to know what's going on." Jessica stood at his side and added her agreement with an emphatic nod.

"And you will, but just not right now," Jill said, putting a hand on each of their backs and turning them toward the door. "Go on and bring something back for us too. Is that okay, Doctor?"

"Of course. Of course," Dr. Brant agreed. "I don't think your dad is going to like hospital food, and I can't say I blame him. He hasn't had anything besides an IV the past couple of days, though, so just make whatever you get at least semi-healthy."

"Fine then, but we want a full report afterward," Jon said as Jessica smiled worriedly. Jill nodded as both gave a last half-hearted pout over their shoulders as they walked out the door.

Dr. Brant immediately returned his attention to Lucas.

"Well, from what I understand, Chief, it's been a bit more than routine. In order for me to help you and make sure you don't come back for another visit, I need you to be completely honest with me. Will you do that?"

Lucas looked to Jill and then back to the doctor before nodding reluctantly.

"Very good. For starters, I'd like for you to rate the level of stress, actual stress, you've been under for the past, say, three to four months with ten being the highest and zero being the lowest."

Lucas sighed. "Ten. Well, actually more like eleven or twelve to be perfectly honest."

"Or higher," Jill mumbled under her breath.

Dr. Brant nodded as he typed notes into the iPad.

"That's exactly what I gathered from talking to your wife," he said as he typed.

"She worries too much," Lucas said with a teasing smile.

"Actually, Chief, I think she's right on target. When you collapsed Wednesday night, your body was giving you a strong warning that it had reached its stress endurance limit. It sounds like you had been stretched past the limit Wednesday alone, and your body just couldn't take any more. Your blood pressure was practically off the charts, and your heart was beating too fast and erratically. That's what caused you to collapse. There were probably some earlier warning signs such as dizziness, short-ness of breath, possibly loss of appetite. Do any of those sound familiar?"

Lucas listened closely, and unfortunately, what the doctor was saying made sense.

"Yeah, Doc. It does. I've been feeling dizzy and short of breath at times too."

Jill looked sharply at Lucas, who just gave a reluctant shrug.

Dr. Brant nodded, making more notes on his iPad.

"Well, Chief, I'm just glad your body saw fit to give you a warning, but it was a serious one. You're strong and healthy, so your body has bounced back quickly. You were a bit dehydrated, so we've been keeping you on fluids. We've run multiple tests and found no damage done—no heart attack, that kind of thing. All the tests pointed to stress, and with what's been going on in Abernathy, you've had a lot to deal with. You've been out more than forty hours. Your body and mind just needed a chance to rest and forced the issue. How do you feel? Better? More rested?"

Lucas nodded. "Yes, Doc. As far as I can tell, I think I do feel better."

"Good! Then let's keep things moving in that direction. From every test we've run, you're perfectly healthy, but we want to run just a few more now that you're awake to be doubly sure. They won't take long, so I don't see why you won't be able to go home tomorrow. That's the goal, but we'll have to see how the tests look first."

Lucas opened his mouth to object, but Dr. Brant held up a hand, stopping him. "I want to make this clear, Chief Matthews. When you do go home, you are to be quiet and rest for the next few days. No stress. No anxiety. Just quiet and relaxation. Got it?"

Lucas hesitated.

"I'm serious," Dr. Brant said. "Otherwise, you'll be staying here longer. It's up to you."

"Well, looks like you've put me in a corner and made your case in front of my wife, so I have no choice."

Jill nodded and smiled knowingly.

Dr. Brant chuckled. "I'm strategic that way. Oh, and by the way, I have to admit that when you do go home, the hospital staff is going to be glad to have their waiting room and parking lot back."

Confused, Lucas frowned and looked at Jill, who just smiled in return.

"I'll check back a little later this evening," Dr. Brant said, giving instructions to the nurse as they left.

"What does he mean about the waiting room and parking lot?" Lucas asked after Dr. Brant left.

"Lucas, the waiting room downstairs is full of firefighters standing vigil for you and has been ever since you were brought in Wednesday night. Some of them followed the ambulance from the gym fire and stayed until they were spelled off. There's been a constant rotation since then, and from what Forney just told me while I was downstairs, there's a waiting list of those wanting to come for however long you're here."

Lucas shook his head slightly, trying to absorb what Jill was saying, attempting to make sense of what was and had been happening.

"But, Lucas," Jill said and suddenly grew serious. "There is something I want to talk about, and then I won't bother you with it anymore."

Lucas's eyes went to Jill's, a frown of concern on her face.

"Well, of course. What is it?" He cleared his throat and waited.

Jill came and sat on the edge of the bed as Lucas took her hand. Her hand was soft and warm as she laced her fingers with his and squeezed his hand. Looking up, Jill said, "Lindsay texted Wednesday afternoon to let me know what was happening—the vote of no confidence." Jill's eyes filled with tears. "That's why I went to the high school when I heard about the gym fire on the scanner. I knew no matter what had happened, you'd be there. When I read that text, it nearly broke my heart. I know how much this job means to you and how much you've poured into it. I can't imagine the amount of stress that put on you, and I'm just so sorry it happened. If I ever see this Carr again—" She gripped his hand even tighter.

A small grin teased Lucas's lips as he looked at her.

"I mean it, Lucas. That guy is—"

"Not worth worrying about so please don't, okay?" Lucas asked, putting a finger under Jill's chin, tipping her face to look at him. "I don't know how things went after I left, but it's out of my hands. We'll just have to see what happens, but I'll make you a deal. I'll try not to worry and stress if you'll promise to do the same."

Jill rolled her eyes and nodded slowly. "Okay, but a final word. I—"

"Final word?" Lucas quirked an eyebrow. "You're not letting me have the final word on this?"

Jill laughed lightly. "Not this time, dear. I just want you to know. I believe in you, and Jon and Jess believe in you too. And . . . I just so happen to know we're not the only ones."

"Oh, you do, do you?" Lucas asked as he smoothed some hair from her face.

She smiled. "Yes, Lucas Matthews, I do. Remember what I told you about the firefighters downstairs and the ones who have been coming and going the entire time you've been out? They're all concerned about you. I don't think they'd be here asking to do whatever they can for you . . . for our family, if they didn't genuinely care about you. But right now, Lucas, my biggest concern is you. So long as you're okay and our family is healthy and well—and together—everything else is going to be fine."

Lucas stared down at their clasped hands. He wanted to believe what Jill was saying, but with the vote of no confidence hanging over him, he just couldn't know for sure. Standing vigil for another firefighter was just something firefighters did but did it ultimately mean he had their respect and confidence? He just didn't know.

Jill placed her hand on Lucas's cheek and lifted his face to look him in the eye before moving it to the top of their entwined hands.

"Lucas, you scared me. Please don't ever do that again. I couldn't bear it."

Lucas pulled Jill close, kissing her with as much emotion as he possibly could.

Leaning back, Jill whispered, "I love you."

"And I love you too," Lucas said, running his finger down her cheek.

Lucas pulled her to him, not caring the IV tube trailed across the bed, silently holding her as the monitors continued beeping and murmured noises drifted in from the hall. Jill lay her head on his shoulder, her arms tightening around him as Lucas tightened his around her.

Minutes passed until someone cleared his throat, and Jon's teasing voice broke the silence. "Is anyone here hungry, or should we make our delivery later?"

Jill sat up, swiping at her cheeks before smiling at Lucas and turning to face Jon and Jessica who stood in the doorway smirking.

"I don't know about you guys, but I'm starved," Lucas said, clearing his throat and squeezing Jill's shoulder. When he smelled the Max burger Jill handed to him, Lucas chuckled at the twins' idea of healthy food and suddenly realized just how hungry he was.

AFTER THEY'D EATEN, JILL and the kids went home for a while to let Lucas rest, but rest didn't come easy. There was too much on his mind. He'd done his best to reassure Jill about the vote of no confidence, but in reality, it had shaken him to his core. He'd always fought his own battles. He'd stood on his own two feet when he had no one else but himself to count on, but now he had an entire department depending on *him*. Had he let them down?

He'd brought self-assurance and self-confidence to this job and thought he was leading the department—its people—in the right direction, but had he been *too* sure of himself? He'd known Carr was infuriated about not getting the chief's job, but maybe Lucas hadn't taken him seriously enough. He should have addressed Carr's behavior more directly, but he'd hoped to bring Carr around. Evidently, the hatred and bitterness Carr carried was deep, too deep, for Lucas to reach.

Lucas closed his eyes and sighed. It was out of his hands, and he'd accept whatever happened. It might not be easy, but as it had been his whole life, the only place to go was forward—no matter what.

Willing himself to relax, Lucas finally drifted into a light sleep until a soft knock at the door woke him. It took a minute to focus on the three hesitant figures in the doorway—Riley Sullivan, Jeremy Ennis, and Cade Marshall.

"Chief? Is this a good time?" Riley was asking without any of them moving.

"Guys, sure. Come on in," Lucas said hoarsely.

"Sorry to wake you, Chief," Jeremy said as they tentatively approached his bedside.

"No worries. Marshall, you look a whole lot better than the last time I saw you. You're even recognizable."

Cade chuckled and then coughed with a wheeze. "Yes, sir. I've just been released and wanted to come by and say thank you for helping get those boys out. The guys told me you gave the go ahead and came in too." Out of breath, he paused, breathing heavily.

"The boys are all fine," Cade went on after catching his breath. "They had some smoke inhalation, so they'll be doing breathing treatments, but they're going to be fine. Their parents asked me to extend their thanks. You'll probably be hearing from them personally, but really, thank you."

Lucas nodded. "That's our job, but it took all of us to make it happen." He paused, studying Cade's pale face and hearing his labored breathing. "Marshall, are you okay?"

"He's got some smoke inhalation. He'll be doing some breathing treatments for the next few weeks himself," Jeremy said, looking at Cade with concern.

"And we're going to make sure he does them," Riley added.

"Great. Two nursemaids," Cade grumped with a smirk then coughed again. "Not to worry. I've already given these guys my word I'll do them," he said, motioning with his thumb between Riley and Jeremy. "I guess I'd better go. Emily will be downstairs by now. I just wanted to come by and thank you personally."

"No thanks needed, Marshall. Take care of yourself. I'll also be checking to make sure you're getting those treatments done."

"Oh great. Now I'm up to three nursemaids," Cade said with a smile and wave as the three walked out.

"And, Chief," Jeremy added as he stepped back inside the door, "I think we might have some news when we get the security camera footage from the gym. I've seen something interesting in the photos of onlookers. Nothing conclusive, but the angle of the gym cameras may uncover what we've been needing."

Lucas nodded. "I hope so. Enough damage and anxiety have been inflicted on this city."

Lucas wanted to ask how the vote had gone and started to call Ennis and Sullivan back but that would be putting them in a bad spot and wouldn't be professional either. No, he told himself. Word would come soon enough.

Lucas watched as Jeremy joined Riley, and Cade took a seat in a wheelchair right outside the door. They left with Riley pushing, Jeremy and a hospital orderly walking alongside. He heard them exchanging greetings with someone in the hall, and a couple of seconds later Jack Weston and Nate Baldwin appeared in the doorway.

"Chief, have a minute?" Baldwin asked as they hovered outside.

Lucas sat up further in bed, his heart involuntarily speeding up. He had a feeling they were here in an official capacity as it was after office hours, and they were in uniform. Word was coming faster than he'd thought it would.

"Sure, Nate. West. Come on in. Everything wrapped up on the gym fire? Have there been any others?"

"Sir," Jack Weston nervously began, "we've been told not to discuss actual department business with you . . . exactly. The Doc says you're supposed to be resting."

"I see," Lucas said. "He's a bit of a busybody, so if it's not departmental business, then . . ." Lucas let the question hang in the air.

"We do have just a small bit of departmental business to discuss with you, sir," Nate Baldwin said with a quick glance at Weston.

"Okay then, let's discuss." Lucas crossed his arms in front of him, schooling his face to as blank an expression as he could muster and braced himself. He looked between the two, who, oddly, didn't look reluctant at having to share the bad news Lucas thought was coming.

Jack West cleared his throat and said with gravity, "Chief Matthews, we would like to report the results of the vote taken last Wednesday. The vote, sir, was unanimous except for one individual."

Lucas's breath caught. He thought he'd at least have both Riley and Jeremy's votes.

"I see," Lucas said, unsure of the appropriate response. "I haven't been in this situation before. Is the city manager expecting my resignation then?"

Looks of confusion crossed Baldwin's and Weston's faces, replaced almost immediately with looks of understanding.

"Oh, no, sir," Weston chuckled. "My apologies. I should have clarified. It was a vote of confidence—*in you*. The entire department voted their complete and total confidence, and enthusiastic support. The only dissenting vote, as you've probably guessed, was Carr."

"What happened to McCracken? I'd heard he and Carr were in this together," Lucas asked, beginning to relax as the news sank in.

Baldwin shot a glance at Weston and then back to Lucas. "McCracken actually stood up and apologized. He said he'd also apologize to you personally. He had only heard the lies Carr twisted out of the truth. When you shared the facts, he realized the extent of those lies. McCracken admitted he was completely at fault for not vetting what Carr told him. He distanced himself from Carr immediately and also voted his full confidence in you."

"That took a lot of courage from McCracken," Lucas said with a thoughtful nod.

Weston smiled slightly but growing serious said, "Sir, everyone was pretty upset with Carr when they realized how he'd been attempting to manipulate them, hell, to manipulate the entire department for his own gain, dragging McCracken along with him."

With a quick glance at Baldwin, and gesturing between them with his thumb, Weston said, "Sir, we took it upon ourselves to have a heart-to-heart meeting with Deputy Chief Carr. We told him, well actually, we *strongly* encouraged him to rethink continuing his career with the Abernathy Department."

Before Lucas could respond, Baldwin added, "And sir, when everyone heard about you—about your collapse, being in the hospital, and why—well, everyone is worried. They feel like they helped put you here, unwittingly."

Lucas shook his head in disbelief, feeling the weight lifting from his shoulders—and his heart.

"Sir?" Weston asked, looking at Lucas with concern. "We thought you'd be relieved—happy?"

Lucas nodded. "Oh, I am, West. Truly I am. This is great news. I'm relieved and happy. Very happy." He smiled, a relieved, pleased smile, and shook both of their hands firmly.

"Actually, this is the best medicine I could have gotten. Thank you." Lucas lowered his voice and whispered conspiratorially, "But don't tell the Doc."

"And would you guys do another favor for me, please," Lucas said, laying back, the bed crackling beneath him. "I understand there's a group downstairs. Would you please pass along my thanks and appreciation to them and let them know they can go home. I'm supposed to be released tomorrow and plan to be in the office Monday, so there's no need for them stay."

"We'll be more than happy to pass the word along, Chief," Baldwin replied with an earnest nod from West beside him. "But you do realize, of course, that doesn't mean they're going to comply," he added with a smirk.

Lucas chuckled lightly. "Well, I'm no position to do much about that right now, am I, but do tell them thanks for me, and that I'll see them Monday. And I admit, I'm relieved the vote has been put to rest," Lucas said.

"Did I hear rest?" Jill said as she came in the room. "Someone I know is supposed to be resting," she added with a pointed look at Baldwin and Weston.

"Yes, ma'am," both said at the same time and, with a nod to Lucas, backed out of the room, smiling.

Jill looked at Lucas, who was trying unsuccessfully to wipe the smile from his face. He patted the bed beside him with soft little thumps. Jill took a seat, a questioning look on her face.

"You certainly look pleased," she said as her phone buzzed with a call. She looked down to see Tucker Delaford, the Abernathy Realtor's name on the screen. She tapped the phone and answered hesitantly. Listening briefly, she said, "Sure, I can hold," before tapping mute.

Lucas raised his eyebrows in question.

"It's Tucker Delaford," Jill said hesitantly. "He's downstairs and started to say something, but then asked me to hold."

"Yes, I'm here," Jill said a few seconds later with a slight arch of her eyebrows. She listened and nodded as Delaford talked for several minutes. "Okay. Let me ask him. Hold on for just a second."

Jill tapped mute on the phone and looked at Lucas. "Delaford said we have the house. He's been holding it while you were unable to respond, but now that you're awake, he can't hold the homeowners off any longer. They need an answer if we don't want to lose it."

"Ask him how soon we can sign the papers and close," Lucas replied and smiled at the surprised look on Jill's face.

As Jill talked to Delaford, Lucas shook his head, marveling yet again at how quickly word spreads at the fire department. Riley and Jeremy hadn't been gone for more than a few minutes and now West and Baldwin were downstairs with Delaford. Lucas had to acknowledge to himself with a grin, they *were* obeying orders and spreading the word.

Relaying Lucas's message and then listening to something Tucker told her in response, Jill hung up and looked to Lucas.

"Are you sure about this?" she asked with a slight frown.

"I'm sure. Those guys brought good news—really good news," Lucas replied with a relaxed, happy smile. "Would you like to hear it?"

Jill nodded eagerly and scooted closer.

I N SPITE OF THE constant interruptions from hospital staff taking vitals or recording monitor readings overnight, Lucas woke the next morning from a solid sleep. He hadn't realized how truly tired he'd been.

The orderly, humming distractedly to himself, brought Lucas's breakfast tray in and placed it on the rolling table near the bed. Lifting the cover, steam rose along with an aroma Lucas didn't recognize as anything to do with breakfast food. He poked around at the food and tested a bite of what might be eggs, but he wasn't sure even after tasting. Smiling to himself, he wondered if they'd brought him a breakfast cooked by a rookie at one of the stations. He only drank the coffee, which wasn't too bad.

Jill and the kids came in shortly after the orderly picked up the mostly full food tray. Everyone was trying to talk at once until Jill finally just rolled her eyes and shrugged. She and Lucas laughed as they looked between Jon and Jessica, who kept talking.

Dr. Brant knocked on the door and walked in, thankfully putting a stop to their chatter.

"How are you feeling today, Chief? Sleep well?" he asked brusquely.

"Actually, I slept really well. I didn't realize how tired I was."

Dr. Brant nodded as he entered notes into his ever-present iPad. "All of your tests came back clear as I thought they would," he said, peering over the iPad at Lucas. "I'd say you're good to go home."

"Sounds great. I'm ready," Lucas said as they all exchanged smiles.

"But," Dr. Brant said, moving to stand closer to Lucas's bedside, "I strongly encourage you to remember what I told you yesterday. You are to be quiet and rest for the next few days. No stressors. No anxiety. Got it?"

Lucas nodded soberly as Jill and the twins exchanged a determined look.

"Very well. I'll get the paperwork started. You should be set to go in an hour or two. It's been a pleasure, Chief. I wish you the best, and don't take this personally, but I don't want to see you back here again. Do we have a deal?"

"Absolutely," Lucas said with a nod. "No offense to you either, Doc, but I really don't want to come back."

Dr. Brant nodded and was quickly gone with brisk clicks of his shoes across the linoleum.

"Great news all the way around, Dad. Keep up the good work, but well . . . sorry. We gotta run," Jon said with a quick look to Jill.

"We'll see you a little later on, Dad, and definitely at home," Jessica added, giving Lucas a quick peck on the cheek.

"Well, all right, kids. See you later." Lucas's brow quirked in confusion as they left. "Where are they off to?"

Jill shrugged nonchalantly as she walked to the room's tiny closet to get the clothes she'd brought yesterday in anticipation of his going home. Lucas hadn't seen her carry anything in so she must have brought them while he'd been asleep.

"I thought you might be ready to get dressed or are you just going to lie there and soak all the laziness in until the paperwork comes through?" Jill teased.

Lucas pushed the sheet and light blanket back and turned to sit on the edge of the bed.

"I think you know me better than that."

A smile pulled at the corners of Jill's lips as she opened the closet door. Lucas glanced over and saw the street clothes she was pulling from hangers.

He hesitated but finally said, "Honey, thanks—I appreciate it, but if it's not too much trouble, would it be possible to get a uniform shirt and pants from home? I'd like to leave in uniform—you know—as a firefighter."

Jill stopped and with a knowing smile, reached back inside the closet and pulled out his white officer's shirt and black pants.

"You mean like these? I brought both civilian clothes and your uniform just to be safe but thought you'd probably prefer the uniform."

Lucas chuckled and shook his head. "Scary that you know me so well."

AFTER A QUICK SHOWER and a few bites of the cafeteria's idea of lunch, Lucas was dressed and more than ready to go. They'd been told that an orderly would be up shortly with a wheelchair to take him downstairs. Jill had called Jon and Jessica, who were bringing the car around, to let them know they'd be heading downstairs any minute.

"Uh, excuse us, sir, but we were told someone here needed a ride?"

Lucas and Jill turned to see Riley and Jeremy in the doorway, smiling with a wheelchair between them and an orderly standing patiently behind.

"Oh no. Are you two driving?" Lucas teased, obviously glad to see them.

Jeremy chuckled. "We promise to be on our best behavior—at least for now."

Jeremy and Riley moved further into the room, angling the chair a bit closer to the bed as Lucas stood from where he'd been sitting on its edge.

Lucas cocked an eyebrow. "I can still walk, fellas."

"We just can't risk anything happening to you on our watch, sir," Jeremy said with mock gravity.

Everyone laughed as Lucas walked the few steps to the wheelchair. "All right then," Lucas said as he sat down. "Let's get outta here. I'm ready."

Jill took the hand Lucas held up to her as Riley pushed the wheelchair to the door, its soft rubber wheels gliding across the floor with a soft whooshing sound. As they started down the hall, Lucas noticed some of the nurses and staff watching and smiling as they passed. Some of the faces Lucas recognized and some he didn't, but he still smiled and nodded in acknowledgment, wondering why he was garnering their attention. After everyone was on the elevator, Jeremy punched the round button with a G on it for Ground Level.

As the elevator doors closed and it started down, Lucas started to comment on the unusual attention from the nurses and staff when Riley interrupted him, looking at Jeremy with a grin.

"Sir, we might warn you, there's going to be—" he began, but the elevator doors opened quickly, making it too late to say anything more.

As Riley pushed the wheelchair across the shiny linoleum floor the short distance to the automated exit doors, Lucas saw firefighters—a lot of firefighters—beyond the glass windows. The exterior walkway was lined with firefighters, several deep, with two fire engines, their lights on, parked on either side of the walkway. As the automatic doors swished open, and Riley wheeled Lucas through, a round of applause and cheers erupted.

It was a beautiful afternoon. The wind was gone, and the temperature had moderated. The sun was shining brilliantly, and the sky was an intense blue. The chrome of the two red fire engines sparkled in the sun while the firefighters who had encircled him continued to smile and cheer.

Lucas's eyes widened and his mouth fell open. Jon and Jessica, smug smiles on their faces, walked up to stand beside Lindsay.

Deputy Chiefs West and Baldwin stepped away from the group and walked toward Lucas, who rose from the wheelchair, his grip on Jill's hand tightening. The group quietened as West began to speak.

"Sir, I speak on behalf of the entire Abernathy Fire Department, in saying that we're glad—more than that—we're thankful to see you up and about. We all want you to know you have had and will continue to have our full and complete respect and support. As you have reminded us by your words and by your example, the brotherhood sticks together."

West looked to Baldwin who then added, "We also want you to know that we look forward to your returning to work, but until then, everything is in good hands, and you are not to worry."

Lucas nodded solemnly and when he tried to speak, his throat was tight and his voice was hoarse with emotion. "I thought I told you guys to go home," he said gruffly, trying to contain his emotions. Low chuckles went through the assembled firefighters.

Turning, Lucas looked around the group and, motioning around the circle, said, "Thank you from the bottom of my heart. This means more to me and my family than you'll ever know. I appreciate each and every one of you, but we still have work to do. As I've said before, let's continue to give it our all, and—"

As Lucas started to say the final words, to his pleased surprise, the entire group recited them together, "and then some."

ONDAY MORNING CAME QUICKLY, and Lucas was as determined to go to the office as Jill was to keep him home. Even though she had signed the lease for the space in the old downtown area and was excited to start setting up her new office, she was putting it off to stay at home with him. On the other hand, he felt great and was ready to get back to work.

"What are you doing?" Jill asked as she walked into the bedroom, carrying a tray filled with some of Lucas's favorite breakfast foods. Just the aroma made him smile.

He was buttoning his uniform shirt and tucking it in as he slipped his shoes on.

"I'm getting ready for work, but that sure looks and smells good."

Lucas reached over and snagged a piece of crusty bacon. She had cooked maple syrup on top just the way he liked it. He had time to savor his first bite before Jill began.

"The doctor told you to rest, did he not?"

"And I have—all weekend. But it's Monday, and there's still an arsonist out there we've got to stop." He took another bite of bacon and chewed slowly, relishing its sweet crunchiness.

"Did you not hear the same things I heard Dr. Brant say?" Jill pressed.

Lucas leaned over, grabbing a biscuit before planting a kiss on Jill's cheek.

"I heard every word and have obeyed—until now. But I feel great and am ready to get back to work. Plus, you've got a new office to set up and clients waiting for you to start their projects. You need to wow them when you meet with them, and you can't do that babysitting me."

Jill cocked her head sideways, studying him. He was right, and he knew that she knew he was right. He grinned.

"Told you so," he said before taking the tray from her and sitting on the edge of the bed and diving in.

Jill put her hands on her hips, shaking her head but smiling.

"Want a biscuit?" he asked with a smile holding one up. "They're really good."

Jill laughed and snatched the biscuit from his hand as she plopped down beside him.

Lucas walked into the office a short while later. While it still had the ever-present smell of coffee, it looked and felt different. It felt like he belonged here—really belonged—and that was a good feeling. As he walked by, he noticed the door to Deputy Chief Carr's office was closed.

"Good morning, Chief!" Lindsay said, jumping up and running around her desk to embrace him in a tight hug.

"Welcome back!"

Lucas chuckled. "Thank you, Lindsay. It's good to be back. What do I need to know? Bring me up to speed."

Lindsay read from her computer screen, rattling off a list of items, but he could tell she was keeping things to generalities. He grinned to himself. It wasn't necessary, but he appreciated her effort to be helpful. Before he went to his office, he made a quick detour to the break room, filled a mug with coffee, and took a hearty drink.

As he went back by Lindsay's desk, she followed him to his office and watched as he sat down, looking at the top of his desk. He saw the key to the desk drawer next to the phone where he'd tossed it in his haste to get to the fire at the gym after securing Carr's personnel file.

He nodded as Lindsay completed her update from the notepad she kept with her.

"Thank you, Lindsay. All good information, but right now, I guess I'd better check in with Kirk Lorimar."

"Oh, sir. My apologies. He asked that I let him know when you arrived. I called when I saw you pull up. He said he'd be down shortly."

Lucas frowned. "He's coming here?"

Lindsay nodded at the same time there was a knock on the door, and Kirk Lorimar stuck his head inside. Looking between Lucas and Lindsay, he asked, "This a good time, Chief?"

"Absolutely. Please, come in."

Lucas glanced to Lindsay who hurriedly exited and pulled the door closed behind her.

"How are you, Lucas?" the city manager asked as he settled into one of the guest chairs and looked at Lucas closely.

"I'm doing really well, Kirk. Thanks for checking, but I'm fine."

"I'm glad to hear it. I've been worried and wracked with guilt," Kirk said with a heavy sigh. "Lucas, I want to offer you my sincerest apologies."

Lucas started to shake his head, but Kirk held up a hand, stopping him. "No—I owe you an apology. I knew when we went through the hiring process that Milton Carr thought he had a free pass to the position. I didn't address his not being selected with him as thoroughly as I should have. I put you in a difficult spot, and for that I am sincerely sorry."

He paused and Lucas could tell there was more.

"I heard about the vote of confidence," Kirk added softly.

Lucas reflexively flinched, and Kirk Lorimar shook his head sadly.

"Again, it never should have gotten to that point. I watched from afar and saw you trying to work with Carr. What I didn't realize is the lengths Carr would go to get the position. I'll have to report the vote being taken to council, but I'll be especially pleased to report the results."

Lucas leaned back in his chair and exhaled a sigh of relief.

"Thank you, Kirk. I have to admit, I was afraid of what even the idea of a vote would mean to my standing with the city."

"Well, the only thing that's changed is that your standing has been elevated. You were well thought of before by council, despite how they might carry on in the public sessions. But from those I've already talked to, they've expressed their appreciation for what you're doing and how glad they are you're Abernathy's fire chief."

"That's good to hear, and I appreciate it, but I think we're all ready to put that behind us and move on. The next big task is getting that arsonist. I think we're getting close."

"Well, that's good news. It'd be great to put that behind us as well and as quickly as possible." Kirk stood and looked at Lucas, adding, "And you have my support in whatever you'd like to do regarding Carr. I think you know where I stand. I'd have already fired him, McCracken too, and kicked them both to the curb, but it's your decision on how you want to handle it. I have alerted Ruth in HR that she may be hearing from you and to assist you in any way you need."

Lucas stood and extended a hand that Kirk took and shook fervently.

"Keep me posted, Chief," Kirk added as he stepped to the door and opened it.

"I will, and thank you, sir."

LUCAS SETTLED BACK INTO his chair, taking another sip of his coffee, pondering what Kirk Lorimar had just said. He unlocked his desk drawer and pulled out his file on Milton Carr. How differently his notes read to him now as he contemplated last Wednesday's events. What needed to be done was pretty straightforward. He just needed to make sure his i's were dotted and t's crossed, and that's what he was going to do right now. He turned on his computer and typed in the familiar password.

The soft early morning light that filtered in the windows had shifted. It was much brighter now, and looking up from his desk, Lucas could tell it was close to midday. He'd asked Lindsay earlier to cancel the morning's staff meeting but was surprised when he saw that it was already 11:30. He hadn't had any visitors or phone calls all morning and had a suspicion Lindsay was running interference. He got up and walked across the hall to her desk, taking his long empty coffee cup with him for a refill.

He nodded to a couple of the admins who hurried by. Lucas frowned, suddenly noticing how quiet the entire office was despite staff being present.

Lucas cocked his head and asked nonchalantly, "It sure has been quiet this morning, hasn't it?"

"Yes, sir, it has," Lindsay agreed without looking up.

"Why do you suppose that is?" he went on in a conversational tone.

Lindsay's shoulders slumped, and she looked up at him sheepishly.

"Well, it might be because I've been taking messages for you and telling others you're not seeing anyone today."

"And . . ." Lucas asked, sensing there might be more.

"And I've asked everyone to keep it down. I thought you might need some peace and quiet."

"Ah," Lucas said, nodding. "I see. Have you made very many of these interceptions?"

Lindsay looked down and nodded, twisting her fingers together. "Yes, sir."

"Would you forward the phone messages and then call anyone who came by and schedule them to come by this afternoon or tomorrow morning by priority?"

Lindsay nodded silently.

"And, Lindsay, thank you," Lucas said with a slight grin. "I appreciate it, but department business must go on as normal, so would you make sure everyone knows it's business as usual around here?"

Lindsay hesitantly returned Lucas's grin before nodding and turning back to her computer. "I'll email the phone messages to you right now and start making calls."

"And, Lindsay," Lucas said solemnly, taking a step back toward her desk, "make the first call to Ruth Bingham in HR. Tell her I need to come down and visit with her."

Lindsay's eyes grew round, but she only nodded.

LUCAS RETURNED FROM HIS meeting with HR to find Jeremy Ennis waiting for him, pacing anxiously in front of Lindsay's desk.

"Chief! I'm glad you're back. You've got to see this."

Jeremy took off down the hall without waiting. Lucas followed him into the conference room being used for the arson investigation. The two police investigators were waiting for them, their expressions solemn. A bank of lights had been turned off, making the image of a dumpster on the large monitor at the end of the room more easily seen.

"Look at this, sir. We got gym security camera footage from the school this morning and have been going through it. We found this."

Jeremy picked up the remote lying on the table in front of the monitor and clicked to start the video he had ready. The four gathered closely around, Lucas in the front. From this camera angle, a dumpster was visible, overflowing with trash of all kinds from paper and cardboard boxes to paper cups and more. It was in the gym's loading dock area indicated by signs on the cinder block wall behind it. After a few seconds, a dark figure could be seen approaching from the right. The figure was dressed exactly like the figure they'd captured in incomplete images in photos of onlookers at each fire scene.

Without hesitation, the figure moved quickly, pulling a lighter from beneath his jacket and clicking the trigger mechanism, sparking a flame. He circled the dumpster, setting fire to several pieces of trash, ensuring that each caught fire before moving on. The flames grew quickly, brightly lighting the enclosed area. The figure moved to leave in the same direction he'd come. Due to the dark hood, his face remained completely in shadow, and even though brightness of the flames grew, he kept his head averted from the camera as if he knew exactly where it was. Lucas sighed in frustration until suddenly, inexplicably, the figure turned and looked up, straight at the camera, his face clearly visible. Lucas gasped as Jeremy turned to him, his face pale. As Lucas continued to watch . . . Chase Carr smiled before turning and running into the dark.

Lucas took a staggered step back and looked at Jeremy.

It felt like all the air had just been sucked from the room.

Police Investigator Carl Manon spoke up, "Each video is time stamped, sir. He made the rounds that night, igniting dumpsters, trash bins, anything that was easily flammable. Each one was easily visible to a security camera. From the time stamps, he moved directly behind the quarter hour patrols we had in place. He had it timed perfectly, so he must have somehow already known or watched for the timing."

"It's obvious it's the same figure in every video, sir," Michael Foster, the second police investigator added, shaking his head. "Each time, except this last one, he successfully kept his face from being visible. But in this one, the one time stamped the latest, he turns and looks at the camera, almost—almost as if it's on purpose."

Lucas pulled out a chair and sat down, running his fingers through his hair before putting his head in his hands. He took a deep breath and leaned back, gripping the chair's upholstered arms.

"It's as if he wanted to get caught, sir. There's no logical explanation," Jeremy added.

"No—because the behavior isn't logical," Lucas sighed.

"There's more if you want to hear it," Jeremy said, easing into the chair next to Lucas.

Lucas nodded reluctantly.

Jeremy pulled several sheets of paper from the closest stacks on the table and held them out to Lucas, pointing at several lines highlighted in bright yellow.

"Sir, once we identified Chase Carr, we retrieved the registration on his car. Even though the title is in Deputy Chief Carr's name, Chase Carr is listed as the driver on the insurance. The make and model match the same car we've noted in the area of several of the first fire scenes. There were no clear shots of the plates in the dark, but now, all of this corroborates," Jeremy said, gesturing to the paper he still held.

"And, sir, the four fires we had in one night? All those addresses are in a one-mile radius of Deputy Chief Carr's home address. On that particular night, the car wasn't seen at or near any of those locations. We checked every surrounding block in a one-mile radius, but the car remained parked at Deputy Chief Carr's address. I'm not sure why he wouldn't drive that particular night, but the addresses are close enough to his own home that Chase could easily walk."

Lucas shook his head. The evidence was building.

Police Investigator Manon's phone buzzed, and he stepped to the side to take the call while Jeremy continued showing Lucas more of the growing amount of corroborating evidence.

Lucas thumbed through some of the sheets of paper scattered across the conference table's dusty top. He was ready for this to be over, but at what a terrible cost to the Carr family and to the Abernathy Fire Department.

After a few hushed minutes of conversation, Manon hung up, slipping his phone into his jacket pocket as he rejoined the group.

"Sir, that was an officer in the area of a discount store where we suspected some of the gas cans were purchased. They carry the same type and style of cans found at the scenes. We sent the suspect's photo over to the officer, and when he showed it to two of the store clerks who work in that department, they recognized Chase Carr immediately. They said he typically bought two cans at a time and always paid cash. The officer is getting a statement from each of them now. We've sent the photo to a few other officers to check auto parts stores and additional discount stores in the surrounding areas."

"Once we had the image from the video, everything fell into place perfectly," Jeremy added. "No gaps, no question marks. He was smart—very smart—and we wouldn't have all of this if he hadn't looked into that camera so boldly. To be so smart and clever all the other times, it doesn't make sense."

"No—I'm afraid it does make sense if you put *all* the pieces together—the taunting, the notes on the gas cans, the timing for each fire. I bet when we learn the whole story, there will be a reason for his targeting the gym. No—he wanted us to catch him this time," Lucas said, staring at the monitor and then turning and looking at Jeremy pointedly. "The gym fire was last Wednesday night. You might recall what happened last Wednesday afternoon. He thought his dad would soon be chief. He didn't think he'd have to worry, even if he was caught."

Jeremy's eyes widened as full understanding hit. He stared at Lucas, stunned.

Lucas looked back to the monitor and shook his head, trying to fathom what this would mean, not just to the Carr family, coupled with Milton Carr's recent behavior, but also what it would mean to the department. A child of one of those sworn to protect was the one destroying property, displacing families, and putting lives in danger.

"Do we have eyes on him?" Lucas asked as he stood and looked between Jeremy and the two police investigators.

"Yes, sir," Carl Manon replied. "Full surveillance until you give the word to pick him up. We've let Chief Harper know. He should be here any minute."

"Good. Let me think about how best to handle this. Give me a couple of minutes."

MILTON CARR PACED DISTRACTEDLY outside Ruth Bingham's office late Monday afternoon. He should have known Matthews wouldn't have the guts to face him. He'd foisted him off onto the HR Director to do any dirty work. He'd probably get a reprimand, Carr thought, maybe a demotion in rank, but really, that'd be fine. He didn't want to work with Matthews anyway. Whatever happened, Matthews still didn't deserve to be chief, Carr thought, whether anyone else agreed with him or not.

He stopped pacing and turned when Ruth Bingham's office door opened and she stepped out, carrying a single folder. They had always been on excellent terms through the years, working together on departmental hiring and training issues. For all of their work history together, today, her demeanor was aloof and distant.

"Deputy Chief Carr, would you please come with me?" she said, stepping toward the hallway. Her face was solemn. She offered no niceties or even a smile. Carr frowned a bit as he held the glass door open for her then followed her into the hall. They walked a few doors down to the City Manager's conference room. When they stepped inside, Carr hesitated briefly seeing Kirk Lorimar seated at the head of the long table along with Matthews and Police Chief Harper on either side, obviously waiting for him.

"Would you like to take a seat?" Lucas motioned to the empty chairs at the table.

"I'll stand, thank you," Carr shot back.

Carr's focus remained on the three men seated at the far end of the table while being vaguely aware of the room around him. It was well but practically appointed with a large bank of windows on one side, extra chairs, and two cabinets on the opposite side with large prints of various locations around Abernathy framed at intervals on the walls. This room was where the department head meeting was held each Wednesday morning and of which he'd had no part, thanks to Matthews.

The group exchanged glances as Kirk Lorimar, a somber look on his face, took the file Ruth Bingham handed him. She took a seat next to Lucas, leaving Carr standing at the far end of the table. The air in the room was heavy and oppressive, and Carr began to feel the first inkling of unease.

"Milton, you are probably aware of why you are here today, and the circumstances sadden me more than you know," Kirk Lorimar began. "After many years of employment with the City of Abernathy, you know that we hold our employees and staff to the highest ideals for the betterment of our city and its citizens. You have always upheld those ideals—until the last few months when it seems you've become focused on marginalizing and demonizing your superior officer, not only to other officers, but also to the rank and file of the Abernathy Fire Department."

Carr opened his mouth to object, but Lorimar held up a hand silencing him and continued.

"City management has also become aware of the vote of no confidence you instigated against Chief Matthews. That vote was predicated on lies that you and another officer you recruited spread among members of the department."

Lorimar paused and sighed heavily. "The situation we currently find ourselves in would normally be handled by Chief Matthews, but I asked him to let me conduct this meeting. I wanted you to hear this directly from me, as City Manager, so there would be no question as to your standing with the City of Abernathy."

From Kirk Lorimar's tone and demeanor, this wasn't going to end well for him, Carr was realizing as the hair on the back of his neck stood on end. A trickle of perspiration dripped down his back. He cleared his throat and shuffled his feet nervously.

"What . . . what are you saying, Kirk?" Carr asked, his mouth suddenly dry, his voice not sounding as confident as he'd hoped.

Kirk Lorimar looked around the group before looking back to Carr.

"What I'm saying, Milton, is that you are relieved of command, and your employment with the City of Abernathy is terminated effective immediately. Your computer access has been discontinued, and your employee access key card has been deactivated. The personal items from your office have been gathered and are in a box in Ruth's office. We'll have it for you at the conclusion of this meeting. Also, the keys to your City vehicle must be relinquished immediately."

Stunned, Carr could only stare at them. He staggered backward before grabbing onto the back of the nearest chair to steady himself, the chair rocking under the pressure. After several long, deathly, quiet seconds, he regained his composure and exploded.

"So, that's it?!" he demanded hotly. His face becoming mottled first with disbelief, then turning red with rage as the force of what was happening hit him. "After all of the years of dedicated service I've given this city, you're walking me out the door because of *him*?!" Carr flung his hand out and pointed a shaking finger at Lucas accusingly. "I'll sue the city for wrongful termination. My record speaks for itself. I won't allow you to do this!" he fairly shouted. His chest heaved, and the hand holding onto the back of the chair was trembling.

The group at the end of the table looked at each other sadly as Carr stood rigid and immobile, glaring at each of them in turn.

Lucas glanced at the others and then slowly stood and walked down to Carr and put a hand on his shoulder.

"Milton," he said softly, "Go home. Your family needs you."

Carr jerked away from Lucas. He dug in his pocket and flung the keys to his vehicle on the table and with a last accusatory look, stormed from the room, the door banging solidly behind him.

Lucas turned and looked at the others and shook his head. They all knew the hardest part was yet to come.

L

UCAS HURRIED IN THE back door of the admin office and walked straight to the conference room. He'd asked Lindsay to contact the command staff and all three battalion chiefs and ask them to wait for him while he was at city hall. As he walked into the crowded room, silence fell and the small talk stopped, any smiles dropping from their faces. He looked around, his face grave, as he took his seat at the head of the table.

"Thank you for coming, everyone. I know it's a day off for some of you, so I appreciate it. I'm afraid we have some unpleasant business to discuss, so it's best to get down to it. First, I have just come from city hall where Deputy Chief Carr was relieved of command, and his employment with the city was terminated."

Glances were exchanged around the table, but no one seemed surprised.

"I assure you this was not a retaliatory move," Lucas went on. "The next bit of news I have to share with you is to be kept within this room for the next few hours. The arsonist has been identified, and as soon as this meeting is concluded, Fire Marshal Ennis and I, along with Chief Harper and his officers, will be making the arrest. The arsonist is currently under full surveillance. I regrettably must inform you that the arsonist has been identified as Chase Carr, Deputy Chief Carr's son."

There was a collective gasp as startled glances were exchanged before darting back to Lucas.

"Sir," Deputy Chief West began after a brief minute of silence. "That's . . . that's just not possible. I've known Chase Carr since he was a little boy. He wouldn't, no, he just couldn't . . ." West left off, shaking his head, his lips pressed into a thin line.

"Sir," Deputy Chief Baldwin began, clearing a catch in his throat, "may I ask—what is the evidence that makes you believe Chase is the arsonist?"

Lucas looked at Jeremy and nodded. Jeremy pointed the remote at the screen at the far end of the room and clicked it on. The video from the security camera began to play, and when Chase turned and looked at the camera, gasps and moans were heard.

"I'm afraid there's a lot more evidence to go along with this," Lucas added when Jeremy froze the video with Chase's face in full view. "Ennis and the PD investigators have done an outstanding job putting a solid case together. We don't have time to share it all with you right now, but we will go into more detail as soon as time allows."

"This is going to rip Chief Carr to pieces, sir. You do know that," West said softly.

"Yes. I do know," Lucas replied heavily. "The arrest has to be made, but I can't tell you how much I'm dreading it."

Silence hung heavily in the room for several minutes before Lucas turned to Elise Stephens who was sitting quietly, nervously twirling a pen between her fingers.

"Elise," Lucas said softly, "I am so sorry, but as the public information officer, you are the point person on this. You have a good relationship with the media, but I assure you their response will be rapid and intense when this breaks. Prepare a statement and let me take a look at it. I'll also need to run it by Kirk Lorimar before it's issued. I will provide you with the talking points to be shared. If someone asks something beyond what's included, tell them it's a developing situation and more information will be coming."

"Lindsay, please make sure the admins know that all media calls or inquiries are to be directed to Elise. No one else. We need a unified and consistent message from this office, and the easiest way to accomplish that is for it to come from one individual."

Looking back to the group, Lucas added, "Please pass the word to everyone in your chain of command that no one outside of Elise is to comment on the arrest, on the investigation, or what this means for the department. Everything—I repeat—*everything* must go through Elise. There is a lot at stake here. We will immediately be in the process of rebuilding the community's trust in this department, and we can't risk having any loose cannons. Am I clear?"

Everyone nodded solemnly.

Lucas continued issuing rapid fire orders, the group quickly discerning Lucas's grasp of what the department's comprehensive response needed to be. Rallying from the shock, each took notes on their assignments and responsibilities in support of what was about to take place. Thirty quick minutes later, Lucas stood and looked at Jeremy.

"I'm afraid Marshal Ennis and I have an appointment. Is everyone clear on what they need to do? As soon as this happens, it's going to be all over the news. We've got to have our game plan firmly in place. Any questions?"

Met with silence, Lucas looked around the room as he moved to the door but then stopped and turned around. "I just want you to know ahead of time how much I appreciate each of you, the sacrifices you've made and will be making for the department. It's a sad and regrettable day for Abernathy and our brotherhood, but it will be up to us and how we conduct ourselves going forward that will reinstate our reputation with the community and beyond. I have complete faith that we have the devotion and ability to make that happen. Feel free to call me personally if you have questions or feel the need to discuss anything privately."

Opening the door, he stepped into the hall with Jeremy close behind. Jeremy looked over his shoulder at Riley who solemnly nodded his encouragement.

T HANKS TO SOMEONE FROM school giving him a ride, Chase got home early. He heard his parents talking in the living room as he walked through the kitchen and was surprised his dad was already home. It looked like his mom had started making dinner from the dishes and food on the kitchen island.

Chase opened the refrigerator door and pulled out a canned Coke and popped it open. He started toward his room, hoping to avoid his parents, but the house was unusually quiet except for their voices, which he soon realized sounded agitated, maybe even frantic.

"How could you let them fire you, Milton?" he heard his mother say. He paused as she went on, "You were supposed to get Matthews fired not the other way around! Did you object? What did you say?"

Chase froze. His father was answering, his voice low, but Chase had stopped listening. No—that couldn't be right. It just couldn't be. Chase choked on the sip of Coke he'd just taken.

It was supposed to have been Chief Matthews who got fired—not his dad. Things were going to get a whole lot better after that. Chase had overheard his parents talking about the no confidence vote on Chief Matthews planned to happen last Wednesday. That meant the so-called chief should be getting canned any day—if he hadn't been already. Chase's dad would then be fire chief and have the job he'd always wanted.

And when that happened, Chase smiled grimly, all of his extra "activities" would have paid off. It'd been fun writing the snarky little notes he'd attached to the gas cans and then watching Matthews' reaction from a distance, but it would all be a waste if it hadn't helped his dad become chief.

His mom was yelling when he heard her again. "We're going to sue for wrongful termination, Milton. This isn't right. They can't let you go just like that! Not after all the years you've put in with the city. You've worked too long and hard just to be turned out on the street!"

Chase hurried down the hall to his room, avoiding the living room. His mind was racing and his heart pounding. He quickly but quietly closed the door behind him. His books hit the floor with a soft thud as he frantically looked around. If Matthews was still chief, that wasn't good. But what could he do—what *should* he do? He was trying not to panic, but his mind was spinning. He'd avoided being caught this long; maybe with a little creativity, he could continue doing so.

But then, he remembered, he'd stupidly looked at that camera. That might have been foolish, but it had been his reward to himself. Burning the gym down had been especially sweet. It was payback to those guys on the Abernathy basketball team that meant so much to his dad, and it was also payback for the extra harsh terms of being grounded his dad had imposed. Now, nobody would be playing or watching basketball. There might have been a bit of a rough patch to get past when they came across him on the security camera video—if they found it. The plan had been for his dad to be chief by then, and he could have fixed it. But now . . .

But now, everything had changed. He had to leave. It was his only alternative. It was a huge step and a frightening one but what else could he do? He quickly grabbed a duffel bag from his closet and began stuffing clothes into it, pulling shirts and pants from his closet. He'd get just a few things and then retrieve his car keys from where his dad thought he'd hidden them and be gone before his parents even realized he'd been home.

After squeezing as much as he could into the bag, Chase eased his door open and stepped into the hall. His parents were talking in low tones now, and his mother was crying. He paused briefly, wishing he could tell her goodbye, but he was out of time. His car keys were in the back of a drawer in the kitchen. Chase inched his way down the hall and had just reached the kitchen when the jarring tone of the doorbell split the uneasy quiet, and his parents grew silent.

AFTER RINGING THE DOORBELL, Jeremy took a step back. Manon and Foster, the two police investigative officers, stood behind him, guns in hand. All three were dressed in protective gear. Lucas and Chief Harper were a few steps behind them. No one expected trouble, but they were prepared just in case. Additional officers had been deployed at the rear and on either side of the house, surrounding the home.

Milton Carr flung the door open, enraged as soon as he saw them.

"Is it not enough that you humiliated me this afternoon? Are you going to harass me now?" he snarled.

Brenda Carr walked up behind her husband, her face red and tear streaked. "What's happening, Milton? What is this?" She cast a confused glance between her husband and those standing at the door.

"We have an arrest warrant for Chase Carr," Jeremy said firmly. "You can either bring him out, or, if necessary, we are prepared to come inside to get him. We've had the house under surveillance, so we know he's inside."

The confusion on Milton Carr's face was evident as he exchanged a puzzled look with his wife.

"Chase? What do you want with Chase?" he asked hesitantly.

"A warrant has been issued for his arrest for multiple acts of arson within the city limits of Abernathy," Jeremy responded pointedly, taking a step forward and holding out a folded piece of paper to Milton Carr. "We also have a search warrant for the premises."

"Arson?" Carr breathed faintly, grabbing the paper from Jeremy's hand and unfolding it.

The sound of a sudden scuffle from the hallway caught everyone's attention. Two police officers emerged from the hallway, each holding an arm of the handcuffed and struggling Chase Carr.

"He was attempting to flee out the back when we apprehended him, sir," one of the officers said, looking at Chief Harper. "He was carrying this," he added and held up Chase's duffel bag.

"Chief Harper," another officer said approaching from the garage. "We found several of these under a tarp in the shop in the garage."

Lucas tensed when the officer held up three of the now familiar shiny red and gold gas cans.

The color drained from Milton Carr's face as he turned to his son, still struggling against the two officers restraining him.

Milton Carr stepped to within inches of his son and in deathly cold tones said, "What. Have. You. Done."

"Milton, please," Chief Harper said plaintively. "Don't make this any worse."

"I did it for you!" Chase burst out in a pitiful wail. "You wanted to be chief, and I thought if I helped with . . . distractions that maybe . . . you'd be happier when you got the job. I just wanted to help, Dad . . . just wanted you to love me . . . to notice me . . ." Chase gulped out between sobs.

It was completely quiet. The cool late afternoon air seemed suspended in a breathless hush. The only sound was Chase's sobbing.

All eyes were on Milton Carr as he took a measured step to within inches of his son. Chase's eyes lit with hope as he looked at his dad through his tears.

In low tones but loud enough that everyone heard clearly, Carr said through clenched teeth, "No son of mine would ever have done such things. And if that's not bad enough, you're a coward—running away from what you've done."

Carr moved a step closer and studied Chase through narrow, cold eyes. "I. Have. No. Son," he said flatly before turning and walking resolutely back into the house.

Chase Carr immediately went limp, the officers supporting him, as he began wailing uncontrollably. "I love you, Dad. Please . . . help me . . ." he sobbed over and over.

Lucas flinched and had to turn away.

Chief Parker nodded to the two officers who moved to take Chase away.

"Milton, please!" Brenda Carr cried hysterically as Carr walked away. Turning, she reached for her son, her arms outstretched.

"Please, step back, ma'am," one of the officers said as they took Chase out the front door, leaving Brenda in the doorway where she collapsed in tears.

Milton Carr had disappeared inside the house without a backward glance.

Lucas exchanged a sad look and a shake of the head with Chief Harper before they walked to their vehicles. As the police car with Chase in the back seat passed in front of him, Lucas saw Chase in the window; a more broken, defeated, lost look than Lucas had ever seen was etched deeply on the boy's tear-stained face. It was a look Lucas knew would haunt him for the rest of his days.

Lucas sat on the sofa in the quiet and stillness of the townhome, his head in his hands. He was trying to stop the tears but the gut-wrenching scene he'd just witnessed felt like part of him had been ripped out on the Carrs' front porch. Jill had an arm around him, her head on his shoulder, rubbing her hand soothingly up and down his back. They sat in silence, Lucas trying to come to terms with what had happened and what it meant for the Carr family and its further ramifications for the department.

"It was awful, Jill. It was absolutely awful," he finally said with a sniff, sitting up and wiping at his eyes with the backs of his hands. "I never want to be a part of something like that again. Ever."

"I know," Jill replied softly. "I'm so very sorry—for all of them." Several more quiet minutes passed, the wall clock measuring the minutes tick by tick.

Breaking the silence at last, Jill took a deep breath, her face lined with worry. Turning to Lucas, she took a long look at him and said, "I know I'm probably asking the impossible, but please, try not to think about it—at least for the rest of the evening. Today was supposed to be a stress-free day you might recall."

Lucas looked at her from the corner of his eye and chuckled humorlessly. "I do recall, and you're right. It's impossible not to think about it." He leaned back and put an arm around Jill. She took one of his hands in her own, looking at him as they absentmindedly laced their fingers together.

"I can't imagine what would possess a father to talk to a son the way Carr did his," Lucas said softly. "That boy has been screaming for help long before today, and Carr didn't want to see it." Lucas shook his head. "I don't know what's going to become of that family."

Jill sat up and looked Lucas in the eye. "I know it's fresh and can't help but weigh on your mind, but what's happened to their family is Milton and Brenda Carr's responsibility to bear—not yours." Squeezing his hand, she went on, "You have such a tender heart, Lucas. It's one of the many reasons I love you, but you amaze me. After everything those two put you through, you're worried about their well-being. If something comes up where you can help, I know you will, but until then please try not to worry about it, and let's not talk about it anymore tonight, for your sake. Okay?"

Lucas gave a slight smile and opened his mouth to agree when his phone buzzed, and he saw a text from Jon: *Wanted to check in. Hope you had a quiet first day back.*

Lucas held the phone out, so Jill could read the text. She smiled and before Lucas could stop her, she replied with a heart emoji.

Jon replied immediately: *Warning: Mom's got your phone again. Emojis in use. Love you too, Dad.*

Lucas and Jill both chuckled as Lucas typed in a reply: *You're spot on. Love you too, Son. Go study.*

Lucas sighed as his smile broadened. Jon couldn't have timed that text any better. Tomorrow was another day, but for tonight Jill was right. He needed to think about something pleasant.

He rested his forehead against Jill's as she wrapped her arms around him. He pulled her close, and they sat in silence, the only sound the gentle rhythm of their breathing. This was what he needed to forget the events of the day—at least for a while.

"JILL, THIS BOX IS just labeled office, so does that mean it's yours or mine?" Lucas yelled toward the kitchen where Jill was unpacking dishes.

"You packed yours, and I packed mine. You can tell the difference," Jill yelled back.

Lucas gave an exaggerated eye roll to Jessica as they passed in the hall, earning a giggle as she carried boxes of her own.

"Pizza's here!" Jon called out.

Work stopped for a lunch break as they gathered in the breakfast nook. Jon lined up the three pizzas they'd ordered; enough for leftovers for dinner Jill had explained, as she pulled out paper towels and paper plates from a grocery bag. Lucas opened the refrigerator, empty except for the soft drinks they'd placed in there last night. Each took a plate, a soft drink, and pieces of pizza, grabbing whatever they could find to sit on in the upheaval.

Renovations had been completed this past week, a couple of months after they'd closed on the house, and today was moving day. The wait had been worth it, Lucas thought, as he looked around, enjoying his pepperoni pizza.

New hardwood floors had been installed everywhere except the bedrooms where new carpeting had been laid. Bookshelves had been added to his study as well as Jill's home office, and the entire house had been repainted. The back deck had been stripped and re-stained. The house had the unmistakable mingled fresh smell of new carpet, fresh paint, and fresh-cut wood. It looked amazing, just like he knew it would when Jill put her design skills to work. It looked and felt like a brand new house, but more importantly, moving their things in was already making it feel like home.

"Sorry you guys are having to help us move on your spring break, but it's greatly appreciated," Lucas said, taking a gulp of his Dr. Pepper.

"Happy to do it," Jon replied jauntily. "Especially after we've been homeless for so long."

Lucas shook his head. "Good lands, Jon Matthews! What you come up with sometimes. Neither of you have been homeless."

"A matter of semantics," Jon popped back and suddenly grew solemn. "But Mom, Dad—Jess and I do have something we'd like to talk to you both about."

Jessica's eyes grew wide as she gulped down a bite of pizza. "Now?" she asked urgently under her breath.

"Nothing like the present. We're all here, so let's do it. You go first."

Jessica rolled her eyes at her brother and took a deep breath.

"Well, somebody had better start talking," Jill said, cutting a quick glance to Lucas who had stopped chewing.

Jessica set her plate on the nearest cardboard box and wiped her fingers with a napkin before standing and looking at her parents.

"Mom, Dad," Jessica began hesitantly, "I have decided, with your approval of course, to transfer to the college here in Abernathy. And . . . and I'd like to change my major to education. I've decided I'd like to be an elementary school teacher."

Lucas and Jill sat back, surprised.

"You started taking majors classes this past semester so what about your business major?" Jill asked, setting her plate on the counter.

"Yeah. I took a couple of business classes this spring—Business Ethics and Economics. They were okay and my grades were still good, but honestly, neither one of them was interesting to me. I don't get excited when I try to picture myself in a business career, but I get *really* excited when I picture myself as a teacher," Jessica said with a nervous smile.

She waited for them to say something.

Lucas finished chewing and swallowed his bite of pizza.

"What changed your mind?" he asked softly. "Did something happen at school?"

"No." She smiled, looking at her dad. "Actually, something happened here."

"Oh?" Lucas and Jill said simultaneously, exchanging a curious glance.

"Dad, I've heard you talk about Andy and Katie Garrett all my life. They were always just some mythical figures I was aware of, but I never really thought of them as real—until you guys moved here. I don't know what all happened with the fire department here, but what I do know is how you handled it, Dad. I got to thinking about you being willing to go through everything you did to be here and *were* here because of Katie Garrett and her husband, so it seems to me she was a pretty powerful influence.

"You've always talked about the impact Mrs. Garrett had on you while she was your second-grade teacher," Jessica said, looking at her dad. "And that's, well, that's what I hope to do as a teacher—make a difference—have a positive impact on my students."

After a brief pause, she looked at Jon. "Too sappy?"

"Eh," Jon said and held one hand out palm down and tilted it back and forth while holding a piece of pizza in his other hand.

Lucas watched and listened to Jessica and looked at both of his children in amazement. He was at a complete loss. He looked to Jill, who was smiling at him, her eyes shining with tears.

"Yeah," Jon said after a few seconds of waiting for their response. "Definitely too sappy."

"Jon!" Jill scolded teasingly. "Give us a second here."

"Oh, and Jess, you left a couple of things out," Jon said, motioning around the room with his finger.

"Oh, right. I checked and all of my credits will transfer with full credit. I might be a little behind in my new major, but I can take summer classes and some extra hours each semester to catch up and finish on time. I know there will be some extra expense trying to catch up, so to be cost effective, I'd like to move back in with you guys while I go to school—if that's okay. This place would be a lot better than a dorm room!"

Jill laughed and clapped her hands together. "Oh, honey! This is wonderful, and of course, you already have your room here." She grasped Jessica's hands. "You'll be a great teacher—don't you think so, Lucas?"

Lucas beamed his approval before standing and grabbing Jessica into a big hug. "You are going to be an outstanding teacher. You have our whole-hearted approval. I am so proud of you. I wish Katie Garrett could have heard what you just said. She would be honored and thrilled to know she's been the inspiration for another teacher." Lucas hugged Jessica again and then looked at Jon. "But what's Jon going to do without you at school?"

Her arm still around her dad, Jessica looked to Jon. "Well, he's got something to tell you too."

"Oh, lord," Jill said with a tease, putting her head in her hands and shaking it back and forth.

"Oh, come on," Jon said, laughing as he stood, and Lucas and Jessica sat back down, waiting.

"I also have made a career change decision. At the end of this semester, I'll have enough college credits to earn an associate's degree. I know getting a college degree is important to both of you guys, but . . . I've also checked into applying at the District Five Fire Academy. I want to be a firefighter."

Lucas sat back sharply.

Jon hesitated but went on. "I've talked to the admissions counselor there, and he said with my grades and credits from school, and a few references, I'll be accepted for the upcoming fall semester."

Lucas and Jill exchanged quick glances but didn't say anything.

"Oh, come on, you guys," Jon went on earnestly. "I saw what happened here too. I saw my dad thrown into the lion's den and come out on top. I also saw the fire service brotherhood I've always heard about in action like I've never seen it before. Dad, that group of firefighters was at the hospital the entire time you were there. They spelled each other off, but there was always a group there. They told me they were ready to do whatever they could to help you and support our family. They didn't leave until you went home. I tell ya, that made a huge impression, and that's when I realized what it means about the brotherhood taking care of their own. Some of them told me about a talk you gave—something about the back of the bay and how important it is to help each other be better together rather than apart. You're leading the way for them, Dad, and when it gets down to it, you're leading the way for me too. I guess what I'm trying to say is . . . what I'm wanting to say is . . . I want to follow in your footsteps."

Jon looked at Jessica with a grimace. "Too sappy?" he whispered.

Jessica looked between her parents, and putting her hands up in a shrug, glanced back to Jon and said, "Well, you had to follow me, and you know I'm a tough act to follow. But yeah, too sappy."

Lucas looked at Jon and then around the room, powerful emotions roiling inside him that he wasn't sure how to handle. He looked down and closed his eyes. "Good, Lord," Lucas prayed silently, "I don't deserve this amazing family you've blessed me with. Thank you."

"Dad?" Jon asked hesitantly.

Lucas opened his eyes and raised his head, looking at Jon earnestly.

"Son, are you sure? Really sure? You've grown up with it. It's a different kind of lifestyle with shift duty. It's being willing to miss holidays or important occasions because you're on duty. It's seeing some things and experiencing some things you'll wish you'd never seen or experienced. This is a huge commitment, and I just want you to be sure."

"Were *you* sure, sir?" Jon demanded, standing straight, looking his father directly in the eye.

Lucas took a deep breath. Standing, he walked over to his son, placing his hands on Jon's shoulders.

"I was sure from the second grade on, and I can see the same determination in your eyes that I always felt." Lucas looked quickly to Jill, who nodded and smiled.

Looking back to Jon, his blue eyes so much like his mother's, Lucas went on, "Jon Matthews, you are going to be an amazing firefighter, and I know you're going to love it just as much as I do. And, Son, I can't tell you how incredibly proud of you I am."

Lucas extended his hand to Jon who, smiling broadly, grabbed it and pumped it enthusiastically before Lucas pulled him into a tight hug.

Everyone took a deep, happy breath and laughed as they resumed their make-do seats to eat their now cold pizza.

"So, is there anything *else* either of you would like to share with your father and I?" Jill asked, glancing between Jon and Jessica who were now busily eating their pizza.

Jon's head popped up as he quickly swallowed the drink he'd just taken. "Oh, good grief! I forgot to tell you something. I'm going to be living with Coach and Patsy while I'm at the academy. In fact, they said I'd probably be staying in your old room, Dad," Jon said, reaching for another slice.

Lucas cocked his head to the side and just looked at Jon. "Did they now? I'm going to have a word with them about running such a thing by me before they agree to it," he said, trying to sound angry but knowing he wasn't succeeding.

"They said you'd say that," Jon laughed around the pizza in his mouth.

Lunch all wrapped up, they'd just started back to work when the doorbell rang.

Maneuvering around the stacks of boxes filling the hall, Lucas opened the door to a porch full of firefighters. Lucas glanced from Riley to Jeremy to Nate to West, and even though he wasn't a firefighter, to Cade, who was definitely part of the group. Even more firefighters were on the lawn, smiling and waving.

The glare from the sun reflected off the windshield of one of the trucks parked at the curb. The trees in the lawn were budding out in fresh growth, and the grass was turning green. The sky was a bright blue, and the air was tinged with just the right amount of warmth. It was a beautiful spring day.

Taking it all in, Lucas stood in the doorway, holding the door open wide, and asked, "And to what do I owe what I'm hoping is a pleasure?"

"We heard it was moving day and thought you guys might need some extra muscle," Jeremy said, bouncing up and down on his toes. "We're ready, Chief. Put us to work. What can we do?"

"I thought you guys were working on the community service projects we've implemented for the high school, and besides that, isn't it the day off for most of you?"

The group looked at each other and shrugged. "We had so many guys show up to help with everything on the service projects that we got done in record time," Riley said. "More to come, of course, but everyone's really pitching in on their days off. It's that brotherhood and the giving back thing, you know."

Everyone behind him nodded.

Lucas laughed and shook his head.

Jon walked up behind his dad. "Cool! You guys are just in time. We're ready to start moving the furniture from the storage unit."

"We've got you covered then," Riley said. "We've got trucks, dollies, and packing blankets. You just tell us where, and we'll have everything back here and set up in no time."

"Yes!" Jon bolted past Lucas and down the stairs to join the group as they moved off toward their trucks. Jon turned and held up the storage space locker key before he jumped in the cab of Riley's truck.

Lucas squinted into the sunlight as he watched the caravan of trucks pull away.

He shook his head and smiled. That boy was already fitting into the brotherhood.

Dark smoke billowed around him as Lucas took a step back, waving his hand back and forth to clear the air and trying desperately to suppress a cough. The rich aroma of cooking meat followed the smoke as it drifted into the evening air.

"Need help with the grill, Chief?" Jeremy asked from the deck chair where he sat across from Jessica, who was holding three-month-old J. C. Ennis.

"Ennis, if you want to eat tonight, you'd be advised to keep your advice to yourself," Lucas said with a teasing glance over his shoulder.

"Ah, come on, Chief," Nate Baldwin said, ambling over and snatching a potato chip from a bowl on the table. "We're all starving. Are we going to eat tonight?"

Lucas shook his head and laughed. "If you guys would only demonstrate a little patience and have a little faith, you'd see. I'm taking everything off the grill even as you speak."

Lucas expertly flipped a couple of hamburger patties onto the platter Jill had brought out earlier before sliding the spatula underneath several more and adding them. He speared the wieners and placed them in a large mound on a second platter.

"When are those burgers going to be ready, Lucas?" Jill asked as she came out of the house, placing a bowl of fruit salad on one of the tables on the Matthews' back deck. Everyone laughed as Lucas shook his head indulgently and placed the platters of meat in the middle of another table. Maggie, Allie, and Emily had followed Jill from the house, carrying pitchers of tea, lemonade, and frosty glasses of ice. West's and Baldwin's wives, Becky and Grace, came right behind them, carrying trays piled high with hamburger and hot dog buns. They set them beside the platters of meat and the other fixings and sides already on the table.

Emily walked to the edge of the deck and signaled to Cade the food was ready. He and their boys had been playing on the grassy lawn below, and all three were red-faced and winded when they made it to the deck.

The sun was just setting beyond the trees at the edge of their property. The inky darkness of dusk was meeting the fiery orange of the setting sun, reflecting brightly off the back windows of the house. Tiny pins of light in the night sky were beginning to emerge through the darkness as a slight breeze caused the strands of overhead twinkling lights to sway in its wake. The rustling and chatter of those in front of him added to the relaxed pleasure and fun of the evening.

Good-natured jostling to go first, or at least close to first took place, before Lucas called everyone to order.

"If I could have everyone's attention, please," Lucas said as the noise dwindled, and everyone grew quiet. All eyes were on him, waiting expectantly.

"Jill and I want each of you to know how honored we are to have you in our home and to thank those of you who helped us move. We didn't know what the future held for us here, but Jill knew how much coming back to Abernathy meant to me.

"We have all experienced some treacherous months, but I'm proud and happy to say we've come through them stronger and better for it. I wouldn't have wanted anyone else but you by my side, and I thank you. And now, I'm looking forward to many happy years ahead for all of us with the Abernathy Fire Department. We're rebuilding the department's reputation and standing in the community bit by bit, and I know that's due in large part to the efforts of those here tonight. And let me just add that we're not going to stop until the Abernathy Fire Department has the highest esteem of everyone in the community once again." Glasses of lemonade, tea, and water were raised in salute.

Lucas asked the blessing and then stepped out of the fray to stand at the rail overlooking the backyard to watch as everyone filled their plates. Filling his own plate after everyone else, he took his seat at the head of the table. He looked down the row on either side of him at family and new friends talking and laughing as they ate.

He glanced over to see Riley watching him.

"This is good, isn't it, Chief?" Riley asked as he looked down the table and back to Lucas.

"Yes, Sullivan. It is. Very good. I couldn't have imagined something like this back in December, but I'm so glad that's in the past, and we're here now."

"What's going on?" Jeremy asked, hearing the last part of Lucas's and Riley's conversation. "Everything okay?" he asked a little too loudly.

Conversation dwindled as everyone looked at each other in confusion.

"Something wrong, Chief?" Nate Baldwin asked, his eyebrows raising.

Lucas chuckled and shook his head. "Ennis, you are such a good investigator, but your hearing sure leaves a lot to be desired."

Everyone laughed and then laughed again when J. C. Ennis chose that particular moment to squawk his displeasure at being hungry.

"I have a good excuse as you can see, or rather, hear, sir," Jeremy quipped. "I've been working on refining my selective listening skills."

"Well, I suggest you refine them a little less—make that a lot less," Lucas said, popping some chips in his mouth as everyone laughed.

Allie left, quickly returned, bottle in hand, and began feeding J. C. while she resumed eating.

"That's amazing," Riley said, watching Allie, an appreciative smile on his face. "I never would have thought I'd see the day my little sis would be so good with a baby. You're a natural, Al."

Allie blushed at her brother's praise.

"And, uh, speaking of amazing," Riley said, uncharacteristically nervous with a glance to Maggie, who was smiling softly as she watched Allie feed J. C. Maggie blushed pink and gave Riley a subtle nod.

"Speaking of amazing," Riley began again as he stood and moved behind Maggie, taking her hand. "Maggie and I have been waiting to say anything until we knew all was well, but now, we were wondering . . . Jill, would you have time for one more client? We're needing a nursery designed—for a boy."

Riley broke into a broad grin as the table erupted. Jeremy and Cade jumped up first and grabbed their friend into congratulatory hugs while Allie and Emily hugged a beaming Maggie. Lucas grinned at Jill whose eyes were bright.

Turning to Riley and Maggie, Jill said, "Congratulations! And, of course—I can't wait to get started!"

"Maggie," Allie said with a nod toward Jeremy, "take it from one firefighter's wife to another. Make sure you get the nursery completed, one hundred percent and way ahead of time, or else you'll have a crew of firefighters painting and finishing it while you're headed out the door in labor."

"Sounds like you're speaking from experience," West said as the group laughed.

"Oh, I am, and I'm never going to let Jeremy live it down either," Allie laughed, lifting J. C. to her shoulder and bouncing him.

"We did have just a little bit going on as you might recall—a few arsons to investigate," Jeremy said, feigning hurt feelings.

"Isn't that trial coming up soon?" Cade asked, grabbing the bowl of fruit salad and pouring a mound onto his plate.

Silence fell. No one answered immediately as the firefighters at the table exchanged solemn looks. The arsons and ensuing fallout were still taking their toll on the department. While the fallout had been immediate and intense, it had also been, thankfully, short lived. The press tried to paint the department in a bad light, but when the city council and city manager gave the department their wholehearted support, the furor had died down quickly. It was also helpful that firefighters were constantly out and about in the community and in the public eye, showing up to help with various service projects, working with youth league sports, wherever and however they could be of service.

Overwhelming support from surrounding fire departments had been welcomed and helped to get Abernathy through a tough couple of months. Cap Rio had called several times to check in and had assured Lucas that he and the Abernathy department had the brotherhood's full support.

Despite that support, the time of the arsons was still difficult to talk about, and with the upcoming trial, it would all be brought back to the forefront again. Lucas looked around the table, knowing every firefighter here had received a subpoena the week before and would be involved in the trial in some way. Lucas dreaded his own participation. Bad memories from those years ago still haunted him.

"It's next month," Lucas finally replied quietly.

Cade looked around the table, sensing everyone's hesitancy.

"Sorry. I probably shouldn't have brought that up," Cade said with an apologetic look. "It's just the kids at school haven't stopped talking about it, especially with the gym gone. You know how kids talk," he finished lamely, forking in a strawberry.

"Speaking of kids, Chief, do you think we should induct Cade into the brotherhood as an honorary member?" Jeremy asked as he dolloped another huge spoon full of potato salad onto his plate. "After all, he did get a commendation for helping save those boys at the gym fire."

"As for that commendation, Marshall," Nate Baldwin said with a smirk. "It was firefighters who pulled *you* out as you might recall."

Cade lobbed a paper napkin back at Baldwin. "I know . . . I know . . ." Cade sighed. "You firefighter types just hate giving us officers any credit."

"Oh, we absolutely give officers credit, but only when it's due," Jeremy looked at Cade with a smirk.

"Well, let's put this to rest once and for all—I hope," Lucas said, shaking his head and chuckling. "Credit is due, and as far as I can tell, Cade is *already* an honorary member of the brotherhood," Lucas said and held up his lemonade in salute to Cade who broke into a broad smile.

"Thanks, Chief! Does that mean I can drive a fire truck now?" Cade asked eagerly as paper napkins were lobbed at him from around the table.

Lucas shook his head an emphatic no as he laughed.

After the laughter died down, Nate Baldwin, concern returning to his face, asked softly, "You say the kids are still talking about the fire, Cade. Are they saying anything about Chase Carr?"

Cade shook his head. "No. Not really. The kid was a loner, and those he did hang out with were not the kind you'd want your kid to have as friends. I know the police questioned several of them, and even they didn't know much about him."

Jill sighed. "I just feel so sorry for that kid. He hasn't had a happy life."

"I guess besides his mom and sister, it sounds like he's in this alone," Cade said, taking the squirming Eric from Emily and setting him on his lap. "I'll check and see if there are any recovery programs available in jail or at the very least, some counseling services for someone incarcerated with similar issues."

"Actually, Chief Harper and I are working on that," Lucas said, turning a plastic fork in circles on his plate. "He's checking with some state counseling services, and I'm checking on some arsonist rehabilitation services. It'd be best if the same programs could be carried forward, so he'd have them while he's in jail locally and then transfer with him to wherever he will serve in the long term. I'm afraid with the scale of the destruction and chaos he created, though, he's going to be locked up for quite some time."

A thoughtful silence fell around the table until Jill asked, "Does anyone know if his family will be at the trial?"

"The last I heard," Jack West said, "Brenda filed for divorce pretty quickly after everything happened with no contest from Milton so it should be final soon if it's not already. Milton moved to North or South Dakota, I'm not sure which, and found a job working with a volunteer fire department in a little town somewhere up there. Casey had to drop out of college. She and her mom are sharing a small apartment and working to support themselves while paying Chase's legal bills."

Lucas had heard all of this before and hearing it again saddened him even more. Carr threw away the most precious possession he'd ever have, his family.

After everyone had finished, gotten seconds, and thirds in some cases, Jill stood. Lucas stood with her and helped clear plates. He was suddenly very glad Jill had insisted on using disposable dishes. He followed her into the kitchen, tossing dirty plates into a large trash bag followed by Jessica with her own stack.

"Lucas, will you take the peach cobbler and a chocolate pie with you? Jess, grab the other chocolate pie and the banana pudding. I'll get the ice cream out of the freezer and be right there. Plates, bowls and utensils are on the sideboard on the deck."

Lucas and Jessica obeyed and were met with appreciative oohs and aahs when they set the array of desserts on the tables, followed by the plates, bowls and the vanilla ice cream Jill had retrieved and just plunged a scooper into. Everyone watched and exchanged contented smiles before they eagerly helped themselves.

Lucas glanced to his right to see Jon talking to Riley, a serious look on his face. Whatever Jon had just told him, Riley broke into a huge smile and then looked to Lucas.

"So, there's to be another firefighter in the family, Chief?" Riley asked, clapping Jon on the shoulder.

Lucas beamed with pleasure. "Yes. I'm proud and happy to say so. Jon just got word of his acceptance into the fire academy. He'll be starting in the fall."

Jon's smile was one of pure joy, which made Lucas smile even broader.

"Well, Chief, it looks like you've got a secure legacy in the fire service," Riley said after the group clapped and expressed their approval. "And I'll even be willing to say that Jon will probably make a great chief one day and continue in his father's footsteps."

"I agree," Jeremy added. "Wouldn't it be something if J. C. and Riley's son and any more sons of ours come to serve alongside him as we do with you?"

Lucas turned and looked at Jon, whose eyes were shining with a light Lucas recognized and knew well—the dream of being a firefighter. Lucas knew the only thing that could possibly outshine that dream was its achievement and becoming a member of the fire service brotherhood.

Lucas reached into his pocket and pulled out Mr. Andy's badge that Mrs. Garrett had given him. He held it reverently in his hand and watched as it sparkled, reflecting the twinkling lights hanging overhead. He looked up at the family and friends gathered in front of him, his gaze going to Baldwin, West, Riley, and then Jeremy before coming to rest on Jon. Lucas smiled and in reply to Jeremy's question nodded. "Yeah, I can see that . . . and then some."

ACKNOWLEDGMENTS

It's a hard and daunting task to attempt to thank everyone who has played a part in helping to make *Embattled Brother* a reality. Whether you've been a voice of encouragement along the Beyond the Badge journey or one who has actually had their hands on the manuscript and helped fine-tune and hone the story, there just isn't a way to adequately express my truest thanks and heartfelt appreciation.

But first, I must thank Battalion Chief Jeremy Wolfe with the Abilene Fire Department. Jeremy was the beta reader and subject matter expert for *Embattled Brother.* His insights and suggestions made the book much stronger and certainly more accurate. Jeremy has been an enthusiastic supporter of my writing and portrayal of firefighters throughout the series. He has played a role in each of the books, from his moving email adapted in *Brotherhood by Fire* to his lending his knowledge and expertise to read and proof *Embattled Brother* for accuracy. One of the firefighters under Jeremy's command on B-Shift said, "When Chief Wolfe speaks, you listen, because he's got something important to say." I certainly found that to be true in his help with this book. Thank you, Jeremy!

A huge shout-out to two amazing people who did a phenomenal job proofing and editing the manuscript for *Embattled Brother.* Judy Barker and Dr. Laura Cheshier lent their time, talent, and expertise to polishing and fine-tuning the manuscript to its finished state. Judy's care and patience in reading and marking up each page (when she didn't get caught up in reading the story!) was an invaluable help. Laura's knowledge and keen insights into not just the grammatical correctness of the manuscript but also discrepancies, plot points, and characters made the story stronger, bolder, and more consequential.

And a special thank-you and my deepest appreciation to Sandra Jonas of Sandra Jonas Publishing House for her advice, guidance, expertise, and industry knowledge that make this book available to readers everywhere. It is a pleasure and an honor to work with such a kindhearted and devoted professional whose goal is seeing an author succeed. Thank you, Sandra!

As always, my deepest thanks and love to my mom whose support and encouragement mean the world to me. When I doubt what I'm doing, she's the one who assures me that I really am a writer. And with those words, I'm able to carry on.

A big thank-you to my nephew, Lieutenant Zac Bell, who is always willing and so very capable of sharing insights, fire station exploits, stories, and his support of my books. That means more than I can ever say. Another big thank-you goes to my brother, Chief Larry Bell (retired), whose story of a fellow firefighter inspired my pursuit of writing in earnest. Special note: The phrase, ". . . and then some . . ." was one my brother used throughout his tenure as Fire Chief in Abilene. I added a bit to it, but the phrase carries a lot of meaning—especially to those who served under his command in the Abilene Fire Department.

And a great BIG thank-you to *everyone* in my family who lends their support, shares my book with others, and encourages me to keep writing the stories and characters I've come to love so much.

And, of course, a HUGE thank-you to firefighters everywhere for what they do day in and day out with humble attitudes and servant hearts. Being a firefighter is a calling of the highest order. I have been encouraged to be an advocate for firefighters, which I'm striving my best to be because as I say often, firefighters can never be appreciated enough.

And above all, I want to thank the Lord for the help and guidance He provides not only in my writing but every day. He guides my words, thoughts, insights, and keystrokes to bring these characters, their stories, and the overall narrative to life. The Lord gives me the words and the heart for each and every story. Thank you, Lord.

DISCUSSION QUESTIONS

1. Lucas defers taking disciplinary measures with Deputy Chief Carr. Was Lucas's choice and his management style the best for the situation and for the department?

2. What did you think of Deputy Chief Carr's reaction to not getting the job he believed was rightly his? How could he have handled his disappointment and anger appropriately? What other measures could he have taken that would have gotten him to a promotion more effectively?

3. If you had a spouse dealing with the situation and issues Lucas faced, what would you do, if anything, differently than what Jill did in support?

4. Lucas chose to try and interact closely and establish close relationships with firefighters and officers in his command. Was this the best approach for Lucas to take considering the situation? Why or why not?

5. As the new fire marshal, Jeremy Ennis faced an unprecedented situation with a serial arsonist. How did you relate to Jeremy's reaction and his handling of the new responsibility and challenges?

6. Was Lucas overconfident in his dealings with the public and City Council? Should he have handled himself differently and if so, how?

7. Carr brings about a vote of no confidence in Chief Matthews. Would you have reacted as Lucas did and confront Carr and the Department face to face? If not, what would you have done differently?

8. What warning signs did Chase Carr exhibit that if the Carr parents hadn't chosen to ignore them might have avoided a catastrophic outcome?

9. How could Milton Carr have handled his frustrations with his son, Chase, differently to reach a better father/son relationship?

10. Discuss the similarities and differences between Jon and Jessica Matthews and Casey and Chase Carr. To what do you attribute their differences?

11. Firefighters have a strong sense of belonging and brotherhood. Do you have a strong group of friends or a strong support system? What drew you together?

12. Why do you think that Chase showed his face to the camera at the high school fire? Have you ever wanted to call attention to yourself when you were doing something wrong?

ABOUT THE AUTHOR

Lindy Bell is living her own dream come true of being an author, seeing her books in print, and being read by those near and far. Lindy's books are recognized for the intensity of the emotions they elicit, the connection between the reader and the characters as well as their powerfully accurate portrayals of the fire service.

Lindy gained her love of writing from her love of reading, and she enjoys a wide range of genres. She is a lover of all things Jane Austen which led her to writing her very first book, *Jane Austen Celebrates: Holidays & Occasions Regency Style*.

Lindy's writing has also brought about opportunities to speak to a variety of groups as well as teach Adult Professional Education courses on Jane Austen and the Regency Era at Southern Methodist University (SMU). Lindy also presents live book reviews to book clubs across the Dallas/Fort Worth Metroplex.

Lindy is a graduate of Abilene Christian University with a bachelor's degree in business administration.

Sign up for *Lindy's Lines* monthly newsletter to get an exclusive peek at the "Heroes Behind the Flames," a subscriber-only series featuring interviews with real-life firefighters. You'll also get a behind-the-scenes look at Lindy's writing process, updates on her books and events, and curated book recommendations. You can subscribe to *Lindy's Lines* at lindybellwrites.com.

Lindy would love to hear from you! Connect with her through her website and social media links:

Website: lindybellwrites.com
X: @LindyBellWrites
Facebook.com/LindyBellWrites/
Instagram: LindyBellWrites
YouTube: @LindyBellwr